MIND GAMES

SHANA SILVER

MIND GAMES

Swoon READS

NEW YORK

A Swoon Reads Book

An imprint of Feiwel and Friends and Macmillan Publishing Group, LLC
120 Broadway, New York, NY 10271

Our books may be purchased in bulk for promotional, educational, or business use.
Please contact your local bookseller or the Macmillan Corporate and Premium
Sales Department at (800) 221-7945 ext. 5442 or by email at
MacmillanSpecialMarkets@macmillan.com.

Library of Congress Control Number: 2018955606
ISBN 978-1-250-19292-9 (hardcover) / ISBN 978-1-250-19293-6 (ebook)

Book design by Liz Dresner

First Edition, 2019

10 9 8 7 6 5 4 3 2 1

swoonreads.com

To Dad,

For making me love science fiction as much as you do,

and for planting the seed of an idea from which this book grew.

00110001

The problem with stealing other people's memories is that you start to lose the difference between what's theirs and what's yours. Luckily, I know how to exploit that—as long as the teachers don't find out, anyway. Normal after-school jobs are over-rated if you have a secret in-school business. When your last name is emblazoned on the school crest—*and* the school letterhead—the other students will let you get away with anything. Like stealing their memories.

On my laptop, I open up my memory-uploading app. A line of students snakes away from me, each one wanting to buy a different experience. And I have loads of experiences to choose from, indexed within the app. I bypass the cool graphic interface normal users of HiveMind see and run the hacking program I wrote back when my dad was first developing the software. It uses a variety of complex algorithms to gain backdoor access to *all* the files stored in the HiveMind cloud, not just my own.

Usually, my partner in crime, Zoey Flint, doles out numbers as though the students are waiting in line at the deli, except she tex-ted me that she's running late today, so I'm doing it myself. Once they receive a number, they disperse across the courtyard and mill about like strangers trying to act normal before they break out in a flash mob.

"Hey, Arden." The first customer out of thirty gives me a quick smile, buttering me up to get the goods. "Can I have the answers to last night's Biotechnology homework?" She lifts a tablet, revealing a mess of stylus-created scribbles on top of complicated math problems. Dark clouds swirl in the washed-out sky, turning the mirrored building in front of us into a sheet of gray. Cold and clinical, more like an office building than a high school for science geniuses. Laboratory chic.

I hold out my palm, indicating fifty bucks. My standard rate.

"Oh my God, you're a lifesaver." The customer digs in her purse and sets the wad of bills in my palm. Once I slide them into my change purse, I get to work transferring over a classmate's stolen memory. The app syncs directly to users' minds thanks to cutting-edge technology my dad invented, so my customer will get an instant download of a memory that doesn't belong to her. But once it copies, it's hers forever, automatically added to her account via a bidirectional sync.

Someone else's fingers cover my vision, and gardenia perfume drowns out the acrid scent of oncoming rain. "Guess who." An excited squeal punctuates the gesture.

"Well, the giggle alone rules out an advancement in robotics. And also someone I'd be friends with." I pause for dramatic effect, ignoring Zoey Flint's scoff. "This mystery may never be solved." I lift one of my best friend's hands off my face, catching a glimpse of the scar that bulges, pink and angry, on the inside of my wrist. I flinch, heart thumping. I first noticed the scar this morning when getting dressed, but I have no recollection of how I got it. It freaks me out every time I spot it.

"Actually," Zoey says. The skeletal trees perform a macabre dance set to the symphony of the wind. A sudden chill descends and Zoey tugs on her white cardigan. "I heard some freshman is working on a robotics project that—" She glances over at my phone, and her eyes widen. "Whoa. Twenty-seven customers this morning! Sorry again for being late. Blame Veronica for taking forever in the shower." She grabs the phone to take over line-control duties and crosses her pantsuit-covered legs. At our school, you never know when a lecture might turn into an important meeting, so she always tries to be prepared. Not to mention we share a parking lot with the lab techs who work on the floors above the school, who may become our coworkers one day.

Zoey handles all the parts of the job I hate: organization, money laundering, and marketing. Without her, I'd be lost. Or at least I'd be without excess cash flow, and every bit of cash helps. It's all seed money for when I start my *own* company one day. I shoot her a big grin for keeping me organized and honest. Well, as honest as it comes when performing illicit tasks that would get me expelled if the administration found out.

I flip my arm downward, covering the scar. Out of sight, out of mind.

Except, of course, if you have HiveMind, version 1.0.

Years ago, my dad developed the cloud-based memory-uploading app. Every memory gets backed up and synced to the brain instantly, meaning nothing is ever forgotten. No more blackouts from a night of drinking. No more study sessions that jumble in the brain as you stare at the test. No more excuses.

Users are only supposed to be able to access their own files. But I never do what I'm supposed to do.

"So you're probably wondering why I'm late." Zoey leans over me, the ends of her blond hair dangling over my computer screen. "It's because I have news! According to the triangular love theory, anyway."

"I already saw the memory." I tap my finger against the file descriptions and thumbnail images that pop up when I hack into Teddy Day's mind. For months, Zoey's had a ritualistic compulsion to dot her *i*'s with hearts when she thinks of him and an obsessive need to know if he's thinking of her back. Which means I've seen so many of his damn memories, my knowledge extends beyond the banal, like what he eats for breakfast, and escalates into I-*so*-did-not-need-to-know-that territory: like what kind of boxers he wears. "Teddy called you last night. Clearly this is the first step to admitting his feelings have progressed beyond the avoid-making-eye-contact phase."

She sighs happily, not picking up on the sarcasm in my voice. After all, he only called her because he was looking for me. He never bothered to find me though.

"It's the only theory that makes sense. He's in love with me."

I laugh. "Yep, a totally logical conclusion." I scroll through Teddy's mind and find his memory of completing last night's homework. As the top genius at a school for geniuses, he's the only person who doesn't need to study but always does. When your spot on the school roster comes from an invitation-only admittance policy and a generous grant supplied by Varga Industries, you tend to only slack off in summer, when free time finally fits into your schedule. A brief preview in the software shows Teddy's view yesterday afternoon as he worked out the answers to the math problems. I drop the memory into the first customer's mind. "Don't forget to alter your answer wording and get at least one wrong."

A few months ago, Mrs. Schlissel discovered three students using the same essay wording verbatim. She gave them all detention and I gave all my customers a stern talking-to about what going to a school for geniuses really means: i.e., use your damn wits. And just in case they didn't have any to spare after their studies, I jacked up my prices to make the market smaller.

The girl instantly straightens, not even thanking me as her thumb sweeps over the keypad while she ambles away.

When Zoey texts the next customer to step up to the plate, he gives us a horsey smile with bright white teeth. "How are you fine ladies this morning? Love that yellow on you, Arden. Really makes your hair stand out."

I wave my hand for him to get on with it. It's never good when people lay it on this thick.

"Here's a secret." He invades my personal space by sitting on my other side. I scoot closer to Zoey. "I have a huge crush on Melody Clarendon. I want to get to know her better."

Time to break out the big guns. I crack my neck from side to side. "Darwin hypothesized that spoken language evolved due to a need for reciprocal altruism, so—"

"What Arden here means"—Zoey shoots me a dirty glare that could only be interpreted as *don't alienate the customers*—"is you should go talk to her."

He strokes his chin. "I was thinking more like . . . biblically."

Zoey's face squishes like she just bit into a lemon.

"Dude, that's creepy." I flick my wrist, shooing him. "You know the rules." I don't mind violating people's privacy when it comes to test answers, but I have to draw the line somewhere. No nudity, no revealing other people's secrets, and no deleting memories.

As the creepy guy ambles away, the next kid in line, Simon Zajek, hurls himself at me. He leans way too close, and I arch my back to avoid his apple-juice breath. "Okay, this is going to sound weird."

"Doubtful." I fake a yawn. I've heard it all. Especially from him.

Zoey snickers, pushing blond waves behind her ear. The leafless trees sway as though they're mocking Simon's jitteriness. Men in white lab coats hustle from the parking lot to the Varga Industries entrance on the other side of the building.

Simon darts his head around the courtyard, knocking his Red Sox cap into my forehead. "You can't tell anyone."

I draw my finger across my lips. My backup dancer nods.

"Is . . . Is Veronica cheating on me?" He holds out a hundred bucks. I shake my head—this falls into category two: secrets.

We can't show him this. It'll crush him. And besides, I'd vowed not to give him any more memories. He asks for something new and more exhilarating every time. I've even noticed him going through withdrawal symptoms—jitters, irritability—when I refuse to feed his addiction. Each time, it gets harder to find a new form of glory from someone else's mind. I got lucky last time when I found a memory of some senior's older brother going skydiving to give him. "Simon, we talked about this. We agreed to a break from memories for a while."

"*You* agreed." He pulls the skin of his cheeks taut. "You're cutting me off cold turkey?"

I swallow hard and take the analog route, the path that doesn't violate my rules. "According to rumors, she is. With Blake." My eyelashes flutter closed to avoid catching a glimpse of his pained expression.

"And Josh," Zoey adds.

We don't mention the rest of the names.

His shoulders sink. "Please," he begs. "I need to see for myself."

He looks so distraught even though the gossip we just shared is practically common knowledge. I started doing this to help people, and seeing the truth might help Simon. He shouldn't be with someone who disrespects him enough to cheat on him with multiple people.

"Fine, but . . . I'm really sorry." I deposit Veronica's memories into his mind. His features fold and crumble.

I have to look away, my chest tight. I focus instead on the sleek silver silo used by scientists conducting experiments in renewable-energy advancements as jagged streaks of lightning barrel across the distant sky.

Simon stumbles backward, his face pinching in absolute heartbreak. Sometimes I wish I didn't have a front-row seat to every one of my classmates' screwups.

A blast of thunder booms. "That was awful."

Zoey rubs my shoulder. "Maybe this will make you feel better about it? I overheard Veronica whispering about reporting you this morning. Consider this preemptive revenge."

I bite my lip. It could also be construed as the first strike of a war.

I spend the next twenty minutes dispensing more test answers and experiences that range from scoring the winning goal for a kid cut from the team to virtually attending a concert for a guy whose parents grounded him the night his favorite band played. Misty drops fall from the sky and plink onto the umbrella Zoey holds over the two of us. She doesn't do a very good job, and rain blends into my now-damp shirt, which clings to me in a scandalous, not-appropriate-for-school-dress-code way. I blink against the rogue drops sticking to my eyelashes. "Is that everyone?"

Zoey glances at the two piles of cash. "For this morning, yep. I'm sure we'll get a new round at lunch." She squints into the distance and points an arm lined with gold bracelets, which makes the umbrella wobble. "Wait! Looks like there's one more customer."

There's an unfamiliar boy loping toward us. He's wearing a button-down shirt and holding an arm over his forehead to combat the pummeling rain. He'd be cute if only he held himself upright. He's got eyes that can't seem to make up their mind between green and blue and golden brown, and a hunched, guarded expression. I squint at him as my brain does a poor job of emulating Google's reverse image search. Admittance into Monica Varga High is a tightly controlled operation and no scenario admits a new student four days before our thesis projects are due.

"Who is *that*?"

Lightning slices between two clouds, drenching the sky in neon colors too ethereal to be captured in Photoshop.

Zoey throws her head back in laughter. "Very funny, Arden."

The boy brushes beads of water from his eyes, then pats down the side part on his sandy hair, as if keeping the strands in place is the only thing he can control. He stares at his feet like he's learning to walk for the first time.

"No, seriously. Who is that? He can't be new here. My mom would have mentioned a new student joining. Especially someone so cute."

Zoey's face suddenly fills with concern. "You're scaring me."

My skin goes cold and the smile drops off my lips. I volley my head from Zoey to the stranger, feeling like I've missed a joke everyone else is in on.

Pressing her lips together, she plants her palm on my forehead. "You need to go to the nurse and lie down, stat. How many cups of coffee did you have yesterday? That stuff rots your brain. And your kidneys."

I leap to my feet, panic clawing up my throat. "I'm not tired and I'm not stressed. Just tell me who that boy is."

Zoey turns white. "You seriously don't remember him?"

"I've never seen him before in my life." My words sound as dire as if they were followed by a *dun dun dun* sound effect.

"He's a student here. In fact, I'm pretty sure you guys are friends." Her words sound equally grave. "I mean, not *best* friends, because obviously I already hold that title. But, you know, school friends. Lab partners."

My heart's hammering so hard it feels like I just ran a marathon. "I would remember being friends with . . . someone like that."

She looks horrified, but then after a few seconds, she snaps her fingers. "Oh wait! I know what's wrong." She beams as if she just solved the Navier-Stokes equation. "Sounds like HiveMind might be glitching. I bet the server just needs a reboot."

Tension drains from my shoulders. "That makes sense." Technically, HiveMind's still in beta testing, so there are often glitches like this, though there haven't been any in quite a while. I twist my necklace in my fingers. The cool metal feels like a familiar comfort blanket. My fingertip skims over the tiny engravings etched into the rectangular pendant:

01000001
01110010
01100100
01100101
01101110

The binary number grooves always remind me of who I am. And what I want to do.

I suck in a deep breath of air tinged with an earthy aftertaste and let the heavy pendant drop against my clavicle.

"Hey, Bash." Zoey ushers him under her umbrella when he gets closer. "What's up?"

Bash and Zoey stand shoulder to shoulder, him rigid, her relaxed, as if they've stood this close countless times before. He blinks at her. "You know who I am?"

"See?" Zoey gives me a triumphant smile. "It's happening to him too. Totally a glitch."

Bash gives her a weird look. "What is?"

"HiveMind," Zoey says.

Bash blinks at us.

I'm still on edge, so I try to end this conversation fast. "What do you need?" I tap a few keys on my computer to run a diagnostic on my mind.

Bash hesitates. "Apparently there's a quiz in my first class. I heard you could help me cram?" The warning bell rings a second before thunder conquers it. His entire body stiffens. "Too late."

"Not if you're with me," I say. "I can help. Not help you cram, but . . ." Much to my surprise, I feel my lips curve into the telltale sign of a smile. "Help."

He hands me a crumpled piece of paper. His schedule, scribbled on office letterhead, as if he wrote it only a few minutes ago.

"Oh crap. You forgot your schedule?" Zoey shakes her head. "Better get that server rebooted fast." She pauses. "Well, maybe not *too* fast. I wouldn't mind if Ms. Kensington forgets about our essays being due this morning."

"I'm emailing IT right now." I pound out an email on my phone as the diagnostic continues to run on my computer.

After I hit send on my email, I snatch the paper out of Bash's hand. "Wait. You have Biochem Software Development first period?" My stomach hollows out when he nods. "That's my class too."

The wind howls and rustles my dark hair, whipping a few strands into my face that stick to my lipstick. Something deep in my core pulses, like a reactor coming to life. First I forget a student and now I forget about a test? This level of glitch has never happened before in HiveMind. Not on this wide a scale. Usually a glitch only results in the loss of a single memory or two. It's supposed to make sure I never forget anything. That's the whole point of backing up my memories and storing them in ones and zeroes, accessible from any device with Wi-Fi. "Zo, why didn't you tell me we had a quiz?" She has Biochem Software Development with the same teacher a few periods later.

Her smile wavers. "We studied for it on Sunday."

Another bolt of lightning zings, illuminating the sky and tangling with an echo of thunder.

"Screw emailing, I'm marching right up to IT to make them reboot the server." I turn to Bash. "Walk with me."

Zoey hands Bash the umbrella. He stares at it for a moment, turning it upside down and letting rain collect in the overturned basin. When he catches Zoey and me staring at him, he scrambles to spin it upright, cheeks red. Water spills onto his head and soaks his shoulders. He moves next to me, body heat radiating, and slides the black umbrella over both our heads. Water drips onto my shirt. "Are you still going to help me?" he asks.

I nod. As we huddle together under the tiny umbrella, his gait slowing when my heels sink into the wet grass, I balance my laptop on my forearm and scroll through the files. Blood whooshes in my ears. I search for someone, anyone, to steal the memory of studying for the quiz from. Despite letting other people cheat on tests for fun and profit, I avoid it myself. But I can't get a bad grade this close to the adversarial review. My entire future rides on the results of that review.

"What are you doing?" He scans his badge to grant access to the school and holds the school door open for me. The air-conditioning blasts in my face, making me shiver. We step into the nearly empty hallway, the click of my heels reverberating off the blue and red metal lockers.

"Helping you cram." I find Teddy Day's file again and set a delay on the memory for twenty minutes before I drop a copy into my brain. I'll study hard for the next one. . . . unless I forget again. "This'll only take a sec." I look for his account on the server, but my search for Bash comes up empty.

He squints at my screen as he shakes out the umbrella and

closes it. "It's Sebastian, actually. Sebastian Cuomo. I don't really know why everyone keeps calling me Bash."

His name pops up and my custom back-end script hacks into his mind with as much ease as everyone else's. I click on his storage, ready to deposit the same memory into his mind, but . . . Sebastian has no memories at all. My arm stiffens.

"What?" he asks, his voice growing more panicked. "What?"

"Sorry, there's an error. One sec." I shut down the program and restart it. Once again, his brain is empty. . . . except for three files. One from this morning, one of our current conversation, and the copy of Teddy's memory I just deposited.

That's not a glitch. That's a complete wipeout. How could anyone seriously have zero memories? How could they even *live*?

My computer dings, the diagnostic of my mind complete. I click on the file and nearly drop my computer onto the floor.

7,694 files missing.

I press my palm to my slick forehead, where a dull sensation throbs, barely noticeable, like the hum of a refrigerator at night. Since I last ran the diagnostic yesterday, seven thousand memories have disappeared from my mind.

I slam my laptop shut and shove it under my arm. I don't care about class or the quiz or the way Sebastian's staring at me with a face full of terror. All I care about is finding out why this boy— who everyone but me seems to know—and I are both missing memories.

One of the perks of being the headmistress's daughter is being able to sneak into her bedroom when she's not home and duplicate her all-access keycard. It remains in my purse at all times, always handy in circumstances just like this. The IT room resides in the basement, along with several other boring, unimportant rooms, locked away from laymen like Sebastian—and me, I suppose—without clearance. The only entrance is via a locked door in the E wing of our school.

I swipe my mom's keycard against the scanner. The light blinks from red to green. I wave Sebastian forward, but he hesitates.

"Are we allowed down here?"

I twirl the keycard at him as if it's the only proof he needs. I'm about to open the door, but it swings open toward me. I leap back, knocking into Sebastian behind me. He stumbles a few steps as I let out a small scream.

Teddy Day's eyes widen at the sight of us, looking as if he's seen a ghost.

I turn to Sebastian with a grin. "See? Everyone goes down here all the time," I lie. "Hey, Teddy, tell Kimmel we'll be a few minutes late." I brush past Teddy, giving him a nod. He stares at Sebastian, blinking a few times, clearly waiting for a similar hello.

Sebastian ducks his head and follows me.

As we descend the concrete stairs, the air temperature drops about thirty degrees. I rub my hands over my arms to combat the chill. The powerful computers stored down here need to be kept cool at all times. We bypass locked rooms that serve no purpose except for storage, as far as I know. The only two places I ever visit down here are the IT room and the server room.

Just before we reach the door to the IT room, my mom steps out of it.

"Arden?" Her dark bob drapes across her eyes and she pushes it aside. "The bell's going to ring in about two seconds." On cue, the final bell rings, making us officially late. Her eyes flick to Sebastian behind me, and she shoots him an expectant look. "How did you two get down here?"

I ignore her question and go straight for the kill. Just the facts, Mom. "My memories are missing. I need to talk to IT. I think Hive-Mind's glitching."

Sebastian's eyes widen.

"Yes, yes. I'm aware. I've had numerous complaints." She jerks her chin toward the IT door. "Brandon's already working on it. It'll be fixed in no time."

I take a step toward the door anyway. I need to talk to Brandon myself.

Mom raises a brow and clears her throat. "Arden, sweetheart, don't make me give you and your friend detention over something as silly as truancy."

"Please, Mom. Give me two minutes with him. I just want to know what he's doing to fix it."

She sighs, and I take her silence as an invitation. I keep my gaze focused straight ahead of me until I hear the click of her heels disappear around the corner. "Listen—" I abruptly twirl around and slam into Sebastian. Again.

Sebastian lets out an "oof" as he stumbles backward. "Is this a habit of yours?" he says. "Because if so, I better get myself some protective gear." He purses his lips. "Though I guess technically it can only be considered a habit after three or more times."

I blink at him, trying to make sense of how calm he is during all this. "Listen, I need a favor. If you see me do anything that I shouldn't be doing in this room, just forget what you saw, okay?"

He chuckles. "That seems in line with how this morning is going."

When I yank open the door to the room, Brandon Chen bolts upright. Red crescent moons curve below his puffy eyes. He sniffles and drops the crumpled tissue on one of the many keyboards surrounding him in a semicircle of humming computer consoles. His lower lip quivers, but he manages to keep his emotions at bay long enough to speak. "Did Leo send you?"

"Leo? Why would he do that?"

Brandon and my brother, Leo, have been dating for years, since they both attended school here as promising students before rocketing into their careers, Brandon as the head IT guru and Leo as one of the scientists working on breakthroughs in biotechnology over at Varga Industries.

Brandon bites his wobbling lower lip. "Never mind."

I take a step toward him. "Are—are you okay?"

"Yeah." He straightens, buoyed by a new resolve. "Yes," he says again as if to further reassure himself. He divides his gaze between Sebastian and me. "Are you two . . . okay?"

We must look equally freaked out. I shake my head. "Seven thousand of my memories went missing overnight. Sebastian lost more."

Sebastian lets out a breath. "So it's not just me?"

"Yeah, your mom told me there's been complaints. I'm making

a backup." Brandon flourishes his hand toward a few of the consoles. "As soon as it's finished, I'll reboot the server. That usually does the trick."

"Reboot it right now." I slide between him and the admin console, ready to do it myself if he doesn't pull the trigger. The admin console is a laptop that's bolted down with chains. If anyone tries to remove the chains or the laptop itself, an alarm system immediately pings several key staff members.

Memory loss has occurred a few times over the years, though not since I helped stabilize the server with new code nine months ago. Three years ago, every user lost twenty-four hours of data, but nothing that bad has happened since. When a memory is deleted from HiveMind, it's just gone, as if it never existed in the first place, so no one got those twenty-four hours back. We like to make up stories of what transpired: random hookups, scientific breakthroughs, and secret confessions.

"It's really best if we wait until the backup finishes. It looks like it'll be done in"—he squints at the screen in front of him—"three days and twenty—"

I shake my head. "We can't wait that long." Because of Hive-Mind's limitations, memories can only be copied one at a time onto each computer, even for routine backups. Though using twenty computers for backups helps speed the process along.

With a sigh, he pushes himself out of his chair and strides over to where I stand by the admin console. Only two admin computers exist: this one and another my mom keeps in a location so secure I don't even know where it is. I circle around Brandon to watch from behind him. While Brandon's back is turned, I fumble into my messenger bag until my fingers grasp a small SSD drive I always have with me. I shove it into the USB port in one of the monitoring consoles that are set up on the side table, where Brandon hopefully won't notice it. As long as the drive's connected, I'll be able to monitor the reboot myself. Otherwise, these computers are off-limits. The network security key is beyond even my hacking skills.

Brandon spins around. "Reboot's in progress. Should be up in a few minutes."

"Thanks, B. I owe you one for sure." I turn toward the door.

"Wait!" Brandon shouts. "Can you tell Leo—?"

I swivel to face Brandon again as his face crumples. He swallows hard, his Adam's apple bobbing. "Never mind."

I squint at him. "You sure?"

He squeezes his eyes shut for a few seconds. "Yeah." He opens a drawer and pulls out two pink hall passes. "Here."

I pluck them from his fingers and give him a tight smile, making a mental note to send my brother down here to give him a great big comfort hug. The dude looks like he needs a serious shoulder to cry on.

When Sebastian and I exit into the hallway, he looks at me with big, hopeful eyes. "I don't know what you did, but do you really think it will work?"

I nod, ignoring the way my stomach clenches. "This kind of thing happened before." Sort of. "The reboot always fixes it." Sometimes.

The two of us head back up the stairs and traipse through the empty hallways. Silence wedges between us like a barrier.

Before we open the door to Kimmel's room, he breaks the silence with a question. "Hey, um." He shuffles his feet. "What do I do?" He jerks his chin toward the classroom door. "In there?"

I blink at him. "What do you mean?"

"When I go inside. What should I do?"

I think back to his account, completely empty before today, and my heart aches for his complete lack of knowledge. "Sit at a desk and follow instructions." I give him a slight pat on the shoulder. "It'll be easy, promise."

In Kimmel's classroom, twenty heads pop up from neat rows of faux-wooden desks—the only part of the classroom on par with average schools. Behind the learning area, the room expands into a sprawling biotech lab filled with state-of-the-art equipment, glossy black tables, and computers so powerful they need their own machine room. This biochem lab is one of twenty-seven specialized labs at the school, each dedicated to a particular field of study.

"Kind of you to join us, Miss Varga and Mr. Cuomo." Mr. Kimmel strokes his beard, bushy and lumberjack-style, as if to draw attention away from the lack of hair on his scalp. In another life, he would have made a great bouncer with his stocky frame and deadpan attitude. "Your peers were thrilled to learn they have eight fewer minutes for this test while we waited for you to grace us with your presence."

Sebastian ducks past me and hunkers down at a desk in the very last row, a row behind every other student.

The clicking of my black stilettos syncs with the pitter-patter of rain pounding on the glass windows that stretch across one entire wall. I pause in front of my seat, every eye still glued to me, when I notice not one empty seat but two, right next to each other. Who used to sit next to me? I try to dredge up memories the old-fashioned way, but in every one, there was no seat next to me. There was nothing at all.

My spine stiffens as I plop into my chair.

Teddy Day, who sits on the other side of the empty desk, shields his tablet screen with his muscular arm. His cheap Fossil watch gleams silver against his dark skin. His hair used to be shaved close to his scalp but now springs in little, curly ringlets that frame his chiseled face. No wonder all the girls swoon in his vicinity.

Mr. Kimmel heads down a row, placing tablets on each desk, and pauses when he reaches the empty seat next to mine. His eyes meet Sebastian's in the back. "For once, you made a good decision, Mr. Cuomo. I think your new desk location will be an excellent choice for you." He taps my desk. "Less chance you'll cheat."

The class snickers while my neck prickles. They all get the joke, but it feels like the joke's on me. They all remember him.

I turn on my tablet and suck in a deep breath that's a mixture of ripe body odor from the boy in front of me and the pungent chemicals in the back of the room. Three short essays, all information I vaguely remember tackling in class, but the details blur like a digital photograph with a weird filter.

1. Describe the process for converting DNA data into binary code.
2. Name three methods of connecting the body to a computer, and give pros and cons of each.
3. Give a brief time line of the history of mind-to-computer conversion, making sure to highlight key dates.

I press my lips together at the easy questions. I don't need those extra eight minutes to ace this. I imagine an alternate version of me sitting at a graffitied wooden desk at Wickham High, the generic town high school. My test there would include some trite paradigm I learned in third grade, like the phases of cell division. Here I get to answer questions that not only challenge me but also propel my career forward. Thanks to a modified curriculum that lets students condense four years' worth of unnecessary classes—such as English and US History—into a three-month intensive freshman year, I never waste time being subpar.

But of course, one failing grade would put me on academic probation, and that would prevent me from winning the adversarial review competition. On the morning of the annual press conference, the seniors present the thesis projects they've been working on for their entire high school careers. We each get five minutes to impress a board made up of key school officials, like my mother, the Ethics Committee, and a few outsiders chosen because of the prominence in their careers. If Einstein was still alive, he would most certainly be on the board. Steve Jobs too.

The board decides which projects get funding from Varga Industries. Monica Varga High operates on a project-based learning environment, where each student works with a scientist mentor from Varga Industries to invent new technologies that will change the world. But most projects never progress beyond a prototype. Out of the one hundred seniors, approximately ten will receive funding. But that's not even the important part. The board selects only one senior whose project will be showcased at the press conference later that night. It's a huge honor *and* a huge career booster. Two years ago, Leo's project won, and after two years of beta testing, it's finally releasing this weekend. If I have any shot at starting my own company in the next year instead of getting the hand-me-downs from my family, I *need* to win. But every other senior in this school feels the exact same way.

I can't afford to fail. Not right now. So I bang out a partial answer for the third question. Eighteen years ago, my dad successfully completed the first binary syncing of brain data with computer files, which paved the way for advancements such as HiveMind. It took him seven more years to develop the first basic prototype of HiveMind and an additional four to deem the product safe enough to hook up the first beta testers—Mom, Leo, me—to the system before expanding the number of users into the hundreds. Only those associated with MVH have the privilege—and requirement—of participating in this final round of user-acceptance testing before the software releases to the general populace. Students, teachers, parents, siblings, and employees of Varga Industries are now required to sync with the software as part of a trial run to make sure everything works correctly before the software debuts . . . in four days.

HiveMind has always been a part of me. I can't wait for it to be part of the rest of the world too. But first we need to find the root cause of this glitch and update the code to ensure it doesn't happen again.

I fill in the date HiveMind was created and work my way backward to the research my dad did at MIT, where he pioneered brain mapping. I also add info about when my mom founded this school for the most gifted science students in the country, since it's relevant to the QA cycle.

Just as I tap the entry box for the second answer, a tiny *ding* resonates in my mind, indicating the start of the memory simulation I had set on delay. A notebook ghosts over the reality of my test, like two images superimposed on TV. I try to ignore the sound of fingers tapping and focus on the new scene playing in my mind like a movie.

I peer out of Teddy's eyes, watching a highlighter race across a line of handwritten text. His thoughts invade my own: *What's the point of this? I don't need to study. But I know being valedictorian would make for a great press release once my project wins the board competition.* . . .

Ugh, Teddy, get to the point. Usually, when I prep for a quiz, I read over the notes to myself for a few minutes so I can see and hear them when I replay the memory. Then right before the quiz, I simulate my own memory in my mind. So much more effective than the archaic method of cued recall via studying.

Teddy squeezes his eyes shut for a second to concentrate, creating an unavoidable black shroud over my vision. I tap my nail against my desk as if I'm thinking while trying to read Teddy's ugly, scrawled handwriting through the image in my mind. But HiveMind memory simulations aren't as vivid as real life, and his writing blurs. His thoughts come louder than my own, distracting me: *I wonder what Eliza's doing later?* Teddy lapses into a replay of kissing her and then the replay morphs into an R-rated fantasy that makes me blush. Oh, Einstein. I do *not* need to know what kinds of perverted things turn him on.

Teddy shakes his head, making the image of his notebook rock like an earthquake. *Test on Tuesday. Biochem Software. Unit twenty-four. Eliza.*

I glance at the clock in a panic. Each moment Teddy gets distracted means another minute wasted for me. The real Teddy next to me types away with his tongue poking out the side of his mouth while the Teddy in my mind picks up a stack of index cards. Finally, he transcribes the necessary information I need for my own test. If I subscribed to the notion of a divine deity, now would be the time I muttered a prayer of thanks to it.

Several minutes later, Teddy abandons studying to play video games, and the memory subsequently ends. I fill in my answers as best I can, making sure to alter my wording, and submit my test to the grade-book cloud. I blink a few times, adjusting to the single image of the bright classroom. When I glance behind me to check on Sebastian, he's hunched over his desk, wiping sweat from his forehead. He lifts his eyes to me, and the horrified look on his face makes my skin go cold.

Mr. Kimmel clears his throat. "That's it. That's all the time you get."

One girl lets out an audible gasp. "I'm on the last question!"

"Submit your answers and bring your tablets up, then resume working on your thesis projects." He taps his wrist. "Time's a-ticking. Only four days left before you present your projects to the school board."

Everyone in the room perks up at the reminder of the competition. The girl a few seats in front of me spins around and eyes me with absolute contempt, then shifts her gaze to Teddy and gives him the same evil eye. She knows we're the ones to beat.

Teddy turns in his tablet and then pulls out his laptop, but his knee bobs up and down beneath his desk. I silently curse Teddy because he must be done with his project. It's some advancement in 3-D bio-printing to speed up the process of producing DNA-specific organs for transplants. Last year he creeped everyone out when he carried around a replica of a beating, bloody heart for a week as part of an experiment.

After I turn in my test, I open my laptop to my to-do list, only to find it empty. My mouth becomes sandpaper, and I rub my temples. All my backed-up versions: gone. Even the ones synced to the cloud storage system. What the hell? I would never have deleted them.

I search HiveMind for keywords like *to-do*, *project*, and *thesis*. A sick dread settles into me at the words staring back at me on the screen: *Your search has returned zero results.*

My pulse beats at the base of my neck. Holy retrograde amnesia, I don't remember the project I've been working on for the last four years at all. I don't have any idea who my scientist mentor was. What else have I forgotten?

I'm in full panic mode now, my leg tapping against the floor as if each revolution of my ankle could speed up time. With shaky fingers, I navigate to the SSD drive I plugged into the monitoring computer in the IT room, run a script I wrote a long time ago to gain control of the remote computer, and use it to pull up the command prompt. This machine is only used for monitoring HiveMind from a Tech Ops standpoint, so it only provides me with a limited amount of read and write access to the software. I type a few commands in the command line to check the status of the last restore. As soon as I press *enter*, a new line pops up:

Reboot successful.

Thunder booms outside, loud and sinister, and I jump. I still don't remember a single thing. I check Sebastian's mind, and his is the same as well: mostly blank. My body begins to shake, skin heating up. I rummage through my messenger bag and tug out the external hard drive I routinely back up my memories onto every night, but when I pull out the case, I hear a sound like maracas shaking. Aluminum shards, twisted plastic, and pieces of a broken and smashed motherboard slide out of the case and skid across the desk.

My heart leaps into my throat, clogging my airway. I gasp so loudly that several heads turn in my direction. I hastily slide the smashed pieces of my hard drive into the case and shove it back into my bag before anyone else can see how easily someone was able to destroy my belongings. Destroy my chances. Destroy *me*.

Students scurry off to the lab in the back, but I ignore them as I rummage through my notebook—the handwritten one I only keep to prevent data loss of this magnitude—searching for evidence that I haven't failed Sanity 101. I bite back a sob. Almost every page has been ripped out, leaving only jagged remnants clinging to the spiral ring.

There are no coincidences in science. Someone erased it all deliberately.

00110011

I shove my ruined notebook in my bag with my destroyed hard drive and turn in panic toward Sebastian. Teddy's skirting around the desks and he seems anxious to go talk to him. Before he can reach him, Kimmel interrupts. "Miss Varga, Mr. Cuomo, can I have a word? It's about your project."

The boy in front of Sebastian contorts his mouth into the requisite "oooOOOoooh" to denote he thinks we're getting in trouble. My pulse spikes.

Teddy rakes his hand through his tight curls and sits back down at his desk.

I push myself out of my chair, wobbling on unsteady feet. My whole body is keyed up and I must look like a feral animal as I bound toward Kimmel's desk in desperation for any information he might have about my project. It takes concerted effort to force myself to stand still even though every cell in my body continues to buzz. Sebastian positions himself several feet away from me, then changes his mind and takes a step closer.

"Have you worked out the last bug in your project yet?" Kimmel tugs at his beard. Chemistry equations and inspirational quotes about science hang on the concrete walls behind his desk. "I need to see it working properly prior to the adversarial review."

"Um." A single bead of sweat forms in the space between my

boobs. A hysterical cry itches to rip out of my throat, but I swallow it back down. *Stay calm*, I coax myself, steadying my breathing the way I have to do whenever I visit my buddy the Hypnotist. Kimmel can't know I've lost my memories. It would be enough to disqualify me from the competition. The teachers here love when you spit out scientific facts, so I do just that, hoping for the love of all things quadratic that I sound like I know what I'm talking about. "According to the expectancy violations theory, surprise increases positive responses to new data." I perform an Oscar-worthy grin. "So the best way to knock the socks off the judges is to keep it a secret."

"This is serious." He pulls at the collar of his striped shirt, loosening it. "I really think your joint project will win the competition, and if you show me before Friday, we'll have time to revise your demonstration."

Joint project. My mouth gapes and I can barely breathe. I place a hand against the wall to keep from tipping over, but the world turns upside down anyway. I can't remember what my project is. Or working on it for FOUR YEARS with a boy who doesn't even exist in my mind. And of course, it's not just memories missing but files and notebook pages.

Someone went to a lot of trouble to make sure I forgot everything related to my project.

My head whips between Sebastian, who wears a caught-with-his-pants-down expression, and Kimmel, who seems to be trying to invent telepathy with the way his gaze bores into mine.

"Can I see the proposal document we submitted?" I enunciate each word to sound as normal as possible. Translation: *What the hell was our project?*

Kimmel blinks. "Gave it back to you last week."

"Okay, well, I need to talk to my mentor first—"

Kimmel's mouth tightens. "That's not funny, Arden."

Not funny? Why isn't that funny? My skin prickles.

I fling my head toward Sebastian for help at the same time his eyes plead with me. It's up to me to rescue us. I latch onto the first thing Kimmel had said and run with it to buy us some time. "We're still trying to iron out that bug issue. I'm not really sure what the problem is or how to fix it."

"Well, you need to figure it out before Friday. Because it's not just about the competition." His tone increases in urgency. "If your project isn't ready by the day of the adversarial review and press conference, someone will die. Do you want that hanging on your conscience?"

I jolt. There's no longer any chance at tamping down the panic rising inside me. "No, but—"

"Unless this goes to beta testing, that one death will become hundreds. Thousands."

He can't be serious. . . . right? I grip the desk to keep myself steady.

"Do you understand what I'm saying? This is a matter of life and death."

My shoulders tremble with the magnitude of an earthquake. "Wh-What do you mean?"

Sebastian backs away, his face a mask of horror at this news.

"Arden, stop stalling and—" Kimmel pauses, eyes wide, mouth parted in horror. He freezes like an ancient Greek turned to stone at the sight of Medusa.

The terror projected on his face strikes me numb. I poke his arm, lightly at first. When he doesn't respond, I jab harder, unable to keep the panic out of my voice. "Mr. Kimmel?"

His face crumples in pain. Students swing their heads in our direction, a few rising out of their seats to see what's going on.

Sebastian's eyes widen. "What's wrong with him?"

I shake my head. If I had that answer, I'd know what was wrong with me as well.

A full minute passes before Kimmel shakes his head out of a daze. He spins to face the wall. The defined muscles beneath his shirt tighten as he chokes on a breath. He uses the bottom of his shirt to wipe his forehead before turning back around. The room is completely silent except for his ragged breath and the racing of my heart.

"Why are you here?" He divides his gaze between Sebastian and me. "Did you need something?" His gaze locks behind us. "Everyone! Back to work."

Goose bumps emboss my arms. He doesn't remember what just happened, like the moment was erased from his mind. Did my face contort in pain when my memories first disappeared?

There's a commotion as the rest of the students scramble to look busy. My gaze never leaves Kimmel. "Did you . . . forget what we were just talking about?"

"We were talking?" Kimmel loosens his tie, pulling it so far away from his neck it's as if he fashioned a noose. "Yes, yes. I—lost my train of thought."

Something in my chest tightens. "We were talking about my project. You said if it doesn't go to the press conference—"

"Right. Right." Kimmel nods to himself. "Give me your verbal pitch." He rests one elbow on his desk and angles toward me, finally managing to perfect a casual appearance a little too late. "You'll need to practice it anyway for your speech to the school board."

"I—" I fiddle with my necklace, twisting it up and down the chain to keep calm. Kimmel claps his hands loud enough to make me snap my teeth together. "Everyone, stop working! Back to your seats. I think we need a little refresher on the importance of your pitch."

There's a mad dash, students rushing across the room. I wobble like I've been hit by a freight train. My head spins. I sink into my seat, my knees giving out halfway.

The boy in front of me twists around. "What just happened?"

I shake my head. I'm still trying to make sense of that myself.

"It's come to my attention that we need to go over the art of a verbal pitch. Any volunteers?" Kimmel's voice is breezy and light, as if he just told a good joke to a fellow teacher instead of telling us our project is a matter of life and death.

Every head turns to pin the target on someone else.

Kimmel's bald head glistens when he stands under the overhead light. "Mr. Day?"

Teddy leans back in his chair, resting his arms behind his head, elbows splayed. Wispy curls frame his face like a dusting of crops on a farm. "3-D bio-print DNA-based human organs at laser printer speed."

"Excellent. Perfect summary." Kimmel presses his hand to his forehead like a sailor and scans the room. "Miss Clarendon? Twitter pitch. One-forty characters or less."

In the back of the room, Melody's cheeks explode with color as she ducks her face behind her frizzy hair.

"Um." She riffles through her notebook.

Kimmel snaps his fingers. "Faster, Melody. Imagine you have thirty seconds to wow the school board. It needs to slip off your tongue."

"It's a device that transmits streaming music directly to your ear so you don't have to wear earphones." She shifts in her seat. "Except it doesn't work yet. I've got the transmission part, but the streaming—"

Mr. Kimmel holds up his hand to stop her. "That's just excess information. You had your pitch down to a single line." Kimmel rotates to the blackboard and scribbles *one-sentence pitch*. "I want everyone to write down your pitch by the end of the class period."

Some of the students groan. A few grab tablets from the stack at the front. I sit there staring at a blank sheet of paper, trying not to hyperventilate.

I tap my pen against the paper, earning a look of death from Teddy next to me. I write down the only thing I can think of, the only thing I know: *If I don't figure out what my damn project is, someone will die, followed by thousands of people.* I tack on today's date as well.

But I don't turn it in. Instead, I shove it into my pocket, where it can't be deleted.

The bell rings, and everyone jumps up, no one faster than me. I spin around to grab my bag from the back of my chair and pivot into Sebastian. Again.

His lips quirk with the slightest of smiles. "Third time's the charm, I guess." I envy his ability to remain calm during all this. He covers his nose when we step into the crowded hallway, making him sound nasal when he speaks. "Look. This is going to sound weird. But what exactly was our project and how will it save lives?"

Someone smacks into my shoulder, so I pull him into a nearby empty classroom and shut the door. The cacophony of the hallway dulls to the buzz of the heater. I'm still shivering from what Kimmel told us. "I don't remember either." I don't remember and people could *die* because of it.

He gazes at me with haunting eyes that seem to be permanently set to *smolder*. "But the server reboot. That's going to fix it, right?"

I shake my head, trying to keep my face as calm as Sebastian's. It takes all my effort to keep my voice steady through gritted teeth. "Didn't work. I just checked your mind again. You're still missing everything before this morning."

He steps away from me and crashes into a desk. "You looked into my head?" The words sound more like an accusation than a realization. I cringe. "You violated my privacy."

That's his biggest concern? Not all the people who might die because of us? "Only because I'm trying to help you." I take a few steps toward him, hands raised in the air to prove I have no weapons. His clean soap scent instills a weird mix of familiarity and longing. "Here's the deal," I say, trying not to inhale. "Something weird is going on. As far as I can tell, it's only affecting you and me. Well, maybe Kimmel too." I'd need to search his mind to confirm. "What else do you remember?" I laugh at how stupid that sounded. "I mean, how do you know English?" His scrawled schedule pops into my mind. "How'd you know to come to this school today?"

"I don't remember anything specific before today, but I know general things. Like how to speak English, that good hygiene requires brushing your teeth, that my bathroom is the second door on my left according to the house schematics, and that my mom is my mom even though I can't recall any conversations we've had. Stuff like that."

"Procedural memory, that makes sense." His mouth parts, so I explain further. "You're remembering only how-to memories, things ingrained in you, like tying your shoe or riding a bike. Actions and knowledge but not moments. That type of stuff is harder to forget." Or more accurately: harder to delete in HiveMind because it's not tied to a specific moment.

"Yeah, but I found out I have a test on *The Illustrated Man* in my creative-writing elective today, and I remember the book verbatim even though I have no recollection of reading it. I can even recite what's on the copyright page. That's not procedural memory."

Weird. "Any other strange bits of knowledge?"

He thinks for a moment. "I'm not taking any graphic design

classes, but I can tell your skin tone is #F8E4CC. Your eyes are #593E1A. Your hair—"

"Whoa." I hold up a hand. "I meant any other bits of knowledge that help you"—how do I say this politely?—"function like a human? As opposed to a vegetable."

He laughs and then bites his lip. "Well, the word *human* wasn't even used as a noun until the early sixteenth century. Before then, it was an adjective meaning 'of or belonging to man' and originally in Latin it meant 'earthly being' to differentiate from gods, so . . . Yes, the etymology of every word in the OED seems to help me act *human*, if you're referring to its modern usage."

I blink at him. "So you know every word ever used in the English language. Good to know."

"*Na kila lugha nyingine.*" He winks. "That's Swahili for 'and every other language.'"

I sputter-cough. "Holy shit. That's not normal."

He nods. "I take it you're not experiencing the same breadth of knowledge?"

"Nope." Suddenly I feel inferior, an unfamiliar notion to me. "Any chance you're good at coding?"

He taps his chin, thinking for a second. "I know all the concepts and commands of most coding languages, but I think I'd still have to practice putting them to use. Same with chemistry and physics. I've got the equations memorized. Just not quite sure how to apply them."

"Well, then at least I have you beat in all things computers," I say. "So just to be clear . . . You don't remember our project. Who our mentor is. Or me?"

Sebastian rakes a hand through his dirty-blond hair. "I don't even remember who my friends are. Or what I like to do." He lowers his voice. "Or who I am."

If someone really did carve our minds deliberately, why would they remove all of his memories but only a few specific ones of mine? And why would he know all this stuff but I wouldn't?

Watching his chest heave in and out, I stifle the overwhelming urge to throw my arms around him and comfort him. Instead, I keep my lips in a straight line, offering nothing but the answer we both need. A scientist deals in facts, absolute truths. Not emotions. "I'll fix this. I'll find a way to get our memories back."

His hazel eyes soak me in, desperate. Pleading. "How?"

"By finding out who did this."

00110100

As I approach the cafeteria, a figure paces back and forth in front of the door. My gait slows as I approach, my stomach knotting when Simon Zajek lifts his head and then beelines straight for me.

"Arden, you have to help me."

"Whoa. What are you doing here? You don't have lunch this period." I shift my laptop to one arm.

"Waiting for you. Help me. Please, Arden!" Simon grabs my wrist, his jagged, bitten-down nails digging into my skin. "Take the memories back. Please." His bloodshot eyes dart around the hallway squirrel-fast, like a drug addict. But I've investigated his mind; the only drug he's high on is love. Well, that and other people's memories. He drags his hands over his face. "I don't want to know. I—I love her. I never should have asked you for this."

"Y-you want me to delete your memory?" A pit forms in my chest at the idea of removing a vital part of him, lobotomizing him one memory at a time with a laptop-shaped scalpel. It's one thing to be a god socially, every student worshipping you because of your brains and your connections. But it's another to play God. "That's against the rules. *My* rules."

I can practically see his heart beating out of his chest. "You have to! It doesn't matter if she cheats on me. It hurt less when I didn't know." His steel-blue eyes plead with mine. "Delete everything! Even this conversation."

Delete everything. My skin goes cold.

A few days ago, I cut him off cold turkey from his extreme memory addiction. Until today, anyway. Maybe last night he tried to make me forget I ever gave him a firm no and then took it a step too far, using a digital hacksaw on other parts of my mind. This morning could have been a test to see if I remembered severing his connection to his main source of thrills.

"Do you know how to delete memories?" I fire questions at him without taking a breath in between. Only HiveMind admins and talented hackers like me have access to the deletion controls in the app. "Were you just messing with me this morning? Trying to throw me off your scent?"

He holds up his hands in surrender. "I—I don't know what you're talking about."

"Playing dumb won't work." I stab a finger into his chest. "I know what you did. I'm going to find evidence and then get you expelled."

Simon wipes a line of sweat from his brow, stepping backward. "Okay, okay. Sorry, Arden. Forget I asked." He darts his head left and right, then lowers his voice. "Just don't get me in trouble, okay?" He lets out a puppy yip and stumbles away down the hallway before breaking into a run.

I suck in desperate gulps of air. I'm losing it. Accusing anyone I can. Simon doesn't have the balls for this kind of sabotage. I push open the cafeteria door and stomp toward my table, heart pounding. Zoey straightens when I slam my laptop down. I sink into the chair and count to ten until my breathing evens out. Heavy rain pounds against the glass, robbing the room of brightness. The high ceilings magnify the acoustics, blending all the chatter and jingle of silverware into one unified sound.

Zoey snaps her fingers in front of my eyes. "Did the server reboot work?"

"No. And neither did the data recovery software I ran. Or defragging the disk. Or the scan for corrupted DLL files. Or the—" I sigh. There's no point in listing every worthless strategy I tried instead of paying attention in my last few classes. The only thing I managed to do for sure was confirm that several minutes were removed from Kimmel's mind during first period. The exact moment when he seemingly blacked out.

I thought the best course of action was to try to recover the deleted data before I tried to find the culprit, but I'm starting to think I've got it all backward.

Zoey's features crinkle in horror. "Yikes. This is bad."

In paranoia, I look around before dropping my voice. "Someone's messing with HiveMind. They deleted everything related to my project, including my notes and my precious hard drive." I slap the case onto the table, the pieces rattling.

Zoey gasps in that dramatic way of hers. "And Bash's too, I gather? Who would do that to you guys?"

"I've got some suspects in mind. First, though, it would be awesome if you could tell me what my project was or even who mentored me."

"It was . . ." Zoey squints and presses a palm to her forehead. "Oh my God. I don't remember."

I swallow past a lump in my throat. "I was afraid of that." I open up my laptop. "I need to do recon, stat." I was so busy trying to fix HiveMind during the last few periods that I didn't have a chance to try to investigate.

Zoey taps the side of her head. "Ooh, I want to see too!"

I do a quick keyword search in HiveMind for project reviews or presentations and select all the ones that include me as a participant. We usually have to do a class review once a semester. I select a few of the memories and set them up in a playlist for both of us to watch.

The first one starts. I peer out of Veronica's eyes as she stands in Kimmel's classroom and presents her progress on her project to the room. Despite her loud blabber in my mind, I do my best to ignore what she's saying and instead focus on her view of me, sitting in my usual seat in the classroom. And directly next to me is Sebastian, in the exact seat he should have occupied this morning. In the HiveMind memory, Bash's face seems a little thinner, his hair shorter and spiking upward instead of neatly brushed to the side, but he wears the same smirk I've come to recognize after only an hour. The sweaters everyone wears and the calendar on the wall indicate this took place in January.

"Good work, Veronica," Kimmel says. "Next time, it would be great if the prototype actually worked."

The class chuckles. Veronica seethes.

"Okay, Bash and Arden. Up you go."

I hold my breath as I watch myself hop out of my seat and stride with confidence toward the front of the room. Through Veronica's eyes, I watch as Past Me opens my mouth to speak—

And then the image jerks and all of a sudden Blake Sanders stands at the front while Bash and I make our way back to our seats. I whisper something in his ear and he giggles. That's it. The memory ends.

Holy shit.

The next memory begins. This one comes from Melody Clarendon's perspective from her seat two rows behind me. Same scene, different angle. I study the cafeteria table and watch an image overlay of Veronica sitting down and Kimmel calling Bash and me up to the podium. And exactly like before, the memory jumps forward before we utter a word about our progress. When the scene replays from another student's perspective, it's more of the same.

Their minds have been tampered with too. The details of my project have been removed from not just my mind but also everyone else's.

Zoey breathes in sharply, air whistling through her teeth. I grip the edges of the table with white knuckles.

A boy heads toward us, and before he even has a chance to stop at my lunch table, I snap, "Shop's closed." He drops his head and shuffles away. I hastily scrawl out a sign that says SHOP'S CLOSED and fold it in half. I can't deal with anyone else asking for a memory right now.

"Arden, I'm scared." Zoey clutches my wrist in a tight grip. "That was awful to watch. What if you can't get them back? What if it's not just you? Oh my God." The corners of her mouth tremble. "What if I lose my favorite memory?"

I lift my chin. "I'm going to get to the bottom of this before that happens."

"Please, Arden. I need to watch my favorite memory again." She bats her eyelashes and gives me her best pout. "*Please.* It's the only thing that calms me down!"

I quickly navigate to her HiveMind account and scan her list of favorited memories to make sure it's still there. "You already have it. Just think about it."

She waggles her fingers at me. "It's so much more vivid when it comes to me brand new. Pleeeeeaaaaaase." She belts out the last word like the chorus to a song.

I sigh and drop the memory into her head again, overwriting the file that already exists in her mind. I know how awful it is to lose a memory, and if this can ease her mind, I want to help. I stole this memory from one of the sophomore's older sisters who goes to Wickham High down the road. Last year, the sister was crowned homecoming queen and spent the evening relishing in all the glory of a tiara, a spotlight dance, the tug of the hot king's arms wrapped around her, and the thrill of two thousand of her closest classmates voting for her.

Zoey's eyes glaze over and her shoulders relax. She lets out a happy little sigh.

Some people find comfort in thinking of a cherished memory when things get rough. Zoey's most cherished memory just happens to be someone else's.

I get the appeal. This memory must make her feel normal. I've watched it myself a few times because it gives me a glimpse into all I missed out on by coming here. Pulsing DJ beats. Clutching my best friend's hand as I wait to see if my name's announced. A spotlight making my satin dress shimmer. A hundred eyes watching me sweep across the dance floor. Don't get me wrong, it's not like I'd rather cry into my false lashes over some high school guy at a dance than go to Varga. But there's something about this one memory that allows me to sum up the high school experience I never got to claim. I imagine Zoey feels the same way.

While Zoey zones out and my computer runs a scan on the var logs to check for errors on the HiveMind server, I glance around the cafeteria at every face, every suspect who might have reason to sabotage my project. Immediately, I spy several promising candidates. Veronica Ackerman—Zoey mentioned earlier she wanted to report me, and she'd have good reason to. After all, I got her put on probation earlier this year when I exposed the memory of her rigging the student election that got her nominated for school president. And I probably didn't help matters today when I gave her boyfriend proof of her infidelity.

Or maybe Teddy Day finally exacted revenge for all the test

answers I've stolen from him. He seemed to be purposefully avoiding me in class, though he was trying to talk to Sebastian, so maybe not. Then, of course, there's the possibility it's someone desperate to knock me out of the running for the project contest. The girl who glared at me in Kimmel's class comes to mind. Hell, maybe it was Kimmel trying to steal my brilliant concept for himself and he was just covering his tracks this morning. It could be anyone.

"Ah." Zoey looks so peaceful and content when the memory finishes playing in her mind. "Best night of my life."

Well, maybe not *anyone*. My best friend swooped in to help me solve the issue. Sebastian's in the same boat. The students in the lower grades would have no reason to stab a knife into my back. And half the people who work at Varga Industries are just names on an org chart and have no beef with me.

"It's Veronica. It's got to be." When I glance over at her, I discover she's already staring at me, her jaw clenching.

Zoey spins around to follow my gaze. "I'm with you on the Veronica thing, but can we switch topics for just a second to discuss Eliza's new haircut? Maybe Teddy won't be able to find her and he'll fall in love with me instead."

My eyes shift to the girl beside Veronica. Eliza Shaw's haircut involves too much bangs and not enough face. My vision catches on someone behind Eliza. Sebastian, burrowing between the recycling bins. He scans the tables in the center of the cafeteria, clutching a tray like a life raft. "Hey, what do you remember about Sebastian?"

Zoey raises her eyebrows a few times in succession. "I know the real reason you're asking, but I'm choosing to believe it's because of a massive crush you're starting to harbor for him. Say the word and I'll sit you down in my vanity chair; grab my trusty, old holostick; and give you that makeover I've been begging to do on you for years now. He'll fall head over heels in no time."

I ignore her and her incessant attempts to cover me in holographic makeup. My temples throb in tune to my heart. I need to talk to him. Maybe if I get to know him, it'll trigger my memories again, the way the scent of wintergreen always reminds me of my dad and his obsession with Tic Tacs.

"Be right back," I tell Zoey, and veer toward Sebastian, who still lingers between the garbage cans, now with his tray propped on the edge of one. He attempts to eat standing up. I grip my binary necklace to keep me grounded as I place one stiletto in front of the other. "What are you doing later?" I ask in lieu of a greeting. "Because we need to figure out what our project is. And where our memories went."

He lets out a relieved breath and lifts his lunch off the trash bin. A portion of the black garbage bag attempts to hitch a ride as it sticks to the bottom of his plastic tray. "I might have plans." He chuckles. Fluorescent beams overhead drop spotlights of color on his cheeks. "No idea."

I laugh too. Even though I just met him a few hours ago, we already have inside jokes. It's nice to find a moment of hilarity amid all this chaos.

A wrinkle indents his forehead when a guy knocks into Sebastian's shoulder and points a finger gun at him. "Looking good, Bash! Feeling okay?"

Sebastian just stares at the guy until he ambles away.

"Do you remember your address?" I sidestep around a guy tossing a heavy brown bag into the trash with a *thunk*.

"That, I do. Only because I wrote it down before I left my house."

I can't help it. I smile. A real smile that stretches my lips from ear to ear, not the cheap half smiles I reserve for all the important people my mom makes me meet with. "Great. Then I'll stop by after dinner and we'll try to figure this out."

He looks heartbreakingly hopeful. "It's a school night." He pushes his lips to the side, distorting a dimple. "I think."

"Why aren't you freaking out? I'm over here snapping at anyone that even dares to look at me wrong."

He shrugs. "I guess it all seems relatively normal to me when I have nothing to compare today to." He cocks his head, sandy blond hair falling into his eyes. "I think your friend wants me to join you guys."

"Come on, then." I stride past him toward my table as wind screeches through the windowpanes. I don't want Zoey to get her hopes up here, not when my invitation to Sebastian was more of a science experiment than the kind of evening that begins with roses and ends with a kiss.

He follows me and plops his tray next to Zoey's. I slide onto the aluminum chair across from him and study his face beneath my eyelashes, trying to spark cued recall for any latent memories lurking in the recess of my mind.

Zoey swivels in her chair to face him. "So. Bash—"

"I'd prefer Sebastian, actually." He swirls his fork around his truffle mashed potatoes.

"Ooooookay, *Sebastian*." She emphasizes the word. "Kind of random that you're reinventing yourself on a Tuesday in April. I would have at least waited until fall. You could have cited seasonal affective disorder as your excuse."

"What's wrong with the nickname Bash?" I start to unwrap my sandwich, momentarily jarred again when my sleeve rides up and I glimpse the red puffy line that snakes from my palm to halfway up my elbow, where it slices across the veins.

He shrugs. "Didn't seem to fit me anymore." He slides a forkful of mouthwatering sous vide chicken covered in artichoke foam from the cafeteria, chewing slowly in a clear attempt to avoid saying anything more. At most schools, the paid lunch is inedible; at ours, it's avant-garde. Some of our classmates experiment with molecular gastronomy.

"Okay then." Zoey leans back. "Why aren't you sitting with your usual table?"

"Didn't feel like it." He swallows a heap of chicken. One guess: He doesn't know where it is.

"But it looks like Teddy misses you." Zoey points a spoon, pink yogurt dripping off the concave basin.

I spin around to see Teddy Day standing up several tables away and giving Sebastian a *what gives* expression.

Zoey waves him over and then squeals when he actually obliges. I finish unwrapping my turkey sandwich, the tinfoil crinkling.

"Hey, man, whatever happened to bros before hos?" Teddy slaps Sebastian on the back, but then watches him in a weird way, almost as if he's studying him.

"There would need to be *hos* for that to apply." Zoey waggles her finger between us. "Only good girls here."

"Considering the word *good* didn't actually mean 'well-behaved' until the sixteen nineties," Sebastian says, "by etymology standards, the girls at this table clearly embody the original meaning of 'desirable.'" Sebastian peels the label off his water bottle and then shoves it into his mouth.

Silence sweeps through the table as everyone blinks at him. Teddy's eyebrow lifts and Zoey's smile wavers. Sebastian slowly pulls the water bottle label out of his mouth and sets it on his tray. I rush in to rescue him. Maybe he forgot how to eat properly. And speak. "So we're desirable, huh?" I bat my eyelashes for emphasis.

Sebastian turns red.

Teddy eyes him weirdly for a second. "I just came by to see how you're feeling?"

"Um. Fine?"

Teddy's shoulders relax. "Good. Glad to hear it."

"I second that," Zoey says in the sugary-sweet voice she uses on classmates she wants to experiment on. "Really glad you're feeling well."

Sebastian squints at her.

Teddy cups his shoulder. "Let's hang this afternoon, okay, man?"

Sebastian and I exchange glances. I nod my encouragement. "Sounds good . . . man. I'm free until dinner."

Teddy starts to walk away, but Zoey shouts, "Wait!" Teddy stops short and pivots back to her.

She bites her lip, batting her eyelashes. "You still mad at me?"

A muscle in his jaw feathers. "That depends. You still want credit for my project?"

Zoey's face falls, and when she doesn't say anything further, he nods to himself and lopes away.

"I did just as much work as him in terms of planning," she mumbles under her breath. "It's only fair."

I place my palm over hers. "You should talk to my mom about it. Plead your case."

She nods. "Yeah. You're right." And then she straightens. "I will."

Freshman year, Zoey had trouble passing classes and presenting a project proposal that didn't get rejected by the board. She submitted thirty-five ideas, and each one was turned down either for being not innovative enough or because the board lacked faith that she could complete them. Thanks to a generous donation from Zoey's parents, my mother agreed to let her remain at the school under the condition that instead of working on her own project, she'd float from project to project among students and Varga Industries faculty, acting as a pinch hitter wherever needed. In addition, my mom started providing her with one-on-one instruction. Since then, Zoey's GPA has shot up to nearly 4.0.

My computer makes a beep and Zoey flourishes her hand as if to tell me to go ahead. She opens her own laptop to catch up on homework while Sebastian studies his food with a curious expression, as if he's never before seen a carrot. When he pops it into his mouth, he chews with extra gusto, using the full force of his teeth with every chomp. After a moment, he starts coughing and clutching his throat before swallowing down the rogue carrot. He eyes the rest suspiciously, then plucks them off his tray one by one and lines them up on the table in front of it like soldiers guarding the rest of his food.

My var log scan completes without picking up any errors in the HiveMind software. I start another diagnostic scan on my mind. On a whim, I do one on Sebastian's too, ignoring the new sensation of guilt spreading through my abdomen over the idea of spying on him after he freaked out about it earlier. When I glance at his account, I notice several new files have been logged since this morning, all from earlier today. That's a good sign at least.

The diagnostic scan of my catalogued memories from today unfolds in short headers thanks to HiveMind's automatic tagging feature. The contents display like the sidebar on YouTube, with little thumbnail previews that automatically play back the video and automatic tags beside each video memory. No sound plays in the previews, just the images. To hear the sounds from the scene and the recorded inner monologue, I'd have to drag the memory from the archive into the live folder, which is essentially the same as dropping it directly into my mind. Our brains are synced so thoroughly with HiveMind that there's no clear indication where one ends and one begins.

Get ready/Breakfast/Drive to school—HiveMind automatically lumps the boring stuff together.

Courtyard business—the thumbnail is of Sebastian walking toward us, as if HiveMind knows this was the most important part of my day.

Visit IT—HiveMind catches me sneaking the SSD drive into the computer via the thumbnail.

Test in Kimmel's class—a 1021 MB dose of smack-me-in-the-face reality.

Try to fix HiveMind in Business and Project Management class—Why couldn't I have forgotten this unnecessary form of torture?

Bathroom break—Nothing to see here, move along.

The catalogue continues up through the cafeteria. Everything seems to be in order. But then my eye catches movement on one of the file's data details. My lips part in a gasp that sends Zoey swiveling toward me.

The file from when Sebastian and I discussed our joint project in Mr. Kimmel's empty classroom is rapidly reducing in file size. The hair at the back of my neck stands at attention. What the hell?

1007 MB

983 K

875 K

I jerk my arm on the track pad to click on the file and knock my elbow into my water bottle in the process. The bottle careens to the table like a soccer player who just got his feet swept out from under him. Water splashes on my arm and across the corner of the keys. I yank the laptop and hop to a standing position. Zoey screams and throws a napkin on the puddle of water while Sebastian sets my water bottle upright. My heart rams.

459 K

"Arden? You okay?" Zoey shakes out her sopped notebook. I

hold up a finger to them and balance the laptop on my forearm, gritting my teeth as I click on the file.

327 K

The preview expands to full screen, showing my perspective as I smack right into Sebastian after taking our test. Did something come after the test? I rack my brain but I can't even remember walking out of class even though the next file in the list shows my view as I chat with Sebastian in an empty classroom. Why did I think this file contained something about talking to Mr. Kimmel when I haven't spoken to him after class in months? Something important happened after that test. I know it. Or at least I knew it a second ago.

My eyes lock on Veronica's, but she's laughing and smiling with her friends, no tech devices in front of her. Teddy's making his rounds to his adoring fangirls. Simon's MIA. I sweep my vision from one person to the next, noting all the open laptops, tablets, phones. All the items that could give someone the opportunity to delete my memory while also having a solid alibi. Though theoretically, someone could have set in motion a deletion script that takes a while to run—they wouldn't need to be on their laptop *right now* if they executed it within the last hour. That means it could be anyone.

201 K

I hit CTRL+S to save, but the file size keeps decreasing. The ESC button mocks me without obeying my command. My pulse races.

113 K

After class? "Hey, did we talk to Kimmel after class today?"

Sebastian's mouth parts and he fixes a grave expression on me. "I have no idea."

Zoey lifts her head as she mops up the water with her napkin. "Oh my God. You're forgetting more?"

The file blinks once before graying out like an expired link with a file size of 0 K. My stomach lurches. When I click on it, an error pops up. *This file does not exist.*

And just to prove itself right, the file itself disappears from the list completely.

I slump into the nearest dry seat and press my palm to my forehead. I'm forgetting something. What is it? And more important, what memory will I lose next?

Sebastian slides over to the seat across from me and mouths, "What happened?" Zoey watches with an extremely concerned expression.

I swallow past the lump in my throat. "I just watched a memory disappear. It's not the first one, obviously."

Sebastian blinks a little too hard. "Then it's probably not the last." He studies me for a moment. "We should go to the police."

I shake my head. "They don't know the first thing about Hive-Mind. No one outside the Varga conglomerate does."

A horrible weight settles into my gut. I frantically click over to last year's files. To the one where my dad looped his fingers through mine and told me he loved me and he believed in me. He believed my talents would take me far. That was the last thing he ever said to me.

874 K. It's still all there. A breath rattles out of my lungs and I press a hand to my chest to still my heart.

I already lost my dad once. I can't lose the precious memories of him too.

My limbs twitch. I pace the floor of the employee lounge on the third floor of Varga Industries, trying to shake it off. Sleek white tables and midcentury modern gray fabric couches make employees feel at home where they feel most comfortable. . . . in a laboratory. There's even an eye-wash station in the corner, just in case. My heels click on the white linoleum floor, leaving black scuff marks. I'm supposed to be in Advanced Software Engineering, but I can't possibly sit still in a classroom right now. Not when every precious moment of my life might be going the way of the digital recycle bin. Not when I have no idea the scope of what I've lost.

I glance at the clock and curse under my breath. My brother said he'd be here in two minutes. . . . twelve minutes ago. I let out an aggravated growl that does nothing to assuage the panic coursing through me. I have to do something. Screw trying to recover the data. I have to preserve what I already know in a way that can't be deleted.

I frantically grab a pen from my messenger bag and uncap it. I roll up my sleeves, flip my forearm over, and overwrite the ugly, creepy scar with thick black letters.

Someone's deleting your memories. Suspects: Veronica, Teddy, anyone else you've stolen memories from.

One long breath slips from my throat. I turn my arm over and write more evidence.

You're working on your project with Sebastian.

I change the size of my handwriting to fit more info on the canvas of skin that stretches between my inner elbow and wrist.

Sebastian: good-looking in a geek chic way; speaks every language ever invented, including Klingon (I asked); knows a lot of useless trivia competition fodder; doesn't remember anything about you, or him.

Memories missing: something involving a test. HiveMind recovery steps: reboot failed, diagnostic indicates 7k+ memories went missing, and var log scan didn't return any errors.

Today's events: Simon begging me for Veronica's memory of her cheating then asking me to delete it. Slipping an SSD drive into an IT monitoring computer. Having a discussion with Sebastian directly after Kimmel's class in the hallway about how he doesn't remember our project either. Making plans with Sebastian tonight after dinner. Watching a memory disappear from my account.

I hastily pull down my sleeve to cover the writing and the scar. Relief washes through me at the information stored in a place that can't possibly be deleted or torn out. Not without going through me. Leo barges into the room, raking his hand over his shaggy hair.

Redness rims his eyes like he hasn't slept in days. As soon as he makes eye contact, his features crumple and he starts to cry.

He barrels toward me with the speed and heftiness of a linebacker and wraps his arms around me. He buries his head into my shoulder and sniffles. "Thank you," he tells me. "I needed this."

"What's wrong?" My voice comes out high-pitched as the cells in my body vibrate on high alert. My mind can latch onto only one thing that can possibly be wrong. "Are you—are you missing memories?"

He pulls back to study me and wipes a tear from his eyes. "What are you"—his breath hitches—"talking about?" He drops his arms from around me and stumbles back. "Didn't you call me so you could comfort me?"

Pretty much the opposite, buddy. "I wanted to know what you remember about Dad." So I can check his version of events and compare it with my own.

Now it's his turn to look at me confused. I wave him over to the couch. He sways for a moment, unsteady on his feet, but follows.

"Okay, you tell me what's going on, and I'll tell you," I offer. Growing up, I was always the analytical one, following in my dad's more technical footsteps to whittle something down to data-driven facts, while Leo and my mom were the same way: focused on biology, the emotional reaction, the parts of you that make you *you*. When something went wrong, I was always the one to assess the situation and make it right again while he sobbed in a pile on the floor. Mom would always take action right away, swooping in to fix them the fastest way while my dad would pause and analyze, trying to find the best solution.

Leo hiccups. "Brandon broke up with me."

My hand flies to cover my lips, hoping I'm misinterpreting his words. Brandon couldn't have broken up with him. Those two were like atoms and protons: magnetic. But then my mind flashes to earlier in the IT room, when Leo's ex-boyfriend sported the same tearstained cheeks and asked me if Leo sent me.

My chest constricts, and I go stiff in a sudden desperation to stay calm. They were my shining ideal model of a couple, flaunting the kind of love I only dreamed to find. They can't possibly be over for good. My heart aches just thinking about it. No, this must be a temporary glitch in their relationship continuum.

"Why?" The tone of my voice rises in volume and pitch. "Why would he be so stupid?"

Leo shakes his head, dark locks bouncing. "He said our careers were going in two different directions. That I'm on my way up and he's probably on his way out once HiveMind goes live and a fully blown IT team takes over." He drags his hands down his face. "I said we can work past that, but he kept saying he doesn't want to hold me back."

I reach for my brother and rub his back. Leo sniffles. My free hand balls into a fist at the thought of that jerk Brandon hurting my brother. "He'll regret it. I know he will. He doesn't realize what he just threw away."

A soft shudder moves through him. "I thought you knew. I thought that's why you called me to meet."

I swallow hard. I was going to tell him about my missing memories, but I don't want to alarm him. Not when he's already so sad. So I come at the question from an indirect angle. "What do you remember about Dad?"

He squints at me, his chest stilling, the sobs subsiding. "What do you mean?"

"Your last memory of him. What is it?" I hold my breath.

"My last memory is at the hospice. He had that yellow blanket pulled way up to his chest."

"The one Mom knitted for him." She learned how to do it, just for him, so he would always have a piece of her with him during his final days. She hasn't knitted anything since.

"His voice was all gravelly. He could barely keep his eyes open for longer than a second. But he looked right at me and told me he wished he wasn't leaving so soon, because now he'd never get to see the great things I would do."

I squeeze Leo's hand.

"You?"

My eyes flutter shut as sluggish relief courses through my veins. "Same."

He tugs my arm toward him, squinting at the writing peeking out of the bottom of my sleeve. "What's this about suspects?"

I yank my arm back. "Nothing. Just a thing for one of my classes."

Leo's phone alarm buzzes. "Shit. My eukaryotic cultures need to be inoculated. Cellular regeneration doesn't like to be kept waiting." He gives me a tight smile. "Thanks for this. I hope whatever I said about Dad helped."

Leo leaves, but I feel more out of sorts than before we spoke. There's a thump in my heart, electricity making my knee bounce. The words on my arm aren't a way to remember, they're an omen. I might lose more, and next time, I won't even know what I've lost. I have no way to fix HiveMind and no way to stop more memories from disappearing. I have to back up every precious memory I have to an off-line source.

With trembling hands, I grab an external hard drive from the supply closet in the room, lock the door, and then open my laptop. I locate some of my most precious memories, which boast little star icons indicating they've been favorited. My heart pounds in my ears as I peruse each and every one. The day Zoey kidnapped me for my birthday. When I won the national hackathon competition in fifth grade. The last day with my dad. And my favorite memory of him. It's only a small moment, but it made a big impact on me.

My throat feels thick as the realization that I might only be able to choose one crushes me like a two-ton truck weighing down my shoulders. How do I decide what to save?

There's a gun pressed to my head, pressure mounting, as I slide my finger down the list and choose which memory is the most important. Which is the only one worth saving. It's the last one that my finger lingers on. The one I can't live without.

Hot tears press against the backs of my eyelids, and the lump in my throat expands. I have to watch it. Just in case. At least then I'll retain a fragment of it if the main memory gets deleted, the ghost of a memory, me watching something that will no longer exist.

I close my eyes and let the moment settle over me like a warm blanket.

"The beach?" I ask in the memory as I get out of the car and teeter on the rock-filled parking lot. The last remnants of blue sky cling to existence. A sea-salty scent rides a breeze that tangles my hair. The ocean looms in the distance, wide and foreboding, white foam rising and disappearing.

I just turned nine years old, and I'm struggling to keep pace with my dad as he trudges through the sand. This was one of the very first memories I synced with HiveMind.

In the distance, wooden planks cover the windows of the Old Crab Shack restaurant, which is usually hopping during the summer. A blue tarp surrounds the lifeguard stand like a wrapped present. The sand stretches for miles in each direction without another soul.

"Not a very good scientist, are you, kiddo?" Dad grins at me before spreading out a large quilted blanket. "You're supposed to analyze the evidence and present a hypothesis."

I harrumph, placing my hands on my hips. "I did." I tug at my wool sweater. "*This* is not beachwear. And dinner at Mama Ferrari's is nowhere near the beach. Which clearly means this beach excursion is merely a distraction while Mom sets up the surprise party."

Dad winks at me. "Well, I guess I take back my earlier statement."

A cold wind rustles my hair and blows sand onto the blanket like a dry tidal wave. I rub my hands along my goose bump–covered arms. "I think what I've proven here is that it's my birthday. And on my birthday, I get what I want."

Dad lounges on the blanket, stretching out his legs in front of him. "You're not guilting me into telling you your birthday present, are you?"

I sit up on my knees and look him square in the eye. "I want you to tell me how HiveMind works." I've already been digging around in it and perfecting my coding skills, but I'm ready for the big guns.

He shrugs. "It's all just ones and zeroes."

I roll my eyes. "I may be a kid, but I'm not an idiot. *Binary*," I say, repeating the mantra he used to tell me every night before I went to bed. A good-night story. "Something made of or based on two things or parts." I tick off my fingers, one two. "Two formats. Two digits."

"The universe at harmony," Dad says, almost absentmindedly, the next line in our nightly script.

"But how does it all work?"

The sunset gives his tan a golden hue. "Everything in the universe is made up of chunks of information—essentially ones and zeroes. This means the human mind is no different from a single atom to time itself to the abstract theory of dreaming. All of it can be broken down to its basics and quantized. And once it's quantized?" He cups his hand around his ear as if waiting for me to shout the answer, but I sit there, my chest stilled. "It can be harvested by scientists—like me."

I cough. "And me."

He nods. "And you. And used in any number of ways. Software, cures for diseases, plastic surgery without ever using a knife."

"Storing memories."

He points a finger gun at me as the wind sneaks puffs of air under his button-down and causes it to balloon in places. "Exactly."

"Show me." I lean closer, my voice insistent. The heavy sun dips, leaving an orange ribbon in its wake.

He shakes his head. "Arden, you're way too young. You—"

"I can help you. I want to work on it. Mom lets Leo help her out in the bio lab sometimes." I throw the last part at him in a petty way, but it's a bold move. A checkmate.

Dad studies me, his pupils swimming back and forth. And then he abruptly stands up. He shakes sand off the bottom of his jeans. "We have an hour to kill before we have to be at the party. That's just enough time to get you synced up to the software. But remember, honey, it's just a prototype. There are only a few others connected."

I nod frantically, hopping to my feet as well. "Yes. Let's do it right now."

"And one more rule." Dad squints into the distance, thinking. "No peeking in other people's heads. Especially mine. The software doesn't allow it, but . . . I suspect you'll find a way around that."

A blush sweeps across my cheek. That's the best compliment my dad could ever give me.

I didn't realize at the time that his warning to stay out of his mind wasn't concern over security breaches, but concern that I'd learn the devastating truth of the cancer that was spreading throughout his pancreas.

I draw my finger over my lips to say they're sealed even though what I really mean is I agree.

"And second." He shoots me with a devious grin. "When you come up with an idea for the program that far surpasses anything I'd come up with, let me at least take a little bit of the credit?"

I shake my head. "Not a chance."

The memory fades. I'll never know what my dad was really thinking that day, or any other for that matter. The emotions that ran through him when he held me the first time and his fading dreams as he took his last breath will forever be stored in the hard drive of his brain, buried in the ground. I never dug into his mind out of respect and request, and now I never will. When he passed away, my mom asked me to lock away his account and preserve it forever, untouched and inaccessible.

Since then it's become policy to lock away accounts when anyone connected to HiveMind dies. Locking an account away means copying it to an external hard drive, encrypting it, and deleting it from the server for good so no one will be able to access it again.

With renewed vigor, I copy the memory onto the external hard drive. If the hacker smashed my other hard drive once, they could probably do it again, which is why I can't let this one out of my sight.

Because of HiveMind's limitations, I can only copy a single memory at a time and each one takes between several minutes to several hours depending on the file size. Copying every file in my account would take days. I don't have that kind of time. I have to do this strategically.

Once the memory of my dad ends, I peruse the list of favorites again and wrinkle my nose. Each one has a value and none of them seem to be as hot a commodity as preserving the information I already learned today. Sure, I have the high-level details scrawled on my arm, but if there's any way to preserve the memories too, I need to seize it.

I start from my most recent memory logged today and work my way backward, copying one at a time. It works much faster when I leave the computer alone, so as much as I want to see if the SSD drive is still connected and hack around, it's way more important to protect everything I've learned today first. When I get to my first memory from this morning, I switch to Sebastian's account and start copying his.

The whole thing takes an hour and a half, forcing me to miss two of my classes. Just as I start on yesterday's memories, movement in the file list on the hard drive catches my eye. A file disappears directly from the backup as I watch. Someone is accessing my computer *right now*.

Heart hammering, I yank the hard drive out of my computer and hug it to my chest. As long as it's not plugged in, it'll be safe. As long as it's in my arms, it can't be destroyed.

But neither safeguard stopped the hacker last time.

00110110

I barge into the waiting room of my mom's office just as Zoey brushes past me to the exit.

I stop short, tilting my head at her. "What are you doing here?" The panic in my voice comes off harsher than I intended.

"Meeting with my mentor." She pushes her blond hair behind her ears and flicks her head back at my mother's door and bites her lip. Her eyes start to fill with tears.

My heart sinks and the panic bubbling through me subsides for a moment. "Is everything okay?" I reach out to touch her shoulder.

She shakes her head and tries to paste on a smile, but a tear still slips out, dripping past her thick eyeliner. "I really don't want to trouble you with this when you have more important things going on."

"You're important too." I jerk my head toward the hallway and she follows after me. "What's wrong?"

She lets out a shuddering sigh. "I'm just feeling really useless when everyone's putting the finishing touches on their projects, gearing up to wow the judges, and here I am, without a project of my own." Her eyes widen. "Don't get me wrong; I appreciate your family's support so, so much. But your mom turned me down when I asked for co-credit on a project. Any project! I'm not even picky."

"Zo, you're amazing. All those people you've been helping out are lucky to have you."

The corners of her lips quirk.

"I'll talk to my mom too. See if she can—"

Zoey shakes her head. "It won't work. Her hands are tied since I haven't provided enough input on any one project to qualify as a co-owner. Not to mention half the things I'm working on are official Varga products already." She wipes at her cheeks, her posture a little straighter. "She said there's a tiny, small, infinitesimal possibility that she can persuade the board to give me co-credit for one of the projects I helped out on, but she won't know for a few days."

I try to inject pep into my voice. "That sounds promising."

"It's a long shot." Zoey lets out a heavy sigh. "Anyway, thanks for letting me vent. This helped. A little."

"Vent away anytime. I'm happy to arrange a dartboard if you want to take out your aggressions with the help of a pointy object."

She laughs, and I feel like I've at least done something good today. I've cheered up my best friend.

"How's the memory situation?" Her voice sounds a little less depressed.

"What's the worst word you can think of in the English language? Because it's that." Damn, I could have used Sebastian and his extensive language knowledge right in this moment.

She frowns. "Any progress?"

"Just in trying to protect the data. Not in trying to stop the data loss."

"You'll stop it. I know you will." The period bell rings and her gaze flicks to the clock. She lifts her bag higher on her shoulder. "Keep me posted on the progress. Gotta get to Molec Bio."

Back inside the office, a copier hums, shooting paper after paper into a neat stack. The secretary gives me a three-fingered wave as she babbles into the phone. I bypass a boy stuffed into one of the uncomfortable plastic chairs, an ice pack pressed to his cheek. The dots of black liquid splashed on his skin indicate he lost a battle with a chemical compound, not another student.

I push open the door to Mom's office. My dad used to hold the principal duties while my mom ran Varga Industries, but when he died, she took over both roles as if she couldn't bear to replace him. They started this place together. They both left their lucrative positions at Harvard when I was a baby to open this place in a small town twenty minutes away. Every nook and cranny contains a piece of him. He picked out the flooring, got on his hands and knees and set up the first network wiring himself, and even donned a hard hat and supervised the construction process. My mom was always better at the business part, and my dad was always better at the people part, so it was a natural split for him to run the school while she ran the company.

Several former students have created huge technological advancements that changed the world. I always dreamed of being the biggest success of the school. Chalk it up to not only wanting to make my mother proud but to prove to the other students that I *deserved* this as much as they did. That's why I need to win the competition.

"Mom?" I say when she doesn't look up at me. Awards hang floor to ceiling on the walls behind her as if she fashioned a wallpaper pattern out of her success. "The reboot didn't work and someone's—"

My words drop off into oblivion as Mom pinches the space between her eyes and blinks at me, wearing a horrified, dazed expression. The leather chair she usually sits so straight in swallows her as she slumps. Her expression dredges up a weird feeling of déjà vu, but I can't tie it to anything specific. A minute passes before she shakes her head, making her sleek bob jangle. "What's that now?"

I let out an exasperated breath. Did she forget our conversation from earlier due to the breach in HiveMind? "Someone's deleting my memories. I don't remember my project. Or my mentor. Or—"

"Arden, sweetheart." She uses the tone of her voice she only reserves for when she doesn't believe a word I'm saying. "No one's *deleting* your memories. It's a glitch. We know that for sure from the Ethics Committee report."

I blink, a glimmer of hope welling in my chest. "What does the report say?"

She puckers her candy-red lips, flicks her mouse, and studies something on her screen. The mahogany table in front of her holds several computers and tablets so she can monitor both the school and the company without leaving this room. She jabs her hand at an Excel document on her screen filled with tiny type and lots of analytics data. "This shows a number of people with archiving activity in the last day. If you look at the graph, it's clear all this activity started around the same time, right around when we last deployed a patch to the software. The Committee's performing a root-cause analysis as we speak, but all evidence so far indicates a regression issue introduced by the patch."

I'm still stuck on the first sentence she said. "A number as in two?" Sebastian and me, for instance. "Or a number as in hundreds?"

Mom drums her fingers against a table as though she's considering how much to reveal. "More than two is all I'll say."

"Can we roll back the patch?"

"We're looking into that too, but a rollback is quite severe. It requires taking the entire system down for days and reprovisioning every single account. If that's what we need to do to fix this, we will, but trust me when I say it's the absolute last resort."

My face pales. I remember working with my dad to process the initial round of provisioning on the first few accounts. Each one took hours. To reprovision every account would take weeks, maybe even months.

Mom gives me a warm smile. "Arden, I promise. We're going to fix this. The Ethics Committee is doing a full investigation; they told me a few minutes ago that they're testing out a new security measure on a few key faculty accounts. If it works, I promise you'll be the first one we roll this out to. I want to ensure all my students are safe, but especially you." She circles the desk until she rests next to me. Her expensive perfume overwhelms the fresh scent of the plants that line her walls like an exotic greenhouse. She strokes my hair the way she used to do when I was a baby to comfort me to sleep.

"How long will it take to test?"

My mom shrugs. "I don't know. A day or two?"

I squeeze my eyes shut. I don't have a day or two. I could lose my entire mind within the next few minutes. "Test it on my account now. Please."

Mom flicks her wrist dismissively, her glittering diamond bracelet sliding down to her elbow. "The Committee would never approve an initial test on a student account."

The longer I stay connected to HiveMind, the more pieces of myself I might lose. "Then I'd like to disconnect my account entirely."

Mom clucks her tongue. "I'm afraid that's not possible. The Committee also put a temporary freeze on disconnect requests." HiveMind works by syncing directly to my brain waves, so the only way to remove my account is through a lot of signatures—my mom and the Committee members—and then to have one of the admins delete my brain wave data from the host server. It's a system of checks and balances. "Don't worry," Mom continues. "I have every faith we'll figure out what happened and find a way to restore your memories."

But the problem is, as a scientist, I don't believe in faith.

"Mom, you don't understand. This is dire. I don't remember my project!" My voice screeches. "I can't present to the Committee if I don't have a clue what my project is!" I grip my silver pendant, the one Dad gave me on the first day of school, and run my fingers over the engraving.

"Wait." She clamps a palm over her mouth. "I don't remember what it is either." Her face morphs into a mask of horror, and I hold my breath, waiting for the severity of this to sink in. But then just as quickly as she seemed terrified, her cool, calm composure takes over. "Don't worry about the presentation to the board. I'll talk to the Committee. Get you an extension on your presentation until they can fix this unfortunate glitch." She tugs at one of my wavy locks, defying nature by pulling it straight. "Your work has always been exemplary and I'm sure the Ethics Committee will understand that this isn't your fault."

It feels as if the rug was just pulled out from under me. I rock in place, my head foggy and dizzy. "But, Mom—I *need* to present at the review competition. I can't win if I don't present. It's the only way I'll have a shot of getting my project announced to the world during the press conference."

She starts stroking my hair again. "It doesn't matter. The world will know how amazing you are soon enough."

Her words make me sink farther into my seat. It matters to *me*.

She places both hands on my shoulders, forcing me to look at her smiling face and the webbed lines cascading from her eyes beneath a smooth layer of foundation. "I'm really proud of you, honey. Don't get upset. This isn't your fault." She taps the edge of my nose, just as she always did when I was a kid. Her signature show of affection.

As quickly as she came to stand beside me, she disappears behind her desk. She hands me a hall pass and gives me another tight smile as she cups the phone with her palm. "I'll escalate this right now for you and get you that project extension. You go to Gym and try to forget all about this until we get it sorted out."

I swallow, a bad taste lingering in my mouth.

Forgetting about this is entirely the problem.

00110111

I hunker down in my last class of the day, General and Special Relativity, and open my laptop. Mr. Chandler drones on and on at the front of the room, and with my rapid typing, I look like I'm taking notes. But what I'm really doing is taking matters into my own hands because I don't trust the Ethics Committee to solve this one. I've already run every recovery procedure I can think of to no avail and took extra precautions to reinforce my firewalls with a new MySQL script I wrote last period to prevent the hacker from gaining access to my personal computer again. Now it's time to dig around and see what else I can find.

Air whistles through my teeth when I navigate to the SSD drive I shoved into one of the IT computers earlier today. It's still connected. A good thing or a bad thing. Good for me at this moment, but bad for the state of security. No wonder someone else was able to breach the system when our fucking IT department doesn't even notice a rogue device attached to a computer on his desk.

I bite my lip, my mind flashing to Brandon's red-rimmed eyes, my brother's wails, the clear distraction blurring his vision. The clear opening for someone to take advantage of. A quick glance at their accounts in HiveMind confirms as much. Several chunks of time have gone missing from both of their accounts since yesterday, according to the time log.

In the command prompt, I type in a few code words that grant me full read-only access to the monitoring tools. The interface is a lot less user-friendly than the sleek GUI most users of HiveMind see. Instead of compartmentalized windows that are easy to read and navigate, I find myself staring at a root-level folder structure. While Mr. Chandler paces the room, the heels of his loafers clicking on the linoleum floor, I execute a data-mine script from my arsenal that'll illuminate any code changes made to the HiveMind server master file since yesterday.

A minute later, the results pop up, and I gasp so loudly that all the students in the room turn in my direction.

Holy isotopes. 56,320 lines of code have been altered since yesterday, touching nearly every part of the system. I feel like I'm on the verge of short-circuiting.

Mr. Chandler stops in front of my desk. "I'm delighted you find the concept of replacing the Galilean transformations of Newtonian mechanics with the Lorentz transformations so engaging."

The class snickers.

My mind is spinning so fast it feels as if the room is a Tilt-A-Whirl. I can barely cling to anything he just said. He keeps staring at me, expecting a response. I pluck out the only word I can remember. "Um. Lorentz?"

"Pay attention!" Mr. Chandler slaps my laptop monitor down until it clicks with the base. I thrust out my hands to stop it, but I'm not fast enough. Blame the Lorentz transformation, which defines the speed at which an object can move between two coordinates.

An itch tingles at the base of my neck, and my leg rattles under my desk. My fingers graze against the edge of the laptop, but Mr. Chandler shoots me a sharp glare beneath his wire-rimmed glasses. I snap my hands back and shove them into my lap, my pulse a metronome in my ears.

His voice seems to drag on, prolonging every second in an attempt to kill me with absolute proof of the theory of time dilation. My eyes glue to the clock, each tick of the second hand racing faster than the beating of my heart. 56,320 lines of code added, deleted, or altered. Shit.

The last official upgrade of HiveMind changed only 25,787 lines of code. 56,320 is massive. Those kinds of changes could encompass an entire plug-in. This is too big for just a patch.

I can't get away with opening my laptop, but I try to calm myself by inching up my sleeve beneath the desk and reading my handwriting. Under *Today's Events* I add:

Backed up recent memories to external hard drive.
Discovered 56,320 lines of code have been altered in
HiveMind.

When the girl next to me looks over, squinting at my arms, I hastily yank my sleeve downward.

With ten minutes left until the bell, Mr. Chandler announces that he wants us to work independently on a worksheet he pings to us via email. I've never opened my laptop so fast. I pull up the sheet and type a bunch of gibberish into the first line so I can load it up when he pauses behind me to monitor my progress. In an adjacent window, I scroll through the list of code changes. To determine what these changes actually do, I'd have to investigate each one, which could take hours. My eyes flash on a few new additions: *get_IsVariable_MemName* and *InitiateMassPurgeMemName* plus a few more related code words to define parameters for mass deletion. There's also new code to support additional memory transfer functionalities that weren't there two days ago, including *TransferSpecial, TransferEmos,* and *TransferFrags*. Who the hell knows what Special,

Emos, and Frags means when it comes to the ability to transfer? Another set of phrases sticks out to me. *SelectFolder, EncryptFolder,* and *HideFolderInvisible.*

I quickly copy those codes onto my blank arm with my non-dominant hand to remember to look into it again.

I tap my fingers against the table. Why would a folder need to be encrypted and hidden? And more important, have any folders actually *been* hidden? In the command line, I type *s-h-r /s /d *.** to bring up a list of any hidden folders. Only one result pops up involving a nested folder buried within nearly a thousand parent folder hierarchy. Whoever hid this folder tried to cover their trail but neglected a vital rule of programming: You can't hide everything.

My eyes widen when I click into it. It contains 7,694 files. The exact number of memories I'm missing.

My shoulders tense, a headache brewing behind my eyes.

HiveMind autotags memories with helpful easy-to-read titles, but every file in this folder contains only a string of gibberish as the title, clearly encrypted. However, about fifty of them retained little stars identifying them as ones I once favorited. I try to drag a few of the files into my account on HiveMind at once, but I get an error warning me I can only copy one file at a time. When I try to drag only one, a new warning pops up telling me that I can't copy encrypted data. Fuck. I'm going to have to do this the hard way.

I crack my neck from side to side and plug in a USB drive that contains most of my encryption tools. Within a few minutes, I have several programs running simultaneously to try to suss out the encryption keys on a randomly selected file and bust that baby wide open.

I smile to myself when my precious, little genius scripts crack the case in only two minutes and forty-seven seconds. A new record. But I don't gloat long, because Mr. Chandler clears his throat behind me and I pretend to work on his dumb assignment for a few minutes. Once he moves on to the next student, I haul ass back to the hidden folder. Without encryption, the file slides directly into my HiveMind account, though I can still only copy one at a time. Like other transferred memories, it starts playing in my mind as soon as it finishes copying.

A black cloud washes over the classroom like a tidal wave as the memory plays in my mind. Pressure tugs at my skull and then releases in one swift swoosh, like pulling suction off a surface. The memory seizes control of my vision, replacing the view of Mr. Chandler's classroom with that of a science lab. Fluorescent overhead lights flood the room, blotting out all traces of blackness. This isn't Mr. Chandler's classroom at all, but one with an entirely different layout, and I'm standing against a wall with Sebastian pressed against me.

Right against me. No room for excess molecules to squeeze between us.

His face hovers only inches from mine and body heat radiates off him. He winks at me behind dark plastic-rimmed glasses. His hair is shaved down to only stubble, and I run my fingers through my own hair from ends to roots, except the ends stop a centimeter below my shoulder instead of falling into waves that reach below my boobs. This must be freshman year, when I had an unfortunate incident with a pair of scissors and a bad idea.

[Not here,] I whisper. Except I say it backward, like I'm rewinding my DVR with the volume on. I lean my chin over his shoulder, peering past my classmates scrambling backward, toward a pile of glass shards on the floor. Black liquid bubbles on the ground, shiny like a puddle of slick oil.

[Now impress me with your idea.] His words are also backward, but I understand him. This memory is happening in reverse while my mind moves forward. He shoots me a grin, lit eerily by the glow of his glasses refracting a light source I can't identify. [Not many people can impress me with a good physics joke.]

[If we worked together, it would be supersymmetry,] I say.

I see a mushroom cloud of fire appear out of nowhere behind his head, followed by a loud boom.

Sebastian lifts away from me, his hands sliding up my arms to my chest as he skids backward. I shoot forward after him, stopping abruptly as his arms jerk down to his sides.

The fire shrinks back down to a puff of smoke as the glass pieces on the floor fly back together, assembling into the shape of a beaker. The smoke turns into a bubbling black liquid inside. My arm stretches out, fingers cupped, and the beaker flies back into my hand.

With my other hand, I grab an empty tube from the counter and hold it over the rim of the beaker. Reverse osmosis occurs as the tube leeches the dark color from the liquid and collects it into the empty tube. [What if I can change your mind, Bash? I'm in need of a physics guru for my project and you seem to be in need of a project in the first place.]

[That's what Mr. Kimmel said, but this is what I want to work on.] Sebastian bites his lip.

[There's a fine line between a project and a product. In order for the school board to approve your idea, you have to cross it.]

[No, but she will. If I can just get—] He hastily picks up a paper and then peruses it, purposefully avoiding my eyes, before setting it back down.

I set the test tube filled with black liquid onto the table. [My mother didn't approve that.]

[Prove the existence of bosonic strings.] He walks backward, and I meet him, stride for stride, the clear liquid in my beaker sloshing. In the background, I can hear the teacher warning students to be careful when choosing compounds to mix because some have dangerous reactions.

[What's your thesis project?]

I spin and face a table loaded with beakers and set the one in my hand down. I pick up another tube from an array labeled REACTANTS and hold it over the beaker. The liquid lifts out of the beaker and flows into the test tube. Once the tube is full, I set it back down on a tray.

He nods toward Teddy across the way. Teddy's head is shaved too, matching Sebastian's, as if they purchased a two-for-one special. [He's the best people.]

[Awww, don't talk about Teddy like that. He's good people. And besides, it got you into this school, didn't it?]

[I was robbed. How does a quantum computing simulator not take first place?] Sebastian leans casually next to me, propping his hands behind his head. On the inside of his wrists, red markings dot the surface, scars like my own, but different. His are dots, mine is an angry red line.

[I also know you ranked number two in the country for your eighth-grade project in the National Science Fair competition.]

[They never have much plot, but there's always a killer ending.] He crosses his arms over his SCHRÖDINGER'S ABS T-shirt. I snicker inwardly at the joke as we walk backward to our station.

[That you read physics books for fun.] I hop onto the black table and straddle the lab report sheet resting there. I grab a notebook from beside me and hold it high over my head as Sebastian tries to swat it away from me. Keeping it high, I flip through it, tilting my head back to read, passing by pages of complex classical mechanics questions. Sebastian continues to try to grab it from me. After a few seconds, I sneak the book back into his messenger bag while he stands in front of me, looking somewhat confused.

His brow lifts. [Hope they were good rumors.]

[Because I heard some rumors about you.]

[Why did you choose me?] He propels himself to his feet and starts to walk away backward.

He keeps skidding backward as if avoiding my siren call. I keep my eyes locked on his, waggling my finger toward my chest.

Blackness seeps over my eyes as the memory ends. I blink against the harsh light that fades back into my vision. It takes a moment to get my bearings, and when I do, I flinch to find Mr. Chandler seated across from me, staring at me with a concerned expression. Every other chair in my classroom is now empty. He snaps his fingers in front of my face. "Arden?"

I rub my fists against my eyes, heart pounding. "What—what happened?"

"Class ended ten minutes ago. You didn't move." He jerks his chin toward the clock.

I press a palm against my forehead. I was so deep in the memory I had no idea what was going on in my current surroundings.

"I'm okay." I scramble out of my chair, wobbling on unsteady feet. Mr. Chandler reaches toward me, but I swat him away. "I'm fine."

I hastily thrust my laptop back into my bag and then fling myself into the hallway, gulping desperate bits of air. I lean against the lockers and try to make sense of what the hell just happened. The memory played backward but when I piece it back together in the correct order, it makes total sense. I propositioned Sebastian— Bash?—to be my lab partner, first for this chemistry experiment assignment that day and then for our larger thesis project. I told him I was in need of a science genius and he was the best there is. Well, second only to Teddy, according to the science fair competition that my mom established a few years ago to find potential MVH candidates. In the last decade, it's become the most prestigious science competition for young people short of the Nobel Prize.

After that, I told Sebastian his own project idea for bosonic strings would never get approved because it's not a product, and I finally won him over with a physics joke about supersymmetry. And he won me over by pushing me out of the way just before my beaker exploded after I mixed the wrong chemical compounds together because I was paying more attention to his adorable smile than the assignment. It all led to him pressed against me, both our chests puffing in and out, while I refused to tell him the one piece of vital info we both need to know: What the hell is our project?

The sensory details were far more vivid than the usual Hive-Mind replay, overwriting everything in my vision until I could only see the moment replaying in my mind's eye. With normal Hive-Mind replay, it's like a piece of tracing paper overlaid on my eyes. The scents from the memory are muted beyond recognition. But just now, the pungent odor of the chemical compounds at my feet were so strong, I wanted to gag. I couldn't even hear the bell ringing or my classmates exiting the room.

And that wasn't the only thing different. *We* were different. The Sebastian I spoke to this morning was quiet and reserved, but the one in the memory was full of wit and energy. *I* acted so different with the way I clearly flirted with him.

Holy shit. I need to experience that again. I need to get back another memory.

I slide onto the cold linoleum floor and open my laptop. With trembling fingers, I navigate to the SSD drive. When I click on it, an error pops up: *Could not connect.*

My shoulders tense. I jab my fingers against the keys, trying a million different things to reestablish the connection and find that folder again, but it's no use.

The drive's been disconnected.

Someone pulled it out of the computer.

00111000

I kick off my stilettos and race toward the IT room in my bare feet, my soles slapping the cold linoleum floor. My shoes dangle in my hands, swinging like pendulums. I keep my gaze focused on the prize and ignore the way my heart pounds so fast it's about to burst out of my chest. I skid to a stop in front of the door and scramble for my mom's access card in my purse. I need to get back inside and hook up to the machine again.

I hold up the card to the scanner. . . . except there is no scanner. Or at least the same one from this morning is gone, replaced by a fancy device with plastic that scoops outward, forming an awning, and a translucent area beneath filled with lasers shining through. There's a tinge of sawdust smell and a fresh coat of paint surrounding the newly installed device.

I cup my hand over my mouth and back up, eyes wide, head shaking. It's a retina scanner, one of the new prototypes Varga's about to release to the world during this year's press conference. Unlike previous iterations on the market from other companies, this one's supposed to be foolproof. No way to trick it.

No way to get inside the basement leading toward the IT room.

Cold panic shivers up my spine.

This might be one of the precautions my mother alluded to that the Ethics Committee was putting in place. I thought it would be digital, like a new firewall or system-wide password reset. Something I could easily bypass with a little time and a lot of hacking. But I can't even bypass this with a crowbar!

Laughter emanates from a few doors down, and Zoey's shrill cackle carries above the beating of my own heart. I drop my shoes onto the floor and stuff my feet inside them, then stomp toward the sound. The breath seething out of my lungs feels wild. Feral. Desperate.

The door's ajar, and I push it open so hard it slams into the wall behind it. Everyone inside jumps and stares.

Zoey leaps to her feet, squealing in delight at the sight of me. "Arden! Oh my God, what perfect timing. We need you!" She waggles her hand toward her chest as she plops back down into Mrs. Catalano's seat and props her feet on her desk, not caring that she's scuffing up her grade book. Giant maps hang behind her, making it seem like she rules the world.

"I. Need. To. Talk. To. You." The words scrape across the gravel of my throat, slamming into my gritted teeth.

"Actually, *I* need to talk to you," Veronica says, though her words imply more *scolding* than *talking* will be involved. Next to her, her BFF Eliza Shaw glares and smooths down her new bangs, which make her seem more English sheepdog than human. "What the hell did you do to Simon?" Veronica continues. "He's freaking out. Thinks you're going to get him expelled." Veronica cracks her jaw. "But clearly *you're* the one who deserves that honor."

Her words are as sharp as a spike through my feet, pinning me in place. Someone's out to get me, and Veronica's right here, confessing as much.

"Do you have a problem with me?" I shoot my accusation at her like an arrow as I march into the room and drop my bag on one of the plush couches arranged in a circle radiating away from the teacher's desk. Some of the teachers take the progressive learning atmosphere a little too far. Sparse droplets of rain peck at the floor-to-ceiling windows, and the howling wind interrupts with a whine every few seconds. An expanse of dull gray sky gives the illusion of dusk invading the early afternoon.

"You mean you don't already know that answer?" Veronica taps her forehead to indicate I must be spying on her. "You. Ruin. Every-thing." She spits each word.

"*I* ruin everything?" I have to laugh at the irony. "*You're* the one destroying *my* life!"

"You got me put on fucking probation and demoted from school president." Veronica ticks off one finger. "You cut Simon off cold turkey." She holds up another finger, which just happens to be her middle one. "And you showed Simon that I'm cheating on him!"

"If I hadn't given him those memories, someone else would have told him. It's not like you've been stealthy about it."

Zoey whistles through her fingers, making everyone snap our attention to her. "Ladies, ladies. Save the catfight until after we get shit done. The entire theoretic foundation of this committee relies on audience participation. The press conference is in four freakin' days and everything's falling apart! The decorations haven't arrived, the lighting company canceled at the last minute, the security team's invoice came in at 100K over the original quote." Zoey lifts her hands in frustration. "And Veronica, *please* tell me you called the media outlets to confirm coverage."

My mom formed a student-run committee to handle all logistics for the press conference. It's more of a marketing ploy than an attempt to give students power. The press loves to run articles about how seventeen-year-olds can put together a press junket that gets more views than Apple. When Veronica got kicked out as president, she joined this committee to beef up her résumé.

"I called the outlets," Veronica mumbles, clearly not happy about being silenced by a classmate. "They're confirmed."

"Great!" Zoey always knows how to turn on the pep. "And Arden, we need you to check if Melody paid the sound technician. Eliza, did you pay for the valet service?"

"Teddy did it for me," Eliza says, and Zoey grumbles.

I stand up. "Zoey, I really don't have time for this. I need to talk—"

"Please," she begs.

I squeeze my eyes shut and sit back down. My best friend needs me just as I need her. I know Zoey wants me to check Melody's mind, but the first thing I do is hack into my mom's account. The list of memories pops up like an enticing array of ice-cream toppings, all of which I want to indulge in. HiveMind automatically divides hers into smaller bite-sized chunks, each packed with potential information.

Meeting with Ethics Committee.

Marketing strategy for Leo's and Arden's projects.

Arden in my office.

There's so many to choose from, and for a moment my finger lingers on the marketing-strategy option. A warning error pops up with an angry bleep. *Operation not permitted.*

My gut twists. *This* must be the new security measure the Ethics Committee is testing out on a few key accounts. Of course my mother's account is one of them. It's the keyest of all keys.

I try again, ignoring the bead of sweat that rolls down my forehead. When my hacking software fails, I manually enter every damn password of hers I've hacked into. Kimmel's. Brandon's. All blocked. I can still get into the rest of the faculty accounts though.

Maybe this is a good sign. Whatever security measure the Ethics Committee put in place seems to be working. Maybe they'll be able to roll it out to a wider set of users in a much shorter time frame than one or two days. My shoulders relax a little.

I find the memory of Melody mailing off a check to the sound company and let Zoey know that's all set.

While the group continues to confirm the last-minute preparations for the press conference, I double-check my own account and compare it with the screenshot list of memory files I took earlier. A relieved breath escapes my lips. Everything seems to be in order, and the backup I made also matches, even if it's still missing that memory I lost in the cafeteria. I covertly reread the information scrawled along my arm, and it all makes sense, another good sign. I add a few more pieces of vital information:

Sloppily hidden folder using amateur encryption tools located on the IT console. Possibly contains every missing memory of mine? The memory I retrieved played backward but indicates that I was the one who asked Sebastian—

I cross out *Sebastian* and write *Bash* instead. I decide to call him Bash in my memories to help differentiate in my mind. The old version of him was just so different from his current self.

—I was the one who asked Bash to work on a project with me. Also, we flirted a lot.

I hug my arm to my chest. A temporary shield of safety enwraps me, flimsy and inefficient. If someone erased all my backups before, I have no doubt they'll do it again.

I search my laptop and the user version of HiveMind for various keywords like *TransferEmos* and *TransferFrags* but come up with zero results.

While Zoey and the girls argue about supplies, I search Veronica's mind, perusing the list of memories from only twenty minutes ago. And there, right before the end-of-school bell went off, is a stretch of memory of Veronica exiting the IT room. The thumbnail image shows her leaving the room, and the automatic tag that HiveMind titled the clip says: *Veronica seeks IT help.*

The time codes sync up to the exact moment that someone yanked my SSD drive out of the console.

Zoey sighs when she looks at the massive list on the whiteboard. "I think we need more help."

"Teddy already offered to help!" Eliza reaches for her phone to text him.

Zoey wavers, balancing from one hip to the other. It doesn't take a genius to interpret: She can't decide whether to agree so she might have the opportunity to get close to him or say no to prevent Eliza from texting him in the first place. "Um, I'm sure Teddy's busy. What about . . . Sebastian? Arden, can he help?"

Eliza squints at me, or maybe looks at me, it's hard to tell behind the bangs. "Who?"

"Bash Cuomo." Zoey writes his name down next to *Catering: confirm and set up.* "He can handle the food setup when it arrives, I'm sure."

"Hmmm." Veronica wrinkles her nose, which is hard to do. She has a lot of nose. "Doesn't strike me as his type of thing."

A staccato pulse begins at the back of my neck. "Oh? And what evidence do you have to support this accusation?" I say, crossing my arms for emphasis.

"Nothing. He usually doesn't participate in extracurriculars, that's all. Calm down."

A million synapses snap in my mind, forming unanswered questions worthy of a cold-case classification. What *does* he participate in? What else do they remember about him? What do they remember about *him and me*? But asking those questions would alert them to my decaying mental state. Plus, I don't trust Veronica to give me the truth. "Well, he's changed."

Veronica just laughs. "Changed how?"

I shrug, effectively ending this conversation. *Changed how?* It was a guess before, a hypothesis to be proven. But now I have a concrete answer. Sebastian from freshman year was funny and outgoing, whereas the Sebastian I met today is reserved and guarded, trading his clever T-shirt only science geeks would get for something his mom probably picked out.

That girl in the memory from the chemistry room was daring in a way I rarely am. Daring with a boy. I can't remember the last time I even flirted with a boy, let alone sat on his desk and forced him to pay attention to me.

After the meeting, Veronica and Eliza hover in the room, whispering about going to the mall.

"You wanted to talk?" Zoey shrugs her purse over her shoulder.

My eyes flick toward the girls, who are clearly waiting here just for the exact purpose of eavesdropping. "Not here. Can we go back to your place? You mentioned needing another test subject for your holographic makeup and I'm game. Though I want to make a pit stop first."

Zoey claps her hands and hops up and down in excitement. "Oh my God, you don't know how long I've been wanting to give you a makeover!"

"Can't wait." To spy in Veronica's room while she's at the mall, that is.

00111001

Something tells me this place doesn't even sell lipstick." Zoey's keys jangle in her hands as we march through the parking lot toward the giant computer center in the next town.

"Oh, come on, don't act like you've never even seen a computer before." I yank open the door. "Have you been practicing at all with what I taught you?" When HiveMind first started beta testing on students and we first started our little side business, I showed her a few tips and tricks for how to do the magic that I do. Once when I had the flu, she filled in for me and kept our customers satisfied.

She shakes her head. "I wish, but there's no time. Not with all the press conference prep and the scientists I'm still helping."

"Let me know if you ever need a refresher."

Every time I walk into this store, my eyes bug out at the wide range of computer products available for me. This store sells all the tools you need to build your own computer.... or hack into one, as the case may be. I could spend hours here perusing the loot and dropping my entire savings, but I stay focused and beeline for one specific aisle.

I drop twenty SSD cards into my little blue shopping basket. I'd buy more, but I took every last one. I plan to stash them in various places: purse, car, home, locker, Sebastian's pockets, Zoey's purse. Basically anywhere I can to ensure I always have one accessible. I grab two more external hard drives for good measure as well.

We pay and exit. Thankfully the rain has cleared at the moment, but a dark cloud promises more later. As we're heading to our cars, three girls pause from their trek between the clothing store next door and the coffee shop on the other side of the computer center. They stare at us as if we might genetically engineer them with no tools other than proximity. One wears a jacket with the Wickham High logo patched to her sleeve.

"God, not this again." Zoey groans. It's the standard reaction from the local Wickham students, who can't fathom how anyone would choose to spend every waking minute learning science instead of dallying in more important activities like cheerleading and art club. "Emmenology!" she shouts at them. The Latin word for the study of menstruation.

They giggle at us, mocking us under their breaths. They might look down on us now, but what they don't realize is in less than a year, when HiveMind and various other projects hit the market, they'll be clamoring to be the first preorder.

"You could also just say hi to them," I tell her.

She shrugs. "Maybe if they didn't ogle us like we're museum attractions."

We get into our separate cars and drive to the student house for seniors. It sprawls in front of me, hidden inside your average mini-mansion. Black shutters against white siding make the house look like a black-and-white photograph. Gray branches punch the sky behind the roof.

Most parents at our school drop their geniuses off and wait for the patents to roll in. I used to be jealous of all the kids who lived here while I'm stuck in my childhood home, but living at home actually grants me *more* freedom. I don't have to worry about a specific curfew or about bumping into my teacher wearing only a towel, and I don't need to log my comings and goings with a key fob like an employee clocking in to work. Plus I get to spend time with my mom and brother, and after losing my dad, I want to soak up all the family time I can get.

I follow her inside. An ornate wooden staircase greets us in the grand foyer, giving the room an air of history even though it was only constructed a decade ago. Laughter emanates from the common room off to the side, which opens to a dining room where bright tablecloths cover rows of long tables. A delicious beef-taco scent wafts from the kitchen, where the house chef prepares a casual home-cooked meal for forty people. There's even a mini–science lab in the basement for those students who get late-night molecular-chemistry cravings.

A boy wearing only boxers crashes into Zoey as he comes out of the guys' bathroom near the staircase. He winks, then slips into one of the rooms along the back hallway.

"Sometimes I think he waits for someone to come by just to do that." Zoey races up the stairs to the girls' floor.

A long hallway twists in different directions, with rooms on either side like a hotel. Zoey kicks open the first door. Her room bursts with life from her multicolored paisley bedspread to the uncomfortably close posters of models' faces done up in garish makeup. Most students have to share with a roommate, but Zoey's parents paid extra just so she could have a single all to herself. "It's a donation," her dad once told me when he was visiting. I see it more as a bribe. The fewer distractions his daughter has, the better chance she'll have at success.

"Okay, sit in that chair and tell me what's *really* going on. I want to help."

"Help me snoop in Veronica's room?" I throw my messenger bag on Zoey's bed. I plan to sleep cuddled with my laptop tonight in case anyone tries to break in and erase my data manually.

"I am *always* up for snooping." Zoey switches on her MP3 player, and loud rap beats pump from the speakers on her desk, a clear attempt to thwart eavesdroppers. A white vanity with an oval mirror contains not makeup but various computer apparatuses plugged into a console.

Giggles from outside the door make us both whip our heads toward it. One of the voices sounds just like Veronica. A quick check outside the door confirms as much, as I see Eliza's backside right before she turns the corner.

"Shit." I plop into Zoey's chair with a heaviness I hadn't meant to carry with me. "They must have stopped back here before heading to the mall."

"Perfect. Gives you time to spill the beans and me time to make you beautiful." Zoey plugs a USB into a tray of blue eye shadows. "That's right. You might have used this as a ruse, but you're not getting out of it."

I blurt almost everything that's happened today—that I remember, anyway. Zoey's face turns horrified and sympathetic in all the right places.

"So you think someone's deliberately deleting everything related to your project?"

"Not deleting. Archiving." I'm out of space on my arm, so I lift up my shirt and take a Sharpie to my stomach.

Someone's archiving everything related to my project.
Not deleting.

I'm about to cap it when I add:

If you're short on SSD cards or external hard drives,
check your messenger bag.

Zoey's watching me strangely. "Okay, I admit, writing this all down on your stomach is pretty brilliant."

I grin at her. "Brilliant, huh? Tell that to the board review committee."

She laughs as she tilts my chin up with her finger and squints, assessing the ratio of eyeliner to eye. "Close your eyes." She plugs the other end of the USB cord into a white plastic wand the size and shape of a makeup brush. Holographic makeup was one of Varga Industries' first products to hit the market. Sales have soared and several popular, high-end makeup brands went out of business as a result. After all, you can't beat smear-proof, smudge-proof, water-proof, twelve-hour makeup at a fraction of the cost. New colors download automatically.

"Who do you think is behind it?"

I shut my eyes. "My best guess is Veronica, but I've got a few other suspects in mind." I bite my lip. "Teddy, for example."

Zoey gasps. "It's not Teddy. Don't even joke about that!" She waves the wand over my lids like a magician performing a trick. I brace for a spray of color or a hissing sound like an airbrush. But after a moment of nothing discernible, she sets the shadow down and twists a tube of lipstick into the same USB port. She purses her mouth like a duck. When I copy her, she traces my lips with the wand and then leans back to admire her work like an artist studying a canvas. "Voilà! It's kiss-proof, so you better do some face sucking tonight."

As part of spilling the beans, I also told her about my Not Date with Sebastian.

"What *are* you doing with him anyway?"

I shrug. "I want to talk to him. See what he remembers. Try to get to know him."

"All of those things are precursors to face sucking, just saying!"

I roll my eyes at her and twist to face the mirror. Soft blues of different shades blend across my lids to create an effect that makes me look both pretty and dangerous. When I touch my finger to my daring red lips, no color comes off. "Wow."

"If the science thing doesn't work out for me, I've got a fallback career as a makeup artist," she says bitterly before straightening. "Let's do this. Mental snooping or physical?"

"Both, of course. Have to be thorough. Let me check if they've left."

I log on to HiveMind and check out the list of recent memories in both their accounts. The last one for each of them shows a thumbnail of the two of them opening their drawers in their room with the automatic tag: *Stop back home to change clothes.* HiveMind is only good up until the last archived memory. It doesn't allow me to sync to someone's mind in real time, so I have no way of knowing what they're doing at this very second. They may still be changing in their room or they may already be on the road to the mall. I won't know unless I knock on their door, which I'm clearly not going to do, or wait until the next memory pops up on the list to tell me their last known whereabouts. "They might still be here, so we should lie low for a bit. Let's do some mental snooping first."

Zoey flops onto her bed and clasps her hands behind her head. "Mental snooping is my favorite kind. I can be lazy while doing it!"

My pulse grinds in tune to the rap music pounding against my skull. "Turn off the music though. I don't want it distracting from the memories."

While Zoey flips the station to something classical and turns off the lights, I do some quick keyword searches in HiveMind for my prime targets—Veronica and Teddy. HiveMind can sort memories by size, date, and relevance, so I select the most relevant memories from Veronica's and Teddy's heads and select the first one from the list to copy into both our minds. "First up: Veronica's memory from yesterday when she wanted to rat on me. Should begin in three, two . . ."

Just as I make myself comfortable in Zoey's chair, the cheery *ding* that indicates the start of a memory simulation beeps in my mind. A bowl of Chinese chicken salad overlays on top of my view of the dark bedroom. A fork carrying lettuce flies across my vision. The colors of the memory are dim and muted compared with the vibrant memories of Bash I got back.

"Maybe I should report her." Veronica's voice blares inside my mind. "It might be the only way to stop her."

"I wouldn't mind making her stop looking in my head," another voice says. The image wobbles as Veronica focuses on the Eliza Shaw from yesterday, who still hadn't made a bad decision about bangs. "I suspect she gave Zoey that memory of me kissing Teddy." Eliza stabs her fork at a piece of chicken. "If Zoey really wants to know what it's like to kiss him, I'll tell her *all* the details. I don't need her living vicariously through me."

"Oh, she's got it all wrong," Zoey says from her bed. It's true, I did give Zoey Teddy's version of the kiss, not Eliza's, so Zoey could hear the quick flash when Teddy started thinking about Zoey instead of the girl he was kissing.

"I know," Veronica continues in my mind, answering Eliza-from-yesterday even though it sounds like a direct reply to what Zoey just said in reality. "It's like Arden doesn't even think about the consequences." Veronica glances behind her, where Past Zoey sits at an adjacent table, reading—or pretending to read—a text-book. "I had to do four fucking weeks of after-school bitch work thanks to her probation stunt."

Without the light, it takes my eyes a moment to differentiate between the dining room image playing in my mind and the shapes that make up the dorm room. Her inner monologue from yester-day shouts in my brain: *Simon's falling apart because of his memory addiction and what does Arden do? She cuts him off cold turkey! He needs to be weaned off this addiction gently. Ugh.*

My chest tightens at the reminder of how I've been hurting Simon. Here I thought I was helping him.

"I say do it," Eliza tells Veronica in the memory. "Get the bitch in trouble. It'll finally make her mother realize she's not the second coming of Einstein." Eliza tosses her hair. "I am."

Veronica groans. "Maybe I should talk to her before I do something rash."

The memory fades out.

I groan. "Bad news: That wasn't very incriminating against Veronica."

"Good news: You have a new suspect to add. Eliza." Zoey turns onto her side to look at me. "Good thing I'm planning on doing recon on her."

I copy the next memory. The one of Veronica's visit to the IT room starts to play in my mind. She holds up her laptop to Bran-don and whimpers that she's been locked out of her student email again. After reviewing her account, Brandon turns to her with a perplexed expression. "It says your account has been suspended due to inappropriate usage."

She lets out a large sigh. "Oh my God. I've already been over this with the Ethics Committee. I'm eighteen. I should be able to send any photos I want!"

Brandon doesn't look amused. "Not on school-regulated sys-tems."

"Please just let me back in," she begs. "I can't turn in my quan-tum entanglement paper without email. Do you want me to fail?"

"Fine." Brandon works a little magic with his admin console.

"But next time, use your personal account for those kinds of pics. And maybe send them to your boyfriend instead of Josh Lazarus?"

"Oh my God!" Zoey says.

"He broke up with me," Veronica says bitterly.

Veronica quickly thanks him for fixing her email block. She doesn't yank out the SSD drive. In fact, I can still see it in her peripheral vision as she heads back out the door with her miraculously cured computer.

It wasn't her.

"When do I get Teddy's memory?" Zoey rubs her hands together when that memory ends.

"Give me a sec." I retrieve the last one in the list, this one from Teddy's mind.

Zoey grabs her spare pillow and hugs it against her chest, as though she can simulate the act of hugging Teddy while his memory plays in her mind.

Teddy's memory starts playing. The image of several students surrounding Teddy in a classroom ghosts over the sliver of light seeping under Zoey's door. The sound of Teddy's laughter fills my head, too loud to be coming out of his mouth as well. He's laughing inwardly.

They better not be using my study session, Teddy thinks. He watches as each one receives their grades on their tablet. A boy squints at the screen as if it's written in a foreign language, a girl's lip quivers, a third spins around and glares at Teddy. All three are my best customers. The boy glances over at Teddy. *They are. Shit. I need to differentiate my answers so I don't get in trouble too.* Teddy goes on to decide that next time, he's going to purposefully study the wrong answers, just to mess with my customer base.

The memory ends there, leaving me with no evidence or leads. He wanted to screw with my customers. . . . but not with me.

"You realize what this means, right?" Zoey bolts upright. "Teddy's innocent! He's the best guy ever! He's going to love me forever!" She delivers each sentence with its own little victory dance.

I wrinkle my nose. "The first two, maybe. The last one... debatable."

She throws her pillow at me. "You're my best friend. You're supposed to support and encourage my fantasies!"

"Okay, fine. Yes, he's going to love you forever," I deadpan.

She squeals as if my saying it makes it fact. "Are we ready for the real snooping yet?"

I check Eliza's and Veronica's accounts again and see a new memory, this one with a thumbnail of the two of them in the car with the automatic tag: *On the way to the mall.*

"Let's go." We step out into the hallway and Zoey shuts her door. She tiptoes toward Veronica's room while I march with purpose.

Inside the room, the glow from my phone illuminates a leopard-print bedspread on the left that could only be Eliza's, so I fly to the shabby chic side and open up Veronica's laptop, which waits on her desk like an invitation. Despite the memory potentially exonerating her, I need to verify what I saw with concrete evidence. After all, I know now that memories can be altered and deleted.

Zoey bounces on her toes as she starts searching through Eliza's desk drawers.

I bite my inner cheek and sync my password-cracking software to Veronica's computer. Not even three seconds later, her laptop opens up to all her secrets.

"Look what I found." Zoey raises a bottle of large pink capsules, the pills rattling like a baby toy.

"Are those Eliza's Sober Up prototype?" I click Veronica's HiveMind and run a quick script to pull up her recent activity. I want to see what Veronica's setup looks like and what her permission controls are, in case she blocked me from accessing any shady memories.

"I think they're a rip-off," Zoey says. "Just a bunch of vitamin B and some enzymes that aid in alcohol metabolism. She's got an unofficial prototype called *Shitfaced*. Supposedly that stuff is a huge hit in the party circuit. Gets you drunk without any hangover side effects."

The display of Veronica's recent activity makes my brow furrow. She only logged in to HiveMind twice in the last six months and neither of those times was recently. The only way she could have deleted my memories was if she'd hacked into the mainframe via the admin console like I did using proprietary software. But I can't find any evidence of that sort of thing on her laptop. Either she's an evil genius who knows how to disguise her tracks even from hackers . . . or she's innocent. A cold sensation races down my spine. Intuition tells me it's the latter.

I switch places with Zoey and flip on Eliza's laptop while Zoey helps herself to a spritz of Veronica's expensive, flowery perfume. She then pulls out Veronica's notebooks from her bookshelf and flips through the top one.

Just as I start the cracking program, the doorknob jiggles, and my heart leaps into my throat. Zoey and I exchange glances. If we get caught in the room, the stupid Ethics Committee would over-rule Mom and expel us all. A sharp jolt of panic propels me under Eliza's bed. My knees trample crumbs, and I kick a long plastic container filled with clothes against the wall to make myself fit into the cramped space. Zoey squeezes into Veronica's closet while I yank the leopard-print comforter down to help cover me. My heart beats fast.

The light pops on and two sets of feet parade into the room.

"...Being so psycho, right?" The set wearing combat boots stops atoms from my nose. Eliza. Her feet rise, one by one, and the weight of the mattress sighs, caving in just above my head. Now would be a terrible time to develop claustrophobia.

"Yeah, it was almost like she was accusing me of something." Veronica's feet carry her toward her desk. "Okay, got my credit card. Sorry about that." There's a scraping sound as Veronica likely slides the plastic rectangle off her desk. "Weird; why is my laptop hot?"

My hair rises on my arms. With a jolt of panic, I notice my thumb drive sticking out of Eliza's laptop. The scent of Veronica's flowery perfume from Zoey's spritz lingers in the air like evidence.

"Did you leave it plugged in all day?" Eliza asks. "Mine overheats when I do that."

"Nope, just started charging it a few minutes ago. It was out of battery, so I plugged it in when we stopped back here." Veronica's laptop charger falls into a clump on the hardwood floor.

A vibration from the phone in my pocket sounds louder than a bomb. I hold my breath.

"Are you getting a text?"

Eliza glances at her phone. "No, but I heard that vibration too."

My phone buzzes again, but if I try to reach for it, I'd make even more noise. My heart pounds.

"Must be coming from next door. Do you have everything now or are we going to have to turn around a third time?" There's a hint of jest in Eliza's voice.

"Sorry; I'm just preoccupied." Veronica's feet stomp toward Eliza's bed. "You think Zoey overheard me complaining yesterday about Arden getting me on probation and told Arden and that's why she was being such a bitch?" She stops in front of Eliza's desk. I clench my teeth.

Another four-alarm-fire text vibrates in the pocket of my jeans.

Cold sweat drips down my forehead. There might as well be a neon sign pointing to my location flashing INTRUDER RIGHT HERE! I prepare excuses: *My mom put me up to this. I'm your new cleaning service! We're playing hide-and-seek and you found us!*

Silence cuts the tension, blooming until it lasts an uncomfortably long time. I imagine all sorts of scenarios: Veronica pointing at the USB drive while Eliza raises a brow, the two swallowing a set of Eliza's pills—the kind not for erasing bad behavior but starting it, both of them too self-absorbed to notice the obvious clues we left behind.

"I think you should just ignore both of them," Eliza says after way too long. "Let's get to the mall before the sale at Forever 21 ends."

"Sure." The metallic clink of jingling keys grows softer as Veronica heads out the door. Eliza's feet land with a thump. A moment later the light switches off and the door slams.

My muscles relax, but instead of feeling relieved, I'm annoyed that my classmates really suck at being smart. Perhaps my mom should consider testing for common sense in her new applicants. I crawl out from under the bed and wipe off all the nasty crumbs sticking to my jeans. Zoey climbs out of the closet, and I check my phone. Four texts from Sebastian:

Sebastian: Seriously? I was friends with HIM?

Sebastian: I asked him if he remembers our project but he keeps changing the subject to video games. He's practically on his knees, begging me to play. He seems desperate to just spend time with me.

Sebastian: I told him after we finish our
homework, maybe. Yep. We're
doing homework. We're cool like
that.

I can't help it; I smile as I scroll past the third one.

Sebastian: Oh, he asked if I thought Zoey liked
him or if she's still mad at him.

I hold the last one up for Zoey. She gasps and plucks the phone from my hand.

"Just tell him it's you, okay?"

Her fingers start typing rapid-fire. "But if I tell him it's me, then the text I just sent saying 'I want to lick you all over' is going to seem really odd."

I shoot her the dirtiest glare I can muster and yank my USB drive from Eliza's computer. My only hope is that she assumed it was one of hers.

She hands me back the phone and I peruse the texts.

Zoey: ZOMG WHAT DID HE SAY?!?!? TELL ME
NOW!!!!!

Sebastian: Hi, Zoey.

Zoey: That's what he said? Or are you saying
hi because you've guessed I've taken
Arden's phone hostage based on the
excessive use of exclamation points. She
wants to do naughty things to you, btw.

Sebastian: Is she okay?

> **Zoey:** She's Arden. Which means she has a plan. Now stop stalling and tell me sweet nothings.

Sebastian: Hmm, it seems like you're the one who should be saying sweet nothings to him. ;-)

I tap out a text.

> **Arden:** Hey, it's really Arden this time. Pick you up in thirty? I have some updates.

He responds in an instant.

Sebastian: Okay, I'll tell Teddy I need to go home.

"Come on." I storm toward the door.

"I can't believe we got away with that," Zoey says. "Best day ever."

"I know. I—" The words die on my tongue as soon as I step into the hallway and come face-to-face with Veronica and Eliza. Both wear fighting-stance expressions despite their protective, crossed arms.

"This time." Veronica pokes me in the clavicle, getting her revenge by invading *my* personal space. "I WILL report you." She stomps back to her room, bumping her shoulder into me on the way. Inside she calls out, "Don't mess with me or anyone I care about again."

Comebacks and excuses pile up in a traffic jam in my throat.

Eliza circles us, bangs obscuring her brown eyes as she glares. "You're wasting your time." She jerks her head toward Zoey. "Teddy's never going to be interested in you."

Eliza swings her dark hair and slams her door. I stew in silence.

"Shit." Zoey grips my shoulders in panic. "This is bad, Arden. So freaking bad." Her eyes grow wide and terrified. "I can't be expelled. I just can't. I'm already on thin ice with no thesis project."

My teeth clench at the realization of what I have to do. I have to delete Veronica's and Eliza's memory of the last ten minutes. It's the only way to ensure she doesn't report us. I'm no better than the person who deleted my memories. I'm playing God, choosing what people remember to serve my own needs.

Suddenly, my lungs seem too big for my chest, and I gulp desperate breaths. I pace Zoey's room, working up the courage. I have to do this. If I don't, the Ethics Committee will cut off my access to HiveMind and I'll lose all ability to figure out who did this to me. And I'm not the only one who has memories missing. Sebastian does too. And he's missing *all* of them.

This is the only way I can save him. Save Zoey.

With trembling fingers, I open the HiveMind hacking app I've set up on my phone and navigate to Veronica's mind. When I select the last ten minutes of her memories, the highlighted files are as glaring as blinking neon lights. I add Eliza's files to the mix. My heart pounds frantically in my chest as I sit here, willing my hand to move with the force of a Ouija board spirit at a sleepover. But then I glance over at Zoey's worried face, and my purpose is reinforced. I have to do this. I have to break my own moral code. I drag the last ten minutes of the girls' minds into the trash.

The little *whir* noise that accompanies the deletion makes me want to throw up.

I wrench my fingers from the keyboard and twist them toward me, glaring at them like I can't believe what they've just done. It feels as if the entire Earth just tilted off its axis and I'm off balance as a result.

I saved my friend but sacrificed a piece of myself in the process.

0011000100110000

As I'm changing into my pajamas for bed, I catch a glimpse of a few words scrawled across my left forearm.

Today's events: Simon begging me for Veronica's memory of her cheating then asking me to delete it. Slipping an SSD drive into an IT monitoring computer. Having a discussion with Sebastian directly after Kimmel's class in the hallway about how he doesn't remember our project either. Making plans with Sebastian tonight after dinner. Watching a memory disappear from my account. Backed up recent memories to external hard drive. Discovered 56,320 lines of code have been altered in HiveMind.

Most of this is familiar, but the middle one makes my pulse race. Plans with Sebastian? What plans? My eyes zoom to the clock. It's nearly eleven p.m. Dinner was almost four hours ago. My stomach gives an uncomfortable lurch. I've just been sitting here for hours trying to figure out what the hell those 56,320 lines of code changes in HiveMind meant to no avail while he's been sitting at home, waiting for me.

I yank off my shirt and skim over every word written on my arm, but this is the only piece of information I don't remember.

There's a horrible weight in my gut. I just abandoned him. Left him without a word or a text.

I'm about to scramble back into my shirt from this morning, but on second thought, I grab a fresh one from my drawer. This one has the added bonus of just a little extra cleavage. I shrug on a cardigan as well in case it gets cold. My fingers bang out a text as I stuff my feet into my shoes.

Arden: Sorry! On my way.

After grabbing my laptop and all my supplies, I rush downstairs and cringe at the creaking third step. Voices echo from the nearby kitchen. With an open floor plan and hardwood floors that amplify footsteps even in socked feet, my house offers no place to hide. I call it a first world problem house: too big for the property, too small for epic parties.

"—don't understand. He said he loved me." Leo's voice makes me pause on the landing. "And after yesterday's success—" A foghorn sounds from the kitchen. Or maybe he blew his nose.

"I know you're upset," Mom says in her soothing voice, the one she uses on potential investors. "But it's good this happened now, before the press conference. It'll make customers feel more secure if the creator isn't romantically involved with the head of IT."

"I just wish we could talk about this. He won't even listen to me." Leo's sobs make something painful shoot inside me.

"I know, honey. I say be upset today and then tomorrow you show him how much better off you are without him." She pauses for a moment. "For now, what I think you need are the two best medicines: ice cream and distraction." The sticky squish of the freezer opening sends a wrench through my gut. I think back to swallowing spoonfuls of that same icy cure next to her on the couch after my dad died. Ice cream didn't cure my heartbreak then or bring Dad back from the dead. Neither did distraction.

Mom wouldn't remember that though. She carved out everything from her mind that reminded her of Dad being sick. "To stay strong," she once told me. "Sadness is a liability." It's one thing to accept his death, it's another thing entirely to erase all evidence of it.

A lump forms in my throat. I used to think the only way to lose someone was to have him or her leave you, whether by force or choice. Brandon chose to leave Leo. Cancer stole Dad from us. But I've lost pieces of myself even though I'm still here.

"Speaking of distraction, we need to discuss the press conference," Mom says.

"I'm not going. Not if Brandon's going to be there."

"Well, he has to be there, honey. He's in charge of the technical setup." She pauses for a moment. "Though I guess I can outsource the technical aspects if it means that much to you."

I had planned on sneaking out, but I can't just walk out of here when my brother's so upset. She's right. Leo needs to show Brandon exactly what he's missing. I plod into the spotless kitchen over to where my brother sits at the reclaimed wooden table. He buries his face in his hands, his mop of dark curls spilling over his fingers.

I place a palm on his shoulder. "You okay?"

Leo shudders. "Not really."

"Don't wimp out on the PC." I scrub his hair, messing up his neat part. "Make him jealous. Look better than him. Act better than him. *Be* better than him." Ever since sophomore year, when late nights in the lab turned into date nights in the lab, my brother and his boyfriend have been inseparable. After Leo graduated, Brandon got a job as the IT manager because even one nanosecond apart proved unbearable.

Mom sets the spoons on the table with a clatter. She pinches the bridge of her nose. Slouchy gray pajamas hang from her thin frame, and strands of hair escape from her low ponytail. Even though she stands with perfect posture, this is her definition of relaxed. I've always suspected she strategically hides crisp ironed suits around the house in case she needs to slip into one at a moment's notice, Batman-style.

"But how can I *be* better than him if I'm not ready yet? I just started the trials and I don't get the full results for a few more days." For his thesis project two years ago, he developed some way to cure diseases on a cellular level. Beta testing didn't go as planned last year—they could only test it on mice, not humans, and the mice kept dying shortly after being cured—but it's still being presented to the public this year. He and Mom are both confident the new trial will be successful and they want to get ahead of the market.

I circle around my brother and pick up the abandoned tub of cookie dough waiting in the center of the table. "He'll regret his decision when he sees the world swooning over your product."

"Yeah, you're right." Leo eyes my cleavage for the first time. "Whoa, where are you going dressed like that? Because wherever it is, it can't be good."

I readjust my lace shirt, pulling it a little higher on my chest. "Thanks a lot, jerkface."

He holds up his hands in surrender. "Hey, I'm not the one parading that way-too-revealing outfit."

"I'm wearing a cardigan!" I tug at my sleeve as if nothing can be risqué when covered up with the article of clothing most worn by librarians. The fabric slides higher on my wrist, revealing the ink written across there. I quickly yank it down.

Mom smooths a rogue wrinkle in her pajamas. "You better have a good reason for going somewhere this late on a school night."

My project provides me with the perfect alibi. "Sebastian's house. We need to try to figure out what our project is before the review."

Leo snickers under his breath. "Bash's house doesn't exactly qualify as a *good* reason."

"No. Absolutely not. You cannot go to a boy's house on a school night." Mom crosses her arms. "Besides, it's not even necessary to work on your project. The Committee granted you the extension. Your final grade won't be impacted in any way."

I rush to change the subject. "I noticed a few key teacher accounts are no longer accessible in HiveMind. Does that mean whatever the Ethics Committee did to lock them down worked?"

Mom's eyes widen. "I hope you're not implying you tried to access one."

I present her with my best halo smile. "Of course not. I would never do something like that. So . . . does it?"

Thin lines cup Mom's mouth when she frowns. "No, memories are still being tampered with, even in the accounts we tested the fix on."

Crap. All that means is the hacker was able to bypass the new security measures but I still can't. It's not often I feel inferior and that thought makes me want to punch something.

"Memories are being tampered with?" Leo's face turns as gray as the steel appliances.

"Someone's deleting all the juicy stuff from people's minds." I place a hand on one hip. "Know anyone at Varga Industries who has a vendetta against me?"

Mom thrusts her arm out into the center of the table like a referee stopping an illegal play. "Arden, don't spread rumors. It's a system glitch, *not* targeted malice. We've got it under control. It's actually a lot less activity than it initially seemed, mostly just concentrated on two users with a few other outliers."

"I'm well aware," User One says. User Two's currently waiting in his room for User One to rescue him.

"Rest assured," Mom continues, "I've got people working round the clock to fix it. We're going to get your memories back, I promise, sweetie."

"Don't take this the wrong way, but I don't trust the Ethics Committee to do it right. I'm going to try to fix this myself." I pivot on my heels. It seems to me that my mom's trying to solve the wrong issue: She's fixing the software instead of finding the culprit.

I storm out the door before she can try to stop me. I can hear her faint shouted threat: "If you walk out that door, you're going to be grounded for a month!"

Maybe there's a bright side to all these memory deletions. Perhaps she won't remember grounding me by tomorrow.

LIGHT RAIN COLLIDES with the nearby tree branches and plunks onto the walkway of Sebastian's townhouse. I huddle under the vaulted porch awning and shake out my umbrella. Wind whips my hair around my shoulders as I press the doorbell. The knob twists, and a woman with dusty blond hair pokes her nose out. "Arden." She spits my name like a curse word. "It's a school night. He's in bed."

"Please, it's important."

To my surprise, she opens the door and crosses her arms over a TGI Fridays uniform. She smells like greasy fries and blue cheese. Several nursing scrubs are folded neatly on top of a laundry basket at the foot of the stairs. Two jobs? The kids who live off campus are usually so rich their parents can afford nannies for their child. "Honey, he needs his rest. I know you want to see him, but can't this wait until tomorrow?"

"I'm afraid not." I brush past her and trudge up the stairs, my feet leaving wet imprints on the mauve carpet.

"Arden! You can't keep coming over like this!"

Photos line the walls. As I ascend the steps, Sebastian grows up before my eyes, starting as a squealing baby with a dollop of hair. His body elongates, his glasses change but remain a constant, he gets acne, he covers it up, and he grows gawky, then fills out, then loses some weight. And at the very top, I startle at one image. He's smoldering at the camera, the glare reflecting off one of his plastic-rim lenses, his arm propped around me.

I look so . . . happy.

A nervous flutter warms my belly at the image.

On the second floor, several closed doors face me. I feel like a contestant on a game show being asked to choose behind Door Number One or trade the prize for the mystery behind Door Number Two. But with Mrs. Cuomo hot on my heels, it's Door Number Three—second to the left—that calls to me based on what I hope is latent empirical knowledge.

Sebastian sits cross-legged on his bed, flipping through a composition notebook. "Arden?" He sets the notebook on top of a heaping pile teetering on his bed. "What are you doing here?"

The hair on the back of my neck rises. "We had plans tonight. Check your phone." I slam the door shut, flip the lock, and lean against it while ragged breaths escape. *This isn't me.* I sneak into the school late at night to do extra homework, not into guys' rooms.

He leans over his bed to grab his schoolbag from the floor. He rummages through it and then unearths his cell phone, which must have been in there since he got home from hanging out with Teddy. He must be the first teenage boy in history to not have his phone surgically attached to his palm.

I wipe sticky hair out of my eyes, but it clings to my forehead as though it's mocking me with its rebellion. I jerk my chin toward the notebooks. "Anything about our project in those?"

"Possibly, but it's hard to tell because it's just pages of quantum physics equations. I must have been really fun at parties." He stands and stretches. His white T-shirt rises an inch above the waistband of his baggy pajama bottoms, revealing creamy skin and the elastic of his blue boxers. I force myself to swallow.

He stares at me back, as if waiting for something. "Uh . . ."

Several hard bangs on his door snap us out of our trance. I give him a dismissive shake of my wrist. "Don't worry about her. I'll take care of it."

"No, I meant, I need to get dressed. . . ."

"Oh. Right. I'll just . . . turn around." It takes way too much effort to drag my feet into a pivot. I face the opposite wall, where a desk resides, covered in more composition notebooks. A periodic table hangs alongside a few posters of emo bands. Dirty clothes drape over the back of the desk chair, which sags in the center, a permanent butt print. The room is lived in, not the room of a boy with no memories. I was expecting blank walls to match his blank mind.

While he slips on a T-shirt, I flip open a notebook on his desk. Experimental data litter the pages, all scrawled in nearly illegible chicken scratch.

"Sebastian!" His mother pounds even louder. "Open up immediately! What did we talk about yesterday? When she's here, you leave the door open."

I close the notebook. "Does your mom know you lost your memories?"

"Yeah, but I don't think she understands. I get the feeling she's not all that technologically savvy." Clothes rustle. After a minute, he says, "You can turn around."

I spin to find him looking way too good in dark jeans and a crisp blue polo. He dressed up for me, and for some reason, that fact makes my heart skip faster. He looks way better without glasses.

"What did she say?" I raise my brow, the universal signal for *I need more info than that, buddy.*

The door jiggles harder.

"It was all so weird. This morning she burst into my room yelling we had to leave for school. I was so confused, but I got ready in a hurry because she was freaking out. When I came downstairs, I walked in on her crying. She pulled me into a hug and apologized for yelling at me. Then I told her I didn't remember who she was, who I am, anything. She stared at me as if she'd never seen me before and I thought maybe she was experiencing the same thing." He sighs. "But she went to a drawer and got out the HiveMind instruction manual. She studied that thing for like fifteen minutes before pointing at a line and saying, 'Oh, you need to restore the backup from the online archive.'"

"And did you?"

"We were already late for school, so not until I got home. I followed the instructions, expecting there to be nothing in the online archive. But there was." His face turns gravely serious. "It's just me lying on a hard metal slab, staring at overhead lights. No inner monologue. Just lights." He swallows audibly. "Arden, the memory was endless."

A high-pitched sound buzzes from outside the door. "Maybe it just felt like forever. HiveMind has a way of distorting the perception of time."

He strides to his computer and flips it on with a touch of his finger. "No, I looked at the file size. It's huge."

I stand close enough to inhale a whiff of his cedar wood scent. "Whoa." The file is over two hundred gigs, twenty times longer than my longest memory. It could cover several days, maybe even weeks.

The knocking gets even louder. With a sigh, Sebastian unlocks the door. His mother stands there with arms crossed. "Out. Now."

Sebastian sways back and forth. "Mom, this is Arden. My—uh—lab partner. We have to work on our experiment."

Mrs. Cuomo cocks her head to the side, looking entirely unamused. And a little badass. "What she is, is a bad influence on you."

"I like to live up to expectations. Come on." I storm past her and charge downstairs. The carpet muffles Sebastian's footsteps as he follows.

His mom races after us. "Sebastian, you need to rest! Remember—you have an appointment with Dr. Sadler in the afternoon."

I pick up the sneakers he abandoned beside the front door. He snatches my umbrella just outside the door but refrains from popping it open. Rain pelts the exposed flesh of our faces. It's not until we slip inside my car that we dissolve into laughter.

"Sorry in advance for getting you grounded for life." I back out of the driveway onto the main road.

"Grounded?" He squints at me. "You're calling me well balanced and sensible?"

"I guess *slang* wasn't one of the many languages you recently acquired. *Grounded* means to be in so much trouble your mom won't allow you to leave the house."

He shrugs. "Didn't stop me just now, did it?"

A wide grin pops onto my face. I like the way he thinks. "Too bad the first rule of sneaking out is not to get caught." Though my usual form of sneaking out involved leaving my house to sneak *into* school to have unlimited access to the equipment.

"So what now?"

I debate how much to tell him before deciding to tell it all. We're in this together, which means I need to trust him. "I got a memory back."

He scrambles to sit up straighter. "You have my attention."

"Hold on. Let me pull over somewhere and I'll show it to you." After parking in a deserted parking lot, I drop a copy of the reverse memory I received from the encrypted folder, when he was wearing the SCHRÖDINGER'S ABS T-shirt and we decided to work together on our thesis. He'll have to watch it the HiveMind way: as an overlay on the current scene with sounds and colors muted, and with my inner monologue from today in his ear. When I retrieved this memory, I had a front-row seat to this moment, while he's stuck watching from the nosebleed section. I practically felt the plastic rim of the glasses he no longer wears. I try to decide which way he looks better, with glasses or without. It's like the glasses transform him into a different person.

"Bash." Sebastian wrinkles his nose to himself. "Nope, don't like it."

As he experiences the memory, his expression grows grave. When it's over, his brow furrows. "How did you get this? And why is it backward?"

"No idea on the latter." I shift in my seat. "It's mine. From my point of view. I found it hidden on the server."

The streetlamps splash pools of light onto the dark road, speckles of rain bathing in the glow. The sharp intake of breath he allows carries over the pitter-patter hitting the windows. "So you're getting your memories back?"

"Not exactly. I still lost whatever happened in Kimmel's class today plus at least one more involving us making plans. And I can't get back to the encrypted folder." I tell him about the retina scanner currently blocking me from accessing the IT room.

He squints at me. "Does this mean if a memory's deleted from HiveMind, it's not lost permanently?"

I nibble on my lip. "Technically, once it's deleted, sayonara forever, baby. HiveMind is so integrated with our brains, it's like cutting a slice of cake and trying to point out where the eggs mixed into the batter." His face falls, so I add, "You can archive them though, which is like moving them to a new computer your current one has no connection to. That's what happened here. Theoretically, you can restore the archived memories later, but only if you can connect the two sources, and currently I can't."

Sebastian's frown drags all his features downward in a landslide. "So it's not a glitch in the software."

I shake my head. "The Ethics Committee flagged a number of deletions, but as far as I can tell, all deletions are memories involving, well, us." I suck in a breath of false courage. "I think—from my quick analysis of the situation—this all boils down to our project."

Because it offers both a motive and an explanation. Someone went through the trouble of removing all mentions of it from every student's mind. There's a strong chance I was the most likely candidate to win the competition, after all; I can't imagine a scenario in which I wouldn't be. Which makes it in another student's best interest to erase all evidence of our project. And commandeer the spotlight for themselves.

Sebastian's mouth parts. "That's not random. That's deliberate. Whoever did the initial purge of memories must be monitoring us via HiveMind and getting rid of anything that brings us too close to the truth." He snaps his fingers. "So what we need is a way to uncover our missing memories without using HiveMind in case it's been compromised."

"Oh my God." My eyes light up with excitement and I practically bounce in my seat in a rush to put the car in drive. "Yes! That's it. We have to do things old school. Before technology. The way a normal person would retrieve a repressed memory." I paste a grin on my face to make the next part seem logical—not insane. "We're going to a hypnotist."

0011000100110001

losed during the day. That's not sketchy at all." Sebastian points to the small sign taped to the door that reads: OPEN EVERY NIGHT 10 P.M.–6 A.M. A blue neon WALK-INS WELCOME sign buzzes on and off like a bug zapper. It hangs askew in the lower window, covering part of the gaudy yellow flowered curtains that should be relegated to a museum showcasing bad seventies decor.

"The man needs to sleep." I twist the knob of the seediest of seedy places on the outskirts of Wickham.

A man stands directly behind the door as if he was expecting us. Every time I come, he introduces himself with a new name—Sam, Cornelius, and the Great Mustafa—so I only ever refer to him as *the Hypnotist*. He's a master of illusion, and without a HiveMind hookup, I have no way to validate his real name. It's one of the reasons I've been eager for HiveMind to release and the rest of the world to wise up that backing up photos to clouds is archaic compared with memories. Though, after everything that happened today, I'm not sure the software is quite ready for its grand debut.

Today he introduces himself as the Enabler and he wears a crisp black suit.

Sometimes he wears sweats, as though he can't be bothered to actually get dressed. Other times he hams it up in traditional magician garb or dons a cape with eyes stitched all over the red fabric.

The sharp stench of frankincense makes my nose twitch. Sebastian doubles over into a hacking cough.

"Arden, my dear. Back so soon!" The Hypnotist opens his arms to me.

I squint at him. "When was I last here?"

"Yesterday. Ah! I know why you returned." He strides toward a desk, where he pulls out a pocket-sized notebook. "You left this behind."

I snatch it from him and frantically flip through the book. I don't recognize this one, but it's the same brand as the notebooks I usually carry. Homework assignments cover most of the pages, including one about Kimmel's test. One particular page catches my eye, written in the back after a bunch of blank pages. Sebastian reads over my shoulder.

> *ThoughtFull?*
>   **Cheesy.**
> *Theseus.*
>   **What???**
> *Famous Plutarch theory about some ship named*
> *Theseus. His philosophical question: If you replace every*
> *single wooden part of a ship, would it still be the same*
> *ship?*
>   **Okay, that's a possibility. Let's keep thinking.**
> *Mimicry?*
>   **The pronunciation of that one bothers me. I wish it**
>   **were: "Mimi's crying! Someone soothe her!"**
> *I hate you.*
>   **You love me.**

I recognize my handwriting in every other line, starting with the first. The other lines are written hastily and on a slant, like we were tilting the notebook back and forth during a class to avoid getting caught.

"What does it mean?" Sebastian asks.

I shrug. "Is that your handwriting?" I point at the *Mimi's crying* line.

"I think so?" He lets out a small laugh. "But I'm not very familiar with it."

The Hypnotist clears his throat. "You want the usual?"

"Couple's special." I shove the notebook into my purse and push my way through beads hanging in a doorway until we enter a room painted all black, dark except for the candles flickering around the perimeter. Sebastian follows after me so close his warm breath blows the hair off the back of my neck and sends shivers down my spine. The beads rattle back into place behind him.

He grabs my hand, and a little thrill courses through me.

The Hypnotist rolls two mats onto the lime-green carpet and waves his hands over them. His eyes zoom to our interlocked fingers, and his brow furrows. "Thought he didn't believe in this crap?" He says the words *this crap* like they taste bad in his mouth. Most people write off hypnosis as psychotherapy nonsense, but there's actually a scientific basis for it called neurypnology.

"I've brought him before?" I've been here countless times, always as part of a quest to fill in the blanks of HiveMind and log all the memories from my childhood that lurk in the recesses of my mind. The ones of my dad.

Memories from before HiveMind existed are often incomplete fragments, sometimes just thoughts, sometimes with multiple versions depending on how your recall of what happened changes when influenced by other people's retellings. Cherished childhood moments are as vivid as memories logged today, but most are so lacking in detail HiveMind won't play them back. It won't even list them in the catalogue unless there's a static image it can display as a thumbnail and it has enough information to assign an automatic caption.

The Hypnotist helps me bring true memories of those moments to the surface, making them vibrant and real and archivable. A rush of buried recollections I unearthed in this room come back to me: Dad huffing behind me while perusing the exhibits at the National Science Fair eight years ago. The stale scent of recycled air mixed with antiseptic that attacked me whenever I visited him in the hospital back when he was first diagnosed. A thought, disembodied from a moment: *Dad is fine. He's doing normal things, like everyone else. He's only bald because of old age, not chemo.* My fifth birthday party disappointment when Leo snuck away and opened all my presents before I got to them. Mom beaming at a newspaper photographer when they first broke ground on building the school.

I blink against tears, shaking my hair behind my shoulders. I have to be strong, like my mom.

"It was several months ago. He sat over there"—the Hypnotist points with the end of his red tie toward a beanbag chair in the far corner of the room—"and watched the entire time with a scowl on his face. I don't appreciate being mocked."

"I won't mock you this time." Sebastian's fingers drop from my own, and he ambles toward the beanbag chair. He grazes his hand over it as if waiting for the object to supply him with confirmation of his past actions.

I turn to face the Hypnotist. "I need you to try to uncover more recent memories this time."

"Lie down."

The cold gym mat jars against my sweaty skin. My necklace settles like a weight on my throat. Sebastian elongates his body next to me, dropping the wet umbrella between us like a wall.

The Hypnotist paces the floor. "Breathe in and out, in and out. Listen to my voice and only my voice."

Each rhythmic inhale makes my chest bloat outward. The air tastes like incense.

"Release all the tension from your toes. Nice and relaxed."

The tension flees from my toenails until my heels sink into the mat.

The Hypnotist works his way up our bodies, having us relax our knees, then our thighs, all the way to the tops of our heads. The mat gets heavier beneath my shoulder blades as my body weight pushes into it.

"I want you to think of what you were doing yesterday. Imagine yourself waking up. . . ."

Yesterday, I crawled out of bed and got ready for school. My car peeled out of the driveway ten minutes before my mother's, and I perched at my usual courtyard table and sold a bunch of memories to students. I ate lunch with my friends, attended classes, and . . . that's it. No Sebastian. No work on my thesis project even though I can't imagine procrastinating with only five days left. No trip to the Hypnotist. As far as I can recall, I didn't even go to bed that night despite waking up under my covers this morning.

"I want you to think back, back, back. Dig deep and find that one memory you've been repressing—the one that lies on the edges of your mind. Imagine this memory has strings. Grab one and pull it toward you."

A glimpse of stairs flashes in my vision, and I concentrate on the image until it washes over me.

I'm thirteen years old and I stumble down the stairs after being startled awake by a strange sound. I remember the floorboards creaking beneath my feet, though I can't hear them now. Flickers from the candles in the Hypnotist's room turn the muted scene in my mind light and dark, light and dark.

Illumination spills from the kitchen. As I approach, the sound that woke me intensifies even though I need to strain to hear it in my mind. Dread fills my body as I remember what comes next, a cruel form of foreshadowing. My fingernails dig into the squishy surface of the mat.

I walk into the kitchen, where I find my dad sitting at the table, sobbing into his own hands. When I place my palm against his shoulder, it only makes him cry harder. I wish I could feel the softness of his worn-in T-shirt or breathe his coffee breath tangled with astringent aftershave, an odor that was decidedly only him. My arms ache to wrap around him and never let go.

Instead, I listen to him tell me all over again that he has stage IV pancreatic cancer and it's spreading.

There's a reason I repressed this memory even within Hive-Mind's archiving capabilities. It hurt too much to think about.

The Hypnotist does a series of pops with his mouth to lull us into a hypnotic state.

Abruptly, an image flashes in my mind as if lightning sliced across my vision. It leaves the afterburn etched into my mind. Sebastian. Wearing glasses. Sprawled out on the beanbag chair. Sticking his tongue out at the back of the Hypnotist's head.

"Listen to my voice, only my voice," the Hypnotist says now. I want to scream for him to stop! I need more time to grab on to that memory and see if it leads anywhere. But the Hypnotist continues. "Slowly become more aware of your surroundings. The mat beneath your bodies . . ." The Hypnotist coaxes us back to the reality of the room with the horrible incense. Once I've heard his voice again, I lose all trace of my deep relaxation. "When you feel ready, you may open your eyes."

I normally allow myself a few moments before I engage with the world again, but I'm so hyperaware of Sebastian next to me I blink against the jarring candlelight and sit up. He lies perfectly still, arms outstretched in perfect meditation position.

The Hypnotist raises a brow at me when Sebastian doesn't rise.

"It's time to come out of the trance now," he says in his jarringly loud non-soothing voice. I cringe.

Sebastian remains still.

The Hypnotist's feet squish on the mat as he taps Sebastian's shoulder.

Sebastian shakes his head. "It didn't work. Try again." A desperate "*Please*" punctuates his plea.

The Hypnotist turns to me with an annoyed expression. He thinks Sebastian's mocking him again. "Sorry, but it won't work if you don't open your mind to it."

Or if you don't have any memories to uncover.

Sebastian bolts upright and hops to his feet. He rushes past the beads, umbrella tightly clutched in his fist. They swing behind him, *clack clack clacking* against one another in sync with his pounding footsteps.

I wobble to stand and rush after him, leaving a bunch of twenties on the table, including a few extras to pay for our session. The cool night air outside hits me with a shock. Sebastian bends over beneath the shelter of a green awning, one palm pressed against the building's siding as he gulps damp air. I rest my palm between his shoulder blades without thinking, but then snap my hand back. My stomach balls up like a fist. This moment is all too similar to the one I just got back: me with my hand on my dad's shoulder. I got the memory back, but I'll never get *him* back. A lump rises into my throat, and when Sebastian glances at me with the same anguished expression as my dad, I nearly lose it right there. But just like that time, Sebastian needs comfort too. I settle my fingers into the folds of his shirt.

"I've been here before. And yet . . . no bells ringing," Sebastian says.

I risk trailing my fingers a few centimeters up his back. "We're going to fix that. This was just the first experiment."

Sebastian straightens, forcing me to drop my hand from his shoulders. "When he said I'd never agreed to the hypnotism, I thought: This is it, a fresh start. A chance to be who I want to be instead of who I was." He rakes a hand through his sandy blond hair; the strands spring back up in rebellion. "But the results turned out the same."

We stand there, the two of us, out of place even in the present as we are in our past. I keep trying to be more like the girl in my returned memory while all he wants to do is separate himself. "Why do you want to be something different? Aren't you trying to figure out who you are?"

Thunder booms, rattling the trees. I lean closer, practically holding my breath.

"I'm already different," he says. "The old me was a physics genius while I can barely decipher the formulas."

Words rush to the end of my tongue. *I like you the way you are, from what I've learned so far. I want to uncover you, piece by piece, and then put you back together. Sometimes a fresh start doesn't always mean a blank slate.* But I hold them back, waiting for his answer.

A cool breeze swirls, carrying a fresh earthy scent to counteract the overwhelming souvenir of incense. "Come on, Watson, let's regroup in the car."

He opens the umbrella above the two of us and shields the pattering rain. "I'd argue I'm the Sherlock in the equation. I've got all the skills." He ticks on his fingers. "An arsenal of knowledge plus proficiency in logical reason, forensic science, and the power of deduction. Not to mention I have every Sherlock book memorized."

"Let's discuss semantics when one of us solves this case." This morning, hunching so close together felt awkward, but now it's welcome. I'm starting to feel like he's the only one who truly understands me right now. My feet crunch over the gravel parking lot, slapping through puddles as I bypass another car, stationed all the way at the back, as if it's trying to hide out of view of the nearest streetlamp.

"What if I told you I had an idea to bypass the retina scanner?"

I stop short, blinking at him. "I'd say tell me more."

"The only thing is, I have the school handbook memorized and my idea would break several rules." He purses his lips. "Actually, I have the state laws of Massachusetts memorized and it would break a bunch of laws too."

I shrug. "Based on my day with you, seems par for the course."

0011000100110010

I start the engine and head toward the school. "Okay, how do we bypass the scanners?"

"You said they just upgraded the security device to be a retina scanner."

I nod cautiously. "Right, and despite what I told you this morning, I don't have proper clearance. Plus it's impossible to trick a retina scanner."

He grins. "Exactly. So we're not going to trick it."

"I don't understand." I shift in my seat. "I really dislike this feeling of not knowing the answer to something."

"The only part I can't figure out is how to get into the Varga Industries side of the building unnoticed."

Now it's my turn to grin. "Leave that to me."

I pull over to the side of the road. It only takes me a few seconds to hack into my brother's email account and send a message to the night security guard at Varga.

> Hey J,
> Forgot my laptop at my office and need it to assess
> urgent lab results. Sending my sister to pick it up for
> me. She'll be there in a few.
> —Leo

The whoosh noise the email makes when it sends my message is almost as exhilarating as the rev of my engine. Before I put the car in drive again, I kick off another backup via my phone's hot spot to add the Hypnotist memory to it and give Sebastian instructions to add the ones before that to the backup in reverse chronological order once the Hypnotist one finishes. I drive to Varga Industries, parking on the corporate side instead of the school side of the lot. Only a few lights inside the building glow, everything else eerily dark at the midnight hour.

"Now will you tell me the plan?"

"Nope." His grin is all teeth and dimples. "I'm really enjoying how frustrated you're getting by my not saying anything."

I growl. "You're lucky I trust you."

I lead him across the parking lot and up the front steps of Varga Industries, trying to commandeer some semblance of the upper hand here. After a swipe of my badge, I pull open the front door to the building and step inside the entryway. Portraits line the wall behind the security desk, each one containing the smiling photo of an employee who has created a world-changing product that brought all the investors to the yard. The bald-headed guy with the subtle smirk invented synthetic plasma. The woman next to him designed a terabyte drive the size of a human cell. And then there's my personal favorite, the guy who developed the ever popular but completely unnecessary LASIK procedure for changing eye color.

Jay, the security guard, raises his brow when he spots me. He shakes his head at me, but there's a smile on his face. "Not again."

"Ugh. I know." I make a grand show of blowing my hair out of my eyes to feign annoyance. The trick to tricking people is all in your delivery. "My brother sent me to pick up his laptop." I tack on a groan, as if doing this task is a huge burden to my social life.

I jerk my head toward Sebastian. "Not exactly how I planned on spending date night."

Sebastian glances down at his feet, and my insides clench. I said it as part of the ruse, but now that the words have fled my lips, I realize how much I want it to be true.

Jay rolls his eyes from behind the desk and clucks his tongue. "He keeps doing this to you!"

I sigh heavily. "What can I say? He's lazy as all hell and I can't refuse the twenty bucks he offers me to do his bidding."

The security guard laughs and I say a silent prayer of thanks that tonight isn't the first but the hundredth time I've pulled this trick. By now Jay can practically expect me to show up on behalf of my "brother."

"You've got fifteen minutes." He buzzes us through.

"Only need five. I'll text you when I'm leaving. Going to stop at my locker on the way out and exit through the school."

Jay points at the various security monitors. "I'll be watching."

I force a laugh at his joke, ending the conversation on a breezy, friendly note. But if Jay ever refused me or tried to turn me away, I have a plan for that too: blackmail. One time I synced to his mind to confirm he was alone before I pulled off this trick, but instead of finding him sitting at his desk, I found him a few doors away, inside the locked office manager's door, using lock-pick tools to break into her desk and swipe a few bucks off the top of the petty cash supply. That wasn't the first or the last day he skimmed from the cash reserves.

We traipse through deserted hallways, squinting into the near darkness, the only lights stemming from the glow of our phones. My mom's access card grants us free rein of the locked elevator. I squint at the numbers. "Which floor?"

"Which one contains the hydrogel biomaterials?"

My eyebrows shoot way up. "The *what*?"

"Bioinks lab. Teddy's project."

I love that he has so much latent knowledge in his brain. "Why? Need a new arm or something?" I press the button for the eleventh floor.

"Don't need any arms currently, but I could definitely use an inch or two in the height department."

"No can do, buddy. I remember Teddy's presentation from last year. Those machines can currently only copy from existing scans. There are a few scientists working on the ability to print biomaterials from scratch using modified 3-D animation software, but that advancement in technology isn't ready yet."

My heels click on the linoleum floor until we come to a door labeled BIOINKS PRINTING LAB. I swipe my mom's card, and the little dot on the access panel blinks green.

I step inside the sprawling space filled with giant gray machines that look as if a computer printer and a crane mated and had a baby. 3-D bio printers aren't new technology and most can only print tissue over several hours, but Teddy developed a more robust process that can print any body part in only a few minutes. The materials are derived from various biomaterials such as gelatins, alginates, and hyaluronic acids.

"What are we printing exactly?" I nudge one of the computers awake and the printer nearby whirs to life.

"It's a retina scanner that we have to fool." He blinks at me. "So we're soon going to be the proud owners of new retinas! Well, and the eyeballs that belong to those retinas."

Holy shit. Holy shit. This is brilliant.

"Okay, fine," I say grudgingly. "You can be Sherlock."

He squints at the machine. "Only thing is, I don't know how to work this."

"I do." Last year, Teddy Day gave everyone in class a demonstration on how to use this machine as part of his project, and I say a quick-whispered thanks for his stupidity. He clearly had no idea how handy that demo would come in for someone planning to use this machine without explicit permission.

A password screen blinks at me, and I crack my knuckles, ready to get to work. "Do me a favor? Find my phone and text Jay that we're exiting through the school." While Sebastian grabs my phone, I run two hacks back to back. First, I gain control of the security monitors and pause all the footage so Jay can't spy on our whereabouts. I replace the one of the bioinks lab with footage from five minutes ago, before we stepped in here, and I replace the footage of the elevator with a still frame of us waiting inside. Jay will think that camera's frozen, and by the time he reboots it, we'll be long gone anyway.

Next, I plug in a drive and run a password-cracking script from my arsenal. Within two minutes, the 3-D printing machine opens up for my prying needs.

Once inside the system, I pull up the list of saved scans. Back when this technology was still in beta testing, Varga Industries requested all staff and students to scan themselves into the system as a test. Which means all the people whose eyes currently pass the scanner clearance are in this system, ready to be copied.

I tap my fingers against the table as I scan the list of options. There's my mother's eye, of course, but that seems like a huge risk. The comings and goings to the basement are going to be monitored closely after the security breach, and she doesn't have a reason to be entering there at random times, such as right now. There are a few other maintenance folks who have access down there, but who knows for how long. There's only one person with guaranteed access, whose business down there won't be seen as a red flag.

Brandon.

I have to steal my brother's ex-boyfriend's eye.

My teeth clench and I get a sudden wave of guilt. "Is stealing eyeballs more or less morally wrong than stealing memories?"

Sebastian considers this for a second. "Well, the frontal lobe of the brain plays a part in both short-term memory creation as well as eye movement thanks to its responsibility over frontal, medial, and supplementary eye fields. So basically, it's all the same."

"I was hoping you'd say that." I suck in a deep, shaky breath. This isn't any different than anything else I've done. Besides, Brandon won't be missing anything. He won't even know I'm taking this. I select his scans, modifying the controls to zoom in on just Brandon's eyeball.

I get the printer all set up to print one copy of the eye, but at the last second, I change my mind and set it to two. If there's one rule of digital technology I abide by, it's this: Always have a backup. I purse my lips. While we're here, I should take extra precautions. Just in case, I also set up the printer to print a copy of my mother's eye in case Brandon's access becomes restricted. A backup for the backup.

"Stand back," I tell Sebastian as the machine lights up. "This might get gooey."

Sebastian stumbles backward so fast he slams into a metal countertop a few feet behind him. The printer lets out a loud buzzing sound, and a little laser zips around, forming the base of the sphere in mere seconds.

"Do you really think this will work?" My voice rises an octave.

"Retina scanners work because the intricate web of the capillaries that provide blood to the retina is unique in each person. It's not genetic though; even identical twins have different patterns."

I blink at him. "So is that a yes or a no?"

"If we're printing a copy of someone's eye, then it's a yes. In theory."

"Then we'll try to get back into the basement tonight. What you just said about capillaries gave me an idea of something to try on you."

"Good." He lets out a breath. "Because I can't stand it. Not knowing anything about myself."

This I can work with. This I can fix for him. "Then let's find out who you are while the oculi print. We can start by figuring out what you like to do." I set my laptop on the counter. In HiveMind, I find the folder containing the list of hobbies I've collected for various customers. "Surfing? Skiing? Being prom queen?"

He raises a brow. "Prom queen?"

"You should try it. It's quite popular among my customers." The printer finishes the ocular nerve, which looks like a jagged string detached like this. It always starts from the inside out, creating the veins and bones first before fleshing out the rest, so to speak.

He wrinkles his nose. "Pass."

I keep sifting through the list. "Skydiving? BASE jumping? Brazilian bikini wax?"

"Um, *what*?"

"Sorry, forget I mentioned that last one." Zoey convinced me to get a waxing before a party last month. Decision: regretted.

"No, no. I'm intrigued. Let me see it." He waggles his fingers as if I could drop the memory into the palm of his hand.

"You realize you don't have lady parts?"

"I am aware of that, yes." He fist-pumps the air. "Finally, something I can validate for sure!"

"Let's go with something slightly less . . . revealing. Here's a fan favorite." I fumble with the track pad on my laptop until I find one of my biggest requests from my customers. "Winning an award."

It's from last year, when I won the school's equivalent of an Oscar. Most Likely to Succeed.

Sebastian closes his eyes as the memory of my stepping onstage to give my speech starts to play. "I've been meaning to ask, when you give me memories like this, does that mean you no longer have it yourself?"

"Nope. It works the same way as emailing a photo to a friend. The original stays untouched while they receive an exact duplicate."

The smile on his face grows wider as he experiences the exhilaration of being the best. "And if you delete it from my mind?"

The printer moves in a radius, and a blue iris with flecks of brown emerges out of thin air. "It stays intact in the original owner's mind, if that's what you're—"

He holds up his hand to silence me, eyes closed in concentration.

"Okay, it's over. Sorry, you started thinking about . . . someone. Someone you wanted to see at a celebration that night."

"Melody Clarendon threw a celebration party that night. . . . but—and I know this is going to come as a shock," I say, unable to refrain from grinning, "I don't recall talking to any boys there." Just the usual mind escape via foamy beer and no obligations.

"You never mentioned a name. I wondered if it was . . ." He arches an eyebrow, one dimple creasing. "Me."

My cheeks ignite.

"What are you thinking about?" Sebastian lowers his voice and leans closer to me, giving me a private view of the faint stubble sprouting along his defined jaw.

Daring. Be daring, Past Arden coaxes me. Instead, I play it safe. What I know versus what I want. And I know how to work Hive-Mind to my advantage. "What activity do you want to try next?" I flourish a hand at the computer screen, which tints my black leather seat with blue luster. "Horseback riding? Paintball? Swim—"

He shuts my laptop. "I don't want someone else's memory. I want to make my own."

Every atom in my body ignites as he takes a step toward me. He leans against me, torso sealing along mine. I swallow and arch my back, hoping hoping hoping that he's about to lean down and press his lips against—

Just then, the printer dings, breaking the moment. He glances at the eyeball wobbling on the table dripping with artificial tears. There's nothing more romantic than the ambience of illegally sneaking into a lab and printing severed organs.

"This one's yours." I jerk my head toward it, heart thumping. "Some girls prefer flowers, but I like to give the gift of detached body parts."

0011000100110011

As the second eye prints, I nestle the first eye in a mini-cooler filled with ice packs and then douse it with a bottle of 0.9% NaCl solution. "It's a living organ, so you have to keep it lubricated and cold. Coat it with saline every thirty minutes or so and switch out the ice packs every few hours."

His eyebrows shoot upward. "Whoa, this is certainly a high-maintenance gift."

I pat him on the shoulder. "Only the best for my partner in crime."

He presses a palm to his chest. "I'll treasure it with all my heart."

"Do it in private though. No one can see you carrying this."

He laughs and traces his fingers over large red letters on the side of the container. "Good thing it doesn't have the words *Human Organ for Transfer* printed large enough for a shuttle to see from space."

I grab a Sharpie marker from my bag and cross out the words with large blocks of black. "There, now it doesn't."

"You're right. This is way more inconspicuous."

I shake my head at him, lips quirking. "Just put it in a different lunch box when you get home, okay? We might need these eyes again."

He squints at the bag. "Wait. Severed organs only last for approximately thirty hours before they go bad."

"Not these. Extending longevity was a major part of Teddy's project. They can last for a full week as long as they're stored correctly."

When my mother's eye finishes printing, I add it to my cooler, which already contains Brandon's eye, separated only by a makeshift glass partition. I scrutinize my copies and then Sebastian's single one. "On second thought, let's switch." I hand him the bag with two eyes.

He squints at me. "Why?"

"Because someone ripped out my notebooks and smashed my hard drive but not yours. Leave my mother's eye at your house just in case." I make a mental note to create a second hard drive backup tonight and give Sebastian that to hold too.

He nods.

I shut off the lights and press a finger to my lips. "Pretend you're a mouse stealing cheese at night. Silent."

"I mean, mice squeak, but sure. I get your meaning."

We tiptoe through the empty hallways. Inside the elevator, we squeeze in tight, getting off at the second floor instead of the first to take the stairwell down to Monica Varga High School. When we reach the basement, the retina scanner sits there, looking oppressive.

I shrug on plastic gloves, and it takes a deep breath to steady my shaking hands. The eyeball feels squishy beneath my fingers. I lift it toward the scanner, my elbow rattling. "If this doesn't work, we're screwed."

"I assume your use of *screwed* does not refer to metal bolts but rather being stuck in a hopeless or difficult situation. To that I say we're already screwed."

"Good point." I hold the eyeball up to the retina scanner and brace myself.

A laser zooms over the retina, casting it in glowing red light. There's a pause that makes me hold my breath before the scanner blinks green and the door unlocks.

Air whooshes from my lungs.

We rush down the steps and bypass the retina scanner outside the IT room the same way. My eyes fly to the monitoring computer, where I deposited my SSD card earlier today. The card's gone, but so is the computer in question. All that remains is a square of dust.

My skin prickles, but I force myself to shrug it off. There are six other monitoring computers in here I can use. Still, before I get to that, I need to reinstall Sebastian's account. It's the one diagnostic measure I haven't tried yet. If this works on Sebastian, I'll try it on mine next.

I head to one of the cabinets and pull out a synthetic metal device that looks like a headband but with electrodes attached to it. "Put this on. It's an electroencephalograph. My dad invented it."

He stretches the material and it snaps back into shape like a rubber band. "It detects brain waves?"

I grin. I guess knowing every definition in the OED has its advantages, such as not looking at me like I'm insane when I mention a word that's as hard to spell as it is to pronounce. "Yep. Brain waves are as unique as fingerprints, so HiveMind uses them as an authentication tool to connect directly with your mind. I'm going to take a new capture of yours and re-upload it to the remote server to make sure everything's still syncing correctly."

Sebastian slips the device over his head, messing up his neat part. His knee bobs up and down. When he's all set up, I press a button on the outside of the band. A glow washes his sandy hair in green tones for a few moments. We stare at each other, waiting for the device to dim. Something about his gaze encourages me that we're on the right track here. That he's with me every step of the way. When the device beeps, we both let out a breath.

"Now I need to input your brain wave data into the admin console."

I head to the back and purse my lips at the new retina scanner installed on this computer too. Thankfully it's no match for my new pet eyeball. While I upload his electroencephalography data to the HiveMind server, he fixes his hair in the camera of his phone, at first messing it up to resemble the spiky version of him from the reverse memory before wrinkling his nose and smoothing it back down into a side part like he had before. Uploading is a one-way street. I can send data to the server, but I can't retrieve it. "Okay, I'm going to restart your account to sync everything. Kind of like rebooting a computer to make sure new software installs properly." I navigate to his account on HiveMind. "Ready?

Sebastian braces his hands on his thighs. "What should I expect?"

"If all goes well, a flood of memories." I click the refresh button on his account.

His shoulders tense.

I raise my brow. "Anything?"

"Nope." He brings his hands to his face, and I fight the urge to do the same.

"Shit." Nibbling on my inner cheek, I disconnect the electroencephalograph from the computer. "I have one more thing to try. Sit tight."

On the monitoring computer, I insert another SSD drive and retrace the same steps I took this morning to find the hidden folder containing what seems to be my encrypted memories. It's there. It's all still there. I squeeze my eyes shut, resisting the urge to hug my arms to my chest.

Trying to select or decrypt multiple memories brings up an operation error again, so I choose one at random from the favorites list and decrypt it. I'll stand here all damn night to retrieve these one by one if I have to. "I'm going to give you something, okay? I have no idea what it is. It might be from my point of view, it might be from yours." Or it might be nothing at all.

He drops onto one of the tall black stools. "I'm ready."

I transfer the file into both our minds.

I have just enough time to sink into Brandon's chair before oppressive blackness floods across my vision, erasing the IT room entirely.

Light blue walls glitch into focus like ink obscuring a sheet of paper, oozing in unexpected patterns until it covers the entire expanse of my vision. Posters emerge onto the surface into the shapes of a periodic table and emo bands. A desk pops into place as dark blue carpet spreads below it. Bash's room.

But I only get a glimpse of it before the image of Bash fills my vision, showcasing the most brilliant grin I've ever seen.

The corner of a soft pillow with a navy pillowcase grazes my cheek. Holy subatomic particles. I'm lying on Bash's bed. And he's wrapped around me. My eyes shift focus to his mouth and secretly, I'm thrilled. Past Arden, who once experienced this moment in real time, is in league with Current Me, who wants nothing more than to suck on his lower lip. My body leans into his and he slides forward until our mouths get closer and closer. Electricity crackles when our lips meet, slow and gentle. He tastes like Coca-Cola, and my whole body heats up from the way his mouth moves against mine.

Holy shit.

The kiss intensifies, turning hard and fierce and oh God, amazing. I want this memory to last forever. I want nothing more than to keep kissing him. But the kiss softens again before dissolving into a series of light butterfly pecks. I slide my mouth down, kissing his jaw, chin, neck, while simultaneously trail-

ing my fingers across his bare arms. When I reach his clavicle with my lips, I shift, cuddling into his chest, his arms cradling me. My fingers continue to trace circles on his arms.

[You won't. Everything you love about me, my entire personality, it'll all still be me,] Bash says. Like the last retrieved memory, he speaks backward, but I understand it all. I fight to turn toward him, but an invisible force holds me in place. Instead, all I can do is sniffle in a very unattractive way. He squeezes me. Wow, it feels good to be in his arms like this. He's stronger than his scrawny frame lets on. He nuzzles his chin into my neck, his nutty shampoo surrounding me. The visceral details are once again stronger than the usual HiveMind rewatch, and I long to breathe it in deeply, but instead I let out another sniffle.

[I've already lost my dad,] I say, my voice shaky. I swipe at my eyes a few times with my palms, each time leaving my cheeks wetter and stickier. [I can't lose you too.]

[You don't have to be.] Goose bumps surface along my arms, popping in response to a hot breath that scorches my skin a moment later. He yanks his arms out from under me and I readjust my body to let him slide off the bed. He hovers over me and I stretch out my arm to him. He tugs my hand up to his lips and plants a delicate kiss. All I can think of is that other moment, a few minutes ago, or a few months, days, weeks later than this memory depending on your perspective. When his hand found mine at the Hypnotist, it was for comfort, but it seemed transient. Now his hand in my own seems like home.

[I'm scared, Bash.]

He drops my hand and treks across the room, spinning away from me. A sob rips from my throat, making my torso convulse. Tears streak across my cheeks, sliding back up into my eyes. The last time I permitted a neuronal connection between my emotions and my tear ducts was when my dad died, and I cannot imagine any other scenario that would make me cry. Of course, I can't imagine a scenario in which I would have been this close to a boy either, even one as cute as Sebastian.

Blackness leeches my vision for a moment before reality fades back in. The bright lights of the IT room make me squint. My head throbs as if I'm standing next to a speaker at a rock concert. Sebastian gasps for breath beside me.

"Holy crap." He turns to me, clutching his head like he's trying to hold on to his brain.

I wrap my fingers around his bicep. "What—what did you see?"

"Us." He holds my gaze. "In bed."

I want to dwell on the *in bed* part of the equation, but his eyes zoom to my fingers. I immediately let go. He pulls his arm into his lap and shifts an inch away from me. I've never been slapped or even stolen anyone's memory of the sensation, but that's exactly what his reaction reminds me of.

I speak slowly to regain my composure. "But more importantly, what did it feel like to you? Was it visceral?"

He shakes his head. "It was like all the others. Kind of subdued. Overlaid over this room like tracing paper. But . . . This one was backward like the one of us in the chemistry lab."

My jaw clenches. That's strange. This was so vivid for me but came to Sebastian like the usual HiveMind memories, yet I transferred it from the exact same source into both of our minds at the same time.

"When you . . ." He studies his knuckles.

My earlobes tingle. "When I . . . ?"

His ethereal hazel eyes disarm me. "When you were trailing your fingers over my skin, I wish I could have felt that."

My face combusts in a blush that radiates across my cheeks. The sensation of his lips brushing softly against mine lingers. I fumble with my laptop in a desperate attempt to occupy my fingers. I didn't just kiss him; I was *in bed* with him. How far did we go? Would I forget something as important as losing my virginity?

"So." I let out a strained laugh. "I guess we've hooked up."

"This is awkward." He twists his hands together, avoiding my eyes. The computer monitor in front of us paints him in tones of blue. "What does this mean?"

My heart quickens in pace. I decide to be brave, like the version of me that sat on his notebook and forced him to pay attention to me. I dislodge the words Current Me would normally hold back. "We can reenact that memory and find out."

His expression drops. "Oh. That's . . . not what I meant. I meant, could we really get all our memories back this way?"

"It was just a joke," I say to save face. My voice hitches.

"I don't even know you." He hops off the stool in a gesture of finality.

I was wrong before. *This* is what it feels like to be slapped. Rejection stings even when it comes from a source I didn't know I wanted until a few minutes ago. A source I was apparently hooking up with, someone who I was comfortable enough to cry—no, to *sob*—in front of. And also, *why* was I crying? Why did I think I was going to lose him?

He might be wondering what this means in terms of regaining his memories, but I'm wondering what I was to him. Clearly my friends didn't know about our clandestine hookup that may have been the first, the last, the only, or one of hundreds. Why were we keeping this a secret?

Maybe it's not a glitch in HiveMind but a glitch in us.

"That came out wrong. I suck at this. Add being suave to the list of things I need to relearn." He pries my fingers from where they grapple for my keys. "I hope I was better at wooing you the first time around." He presses a finger to my chin and tilts my face back to him. "What I'm trying to say is . . . I *want* to get to know you."

The words sound amazing to my ear and make my chest flutter.

"But I also need to get to know me too." He leans back against the desk.

His words make something loosen in my chest. This I can understand. This I can try to help with.

"Let me see if I can find any of your memories." I nudge the screen awake and start to navigate back to the hidden folder, but just before I reach it, the IT room door swings open.

Jay, the security guard, beams a flashlight in our faces despite the bright fluorescent lights streaming overhead. "Arden? You're still here?"

Sebastian freezes. I back away from the computer, hands raised in the air. "Sorry, I—"

"Did you trigger the retina scanner? No one's supposed to be down here right now. How do you have clearance?"

"Oh." I let out a strained laugh, as if what he just asked is hilarious. My rapid pulse beats in my neck. "I didn't need the scanner. I have an access card." I hold up my mom's duplicate card, but it feels like I'm showing him my entire hand.

"That card shouldn't have worked." Jay holds out his palm, his face grave. I wince as I drop it into his grasp. His fingers fold around it tightly. "I need you to leave. Right now."

His words send a cold, crackling sensation down my spine. The blackmail leaps onto my tongue. All I need to say is one word and he'd have no choice but to disobey his orders and oblige mine instead. But the word catches in my throat. I can't destroy someone else's life just to save my own. I can't fault someone else for stealing when I'm the queen thief in this school. Perhaps he had a good reason for taking that petty cash.

I slide my messenger bag off the table. Sebastian ducks his head as he shuffles past the security guard. I take slow, deliberate steps, my heart beating so fast it's about to burst out of my chest. I don't dare look back at the SSD drive still lodged in the computer. *Please don't notice it. Please don't notice it.*

Jay's vision shifts beyond my shoulder. His eyes narrow, his mouth slanting downward. Sweat gathers in the crooks of my elbows.

He stomps toward the SSD drive and yanks it out of the computer. It feels as if he just punched his hand through my chest and ripped out my heart. It takes all my willpower not to scream out in agony.

He holds it up to me. "This yours?"

I twitch. Sebastian sways. Our silence does nothing to exonerate us.

"Gotcha." Jay slips the SSD drive into his pocket. "I'm going to have to report this."

"Do you?" I fumble into my purse and pull out a wad of twenties graciously donated by my cheating classmates. I fan the bills like a poker player checking her hand. He needs extra cash, I'll give him some.

Jay stalks forward and plucks the bills out of my fingers. "Maybe I don't. This time." He pats his pocket. "But I'm still keeping this. If you try to come down here again on my watch, I *will* turn these in. I'm under strict orders to keep this room on lockdown. My job's on the line here."

Air whistles through my teeth. I pivot on my heels and stomp out of here before he changes his mind. Sebastian hustles after me and we don't dare speak until we're safely ensconced in my purring vehicle.

I lean my head against the headrest. "Fuck. That was close."

Sebastian squeezes his eyes shut. "Guessing that means no way to get more memories tonight."

I shake my head. "Sorry, bud. Home it is."

His head tilts, obscuring half his face in darkness like a hollowed-out version of the man in the moon. "But I don't want to go home."

My eyes land on the clock. One a.m. School starts in less than seven hours. "Where do you want to go?"

"I don't know." Sebastian rests two fingertips on the inside of my wrist, over my cardigan, on top of my jagged red scar and the writing temporarily tattooed there. "I'm afraid."

I shift toward him and wince at the squeaking leather beneath my butt. It seems as if even the slightest wrong move might disturb the balance of the entire universe. Even the talkative commercials on the radio somehow fit as if they contain sweeping violins in an orchestra. "Of . . . me?" I ask.

"No. God, no." He rips his hand off my wrist and rakes it through his hair. "Just . . . We both woke up with pieces of us missing. As far as you remember, things were fine yesterday?"

Yesterday, I felt like I was on the verge of ruling the world, not just the school. I nod.

"We know that someone's monitoring us and removing memories as we get too close, but I can't forget that the biggest wipe so far happened last night. While we slept. The only logical conclusion I can draw is that the same thing might happen tonight, once we let down our guard."

"You're afraid to go to sleep." My pulse thrums behind my ears. Already my mind works overtime, making the mental calculations of how much coffee it would take to battle the night, where we could go to rob us of any opportunity to drift off. What other experiments we might try to get our memories back or at least figure out what our thesis was.

"Not to sleep. I'm afraid of waking up again without any idea where I am, *who* I am." He allows his eyes to flutter shut, his long lashes casting dark shadows on his cheeks like cat whiskers. "I don't want to wake up so alone."

"You don't have to." I put the car in motion and head out of Wickham toward the next town, where the students' biggest worry is which college to choose. We can't go back to either of our houses, not when we basically defied both our mothers by stomping out on them. His mom seems like the type that would wait up all night until he walked through the door and my mother barely sleeps as it is. "We'll go to a motel."

We'll fight this together.

0011000100110100

VACANCY sign flashes as though it can't make up its mind between advertising or hiding its status. The once dreary yellow stucco of the motel's exterior received a fresh coat of paint recently and hopefully a full renovation to match. This will have to do.

Sebastian pulls the door to the front office open for me, then rakes his hand through his hair and goes in first, as if he doesn't want to be seen being chivalrous. Because that might make whatever this is seem different. Like the memory, instead of the reality.

I blink against the sharp lights, which seem to have been set to *stun*. Water sloshes in the pipes hidden behind the beige walls, where stock photos hang proudly. Behind the counter, a guy with a ponytail longer than mine pulls out his earbuds. "We don't rent by the hour."

Blushing, Sebastian becomes intensely interested in the peeling gray paint coming off in curls from the counter. A nervous flutter warms my belly as the clerk's insinuation mixes with the memory from earlier of the two of us in bed kissing.

I place my hands on the counter, palms up, like I'm showing him there are no tricks up my sleeves. "Do you have two double beds?"

The man snorts. "I don't know what kind of place you think

this is, but it's not that. We only have kings." He crosses his arms. "You two over eighteen?"

I lift my chin. "This the kind of place that cares?" I am actually eighteen, but I have no idea if Sebastian is yet.

His smirk widens. "One thirty-two a night plus tax. Checkout's at eleven—if you're still here by then." He squints at us.

To shut him and his insinuations up, I slap a bunch of bills on the counter, using up the last of my stash.

"So it's one of *those* nights," the clerk says as he counts out the correct amount from the pile. "Condoms are in the vending machine." He hooks his thumb toward a machine by the door, brightly lit in an inviting way, stocked with a few varieties of condoms—*Ribbed for her pleasure*—along with Twix bars, cans of Coke, and travel packets of aspirin. The essentials.

Sebastian takes a tiny step away from me, and a sting starts in the back of my throat at his reaction. I keep my lips straight and uninterested despite the fact that I'm pretty sure this guy just accused me of being a prostitute. Only strippers and gamblers—and business moguls like me—carry this much cash on them when going to a place like this.

The bell jingles when we exit, offering us background music as we bypass cigarette butts on our way to room fifteen. A wide awning shields the rain.

Sebastian cuts the silence of our walk of shame. "I don't know what my life was like before." He steps over what looks like a dirty towel discarded between two rooms. "But I hope it was always this exciting. And awkward."

I snicker. "I'd say you've reached your quota for awkward situations in one day, but I'm afraid you're about to have another one."

I twist the key—an old-school brass key, not a modern electronic card, and that fact more than anything else gives me a distinct feeling of abnormality—into the lock. A lemon-fresh clean scent fills the air and erases the drenched-asphalt smell. Sebastian gags. The white bedspread looks chic and modern and the decor uses all hard angles and dark gray finish.

"I feel better already." Sebastian plops down on the edge of the bed and lets out a sigh.

I consider the chair in the corner with the stuffing spilling out of a seam. I should give him space.... but instead, I slide next to him. Our knees touch, and when he doesn't move his away, I press mine closer, covering it up as though I'm just readjusting my position to extract my computer from my messenger bag. I find it's not enough. My body itches to slide even closer to him.

His breath heats my shoulder and I close my eyes to savor the sensation. "What are you doing?" he asks. "I thought we were out of luck with retrieving anything else tonight."

I open up both our accounts from the live HiveMind system and then hook up my external hard drive to compare the file list against the backups I made before I left tonight. I have to be like a hawk, watching this with keen eyes in case the hacker invades my computer again. "Seeing if any more memories have gone missing. I've been backing up your mind every chance I get, hope that's okay."

He flourishes his hand as if to say *please, go ahead.*

"It's not a permanent solution because someone smashed my backups before, which means they can do it again, but—" My teeth clench when I compare the file size on the two archives.

Live HiveMind for me: 1.2 TB; for Sebastian: 2 GB. Backup from ten thirty p.m. for me: 1.73 TB; for Sebastian: 216 GB.

My gut sinks, panic jolting me into action. I tilt the screen toward him. He gasps. "I lost so much."

Dread consumes me. Someone must have deleted hundreds

of memories from my mind and the equivalent from his during the last two hours. I think back to when I picked him up in his room and he pointed out the two-hundred-gigabyte memory he retrieved from the online backup storage. "Tell me you remember lying on a metal slab, staring up at lights."

He squints at me, his confused expression confirming what I've already figured out. That memory is gone, gone, gone. That's why his brain seems so empty again; all that's there must be from today, not before. I never had a chance to back up the metal-slab memory and now I won't be able to. It's gone from the online archive too. "Hang tight, I'll run a data mine compare simulation to figure out what exactly we're missing."

While I set up the simulation, Sebastian gets more ice for our newly acquired eyes and lubricates them with the saline solution we stole from the lab. He gently transfers them to the new lunch boxes we picked up at a 24-7 drugstore before we arrived at the motel. A few minutes later, two lists pop up displaying files missing from my live HiveMind and Sebastian's. My jaw clamps tight, heart hammering, as I scroll through the automatic tags.

FILES MISSING FROM LIVE HIVEMIND

Arden Varga's account: 15	Sebastian Cuomo's account: 9
• Discussing procedural memory with Sebastian after Kimmel's class (today) • Discovering there were 56,320 overnight code changes to HiveMind • Searching Veronica and Eliza's room (today) • Hypnotist memory retrieval attempt and notebook discovery (today) • Making plans to meet with Sebastian (today)	• Discussing procedural memory with Arden after Kimmel's class (today) • Poring through composition notebooks for clues (today) • Hypnotist memory retrieval attempt and notebook discovery (today) • Making plans to meet with Arden (today)

None of this sounds remotely familiar. The metal-slab memory wouldn't show up in Sebastian's list because my simulation can only compare live HiveMind against the backups. Only fifteen memories are missing, but I feel a sudden stabbing of longing for those lost memories.

Sebastian points to something written on his own list. "Hypnotist. What does that even mean?"

"I have no idea." I rock in place, making my laptop wobble. My head pounds as I stare at the line indicating 56,320 lines of code, whatever that means. We've only had one day together and it's already coming apart. "I go to a hypnotist sometimes, but . . . I haven't been there in weeks. And I have no idea what a notebook discovery is."

On a whim, I hop up from the bed and start rifling through my purse. Sure enough, there's an unfamiliar notebook that looks like the ones I usually carry with words like *Ship of Theseus* and *mimicry* and me telling someone else I love them. I shiver.

I check every other pocket and crevice for clues. In my jeans, I pull out a sheet of notebook paper with only a single sentence:

If I don't figure out what my damn project is, someone will die, followed by thousands of people.

My eyes bug out. It's my handwriting, dated today. With trembling fingers, I hold it up to Sebastian. "Guessing this doesn't ring a bell either?"

He rips it out of my hands, reading it over and over, as if he could somehow make sense of it.

I sink back onto the bed, my body feeling heavy. My mind is sand, slipping right through my fingers, falling faster than I can save it.

I take one shuddering breath before I grab my laptop again. The last backup doesn't contain the metal-slab or the making-plans memory, but the others are there. I transfer them one at a time to each of us, reliving each moment as if it's a stolen memory from someone else. It feels as if I'm watching another person in these moments. Sebastian buries his head in his hands while they play. My hands curl into fists as the snooping session settles over me and I move Eliza to the top of my suspect list. Once I create new backups for us, I breathe a sigh of relief, feeling safe once again, at least for the next few hours.

But I could lose it all overnight. I turn to Sebastian, grateful he made the suggestion to stay close tonight.

"Just in case this isn't enough, I've been writing stuff down." I shrug off my cardigan and reveal the ink covering every inch of flesh on my forearms. "But I'm running out of space."

Sebastian purses his lips as he studies my arms. He traces my angry scar that runs the length of my forearm. "You don't need all that. You only need one word." He unfurls my fist and spreads out my fingers.

I shiver from his delicate touch. It's the only thing right now that provides any form of comfort.

Inside the palm of my hand, he writes the word *Sebastian* with the motel-issued pen. The pen tickles the delicate skin there, but I'm so entranced by his work, I don't dare giggle.

He hands me the pen, and I glance up at him, mouth parted. "So I remember who you are tomorrow morning?"

He shakes his head. "So you know where to look when you forget everything else."

I squint in question as he swallows hard, his Adam's apple bobbing. He takes a deep, shuddering breath before he lifts his shirt over his head.

My body thrums at the sight of his bare chest, at the little half-moon birthmark just below his clavicle. A nervous flutter pulses beneath my skin. He holds my gaze for a brief moment before spinning around, facing away from me.

"There's more space on my back," he whispers.

My temples tingle in understanding. The pen rattles in my hands as I set it against his warm skin. We've only kissed in a forgotten memory, but somehow this seems more intimate. I'd only held his hand before, but now I get to touch the smooth planes of his back, running my palms over the goose bumps rising to meet the pads of my fingers. He shivers as my pen scrawls across the rippling canvas of his back. I write:

Look at the external hard drive for the folder labeled DO NOT DELETE.

I cringe at the words, but if we do lose our memories overnight, I'll trust my own handwriting.

Be quick though. The hacker was able to connect to the external hard drive and delete a backed-up memory.

"What are you writing?"

I keep my voice quiet, not daring to break the spell, and read out everything else I etch onto his back.

"Your name is Arden Eloise Varga. You're here with Sebastian Cuomo."

I don't write this next line, but I say aloud: "Aka that gorgeous guy sleeping beside you."

The tips of his ears turn pick. My cheeks ignite in the same hue. I can't believe I said that out loud. I can't believe I'm letting the words linger between us rather than trying to make excuses, take them back somehow. But that's the thing about trusting someone: You can tell them anything and know they'll guard your secret as close as their own.

"You don't need to write that part." The tone of his voice lightens. "After all, you'll still have eyes. Quite a few extras actually!"

He can't see the smile that stretches my lips, but he must hear it in my voice when I continue writing down the basic facts about myself I can't bear to lose. Even the thought of not knowing this vital part of me makes a lump clog in my throat.

> "You hack into other people's memories and you think
> someone's deleting yours. Sebastian's memories don't
> exist prior to yesterday."

I add even more information because this is the one place that can't be deleted. Digital files can be erased. Notebooks can be stolen and thrown out. But our bodies are ours to keep.

> "Memories lost for good: Something in Kimmel's class?
> Several hours at my house this evening. Sebastian's
> memory of a metal slab."

I purse my lips as I study his back.

> "Information learned: If our project doesn't work,
> thousands of people will die. The Ethics Committee
> claims it's a system-wide problem, but I think someone
> deliberately removed my memories. The Committee

tested out a new fix on a few key teacher accounts—
my mom, Kimmel, Brandon—but the hacker was still
able to bypass them in HiveMind even though I
couldn't."

I can't hide the crack in my voice on that last part.

Sebastian lifts up slightly, tilting his head over his shoulder to peer at me. My first instinct is to look away, anything to avoid him seeing me like this: so vulnerable. I'm not used to being less than the absolute best and it's a tough position to adjust to. But when I flick my eyes back to him, there's no judgment in his face, only concern and understanding. When he offers me a small smile in comfort, it's exactly what I need to feel complete again.

I continue under the Information Learned header.

"There's an encrypted folder hidden on the IT servers
that seems to contain my missing memories, but I
can't access it via my normal hacking means. I have to
physically get into the IT area and plug an SSD drive
into one of the consoles there, which is now sporting a
swanky new retina scanner to match my swanky new
retina."

"Retinas," he corrects me, and I add an *s* to the end of my previous sentence to make *retina* a plural.

I suck in a deep breath and keep writing.

"Actions taken: Printing Brandon's and my mother's
eyeballs after sneaking into the bioinks lab. Bribing Jay
the security guard to give us access and then turning
over my mom's ID card when he caught us."

There's bitterness evident in my voice. How much would it have cost me to bribe him to let me keep it?

"Electroencephalograph sync did not work. Neither did data recovery software, defragging the disk, or scanning for corrupted DLL files."

I could list the rest of my attempts but they are all just as meaningless. Instead, I sum it up with:

"I've tried everything possible and nothing has worked."

On my arm, I find the suspects line:

Suspects: Veronica, Teddy, anyone else you've stolen memories from.

I cross out *Veronica* and add in *Eliza.*

Tension flees from my shoulders now that everything worth remembering is captured. I keep my pen pressed against Sebastian's back, my palm flat against his skin, for an extra few seconds. For some reason it's harder to let go than it was to let him in. "Done," I whisper, and when he shifts, I instantly mourn the loss of the feel of his skin.

He twists, and when his brief gaze burns through me, I have to fight to keep from sliding off the bed. My shirt's still on, but for some reason, the way he looks at me makes me feel as if he's looking right through me, right down to my bones. I feel stark and naked and empty in front of him, like a glass container.

My heart begins to beat louder. "Your turn." My bones feel watery as I fumble for the bottom of my shirt and tug it over my head. I should feel exposed as I sit beside him, wearing only my white bra, but the way he drinks in the sight of me makes me feel something I've never felt before. Beautiful.

I turn my back toward him and savor the warm sensation of his hands steadying me, and his pen sets a path of sparks ablaze across my skin. His hot breath on my neck makes goose bumps pop all over my arms, warmth radiating across my collarbones. My eyes slide closed and I stay as still as possible.

He relays the words he writes down.

> "I'm Sebastian Cuomo though I used to go by Bash. I live at 1011 Gordon's Corner Road and I've memorized the entire OED. I'm working on some thesis project with Arden that can save lives. I don't like carrots. And I'm falling for a girl I met today but have a mysterious past with."

His words are an electric bolt, zapping through my body and igniting my heart. Every part of me thrums. I'm glad my back is to him, the mirror behind me. This way he can't see my smile or the color that floods into my cheeks.

Past Arden is so brave and daring, but I don't know how to be her. Instead of kissing him like I so desperately want to, I chicken out. I settle for the fantasies playing in my mind of cupping the back of his neck, pulling him toward me, and sucking on his lower lip.

His pen doesn't move for a few moments but neither do his hands. They remain gripping me in a way that's more embrace than an attempt to steady me.

"You—you sure you don't want to add anything else?" My voice sounds foreign to my own ears.

"That's all I need to know." He drops his hands from my back and it takes all my willpower not to lunge straight into his arms again. I twist toward him, searching his face for any indication that he feels the same way, but he just juts his chin toward the pillows and then his eyes flick to my crumpled shirt at the edge of the bed. "Should we . . . ?"

A shaky breath flees my lungs as I slip my shirt back on. My heart races, set in motion by a mix of nerves and I-don't-know-what-comes-next anticipation. I go to unclasp my necklace, and as I'm doing so, he lifts up my hair to help me. His fingers sweep across my bare neck, leaving a trail of tingles in their wake. He pulls the necklace off and my hair drops back down with a heavy flop.

"What does this mean?" Sebastian runs his pointer finger along the engraved numbers etched into the silver pendant.

"My name in binary code. A reminder that everything in the universe can be turned into ones and zeroes. It's like . . . my mantra."

He grins. "Clever and useful. Now you'll never forget your name. Unlike me." There's only a hint of bitterness in his voice. He sets it onto the nightstand.

"Perhaps we should keep everything else on," I say, as his fingers fumble for the zipper on his fly, before this becomes a game of strip poker to see who bluffs first. He nods.

I pull the bedspread from its clutches. I climb into the clean sheets first, keeping my arms pressed against my sides to give him plenty of room. He settles in next to me. We both stare at the stucco ceiling. The empty air that rests between us may as well be an obstacle. We're making a memory, and in my memories, I'd close the distance between us. I think of the flashback—to use the term HiveMind automatically tagged them as—and how similar it was. Not this room, not this bed . . . not this far away from each other.

The kiss in the memory was a glimpse, just a taste, back when we were both different people. Every nerve ending in my body itches to lean over and try it again, for real. When we're both *us*.

0011000100110101

An unfamiliar sound jerks me out of dreamland. Sunlight streams through the billowing white curtains, highlighting the fine blond hairs that decorate the arm resting beneath my neck. An arm that belongs to a guy. One I've never seen before. Wrapped around me.

I bolt upright in panic, flinging him off me. He rolls over, completely undisturbed by the disruption. As my heart thunders, I take stock of the unfamiliar surroundings: a generic room with a geometric art print on the wall, white sheets that are easy to bleach, and stationery with a motel chain logo. I clamp a cold palm over my mouth, biting back my urge to scream. I would never go to a motel with a strange guy. Hell, I'd never go to a motel period.

Suddenly I can't quite catch my breath. How did I even get here? I press a palm to my forehead. The last thing I remember is waking up yesterday and getting ready for school, but nothing beyond that. Latent terror propels me to my feet. I back away from the bed until my shins hit the dresser, anything to put some space between me and this stranger.

A loud *blllllrrrrriiiiiing* from somewhere in the room makes me jump in surprise. The guy opens his eyes groggily and then widens them when he sees me across the way. On his nightstand, an unfamiliar phone vibrates on the shellacked wooden surface. "Who are you?" we both ask at the same time. But then he adds an extra question, one I don't have to ask. "Who am *I*?"

The phone rings again, and he twists toward it, staring at it as if he's never seen it before either. He picks it up, studying it for a moment before clicking the *accept* button, but doesn't say a word. Just continues staring at it. When a muffled voice comes out of the tinny speaker, he finally sets it against his ear.

As he faces away from me to take the call, I reach for my laptop to check HiveMind. It's the only thing that might help me understand what brought me here. My eyes land on a single word written on my palm: *Sebastian*.

My mouth parts and I drag my eyes toward the guy in the bed. Is he Sebastian? I have no idea, but when he leans over to rest his elbows on his knees, his shirt rises just a little bit, revealing a sliver of his lower back covered in pen marks that eerily resemble my own handwriting.

A soft shudder moves through me. I stomp toward him, the carpet rough against my bare soles. When I reach for the bottom of his shirt and start to lift it up, he spins around and squints at me in confusion. My hand falls away.

"Wait, what?" the-guy-who-probably-is-Sebastian says into the receiver. There's panic in his voice and that makes my blood curdle more.

I tug my own shirt upward, my back to the mirror. A gasp breaks free when I use my phone's camera to view the side of myself I can't see and notice scratchy boy handwriting on my back.

Faint yelling resounds through the phone speaker. "I have no idea what you're talking about!" Sebastian shouts back.

I pull my shirt completely off and move into Sebastian's view, forcing him to look at me. I hold his gaze for the briefest moment before I turn around and let him take in whatever words are written on my back. When I face him again, he's already pulling his own shirt over his head while the person on the other line prattles on. He ends the call in the middle of the other party's emphatic speech and tosses his phone on the bed.

My eyes widen at the first line written across his shoulder blades.

Look at the external hard drive for the folder labeled DO NOT DELETE.

What the hell? I have no idea why I would instruct myself to do this, but since it's my handwriting and it's written on the strange guy I spent the night beside, I oblige my own wishes. I find several backups from HiveMind, all captured yesterday. Weird. I sometimes back up my HiveMind account but not every few hours. There's already a compare-simulation script open—though I don't recall writing one—so I run it again, my heart thumping with every tick of the clock as it runs thanks to the warning I left myself to be quick.

A *ding* from the compare simulation resounds. Two lists appear, one tallying the discrepancies between my last backup and live HiveMind, and one for Sebastian's. I grip the white sheets with my fingers so tightly I create starbursts in the fabric. Holy isotopes, something's wrong with HiveMind. Thousands of memories have disappeared from our minds overnight but still exist in my backups. Most memories are from yesterday and contain titles like: *Asking Zoey if she knows what my project is. Backward flashback propositioning Bash to work on a project together. Trying to figure out who might hate me. Deleting Veronica's and Eliza's memories. Writing secrets on each other's backs.*

Panic builds in my body, erupting in a series of shakes. None of that makes any sense. I never asked Zoey about my project. I have no idea who Bash is. With trembling hands, I modify an existing script that will copy over the missing files from the backups one by one into both our HiveMind accounts. This amount of data will take over an hour to transfer.

"What's happening?" Sebastian points at his mind, where the first memory has started replaying.

"We're going to find out." I sink onto the bed beside him. The events from yesterday fall into place in my mind, marching in exact chronological order. *Discovering Sebastian's mind was blank except for latent knowledge. Printing a replica of an eye. Making out with Bash in his bedroom.* All the info we discovered about not remembering our project and all the suspects I dismissed. It all thunders back into me, wrenching my gut.

Sebastian's phone keeps ringing and ringing, but we both ignore it as we let the memories return to us. I kissed him in the past. I held his hand in the recent present. I wanted to do both things again last night.

I swallow hard, my shoulders filling with courage. Before I can second-guess myself, I reach over and grab his hand. I lace my fingers with his and he gives me a squeeze in return. We stay like that, clutching each other, as the rest of the memories steal our breaths.

When they're finally all accounted for, he gasps out, "Holy shit. Someone deliberately erased every single thought related to our investigation while we slept."

"They got rid of the entire day from both our minds to erase any progress we'd made." The words taste vile in my mouth. There's no doubt now: Someone's monitoring us.

Sebastian buries his face in his hands, leaning forward so his head crosses the beam of sunlight streaming through the window.

I graze my fingers along his shoulder, indulging in the contours of his bare upper back. "It's okay. We have everything back now. I hope."

"I can't believe I lost it all again." He breathes out in a huff and rubs the short stubble on his jaw. "At least I didn't lose you this time." His eyes find mine and we share a shy smile.

"Or yourself."

His phone rings again and we both stare at it. "Crap. My mom's calling because I'm late to school. Apparently this is something I do a lot and now she has to drive me to sign me in."

My eyes zoom to the clock. First period has already started. "Tell her you'll meet her at home in fifteen minutes. That you left early this morning to work on our project and we lost track of time."

"Do you think the school will let me come late if I have to leave for a bit later? My mom also has to sign me out for an hour today for some appointment with Dr. Sadler I have after lunch."

"Yeah, they have to let you out for an appointment."

He picks up the call and repeats what I said into the phone while I replace the ice for the eyes and moisturize them again.

After dropping him off, I make it to school just as first period lets out. On my way to my locker, I bang out a quick text to Brandon.

> **Arden:** Hey, having an issue with my laptop.
> Can you let me into the basement?

I want to retrieve another memory, but right now the easiest way to bypass the new security measures is by getting someone else to do it. I march through the hallways, pulling my cardigan sleeves lower to cover all the writing on my arms.

His reply is instant.

Brandon: No can do. Need approval from the
EC in order to let you down here.
You'll need to submit an official
helpdesk ticket.

Shit. A bitter flavor swells at the back of my tongue. There's no way the Ethics Committee is going to approve any request I make, and as long as Brandon's holding down the fort in the IT room, I'm not going to be able to access one of the consoles.

Unless . . . I get him out of there.

I pass Veronica and Eliza in the hallway and both of them sneer at me before falling into giggles. I skirt around them, my temples pounding, and bang out a reply.

Arden: Can you please come to me then to
take a look at it? Meet in the courtyard
at 10:15?

That's the middle of second period, so the hallways will be empty. It'll be my best chance to use the retina scanner and slip inside as soon as Brandon vacates the basement. It would be too risky to try to do this now when the hallway's full of people. Hopefully if Brandon vacates the basement, the Ethics Committee won't flag another log on the scanner.

His reply takes a little longer.

Brandon: I'm not supposed to leave this room.

I squeeze my eyes shut, hating myself for what I'm about to do. But I need to get Brandon out of that room. There's only one thing that would entice him to leave. Leo.

There's a frantic aching in my chest at the idea of deceiving Brandon. But maybe I don't have to be deceitful? Maybe I can turn this into something that benefits both Brandon and Leo as much as it does me. Both of them seemed devastated about the breakup and I think back to Leo's desperate wish for Brandon to just *listen*. Perhaps what they need is a chance to talk.

> **Arden:** Okay listen, you caught me. This is all a ruse. The truth is, Leo is the one that needs to talk to you. Will you please meet him in the courtyard at 10:15 and hear him out?

He writes back so fast, I'm not even sure how he had time to type it.

> **Brandon:** Ok.

Two letters, difficult to interpret without punctuation. He could mean *okay!* or *okay*.... optimistic or begrudging. Still, I let out a breath, feeling like I did one thing right by helping Leo get a chance to talk.

I complete my ruse with a final text to Leo.

> **Arden:** Hey, Brandon wants to meet you in the courtyard at 10:15. He's ready to talk.

I don't need to wait for his reply. He'll be there, pacing the courtyard a few minutes before the meet-up time. Something in my chest flutters at the idea of the two of them being so happy again.

When I reach my locker, Zoey's already there leaning against it, stakeout-style. Her blond hair curls into ringlets that frame her face in an innocent—and completely false—way. When she spots me, her liner-rimmed eyes widen. "Wow. You look like a walk of shame. Where were you this morning and does it have anything to do with your date?"

The corners of my lips curve ever so slightly at the memory of Sebastian's hands on my back, the kiss we shared in a past we've forgotten. Warmth sweeps across my chest at the memory.

The clink of locks opening and metallic slams reverberate around us. "Amazing, actually. We *may* have spent the night in a motel room and overslept."

Two girls next to us hush their conversation to eavesdrop. Alternating red and blue lockers line the hallway like soldiers standing guard.

"Woohoo! An all-night study session of each other's bone structures!" Zoey fans the air in front of her face and then waggles her fingers at me. In any other high school that would be the universal code for *I NEED DETAILS!* But here, she means she wants the memory itself.

"Come closer." I spin around and lift my shirt enough for her to see Sebastian's handwriting on my back.

She gasps. "Wow, not exactly what I would have done without shirts on, but I like your style. Still, I need *more!*"

"How about a trade? You let me dig in your mind to see if I can find evidence of deletions, and I'll show you what happened last night." I'll give it to her, but with some editing. Just the part where we wake up in the same bed, terrified. She can fill in her own details about what transpired before that moment. A modern *Choose Your Own Adventure* story.

Perusing through Zoey's mind is the only recon I can do until

I can get back into the IT room. All my memories of Bash were deleted, but he still exists in Zoey's mind. My guess is that there were so many thoughts and memories related to him in my mind that it was just easier to get rid of it all, but I want to see what remains in Zoey's.

"Deal. But stay away from anything involving Teddy." She presses a palm against her heart. "Those are sacred and personal." Her voice is dreamy.

"Even the one where he tells you not to go into the gym because they're cleaning up?"

"Yes! That one's my favorite. Did you see the way he looked at me when he said such a sweet nothing?" She sighs to herself. "Pure love."

I purse my lips. "You say *pure love*. I say *annoyance*. Apples to oranges."

"But seriously." Zoey enters my combination into the electronic lock for me and hands me my User Interface Design textbook. "I know getting your memories deleted sucks, but let's think glass-half-full. You guys weren't together before, but now you like each other. That wouldn't have happened without all your memories going missing. I call that a win!"

I think back to the kissing memory. "I think we *were* together though."

Zoey squints at me, confused. "No you weren't." She grabs my Business and Project Management book and sets it atop the other textbook in my arms. "As far as I remember, you guys barely talked except for whatever you must have said in class for your project. You never even tried to suggest a double date between you and him and me and Teddy."

She leads us into a mob of students pushing past the traffic jam by the elevators. Video screens hang in intervals from the ceiling and display the countdown until the next bell rings, as if the hallway is a subway platform announcing an oncoming train.

"I kissed him. Not last night but sometime in the past." I give her a high-level recap of the memory I retrieved.

Zoey swishes her hair behind her shoulders like she's modeling for an antidandruff commercial. "That's weird, because once at Melody's party, I dared you to kiss him."

My eyes widen and a smile catches on my lips. Melody's party was the one where I was looking forward to seeing *someone* there. "Did I?" I can't keep the excitement out of my voice.

"Nope. Not even close. I—" She presses a palm to her forehead. "I think you ended the game. Or maybe the game just ended. I can't remember exactly. But I *definitely* do not remember any kissing happening." She wrinkles her nose. "Except between Teddy and Eliza."

Or perhaps only the memory of the game ended thanks to mass deletions of anything related to us or our project. Perhaps I did kiss him that night, but no one remembers it.

"But no worries, because this is *so* much better anyway. You totally need to kiss him for real!" Zoey purses her lips in an attempt to act serious. "You know, for scientific purposes. An experiment to compare the real thing with your memory." She playfully taps me on the shoulder. "I know, I know. This is the best idea ever. I'm brilliant. You can admit it."

"For scientific purposes?" I raise my brow. "What a pickup line. You should try it on Teddy. I dare you."

"Oh no. Looks like this game of truth or dare is ending abruptly too!" She blows me a kiss before heading off to class.

I slide into home plate ten seconds before the bell rings. Since I missed first period, I missed the chance to talk to Mr. Kimmel again today and try to figure out what he might have said in class yesterday that the hacker deleted.

My teacher heads to the board and switches on a projector. Perfect opportunity for me to not pay attention and do something else. I open my laptop and pretend to be really invested in taking notes.

As promised, I give Zoey the memory from this morning, but only the part where we don't recognize each other. She'll hate me for not giving her anything juicier, but it'll have to do. When I open her account, I run a quick search for memories about Bash, but each one that comes up is mundane. Bash ordering food in the cafeteria. Bash answering a question in class. Bash holding the door for Zoey to exit. Even the party memory mostly involves Zoey's obsession over why Teddy isn't talking to her, and the actual truth-or-dare section comprises ten seconds before the memory abruptly cuts off before restarting twenty minutes later, an entire chunk of the night missing. On a whim, I do another search for Zoey + Bash + the keyword *project*. Only one item pops up on the list. It's from two years ago, located in my kitchen.

I click on it.

"Ugh, Dr. Varga." Zoey buries her head in her hands as she leans against my kitchen counter.

I expect her to be talking to my mother, but when she lifts her head, there's someone else across the room.

The world freezes. I squeeze my eyes shut, desperate to hold on to the brief glimpse of my dad sitting at the kitchen table, drumming his frail fingers on the surface. His hair's completely gone, which means this must have been when he was still giving chemo the old college try. It wasn't until the middle of junior year that he told the doctors he was done. That he wanted to live out the rest of his life free of wires and checkups and heartbreaking disappointment.

The rest of his life turned out to be five more months.

He shakes his head at her. "Don't say ugh. Don't slouch. Stand up straight and present your pitch. Be confident!"

She takes a rattling breath. "But Arden and Bash said—" The memory pauses there and then jerks to another spot where she's seated across from him at the table.

"I'm nervous," she says. "My project proposals were all rejected by the board. And this one's only half a project. No, not even half. It's a barnacle on a whale of a project."

Dad shrugs. "So is Arden and Bash's. In a way."

Goose bumps cover my arms. What does that even mean?

"Trust me, the Committee won't see it that way," he continues.

She lifts her head, her gaze focusing on him. "What makes you so confident this one will get approved?"

"Because you won't be on your own." Dad's voice sounds gravelly to my ears and he has to pause to wheeze. "You'll be rotating among the finest mentors and students Varga Industries has to offer. I'm not going to let the board kick you out because of a few measly bad grades. What you showed me just now"—he pats a packet of papers on the table in front of him—"this is the stuff that breakthroughs are made of."

In the distance of the memory, I can hear myself shout from what's likely upstairs. "Zoey? What's going on?"

She stands up. "I should go. Before she realizes I'm not in the bathroom. Thanks, Dr. Varga."

The memory ends there, but the lump clogging my throat remains. There's a sudden stabbing of longing for my dad and for this moment that I was never a part of but now I'm stealing for myself, making it my own. While my teacher lectures, I inch up the sleeve on my right arm and scrawl the only new piece of information gleaned from the memory: *My dad compared our project to a barnacle on a whale.*

When I glance up, I notice the girl next to me watching me curiously. I hastily pull down my sleeves, catching another glimpse of the angry scar on my other arm, and work on capturing another backup for both Sebastian and me. It only takes a few minutes to copy each memory since I restored the last backup an hour ago. I compare the one from last night with the one today. Four memories archived from me, two from him, but at least none of the missing ones happened after the last backup, which lets me restore our minds completely. Well, I use the word *complete* as a relative term, starting with yesterday as the control.

I copy them all back one by one and check the clock. T-minus five minutes until Brandon vacates the IT room. Via a combination of back-end scripts and password-generation software, it takes me less time than that to hack into the school security system. Tiny black and white squares fill my screen, each one showing a ceiling-camera's-eye view of the school hallways.

There's a flash of movement on one of the security monitors. Brandon emerges from the basement and tousles his hair before shoving his hands in his pockets and heading for the courtyard. A quick peek at all the hallways between my location and the basement shows the coast is clear. I leap to my feet, closing my laptop at the same time, and shove it into my messenger bag. "Bathroom," I say, swiping the hall pass from my teacher's desk.

With purposeful movements, I march through the hallways. I keep my pace quick, my nose pointed straight toward the basement door.

My fingers jostle in my bag for the lunch box that contains a body part I should definitely not be carrying around. I clutch it in a tight grip to steady my trembling hands. My pulse throbs when I pause in front of the basement, looking left and right as if I'm about to cross the street. I fumble to lift the lid on the box and pull out the jiggling mass of nerves. It wobbles beneath my fingers, and I have to suck in a deep breath to calm myself enough to hold the retina up to the scanner.

Footsteps somewhere nearby resonate on the linoleum, getting louder with each step. My pulse pounds loud in my ears.

If this eye doesn't work to unlock the scanner or if someone catches me, it won't just be sayonara lost memories, it'll be goodbye to my admission here at this school and, in turn, my entire future.

0011000100110110

Red lasers from the retina scanner sweep over the eye, failing to register it. Shit. It might be too dry.

My heart beats with hummingbird wings. The footsteps get even louder. Closer.

I jam my hand into my bag until I pull out the saline solution. When I pour it over the eye, the damn thing gets so slippery I drop it, but I swiftly catch it in my other palm. Gross. I shove it under the retina scanner once again and the lasers continue to torture me with their ineptitude. A shadow stretches from around the corner, the person about to turn and catch me.

The green light blinks.

I throw open the door and launch myself inside, letting it seal shut behind me. I lean against it, squeezing my eyes shut, my breath ragged in my throat.

That was close.

I drop the eye back into the container and make a mental note to increase my use of saline so this doesn't happen again. And jostling this thing by carrying it around all day isn't helping things—I'll store it in my locker as soon as I'm done here. With the back of my hand, I wipe sweat from my brow and push a tangled strand of hair behind my ear.

I keep to the edges of the basement, the bright light from the

IT room like a beacon welcoming me. But just as I'm about to turn the knob, voices inside stop me short. I risk a quick peek through the rectangular window and quickly fling myself back toward the wall at the sight of my mother and several of the Ethics Committee members walking along the rows of computers and making notes on clipboards.

I swallow hard. I refuse to leave here without another retrieved memory, but there's only one more spot that will allow me the tools to hack into that same encrypted folder.

I duck low to clear my head from the window in the door to the IT room and then scurry around a corner in the basement, where another retina scanner awaits. The server room sprawls across an entire wing, housing the computers that store all the vital data used for HiveMind and several other Varga Industries products. They're a lot more annoying to hack than the ones in the IT room, but I've done it before. My trusty stolen eye grants me access to the server room as well.

Rows of metal shelves fill the massive space with stacks of large black rectangular devices lining each of the shelves. Blue lights blink in the same spot on each one. A chill makes me shiver from the freezing temps that keep the machines from overheating. There's a faint hum buzzing, as if bees are hiding in the darkness. I don't dare turn on the lights, but I tilt my laptop screen upward, and then back, spinning around in the tight space to illuminate as much as I can.

I grab another SSD drive from my newly replenished stash and slink through the expansive rows. I choose one of the servers toward the back, hoping no one will find it all the way over here. I sink to the dusty floor, legs stretched out, back propped against a metal shelving unit. It takes me nearly twenty minutes to connect the device to the server, run a few commands, and hack into the mainframe of HiveMind. *Eureka.*

I let out a relieved breath when the hidden folder's still there, the encrypted contents inside waiting for me to dig my fingers into. There are several more files added to the initial count, probably the ones that have gone missing from our minds during the last day and a half. Once again I try to copy the entire contents at the same time into an external hard drive, but the system blocks me, only permitting me to transfer a single file at a time. I choose one at random from the list of favorites, then decrypt it and transfer it into my head. My shoulders relax, calmness overtaking me, like an addict getting his next hit. My eyes close, waiting for the past to take over.

Blackness sweeps over my vision for a moment before a new scene glitches into place as if pixels are rushing into position before my eyes. In the memory, I'm squeezed next to Bash on a thin hospital bed, fitting my body into the crevices between all the wires and IVs attached to him. A machine bleeps steadily while a heavy antiseptic smell lingers in the air. My wrist throbs where it rests on his stomach, staining crimson the tiny blue flowers dotting his white hospital gown. My forearm scar, slashed open, releasing a metallic scent into the air. I stare at a security guard as he retreats away from the bed and toward the door, not looking where he's going, only focusing on us. Going backward.

[Miss, you can't be in here,] the guard shouts in reverse.

He leaves the room and slams the door shut behind him. [Then we'll have to work faster,] I say, also backward. A cringe forms on my face.

[Six months.] Bash's voice comes out strangled. His glasses display a miniature replica of the fluorescent light above his head.

Gritting my teeth against the pain in my wrist, I jerk to a sitting position as Bash's arms fall away from around my body. The blooming stain on his shirt shrinks. [How long?] I ask.

The bloodstain disappears completely. I slide off the cot, wobbling on my feet. Blood lifts off the floor and flies at my skin as if my wrist is an alien UFO beaming up the droplets. I clutch my bleeding arm with my other hand. My pulse beats under my skin. A strained laugh vibrates in my throat. [They know.]

Bash fumbles for a button on the console beside his bed. [I'll call a nurse.] The tubes stuck in his nose jerk him upright even though he strains against them. [What happened to your arm? Oh my God!] He flops back down on the bed with a heavy sigh.

I backtrack across the room. Without being able to see where I'm going, I worry I'll smack into something but Past Me doesn't care. My throat hitches. [I had to see you.] I secure my bleeding arm behind my back, erasing a streak of red from my shirt in the process.

[What are you doing here?] Bash's voice sounds groggy. His eyes flutter shut.

Instead of answering, I ease open the door and retreat from the room. Clutching my arm, I sprint backward through a long hospital corridor, past an ICU area with nurses observing an array of monitors like producers in a TV control room. I enter an open room and squeeze behind the door. My chest puffs in and out while I wait for something. After a few minutes, I rush out of the room and continue running. Shouts fly at me, begging me to stop. Footsteps jumble with mine. When I round a corner without looking, I fall into step with two security guards and a nurse, who walks backward with me as if this is a synchronized choreography number.

All of a sudden I stop short and plop into a chair that I had no idea was there. My elbows rest on the cool metal of a wheelchair armrest. An orderly wheels me back toward the ER wing entrance. Nurses in bright colored scrubs cross paths with me, all of them walking backward.

Each drop of blood that had been coating my shirt merges back into the flesh on my wrist. The pain grows more intense with every bump the wheelchair hits. Double doors swing open and deposit me in the main lobby. I get off the chair and turn to the nurse who pushed me. [Thank you,] I cry out. Real tears drip upward across the hills of my cheeks and back into my eyes.

The nurse pulls the wheelchair behind a desk and then runs at me. She wears a horrified expression, mouth sliding on a severe slant. [You shouldn't have done that!] she shouts. [Are you insane?] The expression slips off her face.

I hold my bleeding wrist up for her to inspect. She takes one look at it and hands me scissors. I wield the scissors over my wrist like a weapon as she runs over to another patient in the waiting room. She picks up a clipboard from the floor and turns to him.

I clutch my throbbing arm with bloody fingers and bite back a scream of pain. Instead of the excess blood dripping onto the floor, it moves in the wrong direction, seeping back into the gash that traces up the length of my forearm. An impossible task, like trying to glue together shattered glass. I drag the pointy end of the scissor across my flesh, erasing the scar and sealing the blood back beneath my skin.

I take a deep breath, and then amble backward toward the nurses' station. A garland of fabric leaves in fall colors hangs from the front desk, and cardboard turkeys decorate the back wall. Standing on tiptoes, I reach over the desk and drop the scissors into a supply cup.

I stomp back toward the nurse, who spins to face me as if she knew I was coming. Her arms fly up to cross over her chest. [Come back tomorrow,] she tells me in an annoyed voice. Her low ponytail and lack of makeup give her a washed-out, tired-of-everything appearance.

[I have to see him. You don't understand.]

She shakes her head. [Visiting hours are over.]

She turns away from me, and I tap her on the back before grabbing my cell phone from my purse and pressing the end call button. Except since this is happening backward, it initiates a call. I sink into the nearest seat. [No, you're not,] I say into the phone. [We're going to fix this.]

Bash's voice comes through on the other end, heavy along with the words he says: [I'm dying.]

0011000100110111

When the server room rematerializes around me, my heart pounds against my binary necklace. The image of Bash, hooked up to machines, stays etched in my mind like a picture burned onto the TV screen. There's heaviness behind my eyes. I test out the words on my tongue. "He's dying." Does him dying have anything to do with his memory loss?

With mine?

My body begins to shake, my skin going cold.

I trace my hand over the spot where the faint puffy scar marks my wrist. When I piece back the conversation Bash and I had in the correct order, it makes more sense:

"I'm dying."

"No, you're not. We're going to fix this." Then I cut my arm to force my way into the closed-to-visitors ER wing. I ditched the wheelchair escort and found Bash's room, where I crawled onto his bed and asked him, "How long?"

"Six months."

"Then we'll have to work faster."

Six months. If he only had six months to live . . . How much of that sentence is left? Oh God. Thanksgiving decorations littered the hospital walls in the memory. November was five months ago. I shake my head, refusing to believe he only has one month left.

The piece of paper I found in my pocket swims through the fog in my brain. *If I don't figure out what my damn project is, someone will die, followed by thousands of people.* Maybe I'm reading it all wrong. It's not that someone will *die.* It's that my project will save them. Maybe our project could somehow save Sebastian?

The lump in my throat expands and I swallow past it. I will not get upset, not yet, because if my hypothesis is true, then I had a plan to fix it once. I just need to figure out what the plan was so I can save the guy I'm falling for all over again.

Voices from outside the server-room door sound so foreign to me now, with this knowledge swirling inside me. He's dying, but I don't want him to go.

My head spins. Is this what I meant about not wanting to lose him during the memory of us kissing in his bed?

The server-room door wrenches open, and my pulse slams into my skull. I slink down, huddling as small as possible. If the Ethics Committee finds me in here, I'm as good as expelled.

Someone comes inside, sneakers squeaking, and when he turns partially, a crack in the shelves lets me see Brandon. He braces his hands against one of the shelves and drops his head to his chest. His elbows tremble and he sucks down desperate breaths.

My heart aches at the sight of him looking so broken.

A vibration buzzes from my phone, and my teeth snap together, startled. I'm in such a daze that fumbling for the betraying device to silence it becomes an enormous effort. But it's too late. Brandon's head perks up. He squints in the distance before taking tentative steps toward me, running his hand over the short stubble of his jaw.

There's nowhere to hide, no way to run without alerting him. So I scramble to my feet and shuffle as far away from the SSD still planted in the computer as possible. Brandon's eyes widen when he sees me, his mouth set in a thin, grave line. "Arden?" He frantically swipes at a stray tear sliding down his red-tinged cheeks. "You— you tricked us!"

I wince, momentarily caught off guard by the statement that's so far out of the realm of what I thought he was going to ask: *What are you doing down here?* My voice cracks when I try to speak. "You guys needed to talk."

"He stormed off." A breath rattles from Brandon's throat. "As soon as he realized I hadn't invited him."

Guilt ties a knot deep in my gut. "He wanted to talk." I risk a step toward my brother's ex. "He only left when he realized—"

"Why?" The force of Brandon's question sends me stumbling backward a step. "Why did—Wait." His eyes fly over the laptop propped in my arm. "Arden, if someone finds you down here— oh my God, we're both going to be in hell." He straightens, the urgency evident in his flexed muscles. "Come on, you have to get out of here."

His panic jolts my own. I step toward him, mumbling a silent prayer under my breath that my SSD stays hidden. Stays connected. I shove my laptop into my messenger bag and follow after Brandon. "He still loves you," I whisper.

Brandon pauses for a moment, the muscles in his back tightening, before he pushes open the door into the hallway. "He shouldn't."

Our footsteps mask the heavy breaths pumping in our lungs. We round the corner—

—and run smack into my mother.

She brushes herself off. "Arden? How did you get in down here?" Her face falls and her gaze shifts to Brandon and then back to me.

Cold panic sluices through my body. The illegal eye weighs heavy in my bag. My brain's still stuck on Bash dying. "I—um."

"I let her in," Brandon says fast. "Her laptop wasn't working and—"

"I thought you were just going to the bathroom!" There's a hard set to Mom's chin. She turns from Brandon to me. "You know we're under very strict protocols right now with the security breaches going on." Mom switches gears to me again. "Did you fill out a helpdesk ticket?"

I bite my lip. "Yes?" I can always create one later and backdate it.

Mom lets out an exasperated sigh. "Brandon, please go back to the IT room, where you're supposed to be."

Brandon ducks his head and scurries to the room he never should have left in the first place. The room he wouldn't have left except I lured him away. My chest squeezes. Blood whooshes in my ears.

"Arden, really now." She places both palms on her hips in the middle of the dank hallway. "You need at least a 3.75 GPA to get into this school. That means you need to be smart. And yet you continue to ditch class and deliberately disobey school rules."

"Sorry," I say, trying to brush past her. "I should get back to class."

Mom lifts the strap of my cardigan. "Where were you last night?"

I cross my arms to stop my hands from shaking and give her my best Past Arden impression I can muster. After all, the best lies stem from the absolute truth. "I was hoping you wouldn't remember."

She leans toward me and sniffs my hair as if she might be able to detect the telltale scent of motel linens instead of shampoo. "What I remember is making a mistake when I grounded you for a month. Make that two."

I cringe. Two months takes me straight through the end of the school year. But then I think back to what Sebastian said last night about being grounded: *didn't stop me just now*. I could use a copy of his confidence. "Mom, I promise I'll behave once I get my memories back, but—"

"About that." Her expression draws tight. "The Ethics Committee thinks they might have isolated the source of the glitch. Arden—" Her jaw clenches. "According to the latest report, most of the activity related to archiving and restoring is coming from *your* account."

"It's not me." The words fly from my lips, desperate, rushed. They sound defensive, and when I hold up my hands in what seems like surrender, my mom's eyes narrow in suspicion. "I'm just trying to protect my account and stop the hacker, I swear."

Mom crosses her arms, her frown deepening. "Arden, *you're* the only hacker here and all you're doing is making yourself seem incredibly suspicious. Stop trying to bypass the rules. Stop your little investigation right this minute."

I'm already shaking my head, sweat gathering in the folds of my elbows. Hot tears press against the backs of my eyes. "I can't. I won't."

Her nostrils flare. "You will. You need to start trusting the authorities. We have your best interest—" Her forehead wrinkles, cutting her eyebrows into sections instead of smooth arcs. Her mouth puckers like she tasted a really sour lemon. She presses one hand flat against the janitor's door to steady herself.

"Mom? You okay?" When she doesn't answer, I tug on her shoulder. She remains frozen with all her features set to *horror*. Panic amps in my gut.

The next period bell blares. My mom continues to impersonate a mannequin, void of any life except the subtle way she sways. I pull frantically on her sleeve, but she doesn't even flinch. A full minute passes before she shakes her head and blinks at me as if seeing me for the first time.

"Mom?" My voice comes out panicky.

The arch of her brows softens. She smooths down her skirt and checks her watch. "Arden! What are you doing down here?"

My pulse pounds. "What's the last thing you remember?"

"Um." She presses a hand to her forehead. "Sitting at my desk."

I swallow hard. The lie bubbles on my lips, tasting vile. "You brought me down here. To talk to the Ethics Committee." An uneasy knot lodges in my throat, a twinge in my chest. I have to look away from her for a second so she can't see the guilt twisting my lips into a grimace. An itchy crinkle of remorse creeps down my spine. "And now you were escorting me to my next class."

Mom presses the heel of her palm to her forehead. "Okay." She nods as if to reassure herself. "Okay. Let's go."

I hesitate for a moment, biting my lip. But then she starts heading toward the exit. I let out a breath at dodging the detention and grounding bullet. There aren't many benefits to someone messing with HiveMind and removing people's memories, but I'll take this unexpected one.

She escorts me all the way to my second-period class but doesn't say a word the entire time. Instead, she's busy firing off emails and texts and looking extremely worried. After she pops her head into the room to let my teacher know my tardiness is approved, she gives me a tight smile and heads in the opposite direction.

In my next class, I plop into the chair next to Zoey, and she gives me a cheery raising of her brows. After I open my laptop, I continue today's theme of pretending to take notes during lessons and instead attempt to reconnect to my SSD drive to retrieve another memory. I can't get the image of Bash on that hospital bed out of my head. I need more info, anything, about what might be wrong with him. But the device doesn't register on my laptop anymore.

I slam my fist against my laptop in frustration. Two girls across the way giggle at me. I shrug an excuse while my stomach swirls.

The Ethics Committee must have reduced the signal strength, making it impossible to connect directly to the server outside of physical range of it.

Fuck.

I need to see this report that my mom referenced. Yesterday's report should be archived on the server by now because each day's report is only downloaded the following day. I bypass the password to the locked Ethics Committee folder on the public file share drive thanks to the password-cracking script I wrote when I was thirteen.

Zoey shifts beside me, crossing her long legs and whispering, "What are you doing? Please tell me it involves sending dirty texts to Sebastian."

"I think you sent more than enough of those on my behalf last night."

A few heads swivel in my direction, but the squeak of a marker on the whiteboard indicates Mrs. Catalano is still scribbling notes and not catching me.

Since today's report won't be available until tomorrow, I pull up yesterday's Ethics Committee report, and Zoey returns to her own laptop. I skim past the boring analysis and their security recommendations to the section where the affected accounts are listed. I let out an audible gasp. Every single student in the school is listed.

Every single person's memory has been tampered with.

And every single memory removed involves Sebastian and me.

Account Name	HiveMind Tag	Capture Date	File Size	Activity Type	Time of Activity
Zoey Flint	Gives Arden makeover before first-anniversary date	Two years ago	11 MB	Archived	12:07:15

Account Name	HiveMind Tag	Capture Date	File Size	Activity Type	Time of Activity
Veronica Ackerman	Receives physics homework help from Bash and Arden	Two years, three months ago	6 MB	Archived	12:32:27
Eliza Shaw	Overhears Bash and Arden arguing about why their project won't work	Seven months ago	29 MB	Archived	01:29:11
Simon Zajek	Purchases a memory from Arden involving the time she attended a Make-A-Wish trip to Comic-Con with Bash	Four months ago	39 MB	Archived	02:01:48
Melody Clarendon	Truth or dare shenanigans at party	Two months ago	70 MB	Archived	3:07:15
Joshua Lazarus	Arden and Bash present schematic design for personality transfer to class	One year, two months ago	14 MB	Archived	04:45:00

Account Name	HiveMind Tag	Capture Date	File Size	Activity Type	Time of Activity
Leo Varga	Walks in on Arden and Bash making out on the couch	One month ago	40 MB	Archived	05:29:14
Carlos Kimmel	Tells Arden and Sebastian that their project can save lives	Yesterday	17 MB	Archived	10:07:17

My body hums, eyes greedily drinking in every tag and title on the first page. If I went to my first-anniversary dinner two years ago, that means Bash and I have been together for three years. Seven months ago our project didn't work. I have no idea what "schematic design for personality transfer" means, but I copy the words onto my forearm before anyone can catch me, just in case. It seems important.

Using the track pad, I start to greedily scroll down to read the rest of the entries. This document is over three hundred pages long. Except the scroll bar won't budget. When I click on the document again, the screen freezes.

I bang my fist against my thigh to muffle the sound of my frustration. With the document frozen, I have no choice but to X out of my word processing software and restart it. After restarting the program, I try to click on the Ethics Committee report.

An error pops up: *File not found.*

"Fuck." The word comes out so loud that every head turns toward me, including Mrs. Catalano. My temples pound. I thought I was getting answers, but that small glimpse of the memory-archiving activity only raises more questions.

0011000100111000

Zoey and I part ways so we can each head to our respective lockers before meeting up again in two minutes in the cafeteria. When I get to lunch, I stop short at the sight of Sebastian sitting at my usual table as if he belongs there. The wrinkles in his blue polo reveal the secret story of our night together. His shoulders shake from laughing at something Zoey says. I slip into the chair across from him with a heaviness that makes my knees buckle.

I have to tell him he's dying.

Sunlight slants through the windows and illuminates his smile. With his perfectly tanned skin and upbeat composure, he looks healthy. Not like he's on a one-way trip to a coffin. "How are you?" I ask, voice wary. How do you break this kind of news to someone? How do you effectively end someone's life with only your words? I set my messenger bag on the table, nestling the lunch box with the eye between my feet. Anything to keep my heel from rattling.

"Tired." He slides a container of steaming fries drizzled with truffle oil across the table. Buttery garlic scents waft from the kitchen, making my stomach growl. Crinkles of chip packages, paper bags ripped open, and trays slapping onto tables become our background soundtrack. "Got these for you. Ordered them all by myself. Aren't you proud?" His smile could eat me alive. I cringe at the knowledge that I'm going to be responsible for killing the smile on his face. "No carrots though," he continues. "Figured you'd be hungry."

"Thanks. I skipped breakfast," I say through gritted teeth, more for the benefit of Zoey than the boy who skipped breakfast with me. I open my mouth to try to tell him the news but then clamp it shut, chickening out. In an attempt to cover, I pop a fry in my mouth and savor the tangy, greasy flavor as Zoey practically melts into a puddle of *awwws* next to me.

Now. Do it now, I coax myself.

But before I have a chance to tell Sebastian about the memory, Teddy Day swaggers in our direction, chugging a water bottle and carrying a tablet wedged under his arm. His muscles bulge from his tight shirt, causing all the girls he passes to ogle him.

"Eee! He's coming over!" Zoey squeals and sifts her fingers through her hair to comb the beachy waves.

Teddy slaps Sebastian on the shoulder and studies him intensely. "How you feeling?"

Sebastian holds my gaze as he says, "I think the appropriate response to that question is, 'I'm hanging in there.'"

Bile rises in my throat. How much longer does he have to *hang in there*?

Zoey pats the empty seat next to her, winking a dark-rimmed eye. "This spot's calling your name."

"Can't stay. I came to find out if the rumors are true." He turns to me. "Her Royal Spyness is hanging up her crown? You haven't sold anyone a memory in over twenty-four hours now. People are starting to talk." His chest stills and his shoulders rise a fraction of an inch.

I can't answer. I can't say anything at all. The only words willing to rise to my tongue are the only ones I can't bring myself to say out loud.

Zoey pouts, making an exaggerated show of crossing her arms, which also accentuates her lacking cleavage. "Don't worry; I'm trying to convince her she's made a fallible decision."

"Well, I applaud you for it." Teddy offers me a single clap, his springy curls bouncing. "'Bout time the other students had to actually study like the rest of us." He takes a step backward. "Anyway. Gotta go. Have to meet with the Ethics Committee about something."

Zoey wrinkles her nose. "Ew, they're always so invasive."

His words fight through the fog in my brain. I straighten. "About what?"

He shrugs. "Something about a retina scanner? Not sure why they're asking me."

I recall him coming out of the basement yesterday. Maybe they're asking everyone who went down there in the last two days. Everyone except me of course.

"Wait!" Zoey shouts, then calms herself and regains her composure. "What are you doing tonight? We should hang out. Just you and me."

Teddy shoots a glance in Eliza Shaw's direction before aiming his megawatt smile at Zoey. "Can't. Have to work on my presentation for the review board."

He shuffles away and Zoey stabs her pasta with her fork at his rejection.

I rock back and forth on the bench: I have to tell Sebastian now that Teddy's gone. I can't withhold this kind of info from him any longer.

"Hey." My voice comes out shaky and I have to swallow hard to steady it. "I need some water. Accompany me?" I look pointedly at Sebastian and try to hide the utter devastation that must be written all over my face. I wish there was a better way to invite someone to hear about their upcoming demise.

I grab my laptop bag. He rises from the table and follows me toward the concessions line, squinting at me warily.

"I have to tell you something." I hug my laptop bag to my chest like a shield. "Something really, really bad. Do you want to go in the hallway?"

He pulls me into the recess of the open door to the kitchen and we huddle in the half-concealed space. Pots and pans clang. An antiseptic scent dilutes the mix of aromas that wafts from the kitchen. It's as private as we can get right now.

His eyes bore into mine. "There are seven universal microexpressions that appear involuntarily on someone's face for approximately one twenty-fifth of a second. You just displayed two of the seven: sadness and fear." He swallows hard. "Lay it on me."

I squeeze my eyes shut, pacing a short track in front of him, trying to wear off the restlessness in my legs. "You're—" the word lodges in my throat "—you're not okay." My throat feels swollen and my eyes begin to burn. I force the words out between clenched teeth. "You're dying, Sebastian."

I see what he means about microexpressions now. There's an uncontrollable tic in his eye. A muscle feathering in his jaw. His mouth parts ever so slightly in shock. But then his brow furrows. "What do you mean?"

"I saw it in a new memory I retrieved. Your doctor's appointment today. It's with Dr. Sadler, right? I looked him up. He's an oncologist." My voice cracks on the last word and I go stiff in my desperation to stay calm.

Sebastian clutches his chest as if his body's already giving out. Then he presses his other palm to his head. "I feel fine though."

When doctors give bad news, they do it with a straight ripping-the-Band-Aid-off face. But tears are welling in my eyes, blurring my vision. "If my calculations are correct . . ." I squeeze my eyes shut. I was trying to soften the blow by leading into the news with a brief explanation, but I sound as if I'm delivering a lab report and not a terminal diagnosis. The clink of silverware makes my teeth snap together. I steady a palm against the tiled walls to keep from sliding to the floor. Is there ever a right way to tell someone they're dying?

With a deep breath, I decide to say it fast instead of trying to cushion the news. "You have one month left to live." I cringe and force the next set of words out. He needs to know. "Maybe less. I'm so sorry, Sebastian." Tears pool behind my eyes.

He stumbles backward, shaking his head. He knocks into a kid carrying his tray, and the food goes flying, plastic tray clattering to the ground. Sebastian doesn't even notice, just keeps backing up, his eyes unfocused.

A janitor comes running and I sidestep him to catch up to Sebastian. "Wait!" I shout over the din of the cafeteria. I grip his shoulders with firm fingers. "I think—" A second ago I thought telling him he's dying was impossible, but telling him there might be a chance he can still live feels even more difficult. "Listen, there might be a way to save you."

He swivels on his heels to face me, chest still.

"Our project can save lives. Maybe this is all connected. Maybe it can save *your* life." *Please* let it all be connected.

Sebastian's fists curl and he lifts his chin. "Let's go talk to Kimmel, then. Right now."

I grab his hand, lacing my fingers through his, and tug him toward the door. At the exit, I swipe two bathroom passes. "Do you want to see the memory?"

"Um." Sebastian pulls at his collar. "I want it back, but . . . I also don't want to know." He sucks in a deep breath. "On second thought, yes, please give it to me. The more knowledge we have, the better armed we are."

While we head to Kimmel's office, I transfer the memory into his account using HiveMind. As it plays in his mind, he lets out little squeals of horror, and at one point, he stops short and buries his head in his hands. When the memory finishes, his steps are firmer, his grip stronger. He marches with determination toward Kimmel's room.

He's teaching a class, but I don't care. I swing open the door and step inside. Every eye turns toward us, and when Mr. Kimmel sees us, he drops his pen.

"We need to talk to you." I try to keep my voice steady, urgent, and not let it crack the way it did with Sebastian. "It's an emergency."

Mr. Kimmel's jaw clenches when murmurs increase. "Everyone, please continue working on your thesis projects. Make it count. Only two days left."

My heels click on the linoleum floor, ensuring every head volleys to watch us. I tug the shirt from last night higher up my chest, but that makes it rise above my waistband. My cardigan swings open.

Kimmel leans against the back wall, crossing his arms and then dropping them awkwardly to his sides. It's almost as if he wants to appear casual but can't quite master it. He clears his throat. "What do you need?"

I scrub a streak of sweat from my brow and glance back at the other students, each deep in concentration on their projects. "How can our project save lives?" Each word travels over my tongue like gravel, scraping against the roof of my mouth on its way out.

He invades my personal space and drops his voice, huffing coffee-laced breath in my face. "You don't know? Arden, please don't joke about this. You *must* remember." He slams his hand down on the desk so hard everyone in the room jumps. My teeth snap together. A girl holding a beaker drops it. The glass shatters, releasing a formaldehyde smell. "Please tell me you remember."

His words hit me with the force of a gut punch, a knot of pain swelling deep inside me. Latent terror at his wild, pleading expression paralyzes me. Everyone's watching us now. Whispering.

He glances from Sebastian to me and back again.

"Shit." Kimmel's face turns white. "I must have realized my memories were being tampered with, because I wrote myself notes. I keep finding them, hidden around this room." He fumbles around his cluttered desk, lifting mounds of papers and books. "Here's what I know. Your project is called Theseus."

My neck prickles, and Sebastian and I exchange glances. I think back to the notebook I found at the Hypnotist's, which listed out a few title options for our project, Theseus included.

Kimmel swipes a small stack of Post-it notes from the center of a pile. He takes two heaving breaths that make his shoulder blades roll and shoves the stack at me as if handing it over relieves him of a heavy burden. His print handwriting, usually reserved for marking grades, covers the squares. Each one contains a single sentence.

All traces of Varga and Cuomo's project are being deleted from everyone's minds as I write this.

You must convince Varga and Cuomo to complete Theseus BEFORE the press conference.

If Theseus isn't in full working order by Saturday, he will die. That death will be the first death of thousands, maybe millions of people.

My blood turns to ice in my veins and I shudder.

Sebastian massages the stubble on his jaw. "*He* will die. That's me, right?"

Mr. Kimmel nods. Then shakes his head. Then nods again while raking a hand over his bald scalp. "I wish I—" He pauses, his face squishing in anguish. A few seconds pass without him moving a single muscle. But then he comes to and shakes his head out of his daze. He squints at me, confused. "Arden? Sebastian? Why are you at my desk?"

My pulse beats in the base of my throat as I stumble a step away from him, until the edge of the teacher's desk digs into my lower back. "Did you just forget what we were talking about?"

"No, of course not," he says too fast, too rushed, too obviously lying. "But can you please repeat what you just said? I couldn't hear you."

I blink at him, checking to see if his eyes show any sign of recognition. The gossip echoing around the room increases to a crescendo, only drowned out by the sound of pulsing in my ears. It's no use. He's forgotten this moment yet again and it's only a matter of time before I do too.

"Come on." I grab Sebastian's hand, and we stumble into the hallway, clutching the Post-it notes in a tight fist. I yank open the first door I can find—the girls' bathroom—and tug him inside, twisting the lock on the door to prevent anyone else from entering. We both read the Post-it notes again and I nearly vomit a second time. I shove the pieces of paper into my bra, where they will stay safe.

"I'm dying," Sebastian says. "Oh God."

Theseus. Millions of deaths. *Sebastian.* My body sags from the burden of this new information.

I start to sob, my shoulders shaking, and when I glance over, I realize Sebastian's crying too. He wraps his arms around me and buries his head in the crook of my neck. I'm not sure if he's comforting me or I'm comforting him, but either way, I settle into him, breathing him in, and let myself fall apart while there's someone here to hold me upright.

Sebastian might die because of me.

And I have no way to stop it.

0011000100111001

Arden: How did it go?

My knee bobs up and down as I sit in my second-to-last-period class, anxiously waiting for Sebastian to finish at the doctor's. We need answers. Or at least a prescription slip scrawled in chicken scratch. Hell, I'd even settle for an insurance receipt. Anything that might help us figure out how to save Sebastian.

Sebastian: Weird. I know every word in pretty
much every language and "weird"
is the one that sums it up best.

Arden: That's a tall order. Weirder than
everything else that happened in the
last two days?

Sebastian: This one takes the cake. I'm on my
way back to school. Meet you at
your locker before sixth period?
It'll be easier to explain in person.

Arden: You're killing me.

My eyes widen and I snap my hands back from my phone after just realizing what I wrote. Sebastian is actually dying and here I am joking about it.

Arden: Sorry, I didn't mean it like that.

He doesn't respond and the silence makes me want to vomit. I alternate between staring at my phone, willing those three little dots to appear, indicating he's texting, and checking HiveMind against my newly created backups.

When the bell rings, I practically leap out of my seat and run through the hallway as fast as I can before it starts to fill up. I manage to get there before him and retrieve the eye from my locker since I had completely forgotten it during lunch thanks to my anxiety about delivering the news. Thankfully, Zoey stowed it away safely for me. I try my best to lean against the red metal as casually as I can.

When he approaches, I mutter the least cheery "Hey" the world has ever seen.

"Hi." His face is blank, but the furtive glance he darts around at the hallway tells me everything I need to know: He needs privacy. *Real* privacy this time. I jut my chin toward the empty classroom across the hall and pull the door shut behind us.

Sunlight beams through the windows, illuminating the way he shoves his hands into his pockets. "So. Apparently, I'm cured."

I squint at him, waiting for the punch line, but nothing comes. *Cured.* As in . . . not dying? Hope twinges in my chest. "Cured of what?"

He turns away from me for a moment, sucks in a deep breath, and then says in a normal tone of voice, "Last week, my stage four inoperable brain cancer was spreading aggressively. The doctors predicted I'd deteriorate quickly from here on out and my body would start shutting down. I was supposed to be dead in less than a month, probably sooner."

One month. That matches with the timeline I'd already figured out. My tongue hangs thick and dry in my mouth. "And now you're not dying?" I repeat, trying to make sense of this.

"Yep." He steps closer to me in the already tight space, his hot breath tickling my neck. "They ran a million tests this afternoon. All traces of cancer, gone."

"That's—" I start to say but fumble on the end of the sentence.

"Impossible, I know. The doctors are stumped. Don't know how it even happened. They declared it a miracle, but my mom was talking in the car over here about some new procedure I did Monday night. She was calling everyone she knew, saying, 'It worked! It actually worked!'" He rakes his hand through his hair. "My guess is whatever this procedure was, it had side effects." He points to his brain.

I shake my head. "Yeah, but why would I be experiencing them too?" I tap my finger against my lips, thinking back to what Kimmel said about our project saving lives. "I think our project was what cured you."

"No, it wasn't ours." Sebastian leans against the desk next to me, squeezing in beside me. "It's some medical procedure called Duplicell. The thing they're showcasing at the press conference. Apparently, *I'm* debuting as the first successful prototype."

I nearly slide to the floor. "That's my brother's project."

"Well, maybe we can ask him about the side effects, then? If that's why I'm losing my memories."

I hop to my feet and wipe my sweaty palms on my jeans. "That still doesn't explain why I'm affected. And not just me. My mom and Kimmel are still losing memories too."

Sebastian purses his lips. "Any chance you guys were cured as well?"

I sway in place as my legs turn to jelly. "That leaves us with two theories. Yours: All four of us were dying. And mine: The two things aren't related and someone is deleting our memories for an entirely different reason. I like mine."

"Either way, we have a starting place now."

"Yeah. My own flesh and blood." I let out a sigh. "We should go talk to him right now."

Sebastian nods. "Exactly what I was thinking."

We ditch our last class of the day and circle the glass MVH building to get to the entrance of Varga Industries on the opposite side of the school. Puffy white clouds skid across the windows, mirroring the show in the sky. Lavender bushes line this side of the building, tinged with the faint smell of cigarette smoke.

At this time of day, the security guard at the desk lets us in with just a flick of our ID cards and our signatures scrawled on a sign-in sheet. We ride a spotless elevator with several lab coat–clad people up to the sixteenth floor. Inside Leo's office suite, the inviting scent of rose potpourri welcomes us. I stop short. Zoey sits behind the reception desk with a headset strung over her ears. After a beat, she offers a wave. "What are you two doing here? I hope it's to visit me. Yay visitors!"

I cock my head at her. "I was just going to ask you the same thing." She must have raced up here as soon as the bell rang.

"Your brother needed some extra help and I have study hall last period." She slides the headset off her ears and loops it around her neck.

I squint at her. "With answering phones?" This seems beneath Zoey. Even if she's been shuffled around to various scientists instead of working on her own project, she should be in the lab, not behind a desk.

"Oh, I'm actually just making a few calls to media outlets in prep for the press conference."

Cool puffs of air-conditioning chill my cheeks as I nod. "What can you tell me about Duplicell?"

"Not much. I haven't been too involved in the actual procedure stuff." She pats the headset. "Been mostly handling some of the business and marketing aspects for him." She beams at me. "I'm really good at charming people on the phone. And he is definitely not."

"Somehow that doesn't surprise me," I say. "By the way, I have a lot to fill you in on."

"Oh God. Don't tease me with juicy gossip when I've got a list the size of Kentucky to call." She holds up a sheet of paper that unfurls with hundreds of media phone numbers. Her eyes widen with mischief. "Tell me the highlights."

I give her an even shorter recap than the one written on my body: Kimmel's Post-it note and the gist of the Ethics Committee activity list. When Sebastian gives me a tiny shake of his head, I leave out the info about Sebastian being cured. And the part where he was dying in the first place. Zoey's face contorts in horror when I tell her the updates. "Oh man. This is getting bad. What are you going to do?"

"Talk to Leo, actually. I'll catch up with you later, okay?" We turn toward the sleek steel door indented into chic gray-and-white-striped walls. Massive abstract prints of cell data hang on either side of the door. Several uncomfortable-looking chairs with wings instead of armrests circle a table, as if Leo expects a crowd waiting for his services.

I push the swinging steel door open into the sleek lab, my messenger bag bouncing on my thigh. Leo drops the papers he's holding. They flutter to the ground and scatter. He wears his standard uniform of a white lab coat with a bow tie affixed to the collar.

Leo's jaw clenches when he sees me. "Arden! What were you thinking this morning, tricking me like that?" He turns to Sebastian. "Wait, I thought you had an appointment tomorrow?"

"I was thinking I wanted to help you. But now I'm not so sure." I bend to pick up the papers he dropped.

He crouches to my level and helps me scoop up the sheets. When I catch a glimpse, my heart breaks. They're all handwritten but crossed-out love notes to Brandon.

"What. Did. You. Do. To. Sebastian?" I enunciate each word to prevent ferocity in my voice from diluting them.

"Cured him!" He's so excited he practically bounces up and down.

"I know that part." Sebastian leans against a lab table opposite Leo, casual, the good cop to my bad cop routine. "But *what* exactly did you do?"

"Improved you in every way." Leo dances an arc around Sebastian, studying him with a weird grin stretching his lips. "Twenty-ten eyesight now, for starters."

Sebastian touches his temples. "At least that explains the lack of glasses."

I ball my hands into fists. "It doesn't explain anything at all!"

"Your hair grows faster now," Leo continues. "Sharper hearing. Keen sense of smell."

Sebastian sniffs the air as if he might notice a difference.

"You smell that?" Leo slides a beaker filled with clear liquid toward Sebastian, who pinches his nose. "That's perfluorocarbons. Humans normally perceive it as odorless!"

Sebastian glances at me in horror. "It smells like lemon. And auto grease."

I sniff too, but I only smell the permanent chemical stench lingering in the lab.

"What about my memories?" Sebastian's sneakers squeak along the scuffed white floor. We stand side by side, soldiers on the first line of defense. "They're all gone."

Color drains from Leo's face. "Is this what you and Mom were talking about last night? I thought she had it under control."

I roll my eyes at him. "I wouldn't be here if she did."

"The timing of everything's too coincidental," Sebastian says. "We think it's a side effect of your procedure." He laces his fingers with mine, sending the vital message that we're in this together. His hand keeps me grounded.

"No. No way." Leo pulls at the tips of his hair, making it stick out like a mad scientist's. "That's not possible."

I force my mind out of the gutter and back to reality. "Was Sebastian the only one you've experimented on so far?"

Leo drags his hands down his cheeks, pulling the skin taut. "Besides Dad and countless rats, yeah."

I land back on Earth with a *thud*. "You—you experimented on Dad?" Sandpaper coats my throat, making it difficult to swallow.

Leo swallows hard. "And that prototype failed."

"You mean he *died*. They *all* died."

Leo stretches out his hands. "This is not new information. What did you think my thesis project was?"

A way to cure diseases is all I remember. Obviously that wasn't all I once knew. This information has been removed from my mind too. My head pounds just thinking about the data loss.

"I need to see your HiveMind account, Bash." With force, he twists a monitor toward him so hard the display wobbles.

No way am I giving Leo's computer access. "I have it synced here." I extract my laptop from my messenger bag and prop it open, displaying the obvious truth of Sebastian's empty mind in all its glory.

Leo claps a palm over his mouth. "I don't understand. This shouldn't have happened." He backs up a few paces, and when his butt hits the opposite desk, he spins on his heels and yanks the phone off the hook. His finger stabs one of the speed-dial buttons. "Hey." His *hey* sounds anything but cheery. "Cuomo's memories are gone. They're not even in HiveMind. Did something . . . happen during the upgrade process?"

He listens for a moment, face regaining color, nodding. "That's what I thought." His chest puffs out a relieved sigh. "Okay, thanks." He hangs up but refuses to look me in the eye. "My assistant and I both triple-checked the data. Copied everything over. It's not our fault, I swear."

"It's happening to me too." I slam my laptop shut and slide it back into my bag.

"Then that settles it." He throws up his hands in a victory cheer. "It's not a side effect! It can't be." He grins. "We didn't touch you, Arden."

I arch a brow. "Then clarify the procedure for me. How do you replace the cancerous cells?"

Leo beams. "Think of it like find and replace in your word processor. Instead, we sync the body to the Duplicell software, and then the program finds the cancerous cells. After that, Teddy prints them and replaces them by connecting directly to the cell DNA." His voice is confident and rehearsed. He's delivered this line hundreds of times before.

Right. Of course. That's Teddy's entire project.

I grab a sheet of paper from a stack on the desk and quickly scrawl myself a reminder to ask Teddy how he replaces the cells. We can probably catch him after the final bell rings. Still, I need more answers from Leo first. "But how exactly does your software work?"

Leo clicks on an icon on his desktop. As he swivels the screen to face us, a video pops up on the monitor. "This will explain—" He stops talking, then turns to blink at me. "Arden?" He tilts his head toward Sebastian. "Bash?" He looks incredibly confused. "What are you guys doing here?"

My gut sinks. I know all too well what just happened. His memory of the last five minutes has been deleted.

It makes me think we were asking the right questions. Or the wrong ones, depending on your point of view.

Leo's face changes to one of excitement. "But I'm glad you're here." He nudges Sebastian on his shoulder. "How do you feel? Good, right?"

Sebastian and I both exchange glances.

My eyes flick to the video he was about to play. "Hey. Do you have any videos about the procedure? I'd love to see one."

"Yes, actually! I just got it back from production. Came out great." He squints at the screen. "Oh weird, it's already cued up." He hits play.

The video window fades from black to show patients lying in hospital beds. As we watch, Zoey pops her head in and beckons Leo's help on something. Leo holds up a finger to indicate he'll be back in a minute. My attention turns back to the screen.

Six months to live. The words fly at the screen, accompanied by fast-paced music.

Terminal. A shot of a little boy with no hair, waving good-bye to a teddy bear.

Inoperable. A patient in tears as a stone-faced doctor points to a CT scan.

No hope left. Shots of graves, each with patients who died way before their prime.

Until now. A burst of sunlight fills the screen. Leo walks out of it. He's wearing a suit and bow tie that look utterly ridiculous on the guy who always wore T-shirts and shorts to school, even in the winter. "A year ago my father was dying of pancreatic cancer."

My airways constrict, tightening like a drawstring pulled taut. I can't watch this part. I can't.

I back away from the video and bite back a sob. Sebastian slides an arm around my shoulder, pulling me close. My whole body stays tense while Leo relays the details of Dad's disease and deterioration. Every word he says is like a knife plunged into my heart, piercing those memories I still have but don't *want* to remember. Dad first telling us about his diagnosis. The scare when he collapsed out of nowhere in the middle of a family fun trip to the beach. The wires and machines connected to every part of his body. Endless waiting rooms where the good news never came.

It's only when Leo starts speaking again in the video that I relax in Sebastian's embrace.

"I couldn't let anyone else I loved die like that. So I created a way to cure diseases. Not just that, I offer enhancements." The video shuffles through the list that Leo mentioned earlier.

"Here's how it works," Video Leo says. Both Sebastian and I lean into the monitor.

An animation pops up showing a single cell. Leo's voice narrates. "*A tumor is made up of several different cells.*"

Several more cells fly onto the screen and join the first one, linking up together. "*Each cell contains DNA. The DNA of the tumor is slightly different from what used to be there before the tumor grew.*"

A strand of DNA spins around on-screen. One of the links in the DNA severs like a rope chopped in half. "*Most scientists try to cut out the tumor with surgery. But we repair the cell on a molecular level. No surgery required.*"

The animation switches back to the single cell, this time with a dark spot in the center. *"We duplicate each cancerous cell in our lab."* The cell multiplies, forming two spinning versions.

"We then repair the broken DNA on a cell-by-cell basis, altering the molecular data to eradicate the disease." The cell on the right, the duplicated one, turns clear again, no dark spot.

"Then through a simple noninvasive procedure using bio software, we replace the diseased cells with the cancer-free ones." The video shows an outline of a human body with one cell flying out while a new cell whizzes into the vacated spot.

"We don't cut it out, we change it on a molecular level so it never returns." The video shows smiling, happy people dancing waltzes, hugging teddy bears, and throwing fishing lines into sunlit rivers before the screen goes to black.

Sebastian stares at the monitor for another moment before turning to me. "Nothing about the side effects."

I sigh. "Or the actual procedure."

"I wish we knew why I agreed to the cure. And what it has to do with our own project." He taps his fingers on the desk. "Maybe we can try to get another memory and find out?"

I shake my head. "It's too risky. I've already been caught down there once. The Ethics Committee thinks *I'm* the one behind this."

He shrugs. "If they're already onto you, then it doesn't matter if you're caught again."

He's right. We have to do this now. I grab the trusty eye from the table, but there's a weird sound like a maraca shaking. I lift the lid to check and I gasp at the sight of a shriveled mass. An inch of melted ice water covers the bottom of the container, glittering with dissolved salt. The eye is useless now; the retina can't be scanned.

This is sabotage.

I rush out the doors to where Zoey and Leo are huddling over a list on her computer. I thrust the lunch box toward her. "Did you see anyone tamper with this? Anyone at all?"

Her eyes widen. "No! I guarded it with my life before I put it in your locker. Why? What happened to it?"

I squeeze my eyes shut, my gut twisting. Whoever is monitoring me knew I left the eye unattended with Zoey and swooped in as soon as she stowed the eye in my locker. The locker has an electronic lock on it, so if the hacker can fuck with HiveMind, they can most certainly break into my locker as well. Hell, they probably knew my locker combination just from watching me.

Someone wants to keep me out of that basement.

0011001000110000

The fact that the hacker's going out of their way to stop me from going into the basement makes me desperate to get in. Even though the hacker destroyed my copy of the eye, we still have Sebastian's. He had his with him the whole time.

Just as we round the corner to the basement entrance, I plow into someone else. I stumble backward, blinking in a daze. A box crashes to the floor, the contents spilling out onto the scuffed linoleum. Two bobblehead replicas of Leo and Brandon. A mug with the words, I'M DRINKING F5. IT'S SO REFRESHING!, now shattered into three large pieces. A fern, its leaves bent, soil spread in a streak on the floor. Wires and chargers. An empty ID card case. A sweater. And a few other random gadgets.

Brandon dives for the bobbleheads and cradles them in his arms. A burly security guard stands by the basement door, arms crossed. Another hovers over Brandon, kicking his possessions toward him.

A crowd forms a half-moon audience around the chaos. The whispers drown out Brandon's sniffles.

"What's going on?" I crouch down beside Brandon and hand him the plant, scooping some of the stray soil back into it. Sebastian bends to gather the pieces of the broken mug.

Redness rims Brandon's eyes and cheeks. "I was fired."

His words send a cold, crackling sensation down my spine. "Fired? Because of me?"

"Because of all the breaches in security over the last two days. Both in HiveMind and the basement itself."

Shit. So because of me. I'm responsible for half of that. "I'll talk to my mom. I'll—"

Brandon shakes his head. "It was the Ethics Committee's decision. They're moving the HiveMind servers and IT equipment to an off-site data center. They don't trust me to run it." He lowers his voice. "They don't need me anymore."

His words pin me in place, turning my veins to ice. I clamp a shaky palm over my mouth. If the servers and IT monitoring consoles move to an unknown location, I won't have any way to access them. I won't be able to retrieve any more memories. I won't be able to stop the hacker.

A jolt of worry ricochets through my bones. Today might be my last chance to retrieve another memory.

Two men in suits walk past us. The security guard nods at them and lets them into the basement, where they descend downstairs.

But I need to get into the IT room, and Brandon's eye is now worthless given the fact that he's been fired. We still have my mom's eye stored at Sebastian's house, but that doesn't change the fact that I can't get past a burly security guard. Hacking skills don't work on guys who are five times my size. There are no other entrances to the basement, but there are windows.

I straighten. That's it! I'm small enough to squeeze through the window of the basement. I just need a way to bypass the alarms and ensure the IT room is empty since two people recently headed downstairs. And I know just how to do it. I grab Sebastian's hand and lead him through the empty hallway.

"Where are we going?" He amps his pace, struggling to keep up.

"Chemistry lab." We fly down another hallway. "Quick, what two chemicals when mixed together will create a ton of smoke?"

He only needs a second to think before the Google index in his brain picks out the info. "Ammonium and hydrochloric acid." He purses his lips. "There's also hydrogen peroxide and potassium permanganate."

"Which will make more smoke?" After peering in to confirm it's empty, I push open the door to one of the many chemistry labs here at school.

"The first makes a small amount of consistent smoke. The second produces a ton in a short time."

"Second it is." I open the long white cabinets along the wall and trace my finger over the shelves until I find a bottle of each. Chemistry compounds aren't locked down in this school. No one abuses them. Until now, anyway.

"I'm going to take a shot in the dark here, but it seems like whatever you're planning to do is not good news?"

I shove them into my messenger bag along with a beaker and a paper face mask from the supply closet. "Oh, it's great news. For us." Before we exit, I grab the ax dangling beside the fire extinguisher. "Not so good news for the Ethics Committee." I look him square in the eyes. "We're getting into that basement."

"Remind me not to get on your bad side." He plucks two more chemicals plus an empty aerosol spray can. "Plan B," he says. "Phenyl chloride dissolved in hydrocarbon solvents makes pepper spray."

"I love a guy who knows his chemical weapons."

We head around the side of the school, gritting our teeth against the biting wind. I squeeze behind the lavender bush and ignore the way the branches scrape at my jeans. Sebastian twists his body to avoid getting stabbed. There's only a tight space between the bush and the side of the building, and I find myself pressed against him, the wall digging into my back.

"Hi." He grins. Fluffy white clouds float in the sky behind his head.

"Hi," I whisper, fighting back my own smile. My heart amps at our proximity, at the adorable way he's staring down at me. Oh man, I know we're in a rush here, but damn it, I want to kiss his face off right now.

His voice is sultry. "I'm inclined to suggest we forget about getting back any more memories and stay like this instead."

"I like the way you think. But perhaps we rain-check this until *after* we commit a felony?" As much as it pains me to get out of his embrace, I sidestep away from him and crouch down. My knees sink into the soft dirt just in front of the small basement window. It's only about a foot high and covered with sprawling ivy. I settle my laptop onto my knees. "Do me a favor and set up everything. Don't mix the smoke yet."

He takes the ax out of my bag and holds it an arm's length away. "What are you going to do with this?"

I grin. "Cause some chaos."

Sebastian starts by mixing up the homemade pepper spray into the aerosol can. My fingers tap away on the keys. There are some places that are difficult to hack into, like the HiveMind servers, and some that are as easy as breathing, like the town electric company. I connect a device called a "sniffer" to my laptop that will allow me to analyze network traffic, detect problems, and capture the signal data sent via the electrical lines. If I can latch onto the signal from the electrical lines, I can follow it to the main source: the electric company itself. It takes one minute and twenty-two seconds to bypass their firewalls and seize control of the town's power grids. A record. I set up my command prompt to jam the signal to all power lines within two hundred feet of Varga Industries.

Before I hit *enter*, I get out my phone and bang out a text to Zoey.

> **Arden:** I know you're at Leo's, but any chance you're not busy?

Her reply is instant.

> **Zoey:** Depends on why you want to know?

> **Arden:** Do me a favor and hang out by the basement door. Text me if you see anyone come out. If it gets too smoky, leave.

> **Zoey:** Oooh this sounds like a covert mission. Consider me your partner in crime.

I grab the face mask and secure it over my ears. I hope it will buy me enough time to get control of one of the IT computers before I pass out. The small SSD drive fits beneath my waistband, snug beside the aerosol can that Sebastian gave me. When I speak, my voice sounds muffled. "Okay, on my signal, I need you to mix the chemicals together and pour them into the basement. Then take my computer and get the hell away from here. Mix with the crowd if you can. Meet me at my car in five minutes."

Sebastian unscrews the two lids on the chemical bottles. A medicinal smell pierces the air. "What crowd? What signal?"

"You'll know it." I raise my finger high in the air and then zoom it downward onto my laptop. The *enter* key depresses, and the command whooshes away, disrupting electronics everywhere, including the alarm system rigged to this very window. I lean back as far as I can to see the lights glowing in the glass windows snuff out, one by one. The traffic light at the end of the parking lot suddenly goes dim. Honks ring out.

It won't take long for the power company to fix it. Five minutes tops. Which means we have to work fast now.

"Stand back." I lift the heavy ax with both hands and hoist it over my shoulder. This window is at the opposite end of the basement from the IT and server rooms. Hopefully far enough away to prevent anyone inside either room from hearing what I'm about to do. Gritting my teeth, I whack it in a swift arc into the basement window. Glass shatters with harmonic feedback. I run the ax along the edges, trying to clear out any sharp pieces.

I turn to Sebastian and blink. "That was the signal."

He shakes his head out of a daze. "Sorry, I—that was awesome."

"Now it's your turn to be awesome."

He gives me an incredulous look as he dumps both liquid chemicals into the beaker. Smoke instantly forms, making him cough. He throws it into the basement, guessing my intentions. A faint shatter of glass echoes, followed by a scream as the smoke travels toward the IT room.

He bites his lip. "Not sure that counts as awesome."

I pat his arm. "In my book, it does."

I take a deep breath and twist my body, sliding my legs through the broken window while my torso grazes the muddy ground. A rogue shard of glass slices my jeans and pricks my thigh. I gasp but grit my teeth against the pain throbbing in my leg. I keep sliding, sucking in my stomach to avoid slicing that as well. I duck my head to clear it, my hands gripping smooth areas along the window's edge.

I squeeze my eyes shut, counting to three to work up the courage to drop. Glass shards wait below me in the utter darkness. I let go, bracing for impact. My feet land so hard aftershocks ripple up to my knees. One foot starts to slide on a piece of glass, but I stretch out my hands to catch my balance. My palm presses against the wall until my feet remain steady.

Thick smoke clogs the airways, and jarring blackness covers my vision. My lungs compress as if all the wind has been knocked out of me. A dank murkiness settles over the hallway like a film, as if old water collects in the pipes and never leaves. I paw at the wall to guide my way, my feet moving faster than my brain wants them to. My palms trace over cold concrete until my fingers touch the edge of a door.

I pause for a moment, holding my breath, listening for any sounds of stragglers inside, like those two men I saw come down here a few minutes ago. There's an itch at the back of my throat from the heavy smoke, and my eyes start to water. I can't stall much longer. I launch myself into the room, crying out when my hip slams into the edge of a table. I fumble in the dark for the first IT console, but my fingers only trace dust. I get out my phone and shine the flashlight app, illuminating mostly smoke and barely anything else. Nearly every IT console has already been moved out of this room. Except one. Right in the back.

I fly toward it as my eyes tear, obscuring my vision even more. Forced to close my eyes, I fumble against the side of the console until I find the USB drive. I struggle to connect the SSD into the admin console and let out a wheezing breath that dissolves into a cough. My fingers trace along the chains that keep it secured to this room. With the power out, now would be my only chance to steal this thing, but pepper spray won't cut through steel. I armed myself with the wrong tools for grand larceny.

I can't stay here and wait for the power to turn back on and my device to grant me access. Not when I can't breathe.

I run out of the room and toward the basement door, my lungs burning for breath as I take the stairs two at a time. A headache brews behind my eyes, and my mind starts to feel fuzzy from the lack of oxygen. Sweat beads on my forehead. My palm slides off the knob on the first try, and it takes all my remaining energy to fling the door open.

There's a crowd running straight toward the exit, all of them panicked, a teacher frantically shouting for everyone to get out. I rip off my face mask as my legs pump in league with the fleeing crowd. Once outside, I keep running with everyone else toward the parking lot, gulping glorious fresh air.

It's only when I reach my car and spot Sebastian's horrified face that I notice my leg is covered in blood. The gash throbs with dull pain, but I have more important things to worry about. I get inside the car so no one will see me in this state. I glance down at my phone, and the tension eases from my shoulders.

A text from Zoey from two minutes ago. In my panic, I didn't even feel the vibration.

> **Zoey:** About ten guys in suits ran out of there coughing.

> **Arden:** Thanks. You rock! Please get out of there safely too.

Her reply is immediate.

> **Zoey:** I'm good. Don't worry about me!

"Well," Sebastian says. "That wasn't even the craziest thing to happen today."

"It's not over yet." I tie my cardigan around my thigh to sop up the blood. The traffic light comes to life, blinking red and green, red and green. Outside the car, students stand in the parking lot, their hands rubbing their arms, waiting for the signal to get back inside. I flinch from the unexpected blast of air-conditioning against my sweaty skin. "Ready for another visit to the past?"

I open my laptop. When the SSD drive comes to life, I take a moment to hack into the security cameras and delete all evidence that I was the one to cause the chaos. Then I hack into the admin console like before and let out a breath when the device still pings green, still connected. I click on another encrypted memory at random, but as soon as I do, my mouse moves without my permission and zooms across the screen, away from the selected memory. My pulse amps. Against my will, my cursor closes HiveMind and instead opens the notepad app on my computer. Each letter pops onto my screen one by one: S-T-A-Y A-W-A-Y.

Holy shit.

Someone is hacking *me*.

0011001000110001

I have to stop this hacker from stopping *me*.

My pulse pounds as I rip the USB backups out of my computer to keep them safe. Tension eases from my shoulders. If they're not connected, the hacker can't delete all the files on them. But that won't stop them from gaining access to the rest of my computer. Despite my firewalls, a VPN, and other security measures I recently fortified, they clearly found another entry point.

I straighten and forcibly tug my mouse to the corner so hard I elbow Sebastian in the ribs in the process. But the mouse follows my commands before flying to the opposite end of my screen. If I work fast, I can control the mouse in small spurts.

Sebastian leans over, a wrinkle bridging his eyebrows. "What's going on?"

"Someone's onto us. They're hacking me right now." But two can play at that game. I set up an XSS channel using an AJAX application to establish a two-way connection between my computer and theirs. When their IP address shows up in the choices, I squint for a moment, confused. It looks familiar, but probably because it's coming from inside the school. "Quick, write this number down!"

Sebastian hastily scrawls *555.167.111.215* on the inside of his palm.

Adrenaline pumps through my veins. With the connection

established, I can issue commands onto their computer using the XSS Tunnel. I immediately turn on my microphone and blast the volume on their computer. "No, *you* stay away!"

"Yeah!" Sebastian adds like an echo.

I fist-pump the air at finally outsmarting them, if only for a second. I need to hit them with a second attack while they're still distracted by the first. Using the XXS Tunnel, I write a quick command to autoplay the Rick Astley video for "Never Gonna Give You Up." The video fills their entire screen, blasting the classic line of song. I construct the loop so another version of the video pops open right after Rick finishes singing the first line, creating a chorus of round robin melodies the way kids used to sing "Row, Row, Row Your Boat."

Sebastian chuckles. "Really? You Rick Rolled them?"

I shrug. "I had to think fast."

It won't keep them at bay for long, but hopefully it's enough for me to—

Every folder and file stored on my hard drive starts opening at the same time, cascading in diagonal rows across the screen. They obscure my HiveMind app, making it impossible to get to, and if I can't access that, I can't retrieve any more memories. Cold panic makes my spine straighten. Shit shit shit.

I push a tangled strand of sweaty hair behind my ear and take a deep breath. I have to act fast. Using the toolbar, I open my command prompt and quickly click on it before it becomes obscured by all the windows opening on top of it. I'm not sure I was fast enough since I can't see what I'm typing with the hundreds of windows opening to cover my screen, so I enter the instructions slowly, mouthing each one to ensure I don't mess up. The instructions will close all programs at once. My pulse pounds and I brace myself. When I hit *enter*, the windows disappear faster than they started.

Before I have a chance to launch another attack, the hacker rotates my screen, rendering all applications and text upside down. Hot rage boils through me. When I try to readjust it, an error message pops up. I jump at the little ding and curse under my breath. It takes a little bit of back-end coding done upside down and backward to eliminate the error messages and return my screen to the correct view. Thankfully, I've gotten used to things going backward lately.

"I'm done being nice. Time to bring out the big guns." I seize control of their mouse and easily navigate to their command prompt now that they reset the screen display settings on their own monitor. In the command prompt, I type *echo shutdown-s > "Owned.bat"* and copy the Owned.bat file I once created for programming class onto their computer. Immediately, their computer shuts down. It'll create a loop, continually shutting down as soon as it restarts. I have no doubt they'll find a way to stop it within minutes. I need to block their access to my computer before that happens. Clearly this asshole found another entry point into my system, probably via a zero-day exploit.

But that also means I have an entry point direct to them. Every time their computer restarts, the two-way connection reestablishes.

If I allow the connection to stay open, I might be able to write a script that will root out their location down to a precise device. If I type fast, I can whip this up in six minutes, maybe five, and execute it in less than a second the next time their computer connects.

My heart thumps fast. The hacker probably only needs five minutes to prevent the continual restarts of their computer.

A vibration in both our phones makes me jump, and Sebastian and I both scramble to read the alert. My head's still pounding from hack battle, so I need to read the email my mother sent twice to truly understand the severity.

Dear Varga Staff and Students,
Due to an incident under investigation, we insist that
you vacate the premises immediately. All meetings
and after-school activities are canceled for the rest of
the day. We have the utmost concern for the safety of
our staff and students. If anyone has any information
about the events that transpired in the basement
of the building, please call me directly. Otherwise,
we look forward to seeing you again tomorrow and
beginning the adversarial review of student projects
on Friday. Please use the button below to check in so
we can mark you as safe.

My eyes flash on the words *under investigation*. The smoke should clear any minute now, and people will be roaming the basement, taking notes, looking at everything left behind closely. My SSD drive won't stay hidden much longer and this might be my last chance to retrieve another memory before the servers move to who knows where.

I bite my lip and look at Sebastian. "I can either try to retrieve another memory before we're shut out forever or I can use the next few minutes to try to find the hacker's location. I have enough time for the first option, the second is a gamble." Even as I say the words, I know there's really only one option.

His eyes spark in the sunlight. "The first, then. It's the only guarantee."

I nod as a horrible weight forms in my stomach. My pulse pounds so fast it feels like the car is spinning out of control.

While I still have access to the admin controls of HiveMind, I choose a file at random from the Favorites list and decrypt it. I copy the file into both of our HiveMind accounts. I hope it's a good one.

Before the memory starts, I quickly turn off Wi-Fi and Bluetooth to prevent the hacker from breaking into my shit again. I need time to write a MySQL script that will strengthen my firewall by blocking static packet filters originating from the IP address Sebastian wrote down. It'll take me a good half hour to write this, but as long as my computer stays off-line, it's safe from subsequent attacks until I can install the security updates.

Just in case, I lift my shirt and write out an instruction to myself on my stomach:

Hacker found an entry point into your computer. Need to strengthen security firewall via a MySQL script.

Blackness wipes out my vision as I write the last letter, but unlike the previous memories, no new scene glitches in. Never-ending darkness remains while sounds and sensations return. A breath. Something wet in my mouth. The wetness subsides and a voice asks, [Should I get—?] It takes me a moment to connect the clues to the source: Bash's tongue swirls against mine. He tastes like almonds. My eyes remain closed, which accounts for the expanse of black. His body presses against mine, and my arms wrap around his torso to pull him closer, closer, closer.

Warm tingles sweep through my chest as the kiss slows down, going from hot and heavy to sweet and featherlight. I cup the back of his neck and yank him away from my lips. My arms slide downward, my fingers drawing tenuous symbols in the folds of his shirt. [I'd rather skip to what happens after dinner anyway,] I say, backward like all the other memories.

We break out of our embrace but stay close, him hovering over me. Electronics hum in a constant drone, but a faint folksy rock song croons from the tinny speaker of an iPhone nearby. Black lab tables and computer monitors surround us along with a few pieces of complicated electronic equip-

ment on rolling carts. Pinprick stars outside indicate we're at school way past the final bell.

[I was supposed to take you to dinner tonight,] he says, his voice dulcet. He picks up my hand, grinning at me. Bash traces his lips along the bare skin of my forearm, making every nerve ending in my body buzz. When he reaches my wrist, he drags down my sleeves and brings my hand to his mouth, dropping a delicate kiss on each of my knuckles. My scar's there, as angry as ever. He drops my arm and backs up a few steps, the animalistic look in his eyes dulling to one of stress.

[I won't like it, but you'll always have my forgiveness and support.] The words seem to be hard for me to say, evidenced by how slowly I force them out.

Scabs mar his arm from all his injections. [Okay. I'll get the process started. But . . . If I choose not to go through with it, would you forgive me?]

[No. You can't give up like this. Just please, do the scan. Get everything ready for the cell transfer procedure while we figure out how to get our damn project working. This way, you'll have more time to think about it. You'll have a choice.]

Tears glisten in his eyes. [I'm scared. Scared I won't be the same after. Scared I won't be me.] He sucks in a deep breath, chest puffing out. [What if . . . What if I don't want to go through with it?]

[No more classes. No more wasting time,] I say. [We'll try harder.]

[The doctors, my mom, they all want me on bed rest. Deathbed rest.] He swallows loud enough for me to hear the gulp despite the whirs of computer fans. [My white blood cell numbers are diminishing and these meds aren't going to keep my kidneys functioning for much longer. I thought I had three months left, but it's looking more like weeks.] His cheekbones jut from his gaunt face, and his entire body sags in a hunched-over, defeated way. [We can't stop. Not now. My latest lab tests—]

[Let's stop here. We need to think this over.]

Purple crescent moons hang below his bloodshot eyes. [It has to work. I can't lose you. I can't lose me.]

[You really think that will work?] I straighten on my stool.

He snaps his fingers. [That's it. That's what we're missing.] He backs away from me, fist-pumping the air. [Then reverse it during the transfer so it comes in the order of most vivid to least!]

[Right, and we need to quantize the time code in which the memories were formed. Turn them into a variable we can alter.]

[Memories can be quantized and converted into ones and zeroes, then accessed.] He lies down on a recliner chair. [To transfer an entire personality, theoretically, you would have to transfer all memories at once.] He sticks several wires connected to discs onto his forehead, his heart, and his arms, like an EEG machine in a science fiction novel. [Time moves in a chronological direction, but our brains think in nonlinear patterns. Our most recent memories are clearest.]

[Let's go over everything we've done so far to see if it sparks anything. You start. Stream-of-consciousness-style. Go!] I grab my laptop from a nearby counter and balance it on my thighs. [Bash, don't get upset. You still have three months.]

He sighs, shaking his head. [As far as I can tell, the data classification and signal processing are working fine, but it's still wrong! We can still only transfer one memory at a time!]

On my laptop, I move a single encrypted file to another folder. The interface looks similar to the encrypted area of HiveMind I've been hacking into even though it's just crude Linux commands. The date in the upper right-hand corner of the screen announces this moment took place back in February, on Valentine's Day. I'm wearing a red sweater to commemorate the occasion. [I closed the infinite loop. Let me try a transfer.] I navigate back to the mainframe. [How about now?] I stare at object-oriented code and change a few details—adding another If, Else clause and another algorithm to the iteration.

Bash's glasses fog up from sweat and he loosens the red tie he wears over his T-shirt. [Didn't work.]

The memory ends. Reality fades in and Sebastian and I look at each other. I blink against the bright sun streaming through the car windshield, my eyes still adjusted to the memory of the darkening sky. Air-conditioning blasts cold against a spot on my neck.

Piecing it together in the right order, I adjusted code on the computer and attempted something that failed. Bash got upset because he was running out of time, only three months left. That's when I suggested we hash things out stream-of-consciousness-style. He started rattling off the fact that more recent memories are clearest while I supplied the knowledge that we're trying to turn the time codes into a variable we can alter. Somehow that gave Bash the epiphany that we need to reverse the memories during transfer in order to get our project working. But Bash worried we wouldn't get it fully working in time and was second-guessing his decision to go through with Leo's procedure. I encouraged him to just get the process started. Then we made out.

Holy shit. Our project had to do with reversing memories. That must be why these are playing backward when I retrieve them.

"So our project clearly involves reversing memories in an attempt to transfer an entire personality," I say, "but I still don't understand what it's supposed to do. I mean, HiveMind already exists and it can transfer memories."

Unless . . . that's the entire point of our project. My dad only figured out a way to store memories and users were only able to access their own accounts. I must have found a way around that by developing a new method for transferring not just a single memory at a time but a complete personality, more vivid and robust than the normal way of rewatching something in HiveMind.

"That's the part you focused on?" His eyes zoom to my lips. "Because I'm stuck on the first part of that memory."

"Oh. Yes. That." My cheeks combust with heat. *His body on top of mine. Wrapped around each other. Him asking, "Should I get—?"* Get what, a condom? It certainly seems like we might have gone farther than casual surface-level grazing.

"About *that*." Sebastian leans across the car, eyes meeting mine with a questioning gaze. He presses his lips against mine, hard at first, like he's competing against his former self in an aggressive race. After a moment the kiss softens to a sweet flutter. His soft lips tease me with a gentle kiss, brushing against my mouth in a timid way, like he doesn't know how and he's finding his way. The stubble on his chin scratches my cheek in a way that's so purely real. Because I am here, in this moment and able to act, not a prisoner in the past. To prove it, I tease his soft lips open and deepen the kiss.

This is all I have now. Here, now, *Sebastian*. With the servers moving, I can't retrieve another memory. It's too risky to try to log on right now, before I've had a chance to strengthen the firewalls and keep the hacker away from my personal computer.

The two of us are on our own now.

The kiss breaks and I pull his head to my shoulder. He nuzzles into the crook of my neck. "These memories are getting harder and harder to process. I don't like seeing myself like that, so frail, so broken. I'm starting to worry we're going to retrieve something we were better off not remembering." His arms cradle me, and we sit there for a moment, both of us tethered to the only thing we can trust now, two people who have offered only the absolute truth to each other, as we know it anyway. "I'm starting to think maybe I don't *want* my memories back."

"Maybe we can choose." I pull back and he glances up at me. "We're learning more and more each day. Maybe we'll find a way to decrypt the memories first, before transferring, and you can decide what to keep." I swallow hard. "And what to get rid of forever."

He jerks out of my arms, squinting at me. "Why would I do that?" He backs away so fast his shoulders hit the car door. "I lost *all* my memories, Arden. Why would I choose not to relive some?"

I reel back, pulse quickening. "Sebastian." My voice is a whisper. "What do you remember about the last few minutes?"

He presses the heel of his palm to his forehead. "Leo's office." He volleys his head from side to side. "Wait. How did we get in the car? What happened after we left Leo's?"

I don't need HiveMind to confirm the worst: He doesn't remember the chemistry lab, the retrieved memory, the hacker going track pad to track pad with me, our *kiss*.

The sun shines through the car windows, but my mind is full of dark gray clouds. So far we've lost the same memories. It's only a matter of time before this moment gets deleted for me too.

I have to risk it. I have to get back online even though I haven't spruced up my computer's security. I have to save the last twenty minutes before they're gone forever.

My fingers tremble as I stare at the list of memories. I can only save them one at a time and I have to choose which is more important. The retrieved memory. The chemistry lab. The hack battle. The smoke-filled basement adventure. The kiss.

My tongue is thick and heavy in my mouth. How do I even choose? The teenage part of me wants to save the kiss, but the practical part of me knows that's the lowest priority. With white knuckles, I drag the retrieved memory onto the backup. I need that one the most. While that copies, I roll up my shirt and start scrawling on my stomach as fast as I can to try to preserve everything else that just happened, but even as I'm writing, I know I'm already forgetting something. Memory. Chemistry lab. Hack battle.

What else happened?

My gut squeezes with an unsettling feeling like when you can't remember why you opened the fridge but know you needed something. I'll never know what I've already forgotten and I'm realizing now I won't ever be fast enough to save it all.

0011001000110010

As the parking lot empties out, we linger in the car, where it's safe. I turn to Sebastian. "We should write more information down. Before we lose it."

He pulls his shirt over his head while some guy walks by and raises his eyebrows a few times in succession.

We capture the new information gleaned today on the ridges and contours of each other's bodies. His pen feels amazing as it sweeps across my skin. Tingles follow in the wake of his touch. I let out a breath when we both finish capturing all the vital information we want to save:

Sebastian was hesitant about going through with Leo's procedure, but I convinced him to. Our project has something to do with reversing memories and the Ethics Committee report indicated we once presented a schematic design for a personality transfer.

All the servers are being moved to an off-site location. Brandon was fired. The hacker was able to bypass the security upgrades I added to my personal laptop yesterday.

Talk to Teddy about how he transfers the cancer-free cells.

There's a strong chance that reinforcing the firewalls on my computer will only be a temporary solution, but I have no other option except staying off-line forever, and I can't do that. I need to be online to make more backups and try to stop the hacker.

Sebastian keeps me company in the car while I write the script to spruce up my computer's security and keep the hacker out for a few hours. Hopefully. Even though I know the SSD drive must be unplugged by now, it still feels like a punch in my gut when I see the connection's lost. I try to tamp down my panic at being shut out from retrieving any other memories and focus on the things I can control. I spend time making new backups to ensure everything currently stored in our minds stays there. When I've protected us in every way I can, the tightness in my chest subsides.

We stop at Target, and Sebastian runs in to buy me first aid supplies and new clothes since my jeans are sliced all the way up to my thigh and my cardigan's ruined, which means the writing on my arms is completely exposed. He covers his eyes while I change in the back seat, and I smile at the fact that he still wants to be a gentleman, despite all we've exposed to each other: our bare backs, deepest secrets, darkest memories.

I drop him off at home, but we agree to meet up tonight and shower only when it's safe with the other in the next room. Only when we can take photos of the transient words before we wash them off and then rewrite those same words onto each other's damp, bare skin. I write myself a reminder on my palm so I won't forget this time.

By the time I finally pull into my driveway, the sun streaks pinks and oranges across the sky. My stomach lurches at the sight of my mother's car. She's never home this time of day and definitely shouldn't be home today, especially not after the stunt I pulled in the basement. My pulse buzzes. She's caught me. That must be why she's home early. She's caught me and I'm going to get expelled and there will be no way to save my memories or stop the hacker from deleting them all, just like they did to Sebastian.

I shift the car into reverse, preparing to back out of the driveway and get out of this the coward's way: by avoiding confrontation. But my hand stills. Maybe there's another reason she came home. Maybe she finally believes me. Maybe she has concrete information to share with me.

Maybe she finally wants to help me.

That thought alone weakens my resolve, my whole body itching with the desire for her to be on my side in all this.

My hesitation costs me my chance. The front door swings open, and she marches toward the car, holding up her palm like a traffic cop. My fingers twitch. My foot lets up on the brake, and the car starts to slide backward down the driveway.

"Arden! Arden, please! It's important. You're not in trouble!" Her words pierce through my closed windows.

My hands tremble, but I shift the car into park, deciding to risk hearing her out. My legs are jelly when I step out of the car, and the dire look on her face does nothing to assuage my fears. She pivots on her heels, not saying a word, and takes the front steps two at a time as if she's in a great rush. Despite the knot in my chest, I push back my shoulders and follow her inside, preparing my rebuttal for anything she might throw at me.

The spicy scent of her famous chili accosts me as soon as I step into the foyer. I clutch an end table. There's only one reason she'd be cooking during this dire situation: as bait. When my feet stop dead, she twists again, raising a brow. Another form of bait. She reels me in with only that look and I follow her into the kitchen.

Leo's slumped over the table, but he instantly perks up when he sees me. "Oh God, Arden. Way to scare us."

"I've been worried sick that you were hurt." Mom circles me, studying me as if she wants to see for herself that I'm still in one piece. Emotion catches in my throat. She cares. She still cares.

After confirming I'm not injured, at least where she can see anyway, she waves her hand at an empty seat with a place setting waiting for me. A pot simmers on the stove, presumably to keep it warm until I arrived. "You were instructed to return home immediately."

My face burns and I feel like a complete idiot for falling for her ruse. I walked right into the firing squad without a bulletproof vest. I make no effort to hide it from my voice. "Actually, you only instructed us to *leave* right away. And I marked myself as safe."

Mom purses her lips. "You did, but I still rushed home to check on you. Where were you?"

I clamp my mouth shut, refusing to answer.

"Arden." Mom smooths down the blazer of her suit. My teeth clench together with each strike of her heels on the tile floor as she moves toward me. "I need you to be honest with me. Did you steal the admin console? The one that was in the IT room."

Her words knock the wind out of me. I press a palm to my forehead, thinking. *Did* I steal the admin computer? It certainly seems like something I would do and something the hacker might make me forget. But those consoles are bolted down with metal chains. In fact, it was still chained when I left the basement. I can hack all I want, but my science background hasn't taught me anything about breaking through soldered metal. I make a mental note to check the writing on my body the next time I'm alone to confirm I didn't perform such an act. "Does this mean it's missing?" Panic flies into my voice. "What about the other admin computer?"

"That one's secure, but this one disappeared during the blackout. This is an extreme security concern. If you did take it, I need you to give it back." Her eyes plead with me. "You won't get in trouble if you turn it in. Please."

I stifle a twinge in my chest. I've never seen my mom beg like this. And then there's the deeper panic, the one setting me on edge. *Someone* stole that computer and corrupted the other one. Someone still has access to my deleted memories, to all of HiveMind despite the security precautions the school has been taking. I grip her shoulder, trying to make her finally see the truth. "Mom, it wasn't me. It's the hacker. You have to believe me."

Mom nods, finally acknowledging what I've been telling her all along. It's not a glitch.

The hacker must have slipped into the basement the same way I did during the chaos of the smoke bomb. Right after me. If they were monitoring my mind, they knew what I was going to do. They also knew what I wished I had done: brought tools that could cut through the chains and free the console. Maybe they even grabbed a smoke mask from one of the labs. While Sebastian and I were escaping to the car, they must have been *in* the room, stealing the damn admin console and using it to fuck with me a few minutes later.

That's why the IP address seemed so familiar. It's the admin console.

A lump swells deep in my throat. "Mom, I'm really scared."

"Me too." She pulls me into a hug and I sink into her arms. "Me too," she whispers again. All the other times, she's vowed to get to the bottom of this and get my memories back, but this time she refrains. Probably because she doesn't want to make me a promise she might not be able to keep.

I pull away from her. "I can try to fix it if I can connect directly to the servers. Where did you move them?"

Mom shakes her head. "I can't tell you. It's too dangerous. It's not that I don't trust you, Arden, but . . ."

Her words drop off deliberately this time. Because she *doesn't* trust me. That thought hits me like a slap in the face. My mother would rather let entire chunks of her life slide into oblivion than let me help. My throat feels swollen with a lump so large I can barely breathe. My mother doesn't believe in me.

I lean forward, take a step closer, anything to move into her line of vision and show her I'm *here*. Right here. On the front lines and ready to help.

But she won't look at me.

My heart shatters into pieces, and I spin around, pressing my hand to the wall and sucking in desperate breaths. I can't look at her now either.

"I need to call the Ethics Committee and let them know I haven't found it." Her voice sounds determined, not defeated. She ambles out of the room, already dialing, unaware of the arrow she just shot through my chest. Her muffled voice carries from the living room.

This is all on me to fix, whether my mom believes in me or not.

If I can stop this, I'll earn back my mom's respect. Her trust. *Her*.

0011001000110011

Arden: Here

I lean against the beige siding of Sebastian's house as I text and force my leg to stop rattling in tune to my heartbeat. It's just Sebastian. And this is not about kissing him. We need to keep each other safe.

His reply comes a moment later.

Sebastian: Oh cool. Mom just got in the shower.

A few moments later the sliding glass door opens into the kitchen and he presses a finger to his lips. I kick off my stilettos and toss them onto the soft grass of his backyard.

Inside, I take each step with the methodical precision of a surgeon. The fluffy carpet muffles my footsteps, so the only thing audible is the pounding of my heart. We reach Sebastian's room without his mom's door flying open.

Sebastian closes the door with a faint *snick*, allowing me to exhale. "She's working the overnight shift at the hospital." He checks his watch. "Twenty minutes until she leaves."

I bite my lip. "Sorry, I know I'm early. I just—" Couldn't wait another minute to see him.

A wide grin stretches his cheeks. "I was hoping you'd be early."

I tell him the news about the admin console, and his face falls.

We both stand there for a moment in silence, stewing over how royally screwed this makes us.

"I learned some stuff too," he says after a moment. "Apparently, I have a dad? I just assumed he was dead until he called tonight to tell me he heard about my medical miracle and promised to fly me out to visit this summer."

Hearing the word *dad* lodges a bullet in my throat. I can't hide the emotion from seeping into my voice. "Wow. Where does he live?"

"Seattle, which is apparently where I'm from. My mom moved out here with me when I got into MVH and the divorce followed shortly after."

I sink onto the bed, nodding in a daze. "I'm so sorry."

He shrugs and plops down next to me. "I have no memories of him. No connection to him. Nothing except this one conversation and a million questions."

I place a hand on his knee. "We're going to get answers."

"What if—" He swallows hard. "What if I don't want them?"

"What do you mean?"

"I want to know who did this to us and all that. But—I'm starting to wonder if there are things I'm better off *not* remembering. Arden, I was *dying*, for crying out loud, and my dad didn't even bother to talk to me!" He squeezes his eyes shut. "On the phone today, he apologized profusely for not calling me the last few weeks." His shoulders rattle and his hands ball into fists. "I only have this one conversation now stored in my mind." He meets my gaze head-on. "I'm not sure I want to taint it with anything else."

He said the same thing to me earlier today, right before his memory of that moment was deleted while mine stayed intact, though I can't remember what prompted him to say it. It's the absolute opposite of my stance on this. I want all the knowledge back, everything I've lost, but I admire that he can feel complete without all the pieces of him that are missing. "Maybe you can make that choice, then. When we find your memories, you can opt not to download them. But we at least need to keep moving forward so *you* can make that choice. Instead of it being made for you."

"What do we do?" he asks.

"We—" I bury my head in my hands. "Oh God. I don't even know. We're out of options."

"Not all options." He drums his fingers on the table. "What if we break into the new server room?"

"We don't know where it . . ." My words drop off. Within seconds, I remote access my mother's computer in her office. It takes me a few minutes of perusing through her folders and files, but I pull up the work order for the new data center located only twenty minutes away. "I know where." I point at the address on the screen. "But we need to plan how to get inside. It's not like MVH. I don't know it well enough to be able to break all the rules, plus we're never going to be able to sneak in."

Sebastian glances at the clock. "It's too late to go there tonight anyway without raising alarms. That gives us approximately twelve hours to formulate a plan if we want to get there first thing in the morning."

I shake my head. "Not *first* thing. I want to talk to Teddy during first period since we didn't get a chance to talk to him today."

Sebastian nods. "We can go after that."

I bite my lip. "I can try to hack in and put us on the security list, but—" I shake my head. It's too risky to try to hack anything. Data centers are built with the specific purpose of boosting security and keeping out hackers. I have no doubt I'd be able to get through their barriers eventually, but who knows what traps I'll trigger trying to do it. They might be onto me before I even hit *enter*.

No, we need to do this the old-fashioned way. Sans computers.

"Let's think about who might already be on the approved security list. Your mother." He ticks off a finger. "Probably the Ethics Committee folks. Do we know who they are?"

"Yeah, they're board members from the investment firm that funds the various prototypes Varga Industries puts out. Mostly middle-aged men in stuffy suits plus a woman or two for diversity."

"Do you think there's a chance any of them are behind this whole thing?"

I shrug. "There's always a chance, but they normally stay pretty high level when it comes to this stuff, so I doubt the motivation's there. It's in their best interest for our project to be successful."

He purses his lips. "Okay, do we know anyone else that might have access?"

My eyes widen as the plan starts to form in my mind. "We don't need anyone else. All we need is Zoey, actually."

He raises a brow. "I don't think she'll be on the list."

"She won't be. But we don't need her to be. All we need is her holographic makeup skills."

To bypass whatever security protocols are in place at the new data center, I simply need to look like one of the only people the center would allow inside. Thankfully, I already share my mother's clothing size and bone structure: nose too thin, cheekbones too high, face pointed at the chin but rounded upward like a heart. A hair twist will hide my long locks compared with my mother's sleek bob. And Zoey's skills with holographic makeup will cover the rest, adding the necessary tweaks to make me appear older, more severe, and more serious.

More legit.

It's flimsy at best, risky at worst, but it'll have to do.

"Sebastian, I'm leaving!" his mom calls from downstairs. "Call if there's an emergency."

We both pause and wait for the slam of the front door, the rev of her car engine, the safety that comes with the squeal of her tires as she backs out of the driveway.

"I know we have a plan of action now for tomorrow." He grabs his phone off the end table. "But we still need one for tonight. I've been thinking about this." He gestures to the writing on his back.

"About the partial nudity we're about to engage in?" I decide to lighten the mood with a little gutter humor. It at least puts a smile back on his face.

His cheeks turn bright pink. "No. I mean, yes." He rakes his hand through his hair. "I mean, how to prevent data loss."

I purse my lips. "Suuuure. That was the part at the forefront of your mind."

He turns partially away from me to hide the way his blush deepens. "We should take photos, as discussed earlier. And then print them out."

I nod along with him. "Good idea." This way, if someone hacks into our phones and deletes the images, we'll have analog backups.

He flips the lock on his room, an added precaution.

I scramble out of my clothes and try not to blush myself as he whirls around me, snapping photos of my bare back, my legs, stomach, the parts of me I've already exposed and let him cover with his deepest secrets. My nerves dissipate, and I relish the way he drinks me in, careful to capture every hidden message decoded on my skin. We sit there in only our underwear, waiting for the photos to print out, the tension escaping from our shoulders with each warm sheet of paper. When the last one prints, he leads me to the bathroom and keeps guard outside the door.

I set my binary necklace on the bathroom counter, a true sign of trust. The hot water scalds my skin, blurring the words I spent today desperately trying to hide. I close my eyes and savor the normalcy for just a moment, where my skin is just skin and my entire world doesn't unravel with each second that passes.

I take my time drying off and then sliding on the fresh clothes I brought: a tee that's just a tad too loose and polka-dot pants that are way too loose. At least I had the foresight not to bring my retainer. I finally look human again instead of an understudy for *Bride of Frankenstein*. We pass in the hallway like two ships in the night, and I wait in his room while he scrubs the past away too.

His hair drips onto the carpet when he returns, wearing only pants, his chest bare, ready for me to rewrite it all on his torso.

I run out of room on his back as I painstakingly transcribe every word that seems to belong here now. I was wrong before when I thought that I was returning to my skin when I washed this all away. *This* is what feels right. He lets out a shudder when I ask him to flip over so I can continue writing on his chest to capture yesterday's knowledge and the new info gleaned in the last few hours. His muscles clench and he lets out a laugh from the way my hair must tickle him.

I start to cap the marker, but he lifts his hand. "Wait. I think we should try to put the stuff we've learned in chronological order." He sits up and holds out his hand for the pen. "If you don't mind, it might be easier if I try. I've been thinking about this."

We switch places and I lie down on the bed, my head cradled in his pillow, my chest puffing in and out. He stretches out my arm and draws a long black line from the top of my shoulder down to my wrist. I hold my breath to stop from giggling at the ticklish sensation.

I tap the inside of my elbow. "I still need to write stuff there."

"I'll put it all on your back after. I'll write really small, promise." He slashes smaller black lines that break away from the main line on my arm, pointing upward and downward. He leans over my torso, his hot breath making me squirm, as he writes a few words beneath the lines nearest to my shoulder. He works his way down, adding details below each jagged line. He leaves a few spots open and squints at the whole picture before filling those in too.

When he caps the pen and leans back, I lift my arm up and read from left to right, shoulder to wrist:

HiveMind app developed
S diagnosed with cancer
S came in 2nd place in National Science Competition
Started at MVH
Began working on thesis project
Started dating?
S and A continue working on project
S has six months to live
S's Duplicell procedure
S cured
S no memories/A's memories deleted
Projects due
Press conference

"You're missing some things." I point to the space between *S has six months to live* and *Duplicell procedure*. "Here it should say: excessive making out."

I expect him to laugh. Instead, his expression pinches.

I ask him to include a few more items: marking the escalation of security from the installation of the retina scanner, the failed attempt by the Ethics Committee to spruce up security, and the servers being moved to an off-site location. I even include the info about Brandon being fired and the admin console going missing.

And then I add one more. One that kills me to write.

My dad's death. Slotted between *Began working on thesis project* and *S has six months to live.* I'm not sure if we started dating before or after my dad died or if he ever had the chance to get to know the guy I'm learning more about every passing second.

I lift my shirt over my head, wearing only my bra, and flip over onto my stomach. I get lost in the way he transcribes all the missing info onto my skin. The ticklish sensation gives way to pure bliss. He manages to cram all the info that had been spread everywhere earlier into the space between my shoulder blades. When he finishes, he grabs a shirt from his drawer, and I put mine back on.

I teeter on the edge of the bed. My hands wait in my lap, but that feels unnatural, so I stretch them behind me. My arms shake too much like that. I give up and crawl under the covers.

Sebastian slides in and my nerves amp. We both stare up at the spinning ceiling fan, two bodies lying next to each other, not touching except for a few atoms at the elbow. Glowing stars on his ceiling promise a whole universe ahead of us. He smells of hair gel and musky cologne, as though he replenished both on the sly before he slipped in beside me.

I flip on my side to face him. "What are you thinking about?"

He doesn't even hesitate. "That I'm afraid."

That stops me in my tracks.

"I'm afraid I'm still dying. Maybe the doctors made a mistake or your brother doesn't know the real side effects." His eyelashes flutter over his eyes. "And the only thing that could actually save me is our damn project."

My throat burns, thick and heavy. Water swells behind my eyes, droplets piling on top of one another to form a tsunami. Pressure increases until I roll over to face his wall and shove my fist into my mouth to muffle the inevitable. Tears leak, but I let them pool in the crevice between my cheek and the pillow. Because I'm afraid I've failed him too. "And I'm scared I can't save you."

He wraps an arm around my stomach, offering me the comfort I'm too weak to ask for. I'm finally close enough to experience him in real time. I need to touch him, not with a pen but with my fingers. I want to memorize the contours of his skin so this time if I lose my mind, I won't forget. I shiver in response to his warm breath on my neck, goose bumps dimpling my skin.

Turning, I lean into him, hovering above his lips for a moment in case this is moving too fast for him. But he brings his mouth up to meet mine, and that's all the permission I need. I yank him toward me, and the kiss intensifies. He kisses me like he needs to catch up to all the time we've lost.

We kiss until we're breathless. Until only this moment matters, not anything that came before or anything that will come next.

My whole body itches with the need to continue, to knot my fingers in his hair and never let go. But he pulls away, and presses a gentle kiss on the top of my forehead before his eyes slip closed.

You only get to fall in love for the first time once. But we've been given another chance.

0011001000110100

At school the next morning, I pass by the basement with a pang in my gut. It's worthless to me now.

Sebastian and I practically hurl ourselves into Mr. Kimmel's class, ready to see what Teddy can tell us about how his project actually works. The printing part makes sense, but not the transfer part. My feet stop dead when I notice Teddy's empty desk. He's never late.

"I'll text him." Sebastian pounds out a few words on his phone while I watch over his shoulder.

Sebastian: Hey, man.

He grins at me, clearly proud of the way he manages to sound so casual with a friend he doesn't recall having.

Sebastian: You coming to class today?

There's no reply and Teddy doesn't pick up Sebastian's call either. A quick hack into the school attendance records indicates he's been called in with an excused absence.

That's weird. He's never absent. Though maybe he's just putting the finishing touches on his project. A quick glance around indicates a lot of seniors took a last-minute day off to prepare for the adversarial review that starts first thing tomorrow morning. My chest tightens. There's no way I'll be ready for tomorrow. My entire future will be destroyed.

I quickly shake off that thought. There are more important things at stake here. Our missing memories. Sebastian's life.

Movement in my peripheral vision alerts me to Mr. Kimmel shuffling out of the closet in the back of the room. When he sees me, he drops a pile of papers and storms toward me. Everyone in the room turns to watch.

He invades my personal space, forcing me to back up until I slam into his desk. He huffs coffee-laced breath in my face, dropping his voice even though he's already got everyone staring at us. "Arden. *Arden.* Your project. Someone's messing it all up!"

Latent terror at his wild, pleading expression paralyzes me. My mouth goes dry.

He shoves his hand into his front pocket and yanks out another stack of Post-it notes that he must have found hidden in this room. He holds it up triumphantly and then waves it under my nose. He slams his fingers against the stack, making it flap. He's got crazy eyes as he watches me read the words.

Sebastian and I exchange terrified glances as we read. He sets the lunch box with my mother's eye on an empty desk as if he wants it out of the way.

Memories being deleted. They're all being deleted. Bash's entire personality: DELETED.

Someone else tried to run Theseus without A + S and they did it wrong. Only they can fix it.

My stomach clenches.

"Arden, what does this mean?" He pleads with me, throwing me the same question I want to ask him. A few kids in the front row start to snicker. "Sebastian?"

Sweat gathers at the nape of my neck. "I—I wish I knew." I swallow hard to keep my voice steady.

Suddenly, his hands clutch my shoulders, and he shakes me violently. "Arden, you *must* remember. Please tell me you remember." His breathing gets faster. "I don't even know what you need to remember, just that you do."

I go stiff in my desperation to stay calm despite the way my pulse slams into my neck. His fingers sink deeper, digging into my skin.

I try to tug my arm out of his grasp, but he's bouncer strong. Stronger than me. Sebastian tries too, but Kimmel knocks him away with his shoulder so hard that Sebastian loses his balance and crashes to the floor.

Gasps ring out. A few students jump to their feet.

"Mr. Kimmel," I say through gritted teeth as pain radiates from where he's grabbing me. "Let go!"

Melody Clarendon and Josh Lazarus grab on to my other arm to tug me free. I stumble into one of them but catch myself. I rub my stinging arm.

Mr. Kimmel pauses, his face squishing in anguish. A few seconds pass without him moving a single muscle. But then he comes to and shakes his head out of his daze. He squints at me, then at the other students, confused. "Class, why are you all at my desk?"

My pulse beats in the base of my throat as I stumble through a break in the line of kids that step in front of me, protecting me Red Rover–style. My eyes close as sluggish relief pulses through me. Sebastian pushes to his feet and shuffles beside me. When he grabs my hand, it's the only thing tethering me to the ground.

Mr. Kimmel seems utterly confused as his head volleys among

the students. "What's going on? Why are you all looking at me like that?"

"You assaulted two students!" One of the girls already has her phone out, dialing it with shaky fingers. "I'm calling the cops."

"I'm calling the Ethics Committee," someone else says.

Sebastian squeezes my hand, letting me know he's still here, still beside me.

Kimmel holds up his hands in surrender. "I didn't. I don't know what you're talking about!"

"Got it captured on video, right here." A guy hits play on his phone, and the entire terrifying conversation echoes through the room once again.

Mr. Kimmel clamps a hand over his mouth.

It only takes a few minutes for the security team to reach the classroom, review the video, and escort Mr. Kimmel out of the building.

There's a pang in my chest, a swirl of guilt in my gut. He wouldn't have snapped if his memories hadn't been deleted. And they wouldn't have been deleted if he hadn't been involved in my project.

That's two people I've accidentally gotten fired in the last two days.

I slump into the nearest desk as the classroom empties out. Sebastian crouches beside me, clutching the lunch box with my mother's eye, a concerned look on his face. We brought the eye to school just in case any other "security improvements" show up that we need to bypass. He gently pries the Post-it notes out of my closed fist and reads them again. "What do you think this means?" He's pointing to the one about someone running Theseus wrong, but my eyes linger on the other one. The one about Bash's personality being deleted.

When I speak, my voice is grave. "Sebastian, we already figured out that the purpose of our project was to transfer an entire personality. Do you think *we* deleted all your memories as a beta test?"

His face turns white. "But why would we risk doing that if our project still had a critical bug we needed to work out?"

I bite my lip. That's a good point. "And that also doesn't explain why I'm only missing some memories but not all like you are."

"Or why there's a hacker after us," he adds.

I swallow hard. "And none of it explains the biggest question of all: How will any of this save lives?"

"I NEED YOUR HELP." I corner Zoey in the hallway before second period, trying my best to inject pep into my voice in the slim hope that I can fool myself into being upbeat too. I'm still shook from what happened with Mr. Kimmel, but I can't let it stop me. I need to get into that data center. My car keys jiggle in my hands, ready to enact part two of the plan Sebastian and I came up with last night. "Let's go. We're ditching school."

Zoey hops up and down. "Oooh, I don't know what you're planning, but whatever it is, I'm in." She looks around. "Are we waiting for anyone? A certain lover boy perhaps?"

"He has a meeting, but we're going to swing by and pick him up after we get ready." Sebastian got a text from Leo reminding him about his appointment with Duplicell today during lunch. We decided it was too important for him to miss that just to sit around while I get a makeover.

The two of us exit through the side doors. No one stops us today when we utter the magic words: *We need to prepare for the board review tomorrow.*

"Where are we going exactly?" Zoey asks as she buckles up.

"Your room. I need your holographic magic."

She rubs her hands together. "A makeover for the second time this week? Pinch me; I must be dreaming!"

I fill her in on the plan on the way to her room. Zoey plops me into the same chair as before and purses her lips as she switches back and forth between studying me and the photograph of my mother downloaded from the school website. "I haven't used the makeup in this way before, but I love a challenge." She purses her lips again. "Wait. What about identification? And your voice? You sound nothing like your mother."

"If I lower my voice a bit, I kind of do," I say in a lowered voice, and her eyes shine with excitement. "And as for ID, I already swiped my mom's passport before school."

"Brilliant. I love how badass you're being lately."

Zoey hooks up her magic makeup wand to her holographic contouring powder. Her tongue sticks out of her mouth as she moves toward my face. "In exchange for helping you, you do realize you're going to need to give me some more details about whatever's going on between you and the guy you refuse to admit you're dating."

My whole face lights up and the smile jumps to my lips before I have a chance to stop it.

"Oh man. You're already so far gone. I love it."

"We may have made out. And spent the last two nights together." I duck my head and glance up at her beneath my eyelashes. "I really like him."

Her brows shoot way up. "Have you guys . . . ?"

I shake my head on first instinct even though a lead quarry wells in my gut. If we have and we can't remember, does it even count? "We're taking things slow." And by "slow" I mean exploring each other's nearly naked bodies with the tip of a ballpoint pen. "I don't want to rush things." Except of course rushing to get our memories back.

"You have way more restraint than I do." Zoey continues to transform me into someone else.

"Hey, quick question. I know you're helping on Leo's project, but are you doing anything for Teddy's?"

She lets out a heavy sigh. "Not enough. If I had my way, I'd spend every waking minute in the lab with him, pressed up against him. . . ." She stares off dreamily at whatever fantasy must be playing in her mind. "But I think he's mad at me. Ever since I asked him for co-credit."

My brow knits together. "Wow. What did you help him with?" I'm sure I knew this information at one point, before my hacker got the best of my memories.

"Not much, only just *his entire freaking idea*. But I guess ideas are meaningless. He was the one with the knowledge and skills to actually pull it off." Zoey switches her makeup brushes, looking dejected. "Since Teddy did all the execution stuff, he's the only one allowed to demo for the board review, and he's going to impress the shit out of them. It's so not fair."

"What's he demoing?"

"He only needed to print one body part for the review. Instead, he printed them *all*." She rolls her eyes.

Shit. That does sound pretty impressive. "Do you know how the transferring part of Teddy's project works?"

Zoey nods. "The bio software does it. It works in a similar way to HiveMind. With the scans from Duplicell, the entire procedure is completely noninvasive. No surgery required if that's what you're getting at."

I shake my head, my brain stuck on her mention of bio software and HiveMind. "Does he know how to use HiveMind? Is he capable of deleting memories?"

She purses her lips. "I guess so. But it's not him. Stop thinking it's him!"

"It's whoever stole the admin computer. That person still has access."

"That could be a lot of people. Think of it this way: Who *else* would be able to hack into the admin console?" She taps her red nails against her thigh. "Brandon, obviously. You. Mr. Kimmel. The scientists on the seventh floor working on VR stuff."

I shake my head. "Not me. Brandon was fired, so not him. I've never even met those scientists. And Mr. Kimmel's falling apart due to the memory deletions."

Zoey clucks her tongue. "I'm not ruling out Brandon. And there's got to be others. Maybe someone not superskilled but knows enough to at least get inside and do some damage."

I jiggle my keys. "Like Teddy?"

Zoey grips my shoulders. "Don't say that. It's not him. It *can't* be him."

I look her square in the eye. "Zo . . ." There's a frantic aching in my chest. "He's being a jerk to you. And I'm sorry to say it, but . . . I don't think he's interested in you. You're amazing and you deserve to find someone who likes you back and will actually treat you like you deserve."

"He'll like me back. I know it. If I could just impress him, he'd see how amazing I really am *and* maybe give me the credit I deserve too." She yanks her handheld mirror off the vanity and thrusts it in my face with a little too much anger infused in her movements. The mirror is the kind with gold filigree surrounding the oval, as if it came straight out of a fairy tale. With the way she contoured my cheekbones and added wrinkles crinkling in the corners of my eyes and cracking around my mouth, I look way too much like my mother. It's unsettling.

But it's also exactly what I need. My back straightens with the need to lift my chin the way my mother does and carry myself as if everyone I encounter already respects me.

I spin away from the door and lift my shirt over my head to change into the clothes I grabbed from my house before we headed here.

"Wow, girl." Zoey whistles through her teeth. "And you told me nothing happened between you and Sebastian."

My cheeks grow hot and I rush to cover the writing on my back with the new shirt as fast as possible. I tell Zoey everything, but for some reason, accidentally showing her this feels like a secret only Sebastian and I share. "Please don't tell him you saw," I say, even though I know I need to tell him myself. I don't want to keep anything from him right now.

She scoffs, hand going to her chest in mock horror. "Arden, you can trust me. I shouldn't even need to tell you that."

My stomach swirls at this too. "Sorry. You're right." I swallow hard. "Sorry."

Her eyes widen. "Wow, two sorrys in a row? I better go buy a lottery ticket. Must be my lucky day."

And then we head off to add yet another breaking and entering attempt to my growing criminal résumé.

0011001000110101

After a pit stop at the local computer center to buy a bunch of technical equipment to get us through the rest of the plan, I exchange Zoey for Sebastian since she wanted to try to talk to my mother again in a last-ditch effort to get some kind of co-credit before tomorrow's review. The whole makeover and shopping trip took way longer than planned, so I'm over two hours late to pick him up. When Sebastian slips into the car, his eyes widen. "Whoa. It's creepy to look at you like this."

I give him a stern look and drop my voice an octave to sound more like my mother. "You, sir, are in serious trouble for cutting class."

He scoots toward the door an inch. "Okay, I don't like this at all."

I gun the engine. "Convincing, right?"

"A little too much." He folds his long legs up, pressing his knees to his chest. "I know I don't remember much about who I used to be, but I don't think I was the type of guy that ditched class this often."

I pull out of the parking lot. "Correct. Based on the evidence of the retrieved memories, you were the type of guy that snuck *into* school after hours."

He laughs, leaning his head against the headrest. "Well, at least I'm consistent in that regard."

"Tell me about the appointment with Leo."

"He tested my reflexes, took some blood, made me run on a treadmill for a few minutes, and didn't answer any of my questions."

I merge onto the highway. "I wouldn't have expected anything else."

He leans against the side of the car. Sunlight glitters in through the window, tinting his hair to the color of pure gold. "He did test my knowledge, but not of memories. Want to take a guess how I know all that crazy information?"

I don't hesitate. "Upgrades?"

"Bingo." He points a finger gun at me. "Apparently, after the cell-transfer procedure, he took the liberty of also uploading any knowledge I might require in the future. One of the perks of being the first prototype. I'm also an experiment."

"What exactly did he test you on?" I ask.

"Name of the street the US Embassy resides on in the capital of Kazakhstan. Square root of pi to the thirty-fourth digit. The verb 'to be' conjugated in forty-three languages. Third sentence on the one-hundred-sixty-eighth page of *War and Peace*." He twists his hands around his bony wrist as if he's fashioning a finger noose. "I'm not a genius; I'm a file archive."

I change lanes, speeding toward the next exit. "You *are* a genius."

"Actually, it should be, 'I *was* a genius.' That's the correct conjugation of the verb 'to be.'"

"It doesn't matter who you were, just who you are now." I nudge his shoulder and offer a grin.

About fifteen minutes later, we arrive at the new data center in all its glory. On the outside, it looks like a generic brick office building with large windows on the exterior and a security guard stationed at the front of the entrance. I park along the street and stretch my neck high and mighty as I approach, affecting an air of confidence like my mother always exudes. Sebastian follows beside me. When we reach the entrance, I thrust my new fake ID at the guard and check the time on the dashboard as if I don't have time for this kind of delay.

The security guard studies the ID and then me. "Purpose of your visit, ma'am?"

"Checking on the equipment installed yesterday."

"And him?" He juts his chin toward Sebastian.

"Student volunteer," I say, and leave it at that.

"I'm afraid I'm under strict orders not to allow anyone inside except those on the official list. You may proceed, but he will have to stay here."

I give the guard a tight smile. "With all due respect, sir, I *made* the list. I assure you he has received the proper security clearance."

The guard stares at me, stone-faced.

But that's okay. This is all part of the plan. I let out a ginormous sigh. "Fine, but please note that I'll be reaching out to management about this." I turn to Sebastian. "Do you mind waiting here for a few minutes?"

Sebastian shrugs. "I'll take a walk. It's so nice out."

While I'm inside, Sebastian will be scanning the perimeter on the outside, planting little video surveillance devices wherever he can. I want to be able to monitor whoever goes in and out of this place, on my own terms. And if he gets caught by anyone, he just needs to reference the security guard as his alibi.

The security guard buzzes me inside. According to the work order I found on my mother's computer, Varga Industries has rented half a wing of this data center to host their servers. Glossy hardwood floors and a bright lobby welcome me inside the building. I go through the same dog and pony show with another security guard behind a mahogany desk inside. This security guard calls over Ellie, a woman in a sleek business suit, who greets me with a nude lipstick smile and a firm handshake. "I'm surprised to see you again so soon."

I flinch. I was banking on being incognito here by lack of recognition. If she's met my mother, any wrong mannerism might raise her suspicions. I straighten my posture. I try to think what my mother might say. This whole thing would be so much easier if I was impersonating my dad. I know him better than I know myself right now. But my mother has always been a bit of an enigma to me. "Yes, well, I prefer to be thorough."

She squints at me. "But I wasn't expecting you for another hour per your appointment."

Shit. I grit my teeth and wave her off with a dismissive flip of my hand. "We've had a lot of breaches in security lately and I want to ensure that the same level of corruption won't happen here as well. A surprise visit is a necessary step."

Her smile wavers as she studies me, squinting harder. Her eyes land on my binary necklace. "Next time, we do need advance notice."

"Noted." I force myself to hold her gaze as apprehension knots in the base of my throat.

"As I've already explained to you and your team, we take the utmost pride in our security protocols. The two guards you've requested have been posted at each entrance to the storage facility. No one has been inside that room since the machines were installed. You have my word."

"I'd still like to check for myself."

Ellie spins toward a wide doorway and twists a key in the lock. "Very well, then. Please follow me."

As soon as she turns away, I shove my necklace beneath the

collar of my shirt. The two of us march in silence, our heels striking the hardwood floor in a dissonant battle of sound. Rows of metal shelves house black boxes stacked several feet high. Wires snake around the black boxes and coil in neat circles between the rows. Company names glisten in the overhead lights, affixed to the top of each shelf. At the very end of the large room, we face another locked door with a security guard standing beside it. He studies me up and down but makes no effort to budge.

Ellie twists her key into the top lock, but there's an empty lock below it. "Please, if I may have your key." She holds out her palm.

My heart starts to hammer fast in my rib cage. This lock must work like most safety-deposit boxes in a bank. One key from an employee, one from the owner of the box. Both needed to provide access. Shit. Shit. Shit. The work order made no mention of a key. I only have one play here, and it's the exact play that anyone who attends a school for geniuses would cringe at: ignorance. "Key?"

Ellie purses her lips. "I gave it to you personally yesterday."

"Oh." I let out a little laugh. "I thought the key was for any time I needed to access this place after hours."

Ellie and the security guard exchange glances. "We're open twenty-four seven. And you signed a document acknowledging the purpose of the key. I'm afraid I can't let you inside without it."

Panic climbs my spine. I have to think fast. "Okay, listen." I lean close and drop my voice. "The key you gave me? It was stolen from my purse. I need to get in there and make sure nothing else inside was stolen or tampered with."

Ellie flourishes her hand toward the security guard. "I assure you, we've had personnel stationed directly outside here ever since we completed setup."

"And I assure *you*"—I raise my voice, projecting a sense of sternness—"that this method of security is not adequate because there's a significant flaw in the protocol that doesn't account for petty theft." I twist to the guard. "I'm sure you yourself have not been standing here for the last twenty-four hours straight. There must have been a moment when you switched places with someone else. That's a moment of weakness. An opportunity for someone else to slip inside with two stolen keys. Can you assure me that hasn't happened? That every employee key is currently accounted for? Can you confirm no employees from this very data center have been inside since yesterday?"

Ellie opens her mouth but then clamps it shut. "I'd have to review the security tapes, but—"

I don't let her finish with the obvious rest of her sentence, that it's a highly unlikely scenario. All I need is for her to doubt herself. Just a little. Just enough to let me slide past the rules. "This is why I need to check." My voice comes out desperate and earnest. "Please. You can stay by my side. Watch my every move. I just need the peace of mind that everything's okay."

She sighs and grabs a second key out of her pocket. A skeleton key. "Just this once." She slips it inside and twists the lock. "But we're going to have to change the locks later."

"I'd be pulling my servers out of here if you didn't."

She pushes open the door to an identical view of stacked servers, and while her back's turned, I reach into my purse. My fingers graze against the canister of pepper spray Sebastian made yesterday as I grab another SSD drive to conceal in my palm. I squeeze my fist to stop it from shaking. There are rows and rows of servers, far more than we ever housed in the basement of Varga Industries, probably in preparation for the worldwide release of HiveMind at the press conference tomorrow.

Ellie keeps close, watching my every move as I peruse the servers, all neatly labeled in Brandon's handwriting. He must have been helping set this up for a while now. I cup the SSD drive in my hand, palm sweaty. All I need is three seconds of distraction to be able to slip it into the back of one of the servers and gain full access to it. I cough, but Ellie doesn't flinch. I jut my chin toward the window, but she doesn't even glance in any direction but at my face. It's not until she receives a phone call and presses it to her ear, her face turning grave, that she spins away from me. My heart pounds. I brush against one of the consoles and discreetly plug in the SSD drive just as my purse vibrates with a text. I dig my phone out.

Sebastian: I just spotted your mom arriving!
She's at security now.

My eyes widen as Ellie turns back toward me, her face scared. "Ma'am, I've just been informed that there has in fact been a breach in security. As part of our standard protocol, I'm going to need you to come with me. We're placing this room on lockdown."

And her intent is likely to lock down *me* as well.

"I'm actually done here, thanks!" I stomp toward the exit, not bothering to wait for her. Not bothering to let her catch up with me.

But at the exit, a security guard faces me. A pair of handcuffs dangles from his burly fist. He blocks the exit from me.

"I've got her cornered," Ellie says behind me into what must be her phone.

My pulse beats so fast in my skull I can hardly think. I have no place to run. No chess moves left to play. Nothing stored up in my bag of tricks. Except . . .

I do have something stored in my bag of tricks. The aerosol can of pepper spray Sebastian mixed up yesterday. We didn't need to use it then, but it's exactly what I need now.

I fumble into my purse and grip the canister. The security guard's fingers shift to his belt, his eyes on my hand. My heart lodges in my throat. A gun? Before he has a chance to use it, I lift the aerosol can and spray a blast in his face. He screams, hands rising to his eyes. I barrel past him and run straight into the lobby, where my mother stands with an unamused expression on her face, her key dangling in her fingers to prove she's the real deal. Two guards stand beside her, both looking angry. There's a man in a suit with a phone pressed to his ear, probably connected to Ellie.

Mom doesn't flinch at my appearance. "Arden, you're supposed to be in fifth period."

I stop short in front of her and slide the pepper spray back into my purse. "Mom, it's getting worse. I have to stop it. I have to—"

"You have to leave here." She spits her words through gritted teeth. "Right now. Go home and stay there. Do you hear me?"

I nod meekly, feeling suddenly like a cosplayer at a comic convention, extremely uncomfortable in clothes that don't belong to me.

"What did you do in there? Did you touch anything?"

I shake my head frantically, but judging by her heavy sigh, she clearly doesn't believe me.

A new text pops up on my phone and I covertly glance at it.

Sebastian: Side entrance, on your left if
you're facing the main doors. Fair
warning, it's alarmed.

"I'm going to have to let the Ethics Committee know about this." Her voice wavers. "I'm going to tell them I think you're behind this...."

"No!" If she informs the Ethics Committee, that's it. I'm done for. They'll overrule the DNA that links me to her and kick me straight on my ass out of the school. "I'm not. I'm trying to help. I'm—"

Mom turns toward the guards. "You can call off the police. I'm not going to press charges." When she spins back to face me, her face is grave. "Arden, we'll deal with this at home."

"I'm sorry, Mrs. Varga." Ellie's heels click toward us. "But that's not your call. We take our security very seriously and we've already called in the authorities. They should be here moment—"

I lift the can of pepper spray and spray it in the face of the guard right in front of me. While he screams, I use the distraction to dodge around him. There are guards blocking the main entrance, but I switch courses and barrel down the hallway to my left that none of them expected me to take. Sebastian wasn't only planting surveillance equipment outside, he was also casing the place to find escape routes in case I got trapped exactly like this.

I may not be an ace in gym class, especially not in these heels, but the pepper spray slows down the guards enough for me to slam into the exit doors. A loud alarm blares, the sound pounding against my skull as I squint into the harsh sunlight.

My feet pound down the sidewalk and burst through rows of trees. A stampede of footsteps resounds behind me. I'm shaking by the time I reach the car, engine already idling. I'm about to open the driver's side, but I spot Sebastian already occupying it. My getaway driver squeezes white knuckles on the steering wheel as I get into the passenger seat.

Security guards rush toward the car.

"Go!" I shout, gripping the door handle.

"Let's hope the driver's manual I have downloaded in my head surpasses the need for lessons." He slams his foot on the gas pedal, jerking the car backward. "Guess not." Sebastian switches gears, and the car lurches forward again. He guns the engine and zooms forward, finding a smooth pace of twenty miles above the legal speed.

While he drives, my fingers tap so fast on the keys the computer takes a moment to respond to all my commands. I let out a relieved breath when I'm able to use the SSD drive to gain control of the server console. They haven't found it yet. The list of encrypted memories appears for my stealing pleasure. This is it. My last chance. I won't be able to sneak into this data center again. I won't have any other way to get back deleted memories. At least until we find this hacker and prove my innocence.

Sebastian parks in the middle of a strip mall parking lot in the hopes of concealing the car among the crowd.

I select a random memory from the favorite list to transfer into both our minds and hope to hell it's a good one. If I don't transfer it before the SSD drive is disconnected, I'll never be able to. I have to watch it immediately to have any hope of finding the information I need.

Blackness overtakes my vision, blotting out the afternoon sun. When the new scene pops in, the darkness only recedes a little. I'm already running backward through the empty Varga Industries parking lot, weaving around a handful of cars, as lampposts illuminate my progress like spotlights. My bare arms pump along my sides, and flashes of the blue shirt I wore Monday pop into my line of vision. I purchased the shirt last weekend. Cool air blasts and the skeletal trees dance against an inky black sky. Fat tears shimmy up my cheeks and stuff themselves back into my eyes.

Running backward, I race up the marble steps and stop short, spinning to face Mr. Kimmel, who stands in front of the double doors. His casual black T-shirt reveals his bulging muscles.

[Correction. My past. And that's where it'll stay.] A smile stretches my face, weird compared with the tears rolling down my cheeks.

[Because it's your project. Your future.]

I scoff. [This was his choice. Why would I ever help you?]

[And now he can't.] Mr. Kimmel's face changes from all business to crumpled in pain. [We need you to show us how to make Theseus work. Bash wouldn't tell us.]

I shake my head.

Mr. Kimmel ventures a step away from me. [Arden, we need your help.]

[This wasn't what he wanted at all.] I bury my face in my hands and pace in front of my teacher. My heels click out the beat of my heart. [He said no! He told you guys no!]

[He would have died,] Kimmel says in a calm voice. [Not forever. Teddy had no choice.]

My body dips toward the ground and a strangled cry rips from my throat. [I didn't even get to say good-bye! He's gone forever. Oh my God.] My head shakes back and forth so fast, it's like I'm trying to hypnotize him.

[He's gone.] His voice cracks. [It's too late, Arden.] Something inside me cracks as well.

I let out a sob so loud and wounded, it sounds as if I've been stabbed in the gut. [Is it true?] I croak out. [Teddy called me.]

But before Mr. Kimmel can answer, reality jerks back into me like a punch to the throat. Something in my chest squeezes shut and I suck in desperate gulps of air as if I'm about to drown. The raw emotion radiating from me in the memory makes a fresh lump lodge in my throat. I don't know what happened or why I was crying back then, but whatever it was, it was enough to punch a hole in my gut, both then and now. Something terrible happened.

Something terrible that Teddy had a part in.

0011001000110110

ebastian and I both look at each other, panting from the raw emotion radiating from the flashback. "What does it mean?"

I shake my head, trying to piece the memory back in the correct order. I ran up to the school at night, propelled by a phone call from Teddy. Mr. Kimmel was already there, waiting for me, and let me know it was too late, Bash was already gone. I seemed to think he may have died yet Teddy saved him somehow, despite what Bash wanted. But Mr. Kimmel wanted me to tell him how to get Theseus to work, because Bash refused. I refused too.

"The timing of it is too coincidental. That happened Monday night."

Sebastian rubs his jaw. "Hours before someone deleted our memories."

I tear up my sleeve and grab a pen from my purse, squeezing a few more vertical lines onto the timeline sprawled across my arm.

S has six months to live
S's Duplicell procedure/Teddy's procedure
S cured—Monday night
S and A refuse to use Theseus or tell anyone how it works
Kimmel leaves himself a note as memories are deleted
S no memories/A's memories deleted

Admin computer stolen
Projects due
Press conference

There's one more piece of the memory that sticks out to me. Kimmel, asking me to show him how Theseus works. As if it actually *works*, no more kinks to iron out, no bugs to solve. "I think . . ." I pause, testing the words out on the tip of my tongue before I commit them to Sebastian's ears. "I think our project is done. Ready. We got it working."

His mouth parts, nodding. "But we decided not to use it."

"The bug that Kimmel alluded to. It was *us*."

One thing's for certain, I'm not going home like my mother demanded. I need to find Teddy.

HiveMind will tell me where Teddy's last known whereabouts were. When I access his account, I watch the memory that was synced only five minutes ago. I stare out of his eyes at the basement retina scanner. He looks left and right down the clear hallways, thinking about how all the students have headed home already to put the finishing touches on their presentations for tomorrow's board review. Weird. Teddy didn't even go to school today, so why is he heading there as soon as it ends? A red light sweeps over the image, nearly blinding me. But then the light turns green, beeping with acceptance. Teddy swings open the door and marches down to the basement with purpose.

The back of my neck tingles. Why would he be granted basement access?

The only thing on his mind is a phrase, repeated in refrain: *Don't cry yet. Don't cry yet. Don't cry yet.*

He bypasses the now empty IT room and defunct server room. He turns a corner and stands in front of room thirty-four B.

Another retina scanner greets him, this one admitting him without question as well. I remember Teddy coming up from the basement the other day, but I've never been in room thirty-four B. It must be one of the generic locked storage rooms I always ignore.

The memory ends there. I'd have to wait for the next one to complete the capture and sync before I can see the rest, but we don't have time for that. "Still have your copy of my mom's eyeball?"

He reaches into the back seat and pulls out his backpack. "Yep. Too bad I'm not being graded at how well I've kept it preserved."

"You are and you passed. Now let's go find out what Teddy knows."

AS SOON AS we step inside the empty hallway, my pulse beats hard and fast in my neck. If my mom comes back and finds me here, I'm toast. My mouth clamps shut and I force my breathing to leak as slowly as possible through my nose. When we reach the retina scanner, Sebastian carefully unearths his copy of my mom's eye and holds it up. My hands clench until the light turns green. He swings the door open.

Sebastian and I carefully walk down, placing each foot gingerly on the step below. We stop in front of room thirty-four B. It contains no sign, nothing but a heavy door and the same level of recently upgraded security as everything else down here. Sebastian uses the retina scanner to unlock the door and then he gently places the eye back in the ice and hands me the container. I place it in my purse to keep it close. My hands shake when I pull the door open.

White flooring leads up to sleek metal tables. Metal squares line the walls, each with a little hook on the end. The room twists into different sections, and metal drawers line those walls. I shiver from the sudden burst of air-conditioning, loud as thunder, and rub my arms over my sleeves. Sebastian's teeth chatter and his hair dances from an overhead vent.

"This looks like . . ." Sebastian leans close to inspect one of the metal slots. There's a number etched into it. "A morgue."

I press my palm against the metal and yank it back with a yelp. It's ice cold. "Why would there be a morgue in the basement of the school?"

With my pulse beating in my ears, I grip one of the handles and tug it toward me. A long tray slides out, covered with a white sheet. There's a bulge in the center beneath the sheet, too small to be a person. We nod to each other, our silent form of counting one, two, three, before we pull back the sheet. A foot rests on the slab, looking perfectly normal except for the fact that it's not attached to a body. There's no sinew or bone sticking out of it. The top of the foot where the ankle should be rounds off in a perfect skin graft.

I thrust my hand into my mouth and bite down to stop myself from screaming. Sebastian swiftly shoves the cold chamber drawer shut and then clamps his hands over his mouth.

Maybe this is where Teddy keeps all the body parts he printed.

There are so many metal shelves here. "How many parts are there in the human body?" I whisper to Sebastian.

"Two hundred and six bones. Six hundred and forty-two skeletal muscles. But judging by the foot, they're not being printed separately. It's impossible to know how many combinations he's printing."

He pulls out another tray a few rows down, the sound of metal scraping grating on my last shred of nerves. The lump under this one is significantly larger. Body-sized.

I brace myself in every way I can: hand steadied on a cold metal drawer, breath stilled, legs apart.

Slowly, he peels back the white sheet.

And there, lying on the tray, is a body with only half a face.

But it's the face of my father.

My heart pounds so hard and fast it feels as if it's about to explode out of my chest. Panic claws at my gut, and I stumble away, hand clamped over my mouth, until my back hits one of the metal shelves. I spin around and yank it open, sliding out another tray with another person-sized blob underneath the white sheet. With a tug, the white sheet falls off, revealing another copy of my dad, this one sporting a mangled ear and a large gaping hole where an eye should be. Instead of gray skin, this one still boasts a rosy hue, as if he's just sleeping.

Bile bubbles in my throat and I slam that tray back into the wall before pulling out another. There's another body, gray hairs forming an inkblot pattern on his chest, but instead of a head, the neck ends in a smooth stump.

I pull out another and another, each one containing a version of my dad that's somehow wrong. Somehow not whole. Somehow not the same.

But still, they're all *him*.

I stop at one that's nearly perfect, just a small imperfection on the back of his skull. My ragged breaths grow harsh against my raw throat. I haven't seen his face in so long, and even though none of these copies are whole, each one plugs a void so deep in my heart that my chest seems too small to even contain it. I feel like I'm suffocating just from standing here, trying to bask in the image I haven't set my eyes on in far too long. I take in every pore, every beauty mark. I reach out to stroke his cheek, somehow still warm despite his being gone for over a year. The other side of his skull is just a flat plane of skin, like a slab of marble a sculptor has only half chiseled. Hot tears press against my eyes, and when Sebastian wraps his arms around me, I collapse into him, no longer able to hold myself upright.

A sob rings out from somewhere down one of the hallways hidden inside this room. It must run half the length of the building. Sebastian and I jerk apart and I suck in a shaky breath. All I want to do is stay here, staring at my dad's face, but I know we need to follow that sound. We need answers. I can't afford to fall apart right now.

With a gargantuan amount of willpower, I press a finger to my lips and tiptoe toward the sound, my legs wobbly, bypassing more rows of refrigerator shelves that resemble metal laundry chutes. How many contain copies of my dad? I nearly break down from that thought.

Around a corner, Teddy comes into view, his back to us, leaning over an open drawer. There's something resting on the metal slab, a person-sized bulge.

"It's not the same," Teddy whispers to himself between sniffles. "*You're* not the same." Another racking sob rips from his mouth. His shoulders convulse. "God, I miss you so much." He rests his head on the lump beneath the sheet. "No one else understands what I'm going through. It's killing me."

We creep toward him, keeping our footsteps light, but his sniffles cover our movements.

His voice softens. "I'm so sorry, man. I should have honored your request. I should never have let her talk me into going through with this."

Teddy shifts, burying his head in his hands to cry some more. With his head lowered, the person lying on the tray comes into view. Not just any person. It's *Sebastian*, lying cold and dead on a white sheet.

His hair's the same, his body's relatively the same though more gaunt, it's all the same except for one differentiating factor: the bluish-gray tint to his skin. Bash's plastic-rimmed glasses rest on his face. The cloying stench of decay lingers near him like he's dead.

Because he *is* dead.

I let loose a sharp, tense scream. Sebastian vomits onto his sneakers. *Bash is dead.*

Teddy bolts upright, frantically rubbing his knuckles against the tears streaming down his dark cheeks. "Arden. Sebastian. What are you doing here?"

I stare, unblinking, my face frozen in anguish. Clues echo in my head, robbing me of breath.

Why Sebastian woke up without memories but knows textbook information. Information that could be uploaded into a fresh brain even if memories aren't available. Why he had a memory of lying on a metal slab that seemed to last for days according to the file size. How he was cured of cancer. Leo's video talked about duplicating cells and eradicating the disease from each and every one. Teddy's the master of 3-D bio-printing. Zoey mentioned that Teddy had printed *every* body part, and the evidence of every printed body part is standing right beside me, tears leaking from his eyes.

Leo couldn't save him. Neither could Teddy. The only thing they could do was replace him entirely.

The procedure was done in two parts, Leo's mapping and then Teddy's printing. Sebastian must have been created from the mapped data and prepped for days on a metal table.

I look at my boyfriend. But my head volleys between the boy standing beside me and the one on the tray. The boy I love is . . . both of them. The one standing beside me and the one who will never stand again.

I whip my head around the room at all the metal trays, each one likely containing a failed prototype, a 3-D printed clone gone wrong somehow, just like the copies of Dad I found. Leo's words from earlier come back to me, telling me that Sebastian isn't the first person he experimented on, Dad was. The only clone they ever got right is Sebastian.

I whirl on Teddy. He frantically plucks the glasses off Bash's face and throws the white sheet over him. He slides the glasses into his pocket, avoiding my gaze but breathing hard.

"Explain," I demand through gritted teeth.

He swallows hard and scrubs a hand over his face before nudging Bash back into the cold prison with his hips. "You shouldn't have seen this. You should forget—"

"What?" I scoff. "You're going to delete my memories of this moment too?"

He squints at me. "Not sure what you're insinuating."

A hysterical laugh leaves my throat. I have no time for this shit. "Tell. Me. What's. Going. On." The words slide through gritted teeth. "Start from the very beginning." I flourish my hand around the room. "Or I tell everyone about everything in here."

A large sigh rattles his shoulders. "Leo was working on the cell project, but the mice kept dying shortly after being cured. And I'd gotten really good at printing body parts. I was starting to experiment with printing them connected."

Sebastian stares at Teddy. "Y-you mean printing *bodies*?"

He swallows hard but nods.

"And it was Zoey's idea to marry the two projects," I say, putting more pieces together. A barnacle, she called it, because she was latching onto two other projects to make hers whole. Now I understand why Teddy couldn't give her co-credit; she didn't really *do* anything.

"Leo finds the cancerous cells and eradicates them before I print a fresh model. Except"—Teddy rotates his hand at the various metal cells—"it took a lot of practice to get right."

I shiver. "Why are you keeping all the copies of my dad?"

"To study them. So I don't make the same mistake again."

Now I really want to throw up.

"The procedure wasn't refined yet," Teddy says fast, his hands shaking. "I couldn't get it to work in time." He stumbles toward me, and both hands grip tight on my shoulders. "It's for the best. Your dad's still whole, even though he's gone." Teddy's eyes flick toward Sebastian and then back to me. "Your dad's still the same."

My head swims with this news. Hot tears press against my eyes. "No!" I back up, shaking my head. "I would rather have him here. Just like I have Sebastian."

"But you don't have *Bash*." Teddy holds my gaze, trying to get me to understand something my brain still can't make sense of.

"How did I die?" Sebastian's whisper against the silence forces us to turn back to him.

Teddy rakes a hand through his hair before plopping down in the nearest chair. "Monday night Bash came in for another scan. We were just comparing everything in his body with the—the *lusus naturae*." When we both look at him strangely, he clarifies, "The clone." He eyes Sebastian up and down. "You." His eyes flutter shut. "He—he told me he'd made a decision."

"*He's* right here." I jab my arm toward Sebastian.

"That's not *him*." Teddy shakes his head. "Bash told me he wasn't going to go through with it. That he wanted to die as himself and he wanted me to destroy . . . him." Teddy flicks his eyes toward Sebastian. "I held Bash's hand and promised I would." He buries his head in his hands. "Oh God."

Sebastian's expression draws tight. I inhale a shaky breath and then lace my fingers with his.

"He wasn't supposed to die for several more weeks, but suddenly he couldn't breathe. It was just a routine test, nothing invasive, no needles. He clutched his chest, coughed up blood." Teddy bites down on his fist. "He died. Right there on the table. I did some scans—it was a pulmonary embolism."

Sebastian sucks in a breath.

"It's common for terminal cancer patients, brain cancer patients especially—but it was just so sudden. One second he was talking and the next he was gone forever. I called Zoey to come over. You too, Arden. We had to decide, right then and there, what to do. I tried to honor his wishes, but . . . You didn't show up and she started the process with the clone we'd already prepped and I was too numb to stop her. Too *selfish* to stop her."

A spike of horror shoots through me. Zoey *knew*. She knew this whole time about Sebastian and she never said a word.

Fat tears leak from Teddy's eyes. "I betrayed my best friend's dying wish just so I could get him back." His voice cracks and he sets his anguished gaze on Sebastian. "But you're not the same. You won't ever be the same."

Sebastian's jaw clenches. "That's because you deleted all my memories."

"I didn't delete anything. After we got you working, Zoey called Leo over to upload any knowledge he could so he could test the upgrades he was working on. Leo doesn't even know he gave those upgrades to a clone."

He was a blank clone, void of everything. Memories. Knowledge. *Personality.* "To save Bash, we needed to transfer his memories, his *entire personality*. But I refused."

Oh my God. Theseus referred to the moral question of whether or not a ship was still the same ship if every single wooden board was replaced. Every part of Sebastian has been replaced, except for the last step. The final piece of the puzzle. Not just memories but his entire personality.

Sebastian's eyebrows shoot way up his forehead. "But that doesn't explain about your memories being gone."

"It does." My head spins. I grip the lip of the lab table to keep myself upright. "Marrying all *three* projects was Zoey's idea. Not just two. She needs them *all* to succeed because she was denied co-credit for each individual project and this is her last chance. Except I refused to go through with the last part of the project."

My best friend, one of the only people I trusted completely, betrayed me. My chest aches. It feels as if someone punched their way between my lungs and ripped out my heart in the process.

Sebastian snaps his fingers. "And so she deleted your memories of me and our project to prevent you from remembering that you wouldn't go through with it."

"And she's probably trying to get it to work herself so she can complete the personality transfer without my involvement." I taught her how to code. There's a good chance I once taught her how Theseus works. Her hacking skills prove that she's done far more practicing than she let on.

So Sebastian never had any memories because he's a clone, but Zoey deliberately took a pickax to mine, one by one. And once we reunited on our project, she started weeding out our memories every time we got too close to the truth. Kimmel's had to go too—he knew too much and kept trying to remember it just like we did. My mom was probably a liability too. I'd been running to my best friend for help this entire time, but all that did was give her the information she needed to betray me. No wonder my mom showed up for her appointment at the data center early. Zoey probably tipped her off to my presence there.

This also explains why Teddy still has *his* memories intact. Zoey couldn't bear to mess with his personality by removing anything.

Sebastian's shoulders rattle as he takes a deep breath, swallowing hard, his Adam's apple bobbing. "Do you think I'm—" He squeezes his eyes shut. "Incomplete?"

I muster up my most genuine smile. Just being in the vicinity of him makes my cells light up like a circuit board. "You're perfect."

"But I'm not. I'm an experiment that someone couldn't even finish. The guy you fell in love with is dead and the only thing left is—"

"You." I grab his hand across the table and lace my fingers with his. "I fell in love with *you*."

The bright overhead lights illuminate the pain on his face.

"Nothing's going to change my mind." I squeeze his hand, but then I glance over at Bash, lying dead on the tray under the sheet. If I got my memories back, would I even feel the same way about Sebastian?

"I'm pretty sure *I* can change your mind." The click of heels diverts our attention to the end of the hallway, where Zoey comes into view. "When I remove these memories, anyway."

0011001000110111

I stalk toward Zoey, hands curled into fists. "Zoey, I trusted you. How could you betray me like this?" My voice cracks on the last word.

She squints at me, dark eyeliner creasing. "*Betray* you? I'm *helping* you! You were devastated that Bash died. I got your boyfriend back for you." She beams at the way Sebastian and I are clutching each other's hands. "I did this all for you!" She turns to Teddy, her eyes glowing. "And you! Your best friend is back!"

Teddy holds up his hands and rolls his eyes as if to say *sure, whatever*.

My ears perk up at her words. She's telling me everything I want to hear, and for a moment, I lap it all up. I think of the way she's been pushing us toward each other and her confession just now fits like two puzzle pieces connecting. But my mind lingers on the last part of her words. *I did this all for you.* "No." I lift my chin. "You did this because Sebastian's your only shot at getting credit for a project." Plus she told me herself she was trying to impress Teddy.

"Well, yeah." She shrugs. "That too. But that's just an added bonus."

I back away from her, shaking my head. "You've been monitoring us the entire time. Watching everything we do. Archiving our memories as we discovered new things." It's so obvious now; I don't know why I couldn't see it before. She had access to my locker to destroy the eye *and* rip pages out of my notebook.

She saw everything. My feelings for Sebastian. The intimacy of us writing on each other's bodies. When I went to the bathroom. I feel violated. Splayed open on the operating table, my guts exposed.

"Not the entire time. Only the last few hours. Before that I was just going by the information you were giving me, new memories as they popped up, and the automatic HiveMind tags as memories became available to figure out what to archive via Theseus. But it wasn't enough. I kept missing things. And I couldn't always get access to Theseus when I needed to remove something."

Her words tangle in my chest. That's why she didn't get rid of every piece of our investigation except for that one night when she gutted it all: She didn't know everything to remove and had limited access to Theseus to do it. It also explains why she removed some memories immediately after they happened, like the ones where it seemed Kimmel forgot what he was saying: She probably archived those the instant they hit the HiveMind queue. It also explains why she didn't get rid of my version of that same event until later: She lost her access to Theseus and had to wait until she got it back. Until a few hours ago . . . when she stole the admin console. Now, she has full control over *everything*.

"But wait," I say. "I checked your mind. You didn't have any memories of Bash. Plus I found evidence that you had memories archived."

"Yeah, only because I knew you were going to check. You literally *asked* my permission to do so. I transferred most of them back after you did, but left a few archived just in case you checked again."

I squeeze my eyes shut. She was always one step ahead of me, even when I thought I was one step ahead of her. My body winds tight. Holy isotopes. I even taught her the basics of hacking. I gave her every piece of ammo she needed to use against me. I wish I could reverse time, take back all the things I taught her. Take back our entire friendship.

Sebastian clears his throat. "I don't get it though. If all you wanted was credit for the idea of creating me and for Arden to get her, um, boyfriend back, then why go through all this trouble? Why not tell her everything from the start? After all, she was confiding in you."

My chin quivers. I need this answer to make sense. I need her to say something that won't make me hate her.

"I didn't have a choice. We couldn't risk you discovering Theseus and then shutting off access again, just as we've started figuring out how to make it work." She wrinkles her nose. "Though we're not entirely there yet. Personally, I'm cool with Sebastian as he is now, but he's not exactly marketable like this."

Sebastian scoffs. "What does that mean? According to Leo, I'm a newer, improved version of my old self!"

"But you're missing the main selling appeal: immortality. Without the personality transfer, a clone becomes worthless when the original dies."

A chill runs through me. I can hear the marketing pitch in my head. You can never die as long as you can transfer yourself into an empty shell. You can be young again with a simple data upload. With a few "upgrades," you can become taller, smarter, or any other combination with just a simple flip of the switch.

"Wait. Wait. Back up a second. Who is *we*?" There's a hard set to Teddy's chin. "Because it's certainly not me."

Zoey doesn't say anything more and I suspect she's not going to. She's working with someone. Someone who isn't Teddy or Leo. Someone she refuses to name.

"Why come here, then? Why not just delete the memory of this moment as we live it? You've done it before."

"Yes, but your stupid backups keep getting in the way. Besides, I need Sebastian to come with me. Just until the press conference tomorrow. You can have him back after and kiss him *all* you want. Promise."

I scoff. "No way in hell. He stays with me."

"I agree with Arden." Sebastian steps beside me, shoulder to shoulder. He laces his fingers with mine in a show of solidarity.

"Actually, I do too." Teddy crosses his arms. "My board review presentation's at 9:05 a.m. tomorrow. I need Sebastian there."

Zoey lets out a heavy sigh. "I didn't want to have to do this." She sets her messenger bag on the table and fumbles through it. I catch a glimpse of the admin console laptop hastily thrown into her messy bag, and my entire body straightens.

I nudge Sebastian and he follows my line of vision, his jaw clenching.

She unearths a spray bottle and points it toward us. A fabric face mask dangles in her free hand. "You guys are so good at mixing chemicals, why don't you tell me what this does? It's sevoflurane."

Sebastian's face pales. "Same stuff used in anesthesia. Essentially a sleeping gas. It'll wear off in about an hour."

Zoey marches toward us, aiming the spray bottle at Sebastian and me. "I don't want to use this. I really don't. But Arden, I have no choice. This is my only chance."

After all, if Sebastian misses Teddy's review, he can't get credit either. But *she* can. My pulse slams in my neck as I frantically assess the situation, all escape routes. But I won't be able to escape at all if I become incapacitated while she performs mental surgery on me.

"Just don't hurt him. Please." Teddy's face falls and he stands guard at Bash's tomb. It's obvious the *him* he means is Bash, not the guy Zoey's aiming the canister at.

Sebastian squeezes my hand. At first, I think he's telling me that we're in this together. That we'll stay strong, no matter how many memories she deletes, no matter what kind of chemicals she attacks us with. But then he breaks free of me and lunges toward her.

He slams into her so hard they both stumble backward and crash into a wall of cold chambers, rattling them.

Her messenger bag lies on the metal table, open and exposed, the admin console peeking out. I don't think. I just run for it, lifting the entire bag from the table and cradling it in my arms.

Zoey screams, but Sebastian pins her down. She struggles to get out of his embrace, kicking him in the shin in the process. He flicks his eyes to me, then toward the door, the universal signal for *run*.

I can't leave him, but if I stay here, neither of us will get away. Running is the only chance to save us both. I race out of the room, the backpack squeezed in my arms. I hear the telltale sound of an aerosol can spraying just before the door slams shut. I bite back the sob that catches in my throat. My lungs pump painfully as I charge up the stairs faster.

I kick open the side entrance and zoom into the cool night air. At my car, my sweaty palms catch on the steering wheel. I shift my car into reverse and back up at an angle, swinging the wheel like a stunt driver. I lurch the car backward toward the street behind me, the lack of streetlights robbing me of proper vision.

My back tire crunches over a curb and lands on the street with a thud that makes my head hit the ceiling. The car bounces for a moment, wheels spinning in the air. My teeth clench. I rev the gas and take the street at eighty miles per hour. Trees whip by on either side of me, blending into the dark night sky.

I've driven three towns away before I feel safe enough to park in an empty shopping center and catch my breath. The weight of what just happened descends on me.

Sebastian sacrificed himself for me. I'm on my own now, the only one who can stop Zoey.

Something she said earlier swims back to the forefront of my mind: The reason she stole the admin console was in part because she couldn't get access to Theseus when she needed it. From what she told me, it's clear that Theseus is only installed on those two admin computers, and I know all too well how difficult it was to gain access to the admin console stored in the IT room with all the new security protocols. If Zoey had gone through the same lengths I went through to get access, I would have seen the evidence just like the sloppy trail of smoke bombs and severed eyeballs I left behind. No, someone was *granting* her access to the other admin console, the one my mother said was still safe. Zoey possibly even had remote access so she was able to archive memories from her phone without being physically near the console, the same way my SSD drives allowed me to connect remotely. But it still seems that someone only granted Zoey access at certain times, not all day every day like she'd get with a stolen computer.

There's only one person who would grant her access to the other admin console. Hell, there's only one other person in the entire company who would care if we got Theseus to work properly, if we could transfer over Bash's entire personality instead of letting Sebastian wake up a blank slate. With only a few days before the press conference, she would need to be confident it worked as expected before she released it to the public.

Mom.

"Oh my God." My words give way to silence and the heavy rasp of my own heaving breath.

Everything she said to me—the software glitch, the Ethics Committee reports, that she thought *I* was the one behind it all—it was all a misdirection to throw me off her scent and get me out of the way while she and Zoey tried to get my project working. With a gasp, I think back to all the times she seemed to have a memory removed as we were talking, but it was either all an act or she was removing them and replacing them again right after. If I thought her memories were being tampered with, I'd never suspect *her*.

But she didn't have time to monitor me or continually archive my memories, so she recruited the one person who was desperate enough to do anything she said in the hopes that my mother would change her mind and grant Zoey co-credit. My mother knew how to tamper with memories, and she probably instructed Zoey to carve out all evidence of my relationship with Bash from my mind and everyone else's to keep me strong, to keep me from falling to pieces from grief, to give me a reason to figure out what my project is and execute it in a way I refused to previously.

Zoey isn't the mastermind behind this whole thing.

My mother is.

0011001000111000

others are supposed to look out for you. They're supposed to lift up the car you're trapped under without any consideration of the weight. They're the person who brings you chicken noodle soup when you're sick and waits up all night when you sneak out, just to make sure you get home in one piece.

They're not supposed to stab you in the back.

My fingers curl into tight fists. My legs itch to march over to my house and confront her right now. Make her look me in my eye and betray me to my face.

But I can't risk it.

Not after seeing the way Zoey wielded a chemical weapon in our faces just to stop us from fucking this up for her. No, I need time to think, assess, plan. Figure out how to stop Zoey and my mother and then rescue Sebastian.

I slide a key into a generic motel room a few towns away. Emotion clogs my throat at the memory of what happened last time I was in a motel room, when Sebastian and I bonded while we wrote our secrets across each other's skin. Holy isotopes, I miss him so much and it's only been an hour.

But that thought propels me forward, makes me stronger. I plop down on the bed, open the admin laptop, and use my mother's eye to unlock the retina scanner. The laptop boots up with a little chime that startles me.

When I click on HiveMind, I'm automatically logged in to the admin account. I take a deep breath and then navigate to the host server access option in the admin control panel. A new window pops open with a folder hierarchy structure of account authentication details and memories. Before I do anything else, I take another backup of both my and Sebastian's minds in case my mother gives Zoey access to the other admin console.

Once the backups are complete and our memories are safe once again, I find the hidden folder containing my encrypted memories, except this time it's not hidden, because I can view everything with the admin tools. When I navigate to it, I'm transported to a totally different interface with a fancy Theseus logo at the top. I can easily toggle between HiveMind and Theseus from the plug-in panel.

When I dig deeper into the interface, there's a whole lot more open to me. It's not just my folder accessible via the admin folder but many others I couldn't see before, likely because of access controls that prevented me from seeing anyone else's account info. Nearly every student in the school has a folder in here thanks to Zoey's memory games, but two particular ones stick out to me besides my own: Bash Cuomo. And my dad.

My heart bleeds out of my chest and I sink deeper into the bed with a new heaviness. All that's left of my dad is right here. Right in front of me.

I inhale a shaky breath and force myself to keep moving. I click on my own account, and my chest aches at all the memories there for the taking. I know I could transfer them one by one via Hive-Mind but that would take days. I don't have that kind of time. I need to get Theseus working and transfer them all together.

I tap my fingers against the white bedspread. HiveMind restricts more than one memory transfer at a time . . . So maybe the issue is with HiveMind, not Theseus.

I straighten. Holy isotopes. If Theseus is a plug-in for HiveMind as it appears to be, then the firewalls and security protocols the Ethics Committee installed are probably blocking the plug-in from working the way it should.

I confirm this theory by checking the number of code lines associated with Theseus. 56,320. The exact number of lines I found changed overnight a few days ago. *TransferEmos*, *TransferFrags*, and *TransferSpecial* must all be commands for Theseus: Transferring *emotions*, memory *fragments*, and *special* for everything else associated with a personality. In theory, if I disconnect myself from Hive-Mind and connect to Theseus directly, it should work properly.

Switching back to HiveMind, I highlight my folder in the authentication and select *Deactivate*. Deactivating the account will wipe all data that's stored on the server. It'll be as if the account never existed. The confirmation window pops up, and the abrupt *ding* sound makes me flinch. *Are you sure you want to deactivate this account?*

I get up and pace the room, doing a lap around the queen-sized bed. Yes or no. If I'm wrong and this isn't how to make Theseus work, then I risk losing *everything*. But if I'm right, I can get it all back.

I straighten my shoulders and sit back on the bed with gusto. I click *yes*.

My name disappears from the HiveMind user list and all the files in my folders flicker out of existence, one by one. But the memories still remain in my mind because I'm no longer synced.

This account has been deactivated.

Tension eases from my shoulders. My feet remain steady when I walk and my head buzzes with clarity. I'm me again, just me. But I still feel incomplete, missing half of myself, like I've chopped off my hair and my brush stops too soon when I run it through the strands.

When I navigate back to Theseus, there are new controls available on my account that weren't there before when it was acting as a plug-in on my account: a handy *Decrypt All* button as well as a *Transfer All* button. My body tenses as I press each button in turn.

I sink to the carpet and clutch the sides of my head as the memories return with the force of a tsunami, knocking the wind out of me. My vision goes black and then the memories march through my mind in reverse order. They come so fast and fierce I barely have time to latch onto snippets before the next overtakes me. I cry out in pain as I pick up the phone and listen to Teddy's voice: "*Arden, he's gone. He died in my arms. Oh God. What do I do?*" A moment later, I'm back at the Hypnotist's office that same night, trying to fool myself into relaxing under his guidance. I'd just come from dinner with Bash and he was acting weird. Lethargic. Slurring his words. Complaining of chest pains. I needed to escape my own mind while he met up with Teddy for a routine test, if only for a few minutes, if only so I didn't have to face the reality of him leaving me forever.

A week before, the two of us placing our joined hands on a mouse and together adjusting the controls on Theseus to lock out users when accessing the plug-in through HiveMind just in case anyone tried to bypass Bash's decision.

The day before that, Bash sneaking into my bedroom window in the middle of the night. "*I don't want to live in a fake body with a fake life.*" I squeezed his hand. "*I won't ever be able to love another version of you anyway,*" I promised.

Losing my virginity, not on Valentine's Day like my retrieved memory indicated but four months prior, the two of us curling up in his twin bed and finding a way to block his death sentence from our minds.

Falling in love in every way possible, each day bringing me renewed joy just to be with him. I loved him. I loved him so much.

Oh, it hurts to lose him. Sobs rip from my throat. I'll never be able to hold him again or kiss him. He's so different from Sebastian, wild and carefree compared with Sebastian's calm and composed view on life. I'll never feel the rush of Bash's leaping out of a lab chair and spinning me into a waltz to the music blasting from his phone speaker. I'll never clutch his hand wishing I could take away his pain while doctors poked needles into his arm. I'll never be with him again.

Our first kiss, the way I pushed him against the wall one night while working on our project and never let him go.

Bash, my sweet Bash.

And oh God, it goes back even further. Memories of my dad I didn't even know I was missing return, ones my mom carefully archived long before Zoey came into the picture. She must have done this to keep me focused, stop me from mourning. The way I broke down when the funeral director lifted the casket for one last peek at his body before it was lowered into the ground forever. Bursting into tears in front of the funeral director and cursing him out in my intense grief. Crawling beside his body in the hospice and curling against him one last time, his skin already cold. Barging into Teddy's basement morgue and begging him to get his project in working order because my dad had just been moved to hospice care.

Emotions rattle through me, morphing from pain to love to grief to terror as each new memory clangs through my body. When they finally subside, I'm on all fours, panting, my hair slicked with sweat. The memories remain, forever implanted now. It feels like I'm cheating on Sebastian with all these feelings bouncing around in my chest for a guy who no longer exists.

Bash is gone. And I didn't even get to say good-bye.

But I can get him back. I don't have to lose him.

I scramble to my feet and tilt the laptop toward me, my heart pumping wildly. There, right there, are all of Bash's memories. His entire personality. *Him.*

The idea is so tempting that my skin prickles. If I press the buttons, Sebastian will be overwritten, replaced forever. He won't even know he's gone. He only existed for a few days, but Bash was my entire world for years. Bash will forgive me for going against his dying wish. I know he will. I know him better than I know myself. When he decided not to live, the cancer had already metastasized to his brain. He wasn't thinking clearly. He worked for four years on this project. *This* is what he wanted. To be with me forever.

With every beat of my heart, I can only think about one thing: *Bash, the love of my life. Gone forever.*

But I can save him.

This is how I save lives.

Except . . . then I'd lose Sebastian forever. Sebastian, with his Google search brain and his fierce loyalty. Sebastian, who was there for me the last few days, standing shoulder to shoulder with me, my equal. What I lacked, he had, a balance I could never find with Bash, where our strengths often clashed against each other rather than complementing each other. Sebastian, who I fell in love with far faster and more deeply than I ever thought possible.

Sebastian or Bash. My future or my past. Who I want to be versus who I've been.

I can't lose either of them. I can't choose who lives and who dies.

But I have to.

I have to make this choice before my mother makes it for me.

0011001000111001

E ven though I deactivated my own HiveMind account last night, I reconnect myself the next morning. It's the only way, despite all the risks. To rescue Sebastian before the press conference begins, I need the tools that HiveMind offers me. If Sebastian isn't there, my mother has no proof of concept to present to the world.

When I check on Sebastian via HiveMind, all I see is darkness. Cold air. Fear pumping through his body. Longing for me. He woke up like this, in captivity, in a room with no identifiers, in complete panic about what's to come.

I tense, leaping to my feet. I pace the room, unable to shake the feeling of unease.

It's okay, I think. *I'm coming for you. Somehow.* I transfer the memory of me thinking this into his mind, hoping it gives him some form of comfort.

Zoey brings Sebastian breakfast, but the quick glimpse of the door opening and shutting offers only a peek at an empty gray hallway. It resembles the ones on the Varga Industries floors, but there are forty of those and over a hundred rooms on each. This only narrows his location down to what I've already guessed: Zoey's keeping him somewhere in the building.

She tries to reassure him, promises this is only for a few more hours, tries to absolve her guilt with another vow: that she'll delete the memory of this room so he won't ever have to think about it again after today. It's not a reassurance.

My heart aches for him, sitting there all night, in total fear, knowing he's going to lose this very moment just like he may have lost me.

Zoey's careful. As soon as I deactivated my account last night, hers disappeared too. She doesn't want me to be able to access her most recent memories and follow her, one step behind. My mother also took my cue and removed her account as well. Still, they have the admin console and can continue to view the memory tags that populate in everyone's queue. They can still archive them. They can still make people forget everything I need them to remember.

Which means there's only one way I might be able to find Sebastian.

With shaky hands, I dial a number I rarely call. Teddy picks up on the first ring. "Arden." It's just a single word, but the gravity of his emotions comes through loud and clear. I can hear the heavy swallow, the way his voice cracks at the end of my name. "They're making me go to the PC. Told me it was the only way I could get any sort of credit after missing my review this morning. I can't go. I can't."

The two of us have never been the type of friends who vent to each other, but I'm the only one he has now. The only person who understands.

"I have a plan. Sort of. But it does involve you going to the PC."

He groans.

"We need to rescue him. Please. I know he's not Bash, but please." My voice cracks. "If your only motivation is to mess up the PC, then fine."

Teddy lets out a shaky breath. "What do I need to do?"

"Get there early, find Zoey, and flirt with her. Really *really* flirt. I need you to get her to confess where she's keeping Sebastian. But we have to act fast. Before they move him to the stage." If I can rescue Sebastian before the press conference starts, then my mom's entire presentation will be ruined. Without her precious clone to show off, she'll have nothing to demonstrate. It'll all just be talk, nothing to back it up.

Teddy's silent for a moment, though I think I hear a faint squeak from the back of his throat. "Okay." There's another deep sigh, as if he needs to convince himself. "Okay, I'll do it."

We agree that Teddy will text me with the info as soon as he's able to get it out of Zoey. I head to the school parking lot and lie low, ready to make my move. Just in case, I keep Teddy's account open in HiveMind, refreshing for the instant HiveMind logs the memory. Transferring it into my mind is plan B.

An hour passes with no text. I grow more and more antsy, shifting in my seat. HiveMind refreshes and a new memory pops up, this one automatically tagged with the title: *Tries to trick Zoey.*

My heart leaps into my throat. Does *tries* mean he doesn't succeed? And why didn't Teddy send a text?

There's only thirty more minutes before the press conference. I really need answers *now*.

I copy the memory into my mind and close my eyes as I lean back against my car. I peer out of Teddy's eyes as he shows his ID to security. The guard checks his ID and then directs him to a technology checkpoint, where all nonapproved devices must be surrendered for the duration of the press conference.

"Cell phone, please," the clerk tells Teddy, holding out her palm.

Fuck. Sorry, Arden. Hopefully you'll find this via HiveMind.

I let out a breath at his forgiveness for spying on him again.

He turns over his cell phone to the woman and waltzes toward the auditorium. Inside, Zoey's on the stage, looking adorable in a frilly white dress. Her blond hair is curled into little ringlets. She's been keeping my boyfriend captive yet she had time to use a curling iron?

I want to punch her. Teddy feels the same way judging by the thought that surfaces in his mind: *God, she's awful.*

Her sensors ping directly on him as soon as he starts walking toward her. She freezes, backing away from the admin console that's propped up on the stage in full view of the thousands of cameras and an audience filling up with students, alumni, and the press.

Teddy walks right past Eliza, not even acknowledging her, and I have to wonder if Zoey finally removed every thought he's ever had about liking her. I make a mental note to myself to give him back all those thoughts and feelings after this is over. I'll give everyone back everything Zoey stole from them.

Teddy's gaze zooms on Zoey. *I can do this,* he thinks. *She deserves to be swindled.* He swaggers toward her, crooking his finger toward his chest. *Smile, damn it! This is your revenge.* The shape of his vision curves just a little, indicating he forced his cheeks to tilt upward. Zoey's eyes widen and she squeals before rushing down the stage steps and stopping with a hop right in front of him. Her smile is so wide that my heart nearly cracks in two at the sight of it. I used to trust that smile.

Teddy doesn't even flinch. "Hey. Can I talk to you?" The image blurs as he whips his head around fast, left and right. He lowers his voice. "In private?"

Zoey bites her lip. "I'm not supposed to leave the stage."

Teddy steps closer to her, so close her features blur in my vision. "Please. It's important."

Zoey lets out a little huff, flicking her eyes back at the stage and

285

the security guards standing by the stage stairs. "Okay." Her voice is low, conspiratorial. "But I only have a minute."

In his vision, I can see his hand reaching out and stroking Zoey's jaw, gently, from chin to cheek. "This'll only take a minute."

Zoey's eyes flutter closed for a second and she nearly melts into a puddle right there. She follows beside Teddy, beaming up at him with the biggest smile she's ever mustered. When they get in the hallway, he spins around fast and pins her against the wall. Security guards and members of the press mill about in his peripheral vision, but none of them pay attention to two teenagers with VIP passes. "So. I've been thinking."

Zoey gazes up at him, completely lost in his eyes. Her voice is a breathy whisper. "I think I like what you've been thinking."

"I've been thinking about us." He hits her with his megawatt smile again, coaxing himself to turn up the charm as much as possible. "I like you. I just realized that this morning."

"Oh God. You don't know how long I've been waiting for you to say that." She wraps her arms around his neck, stands on tiptoes, and plants her lips against his.

His first thought is to abort the mission and abort it fast! *Just kiss her. It's meaningless.* His lips sink into hers and I'm forced to witness the sound of their teeth clinking together and the wet squish of his tongue against hers.

"W-wow." She wipes her forehead when she pulls back, completely dazed.

"Wow," he echoes despite internally cringing. "I'm so glad this happened." *Is that enough time to butter her up before I start asking questions? Damn, I hope so. I don't want to have to kiss her again.* "I really needed this. Today has been awful."

Her lips pout, playing right into his trap. "How so?"

"I'm just upset about my project. I failed, Zo. My—" *Shit, need to correct that.* "Our entire project is a failure."

She reaches out and rubs his shoulder. "Don't say that. Sebastian is here because of you. Because of *us*. That's a win."

Teddy shakes his head and I scrunch my nose at the abrupt way the image shakes. "I can't find him though. I'm so, so worried about him. I miss Bash so much, but—Sebastian. He could fill the void." A small voice in the back of Teddy's mind echoes this thought, so quietly I'm not even sure he realizes he thought it.

Zoey waves her hand dismissively. "He's fine. Promise."

Teddy's eyes widen. "Wait, do you know where he is? Can you take me to him?"

She bites her lip, glancing around. "I can't. Not yet. But—"

Teddy backs away. *Try to look angry*, he coaches himself. "You don't trust me?"

"No, I do! Of course I do!" Zoey takes a step toward him.

"Then why won't you tell me if you know?"

I can see the decision weighing heavy in her mind, her priorities shifting. The person she's wanted most of all just kissed her and now appears to be mad at her. She can stop this. She can get him back on her side. "I really shouldn't."

"Then I'm not sure we should be together." Teddy starts to turn away, but Zoey circles him, moving into his line of sight.

"Okay, listen. I'll tell you. But you can't tell anyone."

She comes close, her hair blocking his vision. She must be whispering in his ear. "He's upstairs. In one of the empty Varga suites."

"Which one?" Teddy demands.

"Suite 1305. But—"

"Thanks." Teddy reaches out to stroke her cheek again. "I'll let you get back now."

Zoey nods in a daze and practically stumbles back into the room. Teddy stares after her, and the memory abruptly ends.

What the hell, Teddy? She was about to say *but* except he cut her off!

Still, I know where Sebastian is now. I have to act fast. Before Zoey can figure out Teddy liking her is all a ruse.

I quickly type up an email and hit send.

By now, hundreds of cars pack the Varga parking lot. While everyone else ambles toward the main entrance of the school, I weave around the building until I reach the Varga Industries entries. Jay, my favorite security guy, kicks back at his desk, the lone guard for the side of the building no one wants to access.

"Hey." I force desperate breaths in and out of my lungs to sound like I've been running. "My brother just emailed you." I press my hand against the door as if I need to brace myself to regain composure. "He left something upstairs that he needs for the conference and he sent me—"

Jay eyes me suspiciously, the smile he usually greets me with gone. "Funny, because I also have an email from your mother telling me if you came by saying exactly this, not to let you in."

Sweat coats my palms. Shit. "It's an emergency. You have to let me through."

He crosses his arms. "I don't have to do anything."

I reach into my purse and pull out a wad of twenties. "Please."

Jay scoffs. "Bribing me won't work anymore." He lifts his walkie-talkie to his lips but doesn't depress the button. "Leave now or I call for backup."

My skin prickles. The only other entrance to the corporate floors is through the school and I can't go in there without getting caught. Something dips in my stomach and I hate myself for what I'm about to do. "I know about the money you skimmed from petty cash."

"H-how?"

I ignore his question. Most of the nonscientists who are requested to sync to HiveMind do so without having any clue what it does or how it works, despite the training sessions and one-hundred-page manual the Ethics Committee provides. "I don't know what it's for, but it doesn't matter. No one else knows though. Unless I tell them."

We stand there, both of us staring the other down with our respective threats in a game of chicken.

He breaks first. "Fine. Go." He jerks his head toward the door.

My heels clack on the hardwood floors. It's the only sound louder than my beating heart. I jam my finger against the elevator button, silently praying that it drops straight from the eighth floor to the bottom so I can get in faster. When it arrives, I launch myself inside and press *floor thirteen* several times, alternating between that and the *close door* button. The squeal of hydraulics as the elevator shoots upward nearly unnerves me completely.

The doors zip open, and I propel myself out of the elevator, my vision nearly blinded by cold, slick fear. I follow the door numbers until I reach suite 1305.

The door's wide open, lights fully turned on. A sharp jolt of worry pulls me inside. I enter an empty suite, a generic-looking reception desk, cubicles spread out along the floor, all of it place-holders, waiting for someone with a brilliant new product to come in and take over. I race around the room, throwing open every door I can find, revealing empty supply closets and conference rooms and finally what appears to be an office, void of everything except a pillow and a blanket. . . . and the clothes Sebastian was wearing when I last saw him.

I sink to my knees. They've already moved him.

But I need to find him. Save him before it's too late. I scramble to remove my laptop from my bag and hastily prop it open. My fingers fly across the keys until I manage to connect myself into the most recent memory of Sebastian's.

The view of velvety red curtains obscures his vision for a moment until he shifts. A sliver of the stage and the audience beyond comes into view and I nearly vomit. He takes notice of the two security guards standing beside him, the ones by each backstage wing exit, the ones at the stage stairs, the army of them in the back of the room. Zoey, squarely onstage, hovering over the admin laptop on a table a few feet behind the podium like she's the keyboardist at a rock concert. My mother, standing just ahead of Sebastian. *If I run, there's no way to escape. They'll catch me.* His next thought is even worse: *If I expose them, if I say anything at all, they're just going to wipe my memory again. I can't risk that either.*

A shiver runs through me, heart squeezing for the pain Sebastian feels from being so trapped.

I force myself to my feet, a new plan forming in my mind.

I have to be the one to confront them. I have to destroy Theseus and ruin everything my mother and, oh God, my father worked for years for. I have to do it live onstage.

I have to wreck it all.

0011001100110000

everal news stations line the hallway, their main cameramen and reporters already inside and ready for interviews. The press conference live streams on the web, and several Varga employees man a table filled with computer equipment dedicated to keeping the conference free of glitches.

There's only one stairwell that connects the school to Varga Industries, and Jay the security guard was "nice" enough to use his eye against the retina scanner to grant me access to it, looking like he wanted to kill me the entire time. Sneaking into the school that way allows me to bypass the ID checkers at the front entrance, the ones who were probably instructed to turn me away on sight. But the guard in front of the auditorium doors doesn't have the same orders. With more bravado than I've ever mustered, I march up to him. Before I even stop, he warns, "The session's in progress. You can't go in."

I cross my arms, acting annoyed. "I'm Monica Varga's daughter and I'm late for the presentation *I'm* supposed to give."

The guard stands there, stone-faced.

"Go check if you must. But if I'm not on that stage in one minute, the entire press conference will be ruined. Do *you* want that on your shoulders?"

He purses his lips. "Let me see some ID."

I happily show him my driver's license and VIP pass, the one they issued to all seniors last week.

After studying them, he steps aside to let me pass. The tightness in my chest subsides as I push open the swinging doors.

". . . secured the investors needed!" Leo's voice booms from a microphone above the crowd's cheers. "But it gets better." He drums his palms against the podium. He's always had a flair for the dramatic. "There are several customers already lined up for the procedure. We're going to begin saving lives *tomorrow*, folks!"

I scan the stage for Sebastian, but I don't see him yet. He's probably still concealed in the backstage wings. Mom stands next to Leo with a hand on his shoulder. Teddy stays a few feet away onstage, his face full of pain, as if he can't quite bring himself to join them so close to the podium.

I march down the aisle, and when Mom spots me, she grabs the mic straight out of Leo's hand.

"And now—" Mom locks her eyes on me, which gives me momentary pause. It's almost as if she was waiting for me. Or maybe she's just trying to get the info out to the world before I attempt to stop her. "It's time to debut our first test subject. . . ."

Murmurs erupt from the crowd as a security guard pushes Sebastian onto the stage. He hesitates, his feet stuck in place, but Mom coaxes him toward her with her hand. I can see the pain of the choice rattling through him, the way his brow furrows. If he cooperates, he thinks he won't be erased.

But he still can be.

If I choose Sebastian over Bash, the only true way to make him safe forever is to remove the copy of Theseus from the admin console bolted to the table on the stage. I've already deleted it from the admin console I stole from Zoey. But in removing the program from both admin consoles, not only will I erase all the memories

Zoey stole, I'll also lose Bash forever. *Bash or Sebastian?* I have to choose now, before the press conference ends.

Sebastian takes tentative steps toward the podium as I race down the aisle. "Don't listen to a word she says!" I shout as I reach the stage stairs, but then someone grabs me from behind.

A security guard wrenches my wrists behind my back, and I grit my teeth to keep from crying out in pain. Muscular arms keep me from fighting back more than a wiggle of my elbows. My pulse amps, but I calm myself with a deep breath. I won't get free by freaking out.

Sebastian's eyes find mine, desperate, worried, pleading.

Mom smooths down her suit, her calm composure fading into an uncharacteristic smile. "You'll have to excuse my daughter." Her voice booms over mine. "She considers teenage rebellion more important than the news I'm about to share with you all."

The crowd snickers at her joke. To them, the security guards are here to prevent me from ruining my mom's big day, not keep me hostage until the private memories of every damn person in this room fall under her control, to be deleted at her whim. I slam my heel down on my captor's foot. The guard lets out a yelp but doesn't loosen his hold.

"Let me introduce you to Sebastian Cuomo." Mom's heels click along the wooden stage. The audience sits rapt with attention. I think back to something my mother said to me when she first conceived the school/distributor combo. *We're going to sell customers what they don't need but can't live without.* And the prime currency seems to be entertainment.

"Sebastian here had been diagnosed with an aggressive form of inoperable brain cancer." She flips to a new PowerPoint slide on the projector and illuminates a copy of Bash's medical chart. "If you need a closer look, you'll find copies of his chart in the packets provided at your seats." The audience flips through their papers, reading about Bash's personal data.

I struggle against my captor. "Mom, stop!"

Mom frowns at the audience. "As you can see, there was absolutely no way to save him."

"Bash is *dead*. Please!" I elbow my security guard in the gut, my arm throbbing from the impact.

"But the good news is, we *have* saved him! As you just heard, Leo developed a procedure that not only eradicates every cancerous cell from the body, but also eliminates all ailments. No more autoimmune disease! No more blurry vision! No more acne."

A few people in the audience cheer.

"And as you heard before that"—Mom waves her hand in Teddy's general direction—"Teddy Day developed advanced 3-D bio-printing technology that can print any body part in a matter of seconds. And we do mean *any*. In fact, Teddy can print an entire human being."

Leo's eyebrows shoot way up to his forehead. Something inside me cracks with relief. He really didn't know. I haven't lost my entire family.

Mom flourishes her hand toward the back of the stage, where Zoey mans the admin laptop. "But it was Zoey Flint's idea to marry the two procedures with a third I'm about to tell you about to save Bash Cuomo forever."

Zoey beams, her eyes sparkling at finally getting the credit she believes she deserves.

"Arden's right. It's true that Bash Cuomo unfortunately succumbed to his cancer only a few days ago."

"Yeah, and she hid the body!" I squirm harder now, trying to cause as much of a commotion as possible. I think of Sebastian's mother, watching this from her couch, breaking into tears at the news that her son is dead and that no one bothered to tell her.

Gasps ring out.

Mom doesn't even break a sweat. "I did not *hide* anything, as my daughter is trying to claim. I *preserved* him per the contract he signed when he turned eighteen last month."

I let out an aggravated scream. Of course she'd have this all buttoned up legally. "Whatever contract he signed is meaningless. He changed his mind!"

Mom ignores that entirely. "Sebastian here"—she waves her wrist toward him—"is Bash's *lusus naturae.*" On the screen, a slide appears containing the words: *An organism that has characteristics resulting from chromosomal alteration.* "He's a breathing human in every sense of the definition. A *cancer-free* breathing human." She replaces Bash's medical chart with Sebastian's and pauses to let that sink in. "Using advanced personality-transfer software called Theseus developed by my own daughter, Bash will have no pause in his old life. Once we transfer all his memories and his entire personality into Sebastian, Bash can pick up right where he left off, only this time without the threat of dying prematurely."

"But if you overwrite Sebastian, he'll be gone forever! And the software isn't even safe." My face burns from the exertion of shouting at the top of my lungs, but the commotion in the room is too great. My words die uselessly on my lips. "Not when it can be used as a weapon in the wrong hands. You can delete someone's entire mind with a single click."

Mom clicks to a new slide, which gives an overview of what Theseus does.

An innovative new app that enables users to copy
their entire life history into a new shell.

Memories return in reverse chronological order and appear
more vivid so that a user can relive memories in full sensory detail.

Immortality is possible with this breakthrough technology.

When combined with other Varga products, a user can even change their entire appearance by transferring their consciousness into a new, improved model carefully refined via our 3-D technology.

"With this software, we can save lives. We can get our loved ones back." Her voice cracks. "I lost my husband last year. I don't wish that kind of pain on anyone else." She takes a moment to squeeze her eyes shut and swallow down the lump that must be blocking her airway. The entire audience goes silent. When she opens her eyes again, she locks her gaze on me. "When I found out your boyfriend had passed away before you could complete the transfer, I couldn't bear to watch you go through what I went through. The pain. The hopelessness. The utter devastation." She sucks in a shuddering breath.

Something inside me cracks too. I grasp on to this new revelation—that she was trying to protect me—and I clutch at her confession so desperately my hands instinctively form tight fists, knuckles turning white. There's a part of me that wants this to be true. That she did this for me, no matter how fucked up it was. That she hasn't been working completely against me the entire time.

But I know there's also a part of her that cares about the revenue ahead, the fame and fortune. It had been my dad's dream to be the next Steve Jobs, but my mother stood beside him, nodding along with his every goal and figuring out the logistics and marketing.

"Arden." Mom swallows hard. "I did the only thing I could think of to help you get through this: I had my assistant temporarily lock away all your memories of him and store them in the data system you created to keep them safe. Just as I'd done to myself when your dad died. I thought I was helping you cope, but I realize now I went about this all wrong and I'm sorry."

My eyes widen. She just admitted this on live TV, as if this is the most natural reaction anyone would have in this situation. But the audience seems to forgive her by the way they're leaning forward, completely rapt. I was going for sympathy, but she's the one who earned it with her sincerity.

Mom turns back to the audience. "With Theseus, no one has to suffer a loss ever again. I'm going to get my husband back. My daughter's going to get her boyfriend back too. My family will be complete again."

Her words thump in my ears, lulling like a bedtime song. I can have my dad back?

The printed bodies I saw were warped, wrong, so I didn't think it was really possible. But of course it is. Now that they know how to do the printing right, they can re-create him. He can step back into our family and fill the black void that opened when he died.

"Let's see it in action!" some heckler yells from the audience. Commotion rises again, but Mom settles the audience down with a simple hand gesture.

"Now, I admit, there have been some glitches in getting Theseus to work properly. And to be completely honest, we're still resolving the final bug, so unfortunately I can't demonstrate how it works today."

"I can." The words leap from my mouth, projecting across the quiet room. I straighten, every nerve ending in my body buzzing. "I figured out how to make Theseus work."

"You—you did?" Mom squints at me, confused. She glances behind to Zoey, who shrugs.

"I used it last night on myself. Transferred back all my memories. I remember the time I broke down in tears when they lowered

Dad's casket into the ground," I say as proof that I've retrieved even the memories she herself stole from me.

Her eyes widen, and I can see it in her face, the way her brows knit out of concern for me. She believes me. She trusts me again.

I have to look away from Sebastian for the next part or else I'll crack. "I want my boyfriend back. And my dad. I—I miss them."

Mom smooths down her suit and turns back to the audience. "Well then, perhaps you will be getting a demonstration after all."

I meet her eyes. "I need an admin console though."

Mom flourishes her arm toward where Zoey stands behind it. "You're in luck. We used this earlier to demonstrate HiveMind. It's yours to use now." She clicks something on her controller, and the monitors switch to a view of the admin desktop so everyone can watch along with me.

My security guard releases me at Mom's command. I wobble on shaky legs as I take the stairs, painfully aware of every eye in the audience trained on my back and the millions of people watching at home too. But it's only one gaze that bores into me so fiercely I nearly trip: Sebastian's. His face is stark white and terrified.

I shut my eyes, but the image of his scared face is burned on my retinas. I still don't know what I'm going to do, but either way, I'll have to live with this moment, this choice, embedded in my mind forever.

I focus ahead, on putting one foot in front of the other as I suck down desperate gulps of recycled air. Zoey bites her lip, studying me for way too long until she steps aside, checking for any kind of forgiveness.

I won't give her even a glance.

Zoey's already cued up Theseus for me, connected right into Bash's archived mind. All I need to do is unhook Sebastian from HiveMind, hit *select all* on Bash's memories, and transfer them right into Sebastian. I feel the possibility consume me. Bash, mine again. How long will it take for Sebastian to disappear and for Bash to resume his place by my side? Minutes? Seconds?

Teddy pleads with his eyes at me, silently begging me to bring back his best friend. Zoey shakes her head and then flicks her eyes toward the guy she created just for me to love. She has her credit now; she doesn't care if I resurrect Bash.

Blinking red lights of the cameras immortalize my actions through the power of digital archives. When I glance out at the audience, I see nothing but rapt faces, everyone holding their breath. Everyone except Sebastian. The corners of his mouth are trembling, and he drops to his knees, burying his face in his hands as he prepares to be erased forever. A persistent hum trills in my chest and I brace my hands alongside the table to stop them from shaking.

My eyelashes flutter closed to prevent the tears from spilling out, but it's futile. If I choose Sebastian, I have to accept the deaths of my father and my boyfriend to save the life of a boy I've come to love. But if I choose Bash, I'm choosing my mother as well and betraying that same boy in order to bring my boyfriend and my dad back from the dead.

There's no right choice. Either one will leave me heartbroken in the end.

One of my hands slips off the table and reaches into my pocket. I cup an SSD device in the palm of my hand. It contains a script I wrote to destroy Theseus for good. I can remove it from my pocket and save Sebastian or leave it where it is and erase him instead of Theseus.

I take a deep breath and meet Sebastian's eyes. My heart cracks in two.

I know what I have to do.

In my mind, I conjure the image of my dad on the beach that

day when I was younger, his face so full of life, his heart so full of good intentions. I whisper the two words he'll never be able to hear again: *I'm sorry*.

And then I shove the SSD device into the slot and click on the executable file that pops up. Within seconds, the program I wrote over six coffees and four Diet Cokes starts to eat its way through Theseus, destroying every trace of the plug-in.

"What have you done?" Mom grips my shoulders with white knuckles and shakes.

"Bash made a choice, Mom. He's *gone*. And Sebastian is not just a shell!" Tears stream down my face. "He's his own person, completely separate from Bash, and I love him!"

Mom rips her hands from my shoulders and stumbles back a step, a completely shocked expression marring her face. "You don't. You just think you do. You're just a teenager, you're—"

"Smarter than you ever were." The tears are falling faster now, my voice hysterical. "And I'm not going to help you erase him. Not him. Or me. Or anyone else. Not ever again!"

Sebastian runs toward me, nudging my mother out of the way. She doesn't fight it. "You saved me." He studies my face. "You chose me."

"I chose *us*." And then I cup my hand around the back of his neck and pull him toward me. The crowd erupts in cheers when his lips meet mine.

EPILOGUE

I walk up and down the rows of the test lab, checking each computer station, every connection. Trying to ignore the way my hands tremble. I need everything to be perfect for today. You never get a second chance to make a first impression, and this might be my absolute last shot at impressing the entire student body.

I smooth down my blouse and tuck it into my jeans, then immediately untuck it. I considered wearing a suit for today, but I didn't want to separate myself too much from the rest of my classmates. Former classmates, I guess. Plus, suits remind me too much of my mother. Too much of her mini-me, Zoey.

A lump lodges in my throat, but I swallow it down. I've gotten really good at that over the last few months.

The door swings open, and I jerk to my feet, startled. I curse myself for not standing at the entrance, ready to welcome anyone who might filter in. Sebastian lopes into the room, grinning at me when he spots me. His mom trails behind him, taking tentative steps and swiveling her head around the room in awe.

He turns to her. "Thanks, but you didn't have to escort me all the way to the lab."

She studies him, her face a mix of concern and awe. "I just wanted to make sure you got here okay."

Sebastian rolls his eyes. "Mom, I'm okay. It's just a cold."

I don't need Sebastian's handy arsenal of language translations to decode what's going on here. After losing her son, she's terrified that something will happen to Sebastian now. One little sneeze and she wants to wrap him in bubble wrap and maybe steel armor.

"Don't worry, Mrs. C. I'll make sure he's well cared for over the next few hours. I'll even buy him chicken soup."

She gives me a tight smile before planting a huge kiss on his forehead. She looks at him so lovingly, my heart nearly breaks. When she first found out her son died, she mourned, cried, and threw a funeral for him. But she also embraced Sebastian. Maybe a little too much.

"Sorry about that," Sebastian says when she leaves. "She's being a little too overprotective lately."

"Hey, I'd choose overprotective mom over backstabbing mom any day." I rush toward him and nearly knock him into the closest table as I crash into him, wrap my arms around him, and plant my lips on his. He laughs at my attack, securing his arms around me and kissing me with the same amount of fervor.

"How was your group therapy session?" I pull back a little to study the way his face creases at my question.

"As awful as yesterday. Simon spent the entire session crying again. I'm pretty sure Eliza was high on one of her Sober Up pills, her way of coping, I guess. Veronica was shopping on her phone and complaining that she's having no withdrawal symptoms so she doesn't need to be there. And then—" He pauses, turning away from me partially.

I brace for what he's about to say. Ever since the Ethics Committee made the decision to pull HiveMind from beta testing in order to perform a full security analysis and overhaul, they've required anyone connected to attend daily group therapy sessions, Sebastian's mom included. Some students are handling the complete disconnect from HiveMind better than others.

There's a pang in my gut. A momentary lapse. Muscle memory surging into focus. Jitteriness that buzzes in my veins and makes me feel incomplete. Untethered. It feels like getting my leg chopped off and wobbling, off balance, every time I try to stand up. I've heard that amputees report phantom sensations in their missing limb—a tingle, an itch—and losing my connection to HiveMind leaves me with a worse feeling. I feel completely out of control.

I suck down three big breaths in a row to tamp down the feeling of unease, a technique courtesy of the Hypnotist. *It's for the best*, I remind myself, but even I can hear the bullshit in my thoughts. *It's only temporary.*

That last thought allows my muscles to relax, tension draining from my shoulders.

Sebastian waits patiently, watching the play of microexpressions on my face while I rein in my emotions.

"And then?" I prompt when I'm finally ready.

He studies his shoes. "The other students kept ranting about how this is all your fault and they're not going to participate today."

I squeeze my eyes shut, swallowing hard. "I was afraid of that."

If no one shows up today, I can't make it up to them by making HiveMind safe to use. I can't help them. I can't fix everything I broke. I can't fulfill my dad's dream.

I force a tight smile onto my lips. "Well, then. It might just be the two of us bashing some bugs today."

Sebastian cracks his knuckles. "Point me at those SSD drives."

But then the door swings open and a few students come in. Simon stares up at me with red-rimmed eyes. A few students behind him all wear equally distraught expressions.

"After this, can we have HiveMind back?" Simon holds his breath, chest pumping raggedly. The others mirror his pleading expression.

I flinch. My whole body feels heavy with the weight of my dad's dream on my shoulders. *My* dream. I've been asked this question nearly a hundred times a day since I announced this bug bash. The answer is always the same. In fact, there's an official press release containing all this info.

Before I have a chance to quote from the press release, a new voice does it for me. "The purpose of today's bug bash event is to find vulnerabilities within the product itself and the security system so we can then fix them," Brandon says as he takes his usual spot at the front of the room to supervise from an IT standpoint. The one thing I did right was get him his job back. I still haven't managed to get him and Leo back together, but they're having dinner tomorrow night. *Not* a date, Leo claims. I suspect otherwise. "This is only the first of several iterations planned with different audiences. We do plan to release HiveMind eventually, but not until we're one hundred percent sure there are no security flaws. Timeframe-wise, we're probably looking at least a year out, maybe more."

The group groans.

I inject as much pep as I can muster into my voice. "But the faster we find bugs, the faster we can fix them. I promise, you'll all be notified as soon as we release the product for beta testing." I flourish my hand toward the waiting computers, and the students scramble for a chair, circling far away from Sebastian to avoid him, like he's wrong somehow. When I spot the way he cringes, I clutch my hand in his and squeeze, my silent reminder to him that in my eyes, he's absolutely perfect.

The students huddle up in their desks, studying the sheet of papers left on the keyboards. Each desk contains a test script to help guide them.

This is all part of the multistep plan that I presented to the Ethics Committee, and to the new CEO, Leo, to plug the holes in Hive-Mind and make it safe for everyone. They hired me to do exactly that and I'm going to damn well make sure there is no possible way to hack into someone else's account.

The door opens again, and Teddy waltzes in, holding Eliza's hand. Like me, he's been working part-time the last few weeks until he can make it permanent. The Ethics Committee is allowing him to continue his research under close supervision by Leo and other scientists.

Teddy focuses only on Sebastian. "Busy later? That new game just came out." There's strain in his voice, and I can tell he's trying. Really, really trying. I know how it must hurt to look at Sebastian and wish desperately he was Bash. I sometimes slide too.

Sebastian laughs. "You sure you want me to play? In case you've forgotten, last time I eviscerated your butt."

Teddy rolls his eyes. "That's only because you had that game manual downloaded into your brain. This game's new." Teddy grins. "We're even here."

Sebastian pretends to consider for a second before breaking out into a huge grin. "I'm in."

"Cool." They exchange a complicated handshake, a new marker to their friendship.

The smile that spreads on my face hides the pang in my gut. I have to look away at the way they're starting to bond. I press my palm to the wall and take a deep breath. The void that Zoey left on my heart still remains.

There's a hand on my palm, calm and reassuring. "Hey, it's okay." Sebastian's soothing voice lulls me back into complacency. It's nice to know that someone can read my mind just by looking at me and not by accessing my thoughts. "Just think about how miserable she must be too, all alone back in Minnesota."

I swallow hard. "I heard she's trying to appeal her expulsion. Claim coercion. Sue."

Sebastian shrugs. "She won't win."

Neither will my mom. The thought robs me of breath. I dig my phone out of my pocket and scroll to the calendar app. The blue-shaded box on Sunday from three to four p.m. gives me a sudden stab of apprehension. *Visiting Hours—Massachusetts Correctional Facility.*

I haven't decided yet if I'm going this week. I haven't been able to bring myself to visit her any other week.

One day I hope I'll have the courage to confront her. Maybe one day I'll find it in me to forgive her.

Commotion rattles through the room, and Sebastian clears his throat. "We might want to get started."

I spin around, and my eyes widen, as nearly every desk in the room is occupied. I square my shoulders and head to the front of the room.

"All right, guys. This isn't just a bug bash. It's a competition." I head to the board and write the number $1000. "Whoever finds the most bugs in the least amount of time earns this baby." I tap the number.

Murmurs of excitement rise through the crowd.

"And as promised, everyone who helps today will get twenty bucks."

Okay, so I may have bribed them. I never liked to do things by the rules.

"I want no piece of the software untouched. I want you to do everything you can to try to hack in. Please make sure to log every issue or bug you find in the shared spreadsheet. You have five hours."

"Go!" Sebastian says, and then grins at me. "I totally helped."

Fingers start flying across keys as the students work.

I nudge him with my shoulder. "You don't have to stay if you don't want to. I know you've got way more important things to do."

"I want to be here. With you. Figuring out how to transfer cancer-free cells properly can wait. I mean, technically I'm not officially on the payroll until next week."

We both grin. We may not be working on the same project anymore, but I'll still get to see him every single day at work. And after work too, even though we're still taking things slow. Neither of us likes to sleep alone after what happened.

I watch the room, everyone tapping away. This is what Dad wanted. Not for people to exploit his product but to band together to make it stronger. My chest tightens at the thought of him, but it fades quickly. This is the way I can resurrect him. This is the way he can live on. Through everything he left behind: his notebooks that I read every night, his software, his legacy.

Beneath the table, I reach down and lace my fingers with Sebastian's. I sit here and stare out at the eager looks on the students' faces, the guy next to me who I love so much. I think of HiveMind and my list of favorite memories. There was a time when something like this wouldn't even rank. But every moment these days is something I try to cherish. Even the most ordinary, most mundane, most trivial. They're all mine now, and mine alone.

Sebastian turns to me and gives me a look that can only be described as adoration. I melt into his gaze, letting it warm me.

I'm going to remember this moment for the rest of my life.

ACKNOWLEDGMENTS

IF I HAD the ability to relive my favorite memories using HiveMind, my list of greatest hits would consist of memories involving every person named below. This book would not exist without the support and guidance I received along the way, and I'm so thankful to every one of you.

A big thank-you to Holly West, my amazing editor. You helped me find the real story hidden within the bones of my original version and bring it to the surface. You totally got my book and my vision, sometimes even more than I did, and helped me make it the best it could be. I loved our chats about *Supernatural*, Navi from Zelda, and hack battles.

Thank you to Jean Feiwel for taking a chance on me and making my dreams come true. To the rest of the Swoon editorial team: Lauren Scobell for everything you do at Swoon Reads and for being my cheerleader, Kat Brzozowski for your fabulous line edits, and Emily Settle for your tireless efforts running the amazing blog. This book would also not be complete without my terrific production editor Lindsay Wagner, my awesome production manager Raymond E. Colón, my astute copy editor Jessica White, and my talented cover and interior designer Liz Dresner. I also want to extend thanks to my publicist, Madison Furr, the subrights team headed by Kristin Dulaney, the audio team, and everyone else at Macmillan who had a hand in the publishing of this book.

To my incredible agent Brent Taylor for your upbeat attitude and for being my advocate. Thanks also to the entire team at TriadaUS agency, but I want to extend a special thanks to Lauren Spieller for being my critique partner and for always having my back.

Thanks to Chandler Baker and Diana Urban. You both keep me sane (and motivated!) with our accountability gchats, discussions about writing and *Bachelor in Paradise*, and word count sprints. Chandler, thanks for brainstorming every little detail of this book and helping me find the right solution for every writing problem. Diana, thanks for your friendship, your marketing wisdom, and your insightful critique.

To my early readers Denise Jaden, Jessica Love, Cyn Balog, Guinevere Robin Rowell, and Jim McCarthy: Your feedback helped shape this book and I'm forever grateful. I also want to thank all the readers who read my book on the Swoon website and rooted for it.

To Meredith Moran, thank you for being such an amazing boss and friend. To Amanda Nietzel, for encouraging me to submit. To Erika Shenker, Crista Finnochio, Chelsey Wolfe, and Amanda Simon for decades of friendship and memories. Additional shout-outs to Rachel Simon and Laura Benson.

To the Swoon Squad for all your great advice, the Novel Nineteens for embarking on this journey alongside me, the Summer Moms 2012 Facebook group for your support, and the Pokémon Go NJ Mystic Discord group for putting up with my endless computer science questions. Special shout-out to Roger and Paul.

To Rivers Cuomo of Weezer, thank you for the music that comprised my writing soundtrack and for letting me borrow your last name for the love interest in this book.

I want to thank my in-laws, JoAnne and Richard, as well as my brother-in-law Dan, and my sister-in-law Marta. Thank you all for your love and support, for watching Quinn so I could write, and for the amazing meals you all put your heart into.

To my sister Becca for always being there for me. You're the first person I text with any news—TV or celebrity news especially. I know it's cheesy to say, but you truly are my best friend. Thanks also to your family: Eric, Casey, and Eliza. Sorry I stole your daughter's name and gave it to an antagonist in this book.

Thanks to my mom and dad for all you do for me and for being the best parents in existence. You gave me a love of reading and fostered my creativity, both in art and writing. I hope you guys skipped over the kissing scenes, and if you didn't, pretend they were a figment of your imagination.

Last but certainly not least, I want to thank my wonderful husband, Josh, and my daughter, Quinn. You are my rocks, my partners, and my inspiration. I love you both so much.

Check out more books chosen for publication by readers like you.

DID YOU KNOW...

readers like you
helped to get this
book published?

Join our book-obsessed community and help us
discover awesome new writing talent.

1

Write it.

Share your original YA manuscript.

2

Read it.

Discover bright new bookish talent.

3

Share it.

Discuss, rate, and share your faves.

4

Love it.

Help us publish the books you love.

Share your own manuscript or dive between the pages
at **swoonreads.com** or by downloading the **Swoon Reads app**.